I KNOW ABOUT YOU

Visit us at www.boldstrokesbooks.com

I KNOW ABOUT YOU

by

Erin Kaste

2023

I KNOW ABOUT YOU

ISBN 13: 978-1-63679-513-3

This Trade Paperback Original Is Published By
Bold Strokes Books, Inc.
P.O. Box 249
Valley Falls, NY 12185

First Edition: October 2023

CREDITS
EDITOR: BARBARA ANN WRIGHT
PRODUCTION DESIGN: SUSAN RAMUNDO
COVER DESIGN BY TAMMY SEIDICK

Dedication

For Betsy, my beautiful partner in crime.

Chapter One

Natalie was the first to move. She looked up at me, her eyes glazed with a bottomless emptiness. "Okay, then."

There was no feeling in my head, no feeling in my body, just the high, nauseous tremor that had begun some time ago. "I—"

"Don't." She turned toward the embankment, straining to see the road above us. "You need to go."

"I can't just—"

"Go," she begged. "Before someone comes."

I bent to pick up the crowbar that lay on the bottom of the viaduct, just inches from the body between us, but Natalie shook her head.

"Leave it. You were never here, got it?"

My eyes met hers, then traveled to her bloodied clothing. "What about you?"

"I'll take it. You were never here," she repeated.

Everything that statement entailed washed over me in an awful, suffocating wave. "I need to know that you're okay."

"I'm okay," she said. "Are you?"

I nodded.

"I'll take care of everything. Do you trust me?"

We stared at one another for a long time, far too long. "Yes," I said, my voice almost nonexistent.

"Go."

I didn't turn back. I didn't look down at Jonathan, I didn't look to make sure I hadn't left a trail of bloody shoe prints. I didn't touch

Natalie, or even say good-bye, just trusted her absolutely. I ran back to my car, slammed the door behind me, and turned the key in the ignition. The blood was on my hands, on my clothing, absolutely everywhere.

❖

Ten Years Later

George Herbert Walker Bush Elementary School was a squat building that occupied a full block of South Fourth, right across the street from the Pronto Taqueria and a three-walled shack with a corrugated metal roof. My classroom, D-6, sat closest to the back door on the north side, between Marisol Ayala's bilingual sixth grade and a generous expanse of brown scrub grass. The walls were supposed to be white but had turned more of a yellowish gray, and the floor was covered with the thin, deteriorating tile indigenous to Methodist church basements. My bulletin boards were covered with brightly colored butcher paper, posters tacked over the ugliest stretches of wall, and a hot-pink diagram detailing emergency procedures hid two bullet holes next to the pencil sharpener.

Some of the other rooms at Bush might have been more attractive, but mine was a commodity. It had windows. They overlooked the parking lot, but they were windows just the same, a large bay stretching the length of the north wall. We opened them wide on the days it wasn't too hot or dusty, and even when the weather was bad, I kept the blinds raised.

For three years, two months, and some odd days, I'd lived in West Grove—population ten thousand, two hundred, and seven—deep in the left armpit of the great state of Texas. I'd lived a lot of places, some bustling like the Chicago suburbs and others quaint and still, like the town in upstate New York where I'd spent first and second grade. Nothing was quite like West Grove. I knew it the moment I'd entered the city limits, and any native would proudly agree.

I'd taken the job of sixth-grade teacher straight out of graduate school, when the threat of college loans coming due was more terrifying than the idea of transplanting myself into a backward, hyper-conservative little crucible. I did wonder from time to time what my life would have been like if I'd waited for a better offer, but most days, I was thankful for what I had. My sixth graders kept me on my toes, and the pay was decent, considering the outrageously low cost of living. I did tend to stand out like the proverbial sore thumb, but nearly everyone blamed that on the fact that I was from The North and stopped short of questioning my voting record, my religious beliefs, or my sexual orientation.

While fall meant cool, beautiful weather in some places, it was still hot and dusty in West Grove. As usual, the first Monday morning in October was a comedy of false starts. Collection of lunch money and homework. Forgotten lunch money and incomplete homework. Christian, a lanky white boy with floppy hair and long eyelashes, tried to slip into the classroom ten minutes late without stopping in the office for a tardy slip. He was sent back out the door. We pledged allegiance to the flag in the corner of the classroom and listened to morning announcements. Christian returned with lunch money and homework to integrate into the existing stashes. As soon as we began discussing current events, Selena, the head secretary, returned to the public address system to read the license plate number of a car parked in the fire lane. School had been in session for forty-five minutes by the time we could settle into actual learning.

After language arts, we went to the computer lab, then returned to the classroom to work on word problems. Lunch smells started wafting through the halls, and as I drifted from desk to desk, helping students through an equation or two, trying to keep the peace, I could hear stomachs rumbling. Mine felt cranky enough to join them, and for once, I didn't try to quash the feeling. Today was enchilada day.

Nine days out of ten, lunches at Bush sucked. Sorry-looking meat floating in a sauce rife with grease bubbles, vegetables stewed within an inch of their lives, cakes and cookies with the distinct taste of paraffin. Our lunch ladies were all short, wrinkled grandmothers, and they did not care about the edibility of meatloaf or fish sticks. Where enchiladas, burritos, or tamales were concerned, though, their cooking was to die for. Only three of my children had brought lunches from home, and they wandered glumly to the tables while the rest of the class joined the cafeteria line. Had I not had the teacher privilege to cut, I would have likely wasted half my lunch period waiting.

Maxine, the shortest, pruniest lunch lady, had just slopped an extra-large helping of cheesy goodness onto my plate when Jody, the music teacher, caught my eye. She was my best friend at Bush, and I knew her well enough to suspect she had something to say. I got a plastic bag of milk, stopped at the cashier, then threaded my way through the maze of tables toward her.

After twenty minutes of lunchroom duty, Jody's face had gone nearly as red as her hair, and she was busy barking directions in a distinctly outdoor tone. When I got close enough, she gave me a tiny, discreet nod, the kind that meant I was supposed to wait for a second, then glance disinterestedly in that direction. I ducked next to her, counted to three, then peered around her toward the door.

There was no way I could stop at one glance. "Oh," I whispered involuntarily. "Oh my. Who is that?"

"They hired a new bilingual kindergarten teacher."

"Really?" The woman was flanked by a line of tiny, dark-haired children, but I refused to believe she could be a kindergarten teacher. Mrs. Shore, who had been substitute teaching the bilingual class since the beginning of the year, was what I thought of: comfortable and gently maternal. This one wasn't just pretty, she was downright hot, with thick, silky hair down past her shoulders and luscious, imploring eyes. Her blouse was dark blue, and her skirt was so short that every last one of her students could surely walk straight under it. She looked very young and very frightened. I longed to hold her close under the guise of friendly reassurance. I hadn't felt so urgently uncomfortable in a long time.

"Must be. That's the bilingual class," Jody said.

I chewed my lip as the woman guided her students right past us and toward the steam tables. Nice ass, too. Really nice. I glanced quickly around to make sure nobody was watching us watch. Jody's look suggested that she was merely amused that anyone would dress that way to teach kindergarten, but how could anyone help but be smitten with this woman, even if they were straight?

"Goodness," she finally said, smiling and shaking her head. "Save me a spot, okay?"

By the time I got to the staff lounge, Daniel and the two other fifth-grade teachers were alone at the big table. He descended upon me the second I pulled up a chair. "Have you seen the new chicky chick?"

I barely raised my eyebrows. Fortunately, Bev Spardo started in with a completely clueless fervor. "She is so nice, you guys. Those babies loved Mrs. Shore, you know, but they really need someone fluent."

"Where did they find someone in the middle of October?" Sally Schumacher asked.

"I think she's straight out of school, but I don't know where she came from."

Sally nodded. "Maybe she's on emergency certification."

Daniel sighed noisily. "Why don't you just ask her?"

Bev and Sally gave him a collective nasty look and picked up their trays. Most of our colleagues were okay, but Bev and Sally were of the ilk who insisted upon calling us "Ms. Smith" and "Mr. Crenshaw," even when there weren't any students present. They were both clad in patriotic vests and too-tight chinos. We put up with them, and they put up with us, but we never mixed for long.

The moment they were gone, Daniel's eyes lit up. "So have you seen her?"

"Yes."

"That's all you have to say?"

The door opened, and the bilingual kindergarten teacher approached hesitantly with her tray, her eyes right on me. "May I join you?"

"Of course," I said, clearing a newspaper off the table a bit overzealously and making Daniel's Diet Coke wobble. "Cary Smith," I offered. "Sixth grade."

She set her tray down and accepted my handshake. Her grip was surprisingly firm, but that wasn't what made the back of my neck prickle. The disarming, intense eye contact continued. "Tina Flores," she returned. "Kindergarten. Well, you probably knew that."

"This is Daniel," I said, less to be polite than to direct her attention elsewhere long enough that I could breathe.

"Fifth grade," he told her. "Charmed to meet you. You're lucky it's good lunch day. Cary never comes out of her cubicle unless it's good lunch day."

I shot him a look telling him to shut up, but the same delicious look of confused innocence Tina had worn in the cafeteria returned to her face. "Pardon?"

"I usually stay in my classroom 'cause he's a butthead," I translated, then wanted to take it back. A tiny grin appeared on those fuck-me red lips, so I continued hastily, "Are you having a good first day?"

"Yeah, it's going fairly well." As we ate, she elaborated on getting set up and on how so many of her kids didn't speak any English at all. Her eyes mesmerized me; they were amazing in their intensity, amazing in their endlessness. They jumped from Daniel to her lunch as she spoke, but they seemed to spend most of their time locked with mine. They were huge and dark brown with long, thick lashes.

"Are you from West Grove?"

She shook her head. "I just finished at UT Austin."

"Your bachelor's?" Daniel asked.

"My master's. Are a lot of the teachers from here?"

"Most of them. He is," I added, thumbing at Daniel. "I am not."

"She's a Yankee," he said, wrinkling his nose.

Jody arrived on the scene with an extra-huge pile of food. "Jody Finnegan," she announced in her usual bullhorn tone. "Welcome to Bush."

"Tina Flores. You're the music teacher, right? I don't think we have music today."

"Ten o'clock tomorrow. You should've had library this morning."

"So anyway," Daniel interrupted. "Where did you say you were from?"

"I've lived in Texas for a while," Tina began, "but I'm not really—"

The door opened yet again, and Mr. Dunlop, the assistant principal, entered. As always, all conversation ceased. He jingled a handful of coins and pushed three of them into the Coke machine, watching us the whole time. I wondered if he had any idea which beverage he'd chosen. He retrieved it without complaining and finally sidled up to our table. "Miss Flores, how's it going?"

"Well, I think. They're good kids."

"They are," he said. "They are. Have you gotten settled?"

"Somewhat. It'll take a few late nights to figure everything out, but Mrs. Shore did a really nice job."

"Well, if you do stay late, make sure the custodians know you're still here. You want to stay safe."

"Someone stays late most days," I assured her.

"Yeah, you," Daniel said.

Dunlop's rat eyes shifted grimly between us. "Did you find an apartment, Miss Flores?"

"Yes. Everything's still in boxes, but it'll be fine in another couple weeks."

"Good. Good." He cracked open his soda and took a long sip. Some of it clung to the bottom of his mustache when he lowered the can. "It's hard to be new in town when you're all by yourself. I see you've met Miss Smith and Miss Finnegan...and Daniel Crenshaw, of course." With that, he patted Daniel heartily on the shoulder. "I'm sure they'll help you out and answer any questions you might have. Well, have a nice lunch. Oh," he added, turning those beady little eyes back on me. "Two fifteen. Don't forget."

I stared at him, surprised. "What?"

"Check your mailbox," he said, shaking his head.

We were silent until the door clicked, at which point Daniel made a face like he was going to vomit. "He *touched* me."

"You know he's out there disinfecting," I said.

Tina stared at the door, a look of unmistakable distaste on her face. "What was that about?"

Jody smiled brightly at her. "I hear you're single."

"'I see you've met Daniel Crenshaw, resident eligible bachelor,'" Daniel mimicked.

"Well, you are both eligible and a bachelor," Jody said.

"If he marries us off, we'll stay," I said. "Dunlop started working on me before I even signed my contract."

Tina's eyes lit squarely on me, and the end of one eyebrow edged up almost imperceptibly. "And you signed it anyway?"

I couldn't help but smile. I could also feel my cheeks going hot, so I took that opportunity to push my chair back and pick up my tray. "A rather characteristic moment of weakness. Have a good afternoon."

❖

I had just a few more minutes before getting my class from recess, so I went down to the office to look in my mailbox. When I got there, Selena, the foul-tempered secretary whose tiny black eyes followed me as if she expected me to pilfer staplers and ballpoint pens, was pretending to take care of something at her desk.

I nodded at her. "Hello."

Selena said something like "Hmm," and shuffled papers loudly.

I moved past her desk to the mailbox and saw a yellow sheet of paper waiting in my slot.

"Oh, Miss Smith? You have an observation notice from Mr. Dunlop."

I stared at the pattern on her sweater for a moment, wondering why she was paying attention to what was in my box. I folded the paper in half without reading it and considered thanking her, but her back was to me, so I left the office without another word.

Since I'd achieved tenure, only one observation was required of me per year, and that usually happened during the spring. Nevertheless, the assistant principal would be gracing my class with his presence at two fifteen. I had no idea what I'd done to deserve the attention, but it couldn't be something good.

My original plan for the end of the afternoon was to assign a dozen vocabulary words, then have the kids define them and use them in a short story or poem that they could work on quietly until dismissal time. I was fairly sure I couldn't do that and come out looking intelligent, according to Dunlop, so I scrapped it in favor of reviewing fractions.

The instant I wrote an equation on the whiteboard, the groans began. "You've got to be kidding," David wailed. "Fractions again?"

Mr. Dunlop had settled in the back of my classroom with the stealth of a Navy SEAL. One butt cheek balanced on the edge of a shelf as he scribbled feverishly on a legal pad. I hoped the shelf wasn't as sturdy as he thought.

"Yes. Fractions again. Necessary for algebra. First step? Zack?"

His eyes widened, and he stared at the textbook in front of him. "What page are you on? That isn't what it says in the book."

"It's not in the book," I said. "We need more practice, so I'm making this up. First step?"

He glared at me. "Get the common denominator?" He glanced around warily, as if daring the others to laugh at him.

Dunlop scribbled so hard that several kids turned to look. "Hold that thought," I told Zack. "Nestor?"

"I have the answer."

"I know you have the answer. We need to show our work first."

He rolled his eyes. "Turn the whole numbers into fractions."

"And how do we do that? Cristal?"

Slowly, painfully, we created improper fractions and returned to Zack for our common denominator. The entire time, there was an undercurrent of whispers, the very sound of boredom. *Please, please let me get through this without major behavior problems.* Lisa passed a note to Ashley. I thought about confiscating it but decided to just pretend Dunlop hadn't noticed.

When I reached to swap my blue marker for a green, an unsolicited voice came from the middle of the room. "How come you always use green for the common denominator?"

I closed my eyes and tried not to scream. The comment belonged to Christian, and the requisite smattering of girly giggles followed it. "I don't remember calling on you, Mr. Benson."

"You didn't," he said. "I just want to know."

"Do you have a favorite color you'd like me to use instead?"

Nestor kicked at Christian's desk, his eyes wide, and nodded toward the back of the room as if any of us had forgotten that Mr. Dunlop was there. A few of the other boys snickered.

"How about red?" Christian asked sweetly.

"I'll leave it here for you when you work the next problem for us. Where were we?" We continued to work through the problem until I finally asked Eric for the sum.

"Seventeen eighths."

Dunlop snuffled, and Michael laughed out loud. "Idiot."

My eyes found Michael before the word was all the way out of his mouth. "Pardon?"

"Wait, seventeen fourths," Eric said quickly. "Seventeen fourths."

This time, I wrote his answer on the board. "Exactly. Good save. Any guesses as to what answer C is likely to be on your TAAS test?"

"Seventeen eighths," Eric muttered.

"Or two and one eighth. The TAAS people are tricky that way. You caught your mistake, but they know some people won't go back and check their work. Last step? David?"

"Four and one fourth."

"And can you share with us how you came to this conclusion?"

He sighed loudly. I was thankful he didn't add a belch for effect. "I reduced it."

"Thank you, Mr. Mackey. Mr. Benson, I believe you're going to walk us through the next problem."

Giggles and a few snide comments moved through the classroom as Christian slouched to the board. I watched from atop my desk as he worked the problem in front of the class and refused to react when he looked at me sideways and wrote the common denominator in extra-large font. When he tossed the pen down with the others and took a bow, David clapped for him.

He stared at me expectantly. "What? It's right, isn't it?"

"Almost."

Nestor giggled. More scribbling in the back of the room.

"Aw." Christian grabbed a marker, green, and reduced his fractions. "There."

"Excellent. It's the magical green marker."

He cracked a grin as he took his seat. "Whatever."

After working three more problems, the classroom was threatening to erupt. I asked everyone to explain one problem to their neighbor step-by-step, then moved slowly through the aisles, pretending to listen, daring to check the clock. Nearly three. My throat hurt, and my shirt felt wickedly sweaty. I wondered if Dunlop was ever going to leave.

Ten minutes later, I posted the day's homework assignments on the board in larger, clearer handwriting than usual. I waited for a pithy comment from Christian or Chelsea, but it didn't come. Instead, Lisa's hand popped into the air. "Read us another chapter?"

Damn it. I refused to look at Mr. Dunlop, but I heard him click the cap back on his pen. I could picture him quite well, arms crossed, regarding me with a gloating gotcha look. "Not today."

"You don't have to do a whole chapter," Will begged. "Just a page or two."

Please don't mention the name of the book. "Maybe tomorrow."

That was when the speaker clicked, and Selena's afternoon announcements ended the discussion. As she reminded us about class pictures on Thursday and plowed through the lists of which students were to walk home, take the bus, or wait for their parents in the cafeteria, Mr. Dunlop ambled back toward the door. "Miss Smith?"

"Mr. Dunlop."

"I'll leave a note in your box."

I nodded as pleasantly as I could. "Thank you."

"No," he said, his smile wide enough to turn his beady eyes into slits. "Thank *you*."

Chapter Two

Accoording to many of the West Grove Independent School District administrators, standardized tests like the Texas Assessment of Academic Skills accurately demonstrated each student's comprehension of subjects and each teacher's capability to relate information to their students.

I viewed them as a gigantic waste of time, but Mr. Dunlop was a firm believer in the ability of TAAS scores to determine which students were going to succeed in life and which teachers were worth the space they occupied. Since my students' scores generally hovered a good ten to twenty percent above the other classes, I had no idea why Dunlop had called the impromptu observation.

I was well aware that neither I nor my students had come off particularly well the day before, but I arrived at school Tuesday morning assuming that he would memo me, and it would be over.

No such luck. My box was empty when I signed in, and that was far worse than any nasty memo. I tried to go about my business as if nothing had happened, but on Tuesdays and Thursdays, I taught all morning without so much as a jaunt to the library, and I couldn't focus to save my life. Our geography textbook was not exciting. I noticed one of my overhead lights flickered on a fifteen-second cycle, one of the thumbtacks was missing from John Quincy Adams's portrait in the line of U.S. Presidents on my wall, and the top of the blinds needed dusting. Justin was wearing his squeaky shoes. Brianna's socks didn't match. I caught myself staring outside at a dark blue SUV in the parking lot, wondering if it belonged to Tina Flores.

I hoped she would eat lunch with us again.

I was scribbling terms from the chapter on the whiteboard when I heard paper crumpling behind me. A moment later, something hit me in the back. *Little fuckers.* I turned quickly and saw a ball of notebook paper on the floor under my desk. I decided to ignore it and kept writing.

A minute later, a second missile hit my shoulder. I jumped like the first time. I hadn't been expecting it since there wasn't any telltale noise, and giggles spread through the class. I turned and gave a sharp look but didn't say anything.

More crumpling, only this time, I was ready. After pausing a beat, I turned to see David letting loose with another toss. I reached out and caught it. My marker made a thick blue line on my pants, but I managed to not drop it.

"Nice grab," Christian said, his voice only half-condescending.

"Pick them up now," I said to David, holding out the paper I'd caught.

He threw me a you've-got-to-be-shitting-me look.

I didn't break eye contact. "Now."

"Do it," Nestor whispered.

David got up and took his time fishing the other two papers from under my desk. Instead of taking the third from me, he tossed them in the trash, then sat back down.

I closed my hand on it, feeling the redness creeping up my neck. "Get back up and get your things."

"Why?"

"Shannon, please switch desks with David."

"Oh for…" David didn't move until Shannon stood next to him, her books and backpack in tow. She was bigger than he was and wearing a sour look, so he gathered his things and headed to the back of the room. That wasn't a good place for him, but at least I was no longer within range unless he started throwing shoes or something.

It felt like lunchtime would never come. My intent was to drop off my kids, run to the office to check my box, then pop into the staff lounge late enough for Tina to already be there. I'd pretend to be busy with something important, maybe just running in to grab a Coke. I'd catch her eye and agree to sit, well, maybe just for a minute.

The office was buzzing when I finally got there. Selena was on the phone arguing the tardy policy with a parent, someone was signing their child out, Mavis Brewer was juggling half a dozen doses of Ritalin, and the line of kids waiting for her attention spilled out the nurse's room into the office itself. The copier was humming. Both principals had closed their doors, and I couldn't blame them.

I made my way to the mailbox where a short stack of papers sat. Next to me, Javier Sotelo tripped over a backpack and spilled his coffee. Mavis handed him a length of paper towel without missing a beat. As he crept around my feet sopping up his spill, I tried to ignore how the paper towel had turned black. Nothing from Dunlop.

"Did I get you? God, I'm sorry," Javier said, staring at my pants in horror. He was on his knees, the ball of nasty, crumpled paper towel still in his hand.

The bottom of one leg, maybe, but not my butt, that was for sure. "Don't worry about it," I told him, eyeballing my escape route and praying he had the sense not to try to dry me off.

"Miss Smith. I thought I heard your voice." Mr. Dunlop's head popped out of his office so quickly that it took a moment for his tie to catch up with it. I wondered if he'd been standing with his ear pressed to the door. He wiggled a yellow paper. "Do you have a minute?"

"I guess," I said, feeling my grandiose lunch plans dissolving. By the time I could extract myself from the bustle without kicking Javier in the face or slipping on what was left of his coffee, Dunlop had pulled out a chair and was waiting.

He closed the door behind me and hurried back behind his desk. "So Monday."

"Yes?" I sat carefully in the hard plastic chair, then wished I hadn't. He was still standing, leaning over his desk at me, arms spread wide.

"I've documented the details," he said briskly, scooting the yellow paper across the desk toward me. "You'll want to read through this later. In general, not bad. An appropriate level of student participation, a decent amount of feedback. Your strong point, as always, was having the students demonstrate their understanding to both you and their peers. You also threw in some great tips for dealing with those problems on the test." He gave me his Cheshire Cat smile again, then tapped the paper. "You can read about all of that later."

"Okay."

"I did note…" He sighed dramatically and looked up, apparently searching the light fixtures for just the right words. "Quite a bit of sarcasm, Miss Smith."

I stared at the wall behind him. It was covered in faux-wood paneling and certificates documenting everything from participation in leadership exercises to being Dad of the Year. "They're sixth graders. Sarcasm is their native tongue."

"That doesn't mean you have to stoop so low. It's your job to expand their vocabularies."

I'm twenty-seven years old, five foot three, and the word Ms. comes before my name. If they think for a second that I can't play their game, it's all over. "I can assure you that no tender adolescent-boy egos were harmed in the making of that lesson plan."

"And there it is again. This is such a critical age, Miss Smith. If we don't show them that we respect them and that we'll be supportive when they make mistakes, we're going to lose them."

I didn't remember being particularly disrespectful, but I had the feeling that my ideas of respect weren't quite the same as his. I didn't say anything.

"I don't want to take up your time," Dunlop finally said as if he hadn't already done just that. "Keep working on that tone and classroom management."

I palmed the yellow paper, edged past him to the door, and forced a smile. "Thank you."

"Oh, my pleasure, Miss Smith. My pleasure."

The office was no longer full of activity. The copier was still running, but Selena was sitting back at her desk, filing her nails. It was twenty after twelve by then, and the first two wings of the school had already returned to class.

I tried to decompress a bit as I headed down the hall, but I was still pissed by the time I reached the staff lounge. Now all I wanted was a Coke and to shut myself in my classroom for a few minutes. When I arrived, Jody and Tina were bent over some newspaper article along with one of the other kindergarten teachers. Daniel was cleaning up his lunch tray. I felt eyes following me to the Coke machine, but I didn't care to whom they belonged.

"Thought you could blow us off, hmm?"

I fished my soda out of the machine and turned on Daniel. "I had a meeting with Dunlop, okay? I have to go."

He reeled in his arms and sucked in his gut as if he had to hug the wall in order to avoid me. "We'll stay out of your way, then."

"Sorry," I muttered to everyone else on my way out. "I don't mean to be a jerk."

I did get to spend most of my prep period with my head down on my desk, but it didn't do much for my attitude. I knew there was no use in fighting it, either. After picking apart a reading comprehension paragraph for five minutes more than any of us could stand, I asked my class to pack up, sat on the front of my desk, and read the second chapter of *Coral Sharkey and the Bat*.

Nearly all the teachers at Bush read aloud to their kids each day. While I didn't do it every day and thus was not considered a fun teacher, I did break out the book on the days we managed to finish our assignments early. There had been enough of those days during August and September to finish *Coral Sharkey and the Pharaoh* and conduct a bit of research on ancient Egypt and mummification. Today, I could feel the stress begin to drain from my body the moment I reached into my backpack.

This chapter was a good one. Often, I used ideas from books for writing assignments or class discussions, but this chapter was just plain goofy. Everyone was groaning as I read about how Coral's vampire ruined the uber-cool Margaret Bantock's slumber party when the afternoon announcements began.

"Come on," Gina said, glaring at the speaker. "It was just getting good."

"Shh," I said. "You might hear something important."

"Yeah, no," Christian grumbled.

Selena rambled on for a good three minutes about who was leaving the school under which mode of transportation, then reminded us to come cheer on our soccer team that Friday. Everyone looked hopeful for a second, but before I could find where I'd left off, she started in about report cards.

"Thirty more seconds," someone suggested when the speaker finally clicked off.

I shook my head. "Next time."

"I did not hear anything important," Christian said.

"Nestor is parent pickup today."

"I'm always parent pickup on Tuesdays," Nestor reminded me.

The bell rang. I tossed *Coral Sharkey* back into my bag and went to direct traffic as my kids grabbed books, jackets, and lunch boxes and crowded through the door. I lingered, running the usual interference, accepting armfuls of copies from a parent volunteer, listening politely as she told me about her teenage daughter's new boyfriend and her broken water heater. By the time she finished and the halls cleared, it was time to lock up and go to the faculty lounge.

Tuesdays were mandatory staff meetings, as predictable as Nestor's transportation. I decided to pretend I hadn't been a raving bitch during my last trip to the lounge and joined the handful of teachers already congregating there. Some people gravitated toward the more comfortable furniture in the far end of the room or the tables and chairs near the door. Others deliberately stood in awkward places, doing their best to look irritated. I took my usual spot between the paper cutter and Daniel on the countertop that ran the length of the back wall.

Several of the matronly teachers gave us looks full of shock and disdain every week, but I didn't care. There were more of us than there were chairs, and it wasn't as if I was removing my pants and doing a little dance. I was just sitting next to Daniel, wishing I could go home.

"How was your afternoon?" I asked him.

He glared. "How many TAAS vocabulary words can you find in this puzzle?"

"Yuck."

"Jasmine found *fag.*"

"That's a TAAS word?"

His eyes narrowed. "How was your afternoon?"

"Fine. Reading comp. North American trade routes. No bloodshed."

The room continued to fill with discussion and laughter, and the steady ostinato of sodas dropping out of the Coke machine began to lull me into a tired complacency. I had a few things to do back in my room, but the prospect of getting home early enough to cook dinner made me feel better. All four of the third-grade teachers were huddled by the copier, churning out worksheets. The first and second grade teachers were laughing about something so hard that tears were running down their faces. Bev Spardo's Diet Dr Pepper exploded all over the rug, and Sally Schumacher ran to get paper towels. Mr. Dunlop stationed himself next to the door, his legs planted firmly apart, his arms crossed like a balding, potbellied action figure. When Kathy finally entered the room, he glanced obviously at his wristwatch but folded his arms again without comment.

All the chairs were taken, so Kathy headed straight for the back wall. "Scoot," she told me, and as soon as I squished closer to Daniel, she was on the counter at my side, legs crossed at the knee, three-inch heels dangling precariously from her feet.

Kathy Sutton was an excellent principal. In the six years she'd been at Bush, attendance had stabilized, test scores had steadily crept out of the cellar, and parental involvement had increased dramatically. She was smart, personable, calculated, and owned a kick-ass repertoire of business suits with short skirts and painfully chic shoes.

From the beginning, I'd gotten along exceptionally well with her, and that had just fueled my fire. Frankly, I had a ridiculous number of fantasy scenarios in which I slept with her. She had intense, intelligent, dark eyes; spiral curls dyed a maroon-auburn; strong, fine hands with severely manicured nails; and a general air of such self-confidence, it gave me chills. She was quick to acknowledge there was no husband, but she shared her house with three terriers and a teenage daughter. I knew she wouldn't be interested in me even if she wasn't my employer, but that detail didn't at all discourage my daydreams.

"This one will be short," she announced, sending a sizzle of excited whispers around the room. "We need to speak briefly about the Christmas program, I have a few new details about next year's testing regimen, and I believe Mr. Dunlop has something to add about last week's in-service."

The door swung open, and Kathy paused to look up from her list. Jody covered her mouth and crept in, shoulders by her ears. Dunlop gave her a nasty look, even though she'd obviously just finished hall duty. Amy followed, holding the door so it wouldn't slam. Since everyone was looking at her anyway, Jody cut straight through the middle of the room and hoisted herself up on the counter beside Daniel. Amy started the same way but caught sight of me and quickly diverted to her right where the first-grade teachers made room for her on a sofa.

"Before we delve into business, though, I'd like to welcome our newest staff member. Tina Flores has come to us from Austin to take over the bilingual kindergarten class. When you see her in the halls, please make her feel welcome."

This was punctuated with a smattering of applause, and several people craned their necks to get a look at Tina, who was sitting with the other kindergarten teachers by the Coke machine. I smiled in her direction, then caught Amy watching. In turn, Amy's eyes darted floorward so quickly, I couldn't help but feel like the hunky football star to her dorky freshman in the middle of algebra class.

Amy Davis, head coach, wasn't an out-of-my-league fantasy lay like Kathy. I actually *had* slept with her. The coaches I'd had crushes on as a teenager had been tall, sleek, and powerful, and had winning smiles and the coolest brand-name warm-ups money could buy. Amy was little and stocky and had a closetful of khaki shorts and crisp white T-shirts bearing the logos of athletic shoes. She wore her grandmother's wedding band on her left hand as a decoy, and her whistle hung from a cord that wondered what Jesus would do.

I'd gone out to dinner with her during my first year at Bush for lack of anything better to do and had fallen into bed with her two weeks later for largely the same reason. We'd fucked off and on over the past three years behind the backs of our colleagues, her parents, and all the members of her church group, but I hesitated to think of her as my girlfriend since she certainly would never admit I was hers.

I turned my attention from Amy to Kathy in a hurry. She was talking about the Christmas program, something about the lower grades making decorations and the upper grades submitting the names of students to read texts. We would receive memos later. Daniel yawned and stared at the clock. Dunlop glared at him. Maggie McDaniel had a coughing fit and headed for the door. I assumed she would not be returning. It pissed me off.

Kathy went on to discuss the TAKS tests, scheduled to replace our TAAS battery during the next school year. Carefully, trying to appear interested in the chalkboard over her head, I looked back at Tina. She was in another short skirt, paired with a sweater today. Her legs were crossed demurely, her hands folded in her lap. Before I could look away, her glance moved almost imperceptibly to the right and focused on me. It would have been like me to panic, to blush, to do absolutely anything stupid and awkward, but I held her eye contact and smiled.

With absolutely no hint of apology whatsoever, she smiled right back at me.

That was when I felt a pinch on my ass. As Dunlop began to talk about the in-service, Daniel rolled his eyes and whispered close to my ear, "Please, darling. Do you think you could be any more obvious?"

❖

I lived on Parker Road at the extreme north edge of town, nearly as far as I could get from Bush while staying within the city limits. My apartment complex, like all the others of its vintage, looked like a compound of Motel Sixes: chunky, off-white, two-story buildings with exterior staircases grouped like Stonehenge around a parking lot full of El Caminos and F-150s.

I lived on the second floor of unit twenty-nine and shared an entry landing with a young Latino couple and their miniature Chihuahua. Just beyond my address, West Grove disappeared into an endless stretch of scrub grass pasture flanking Highway 669. From my living room window, I could watch the sunset in amazing pinks and golds above the silhouettes of longhorn cattle and oil derricks.

My two-bedroom rented for less than half of what Billy Jessen and I had paid for our apartment in graduate school. The carpet and linoleum were worn, and I didn't have much real furniture, but it was the first place I'd had all by myself, and I loved it. My sofa was a garish hand-me-down, the two wooden dining room chairs were mismatched, and the other two were metal folding chairs I'd borrowed years ago from some student group in Illinois. My end tables and coffee table were large packing crates I'd found at a flea market, the dresser in my bedroom was distressed at best, and my bookshelves were built of bricks and boards. The computer desk and shelving in my second bedroom were new, though, as was my bed. It had solid wood head- and footboards and was far superior to sleeping on the floor atop a mattress a friend's ex-girlfriend had once pulled out of a dumpster.

I would have felt like an adult if I had anyone to share it with, but I didn't, so I still spent most nights eating frozen dinners in front of the television. When I did cook, it was fun until I realized the futility of bringing that lovely meal to the dining room table to eat opposite nobody.

It was my own fault that this was one of those nights. When I arrived home, I found a message from Amy asking me to call her, but the thought of explaining what had gone on with Dunlop made me feel exhausted all over again. I opened a bottle of cabernet while my chicken was sautéing and had my second glass while I tossed it with penne and a rather pleasing marinara. Instead of returning Amy's call, I went into the living room to share my dinner and the rest of the bottle with Pat Sajak and Vanna White.

By ten, the dishes were done, and I'd run a load of whites through the laundry. I'd corrected homework, skimmed my lesson plans for the next day, and watched the early news to prepare for a discussion of current events. I'd also replayed my meeting with Mr. Dunlop in my mind more times than I could count and downed the rest of the bottle of wine plus half of another.

I hated it. Dunlop made me feel like a stumbling, unprepared child. Since my first day at Bush, he'd treated me like an outcast, like something disgusting and half-rotten that a dog had dragged out of the trash can. His imposing, self-righteous stare followed me everywhere I went in that building.

The worst of it started the day he'd asked me to his office to discuss my very first observation. He'd closed the door, sat me down, and paced the room with a sly, disgusting smile. The evaluation paperwork was nowhere to be seen. "You're such a Yankee," he'd said, his voice dripping with disdain. "You look different. You talk different. You act different. You even walk different."

I'd sat across from him, hands shaking, really wanting to correct him. The lack of Southern twang could, in fact, have been attributed to growing up elsewhere, but I'd suspected that my other differences stemmed from something else. I'd never considered myself to be a butch, but it was rather obvious that Wayne Dunlop had never before met a woman who insisted on holding the door for him.

If I'd had my wits about me, I might have filed a harassment report, but I was twenty-four years old and two years away from tenure. It had seemed like this town, this man, and this school were all stuck in some wicked time warp, and like a character in their drama, I'd sat there and taken it. I'd sat there, stared at the plaques on his wall for the first time of many, and taken it. Three years later, I still hated Dunlop for sneering at me and hated myself more for shrinking from him.

I wanted to daydream about how Tina Flores had caught my glance across the room, but I couldn't get Dunlop out of my head. I was going to have a horrible time getting to sleep thanks to that, but I finally gave in and headed to the bedroom.

The message light was flashing on my answering machine again. *Damn everything.* Amy must have called again while I was in the laundry room, and now it'd be obvious I was ignoring her. I felt foolish enough the way it was. The last thing I needed was to add guilt to the mix.

I pressed the button, not really wanting to hear what Amy had to say. It wasn't her, though. It wasn't anybody, actually, just a long enough silence for my machine to register a call, then a click and a dial tone.

Whatever. It probably was Amy, and she was too pissed to leave a message. Between putting away socks and returning my laundry basket to the closet, I stopped by the phone itself to check my caller ID.

West Grove, TX, it said, *230-9950*. Somebody's cell phone, probably a wrong number since the call had come in at ten fourteen. Nobody I knew in West Grove would call so late on a weeknight, especially Amy.

After getting ready for bed, I walked the same path through my apartment like a large cat pacing the perimeter of her cage at the zoo. I checked the lock and the dead bolt and eased the shades down. I set my wine bottle on the counter, ready to take out the next morning, and took a second to tidy the living room. Once back in my bedroom, I stripped off my T-shirt and set my alarm clock for six thirty, but before sliding between the covers, I moved to the back of the room, into the closet, where I took just a second to feel for the shoebox that sat atop the high shelf.

As always, I heard the reassuring scrape of my fingertips against cardboard. Now I could finally turn out the lights, burrow into the covers, and allow the vision of Tina in her short skirt and dark lipstick to sneak into my subconscious and conjure a decent night's sleep.

Instead, I awoke abruptly around three, heart pounding, the residual terror of a horrible dream clinging to my brain. All that blood. I couldn't shake the vision. For just a second, I longed for someone to call out to, to roll over against, to hold, but there in the chilly, silent darkness, it was only me.

Chapter Three

I ran into Tina again on Friday morning. I was on my way back from the office, trying to pass the gym without catching Amy's eye, when Tina rounded the corner of C-wing, ostensibly returning from the staff lounge.

Just like Tuesday afternoon in the faculty meeting, our smiles came easily. "Hey," she said. "Cary, right?"

I nodded. "How're you?"

"Fine, thanks. How was your meeting with Mr. Dunlop?"

"Oh, it was fine," I said dismissively. "How's it been going?"

"I think I'm starting to get the hang of it. Of course, nobody said anything about casual Friday."

I wasn't offended by her skirt and blouse. "Not everybody dresses down. Anyway, it's your first week. You're allowed to look good for a week, right?"

"I kind of feel like an idiot."

"Oh, don't." It came out sounding a lot more emphatic than I'd intended, in a way that totally betrayed what I really wanted to say: *you look fantastic*.

One of those should-have-been awkward moments followed. I stared at her. She stared at me. I had the feeling that we could've stayed there all day if Daniel hadn't smacked me on the shoulder.

"David Mackey has arrived. You might want to scurry on down there before he sets your classroom on fire."

"I should go," I said, at once very aware of the traffic milling past us.

"I'll see you at lunch," she said. "That is, if you grace us with your presence."

I knew I was setting myself up for a huge, stupid crash. I knew she was probably straight, just new in town and looking for friends. Still, I couldn't keep the smile off my face as I took attendance, led the class in the pledge, and sat through the usual excruciating morning announcements. I knew it was still there as I pulled down the world map, intending to discuss the Middle East, but I didn't expect to be called on it.

Shannon started it with, "Somebody's in a good mood this morning."

Cristal leaned across the aisle. "Bet she has a date tonight."

There came an eruption of whispers, giggles, and a few nasty catcalls. This happened sooner or later every year; there was no way it wouldn't, considering the very title they were supposed to address me with betrayed that I was single. It had made me nervous my first year, especially since I'd happened to get together with Amy just days before the questions had started, but in time, I'd come to realize how harmless most of their suppositions were. These were small-town sixth graders living in the middle of nowhere and were a lot less worldly than expected. Their idea of me dating usually involved a big, strong, oil worker who would take me out for dinner and a movie and, if he was bold enough, try to sneak a good-night kiss.

I hadn't been so innocent since junior high, but with Dunlop breathing down my neck, I welcomed the angelic reputation.

"So," Gina said deliberately. "Do you?"

I glanced over the class, taking in the last few whispers. *Bet she does. Bet he's cute. Nasty...Have you looked at her?* "What do you think?"

The room went dead silent, and glances were exchanged. Before the commotion could start again, I grabbed a marker. "How many of you think I have a date tonight?"

Hands shot into the air, but the shocked silence continued. I counted twenty-one and wrote that number on the board.

"How many of you think I'm going to sit at home by myself watching sitcom reruns?"

Now, a few of the boys waved their hands, most of them higher than necessary. One of those hands belonged to David Mackey. I documented that, then nodded.

"How many of you don't care?"

Christian cocked an eyebrow at me. "Can I change my vote?"

"Too late. Our total, Nestor?"

"Twenty-eight."

"We're all here. Thank you, Gina. This was quite illuminating."

"Are you going to tell us who's right?"

Hell, no. "We'll graph it after the spelling test."

There was a collective groan. "Ugh," Chelsea muttered. "You are absolutely incorrigible."

"Oh, and ten points for the word," I said, scribbling *incorrigible* on the right side of the board. "You guys are rocking my world today."

The rest of the morning was just about that good. Twenty-six out of my twenty-eight kids had turned in all their homework, and I got a head start on grading tests during their period in the library. We were a few minutes late to lunch, and by the time I finished talking to Jody, the bilingual kindergarten class was marching into the cafeteria.

Tina followed me back out the door. "Sorry…my lunch is in my classroom."

"Not going to brave the fish sticks?"

She made a face. "I live next door to Captain D's. My parking lot smells like this all the time."

"At least you're not by the refineries."

"Is there anywhere in town where you can't smell the refineries?"

"Not really." I realized I'd followed her all the way down A-wing. I peeked inside once she unlocked the door to A-3, hoping to make that less weird. "Oh, this looks great."

"Thanks. Mrs. Shore did most of it, but I'm adding to it."

While Tina dug for her lunch, I admired the room. Instead of desks, the kindergarteners worked at tables, and each child's name hung in bold letters on the back of his or her chair. An entire bulletin board was covered with huge swatches of color. *Rojo* - red. *Azul* - blue. *Amarillo* - yellow. Fat crepe-paper-covered fish dangled from the ceiling. The dry-erase board at the front of the room displayed the day of the week, the date, and a list of two- and three-letter words, all written in that lovely, round teacher hand I'd never managed to achieve.

A vivid image of what Tina must have looked like on a ladder, hanging those fish from the ceiling, popped into my head. As she reached upward with the string and the thumbtack, her sweater rode up, revealing just a hint of bare flesh. It took a moment to shake it when she returned with her lunch bag.

"Well," she said, closing the door behind us again, "I guess if it weren't for the oil, we wouldn't be here."

"You *are* a Texan."

She grinned. "Sounded that way, didn't it? I lived in East Texas for long enough to call it home. I hear you're a Yankee." Her voice carried none of the disgust Daniel's usually did.

"Really? Someone told you that?"

"So where's home?"

I shrugged. "Here and there. We moved around a lot."

"Always carefully staying north of the Mason-Dixon?"

"Actually, we lived in the south for a couple years, but don't let Daniel know that."

"I won't tell. How come you moved so much? Were you an Army brat?"

I shook my head. "My mother wasn't really into roots." That sounded as weird and dismissive as it usually did, but I'd never found a better way to explain it. I held the door to the lounge for Tina, then for Bev and Sally as they left the room discussing Weight Watchers' points.

Daniel raised his eyebrows at us. "Well, hello."

"Good afternoon," I said. "How are the fish sticks?"

"Better if you don't think of them as fish."

Jody burst through the door several minutes later. "You know what tonight is," she sang, plopping her tray on the table and beaming at us.

Tina caught my eye, then turned back to her lunch. I could tell that she assumed whatever it was, she wasn't invited.

"Friday?" I guessed, fairly sure I hadn't forgotten anything. The week before, Friday had meant some retreat at her church. It wasn't as though we had some kind of standing date.

Jody's eyes went wide in disbelief. "Half-price at the Ranch Hand."

Daniel swatted at her. "Talk dirty to me."

"I know you're in," Jody said to me, then turned to Tina. "You have to come with us. Their sangria is to die for."

Tina glanced toward me as if I was the one who had asked. "I'm sorry, I can't."

"Oh, you don't have to drink," Jody said quickly. "Get some dinner, shoot the breeze."

"Really, I'd love to, I just can't tonight."

Daniel sighed impatiently. "How come?"

"The other kindergarten teachers are taking me to Denny's."

I nodded coolly, but Jody's face screwed up in horror. "*Denny's?*"

"Oh honey," Daniel said, "that just ain't right."

Tina got up and gathered her trash, a lovely, almost-bad smile on her face. "I know, but they're all excited about it. Mrs. Shore is coming and everything."

"Oh," I said. "Say hello for me."

Daniel groaned at me before the door could even close behind Tina. "Say hello to the old bat substitute? Hot, Cary. Really hot."

"Shh," Jody interrupted, covering his mouth. "There'll be plenty of time for that later."

❖

My last students were barely out of the classroom when Jody closed my door and did a little hippity-hop between the desks. "You know what time it is?"

"Are you signed out already?"

"I would've signed for you, too, but you know how the trashy bitch feels about that."

I grinned. "Our friend Selena. Give me five minutes. I have a lot to put together."

"What, homework? You don't give them tests on Fridays, Cary. Look, if you run right now, you can probably still catch Coach D."

"I don't know."

"See if she can come! I haven't seen her outside school forever. Come on," she teased. "You know you want to."

That was the trouble. I *didn't* want to. Things had been worse than stale between Amy and me for a long time, but the way she'd stumbled during the staff meeting Tuesday confirmed my suspicion that she hadn't come to that conclusion yet. I was afraid I was going to have to make up some stupid excuse when a low, indistinct hum came from the speaker on the ceiling.

Neither of us spoke, and Jody looked up and frowned. The PA system at Bush was intended both to broadcast announcements throughout the school and to facilitate communication during an emergency. There was a little white button on the wall of each classroom that allowed us to page the office. Mine was just above the pink piece of paper hiding the bullet holes. Of course, this meant that the office could listen in on the classrooms, and I secretly suspected that Selena spent most of her time eavesdropping and reporting everything she heard to Mr. Dunlop.

The speaker buzzed for a good thirty seconds before Selena spoke. "Miss Smith?"

I spoke loudly toward the ceiling. "Yes?"

There was another appreciable pause. "You have a parent here to see you."

She could have just sent them down. More fun to buzz me after hours, though. Who knew what filth I could be spewing? "I'll be there in a second."

Another long pause. "All right. Thank you, ma'am."

"Thank you," I said, making an obscene gesture toward the speaker as the hum finally ended. "The day they install cameras?"

"The first day of your unemployment," Jody agreed. "You still don't call her ma'am? It's no wonder she hates you."

I rolled my eyes and headed for the door. "I'll be back."

"I'll go see if Daniel's ready."

Just as Jody hoped, I hit the main hall at the same time Amy left the cafeteria. I thought about turning around as if I'd forgotten something, but I didn't want to keep the parent waiting. Amy glanced in both directions, then pretended to fix something on the cafeteria door just long enough to fall in step with me.

I didn't look at her. "Ranch Hand?"

"Soccer game."

"That's right. I could get them to go later?"

"Can't. My Dad's going to the game. Saturday night? Maybe just you and…Hey, Edgar, go warm up, okay? Coach Johnson's out there already."

I paused to let a throng of students past. "Can't. Sunday night?"

"Bible study. Look," she whispered, leaning in as we neared the office. "Call me, okay?"

"Okay."

She looked directly at me for the first time in the conversation. "Okay?"

"I will."

Twenty minutes later, Daniel, Jody and I met at the Ranch Hand. It was one of the better steak houses in town, featuring a menu of large, reasonably priced cuts of beef and Tex-Mex favorites. The decor was Gene Autry-meets-Applebee's, but at least it wasn't Denny's. We requested a table in an empty corner and were seated beneath a huge yoke and a pair of grubby boots. Daniel spent an embarrassingly long time appreciating the spurs. Jody ignored him and ordered sangrias all around, and I got carded as usual. As if that wasn't bad enough, Daniel made such a fuss about how he never got carded that the server finally asked for his just to humor him. While he didn't necessarily look thirty-four, nobody with half a brain would have mistaken him for underage.

By the time our food came, the other tables were filling, and Daniel already had a few drinks under his belt. Jody had blown through her first sangria, but she'd taken three tiny sips of her second so it would outlast her sirloin. I was still nursing my first. I wasn't much for sangria in the first place, and drinking in public made me nervous. The walls had ears in West Grove.

I was afraid Daniel would start right in about Tina, but we didn't touch the subject. Jody went on for over thirty minutes about ideas for the school play, and then Daniel giggled about things that had happened in his classroom that week. "So I drag Tanya down to the office, right, and Selena takes one little glance and gives me the, *ugh, deal with it yourself,* look, the lazy ass."

Jody set her fork down abruptly. "Cary still doesn't call her ma'am."

He looked confused for a moment, then turned on me like I had three heads. "What is wrong with you? Have we not spoken about this before?"

"I don't call anybody ma'am. I mean, if I need to get a stranger's attention, maybe."

"What *do* you call Selena, then?"

"Nothing, usually."

"And this is why she hates you," Jody said.

Daniel shook his head. "She'd hate you anyway. What do you call Kathy?"

"Kathy. Ms. Sutton if there are students around. I don't see the big deal."

"This is why we still call you a Yankee, hon. You're treating people like the help."

"I'm not. I'm always polite to people."

Jody picked up her fork again. "But you don't call them ma'am."

"Look, I hate it when my kids *ma'am* me," I said, turning my attention to my dinner. "It's contrived and annoying. If I would've dared call my mother ma'am, I would've gotten smacked for being cocky."

Jody shook her head as if declaring me a hopeless case. "That's your problem with Dunlop, too, if you ask me."

Daniel grinned. "That she doesn't call him ma'am?"

I didn't look up from my steak. "He says I'm too sarcastic to my students."

"Baby, you're not nearly old enough to be their mother, and they all know it. If you don't give it back to them every once in a while, they're going to have you for a snack," Jody said. "Next time he picks on you, you uh-huh, *sir* in all the right places and leave it right in his office."

"Yeah," Daniel said. "I'm sorry, but have you figured out any other way to deal with David Mackey and Christian Benson short of duct tape?"

Cary shook her head. "I have not."

"He's just an ass," Daniel told me decisively. Over the course of his drinks, his face had grown considerably redder, his voice louder, and at some point, he'd unbuttoned his polo shirt one more digit. Now, he ran his hand through his hair, shifting the product around enough to make it stick straight out in several places. It was a huge improvement. "Just a big, overinflated ass. And if he tries to set me up with one more *woman...*"

I snuck a look at the tables directly flanking ours. The one behind Daniel was still empty, but the one behind Jody was full of large men wearing coveralls. They seemed to be absorbed in their own conversation in Spanish.

Jody looked a little wary, too. "Come on," she said with a forced laugh. "Some of us aren't so bad."

"Oh, don't get me wrong, I love my hags. I'd just appreciate it if they hired me some eye candy for once. Excuse me, ma'am," Daniel said, flagging the server down. "Another sangria, please?"

Jody clicked her tongue. "Two words," she said, her voice barely above a whisper. "Morality clause."

"Oh, please. You think I'm drunk?"

"I know you're drunk. I'm going to have to take you home."

"I've only had—"

"Four?" Jody asked as the server set the latest down. "Or is this five?"

"It's five," I said.

"You're cut off. Could I look at a dessert menu, please?"

"Yes, ma'am." The server pulled one off another table, took Jody's order, then brushed against my purse and knocked it off the back of my chair. When I bent to retrieve it, Daniel started singing.

"I see London, I see France, I see Cary's butt floss."

I came back up as quickly as I could and pulled my sweater down. "Your rhyme needs some help."

"Butt floss pants would work," Jody suggested.

"I've known you for a long time," Daniel said, leaning toward me and touching my arm as if he was about to say something tremendously profound. "Never would I have imagined you wearing a thong."

My cheeks had gone red-hot, but I tried to sound indifferent. "That's good, since it would seriously disturb me to know you were imagining me in my underwear."

"Gonna get some tonight? Where is Coach D, anyway?"

"That wouldn't be your business even if you were sober."

"Does Coach D wear a thong?"

I gave him a warning look. "Shut up."

Daniel shook his head at Jody. "Now you're going to tell me *you're* wearing a thong."

"Well, if I had a tight little butt like that, maybe."

Daniel made a face. "On the topic of getting some, I think little Miss Flores has a bit of a crush on you."

It would have been completely egotistical to assume Daniel was talking to me if we were at dinner with anyone other than Jody. It wasn't that she was unattractive; she was just so blatantly asexual that most people had long ago stopped wondering which way she went. His words rattled me more than a little, but I tried my best not to let on. "Oh, please."

"When I went to sign out today, Kathy asked her how it was going. I distinctly heard her say how helpful and encouraging Ms. Smith has been."

"What am I supposed to do, pick on her like you do? Anyway, she's straight."

Jody frowned. "Is there a boyfriend? She doesn't wear a ring."

"I don't know."

Daniel's eyes went wide. "Then how do you know she's straight? Ten bucks says you guys are in the sack within two weeks."

I didn't get a chance to kick him. Jody's eyebrows arched, and her voice was low and incisive. "Would you like to remind us where Amy fits into this equation?"

"You are no fun, Jody Finnegan. No fun at all." Daniel watched me for a second, then stepped on my toe. "Would you do her?"

I glanced around the restaurant. "I'm not going to answer that."

"I think you like her."

Jody's eyes narrowed. "She's sweet, she's nice, and she's drop-dead gorgeous. What's not to like? Can we please leave it at that and find another subject before the flying monkeys descend upon us?"

Daniel only leaned farther onto the table. My fork fell off my plate, and the salt shaker tipped over. "Wouldn't you like to find out what *she's* wearing under those little tiny skirts? If she's wearing anything at all, that is."

"Daniel," Jody hissed.

He winked. "So Cary's taken. Maybe you're the one I should put my money on."

As usual, Jody didn't substantiate or deny anything. "Maybe," she suggested, setting her credit card on the table, "we should get out of here before you get your butt in trouble."

Chapter Four

The very first document I was handed upon arriving at the West Grove Independent School District's administration office in August of 1998 was not my contract. It was one sheet of white paper covered front and back with eight-point legalese stating that if I, as an employee of the West Grove Independent School District, was found to be engaging in any sort of "immoral" behavior, my contract would immediately be terminated.

Nowhere did it define "immoral," nor did it specify any recourse in the event of an accusation. While I understood that I was giving my employers the right to discriminate, I signed the infamous morality clause, desperate for a job, desperate for a paycheck. I'd been terrified of it ever since. While I didn't give a second thought to pushing a cart around Walmart at eleven o'clock on Sunday morning, I did hesitate to have more than one drink in public. When I dated, I felt like a contestant on a reality show, half expecting to find cameras wedged between the towels in my linen closet and amid boxes of macaroni and cheese in the pantry. Anytime I had sex with a woman, I imagined the SWAT teams were waiting to break down the door. Anytime I did it by myself, I wondered if the good people of West Grove had made special arrangements with God to suspiciously increase my contact lens prescription each year.

Jody usually did a good job of policing Daniel in public, but he didn't hold his liquor well. He'd never been called on the carpet for his sexual orientation, but he had been warned about drinking. Amy and I had gone out with him one evening during my first year at Bush, and after consuming several beers, he'd turned in the middle of a remarkably realistic RuPaul imitation to find Mr. Dunlop and his wife waiting to be seated.

Amy had cried on the way home, certain Daniel would be fired, but he'd gotten off easy. After sitting through what he described as an interminable meeting with Kathy, Dunlop, three supervisors, and the assistant superintendent, it was determined that he had displayed admirable character in his eight years of service to the district, and he was placed on one year's probation. He'd slowed down for about six months, but he'd never taken the threat very seriously. It still frightened me, though, and it absolutely paralyzed Amy.

That being said, Amy's dogged persistence surprised me. For someone who all but pretended not to know me at school, she'd pursued me with a vengeance. I didn't understand how she could enjoy the nearly silent dinners we shared at restaurants. The way her eyes darted back and forth from the servers, to the other patrons, to the door made my stomach so tight, I could barely push food past my lips. She managed to relax considerably once we were alone in her house, but her parents, neighbors, and church friends felt so comfortable stopping by with no notice that most of our sexual encounters played out like a comedy of errors. The one time I'd convinced her to avoid the interruptions by coming to my place, she'd spent the evening nervously checking her messages and worrying about her dogs.

I did feel bad about putting her off. Beyond the frightened, uncertain facade was an undeniably lovely human being, a sweet, gentle person who wanted nothing more than to please everyone. We'd talked for hours over the years when her parents were occupied, and her dogs were asleep. She'd done an admirable job of baring her soul to me, and I'd given her an abridged version of mine. She was a decent lover when everything went without a hitch. There really were several reasons I hadn't managed to break up with her.

My promise to call her still fell between the cracks. I was on the phone Sunday evening with my college friend Billy in Killeen when another call clicked in. It was Amy, so I went on about how ridiculously busy I'd been all weekend, then lied and said my mother was on the other line. By the time I had gotten off the phone with Billy, I knew she was at bible study, so I left a message on her phone and hoped she wasn't as mad as she deserved to be.

She was, but it didn't last long. After disappearing into the storage room and moving to the opposite side of the playground at exactly the right times to avoid me for two days, she emerged from her tiny office Wednesday afternoon to watch as I helped Jody rehearse the sixth graders for an all-school assembly.

Jody was creating quite a scene trying to line the kids up, place them onstage, and warm up their voices, so it was completely reasonable for Amy to lean in the cafeteria doorway with a grin on her face. Kathy was busy doing the same thing in the entrance closest to the office.

When it was time for the assembly itself, I spent the first few minutes at the edge of the room where Jody had my students sit crisscross applesauce, running interference. When she brought them onstage, though, I moved past the whole crowd and parked against the back wall. It was there that Amy sidled up to me.

At first, neither of us said anything. We just stood there, arms folded, eyes darting from the glut of squirmy kids on the floor, to the stage, to Dunlop, who was prowling back and forth down the hall.

As Jody settled at the scarred upright and started plunking out the piano accompaniment, Amy eyed me sideways and spoke without moving her lips. "Come over tonight?"

I'd expected to be chastised, not propositioned. "I'm on the rag."

"You're a fucking liar."

I turned toward her quickly, but her eyes were on the stage, and her expression was blank. "What?"

"You used that excuse two weeks ago."

"Well, I'm really screwed-up, then."

No response. I turned everything around in my head, kicking myself for being so stupid. I didn't particularly want to sleep with her, but I didn't want her to stay mad at me, either. Maybe we could cut some kind of deal. Maybe she could call everyone she knew, feed her cats, do her laundry, and bring her dogs over to my place.

"Yep," she decided after another excruciating moment. "They sound pretty good."

"They do," I said. "Look, how about Friday? I could come over Friday."

The blank look returned. "Sure you're going to be off the rag by then?"

I closed my eyes. "Look, if you don't want me to…"

"I'll see you Friday." With that, she meandered along the perimeter of the room and back toward the hall. Once upon a time, it had been a little exciting to covertly watch her ass as she walked away. Now, the very thought made me tired.

I dragged through dismissal feeling somewhere between bitchy and slutty. I hadn't helped her wash her dogs last week and had avoided a phone conversation all weekend, but I was willing to come over for sex Friday night?

I had a ton of papers to correct and a week's worth of lesson plans to write, so my goal was to sit at my desk for a few hours with my red pen and my frustration. I'd barely settled into the first essay when Marisol Ayala knocked.

"Hey, did you mention the other day that you have a blank map of the waterway network?"

I needed a Coke. I grabbed my purse and went with her to copy the map. The halls were still bustling. Parents were talking to Daniel outside his classroom. A backpack flew over a small boy's head and smacked against the door to the girls' bathroom. Jody's voice boomed down the hall, demanding that the thrower *come here right now*. When we turned onto the main hall, I saw Amy squatting to help a first grader tie her shoe outside the cafeteria. It reminded me of the thong discussion at the Ranch Hand. Amy wore pastel cotton bikinis, the kind that came in a multipack. I'd never seen her shirt untucked at school.

Marisol said something about it being a mess out there as we ducked into the lounge together, but if anything, that was worse. Not only was it crowded, but there were three people waiting in line to use the copier.

"Worse than usual," I agreed, joining them.

"What kind of Coke?" Marisol asked.

It had taken me two years to get used to the fact that in West Grove, that could mean a Sprite or a Dr Pepper, not just regular or diet. "Just a regular Coke," I said, handing her change.

Marisol was one of those sweet, clueless, West Grove natives, absolutely incapable of understanding me no matter how she tried. She lived in a beautiful ranch-style house in one of the newer developments on the east side of town with her husband and their baby girl. Her parents and grandparents lived just minutes away. Her degree was from the college in the next town over, and she'd lived at home while studying there. To my knowledge, the only time she'd been outside the state was her honeymoon trip to Florida. She had invited me over for a barbecue once and spent the entire evening trying to set me up with her husband's brother. While he was nice, gainfully employed, and good-looking, I was fairly sure he had a penis, and I spent the next month and a half worrying that I'd offended Marisol by avoiding his advances. She hadn't been mad, though, just a little disappointed. She asked from time to time if I was seeing anybody but seemed satisfied when I'd smiled secretively and shrugged that I was too busy for that stuff.

Fortunately, we talked about her daughter instead of my love life as we waited for the copier. It jammed on Maggie McDaniel, and I had to get on my knees and dig the paper out. Sally Schumacher was so busy telling Marisol when to start her baby on solid foods that she didn't notice Maggie had finished. When she finally started her copying, the paper ran out, and she had to open a new box from the supply closet. I really wanted to just hand the map to Marisol and tell her to copy it herself after all, but it seemed rude, so I stood and waited. By the time I was done and could go back to my classroom, the halls were empty.

Surely, the stack of essays on my desk had multiplied in my absence. I ran my fingers through them dully, wondering how long this was really going to take. When I went to sit and resign myself to the task, though, I found my chair pushed to the wall, away from my desk and over to the side.

It was the oddest thing. I didn't remember shoving it back that far when Marisol had entered; to move it to that angle would take a conscious effort. I couldn't tell if the custodians had swept yet, but there was still trash in my wastebasket, and the board hadn't been erased.

An unsettled feeling began in the pit of my stomach. I rarely left my classroom door unlocked, even to run to the bathroom, and I couldn't believe that the one time I had, someone had taken advantage of it. I returned the map I'd Xeroxed to my file cabinet, then surveyed my room. My disc player still sat on the shelf behind my desk, and the computer was still tucked next to the locker area on its cart. Nothing seemed to be out of place, save for my chair.

I tried my desk drawers and found everything intact. The two that locked were still locked, and the two that didn't held nothing of value. My backpack was on the floor where I'd left it, my copy of the sixth-grade math book and the bright pink and turquoise cover of *Coral Sharkey and the Bat* barely visible from where I stood. My purse had been with me. Someone had probably been looking for that.

Just stop it. I was tired, upset with myself, perhaps a little bit afraid that someone could've overheard me with Amy. Nothing was missing, after all. Before my mind could play any more tricks, I zipped up my backpack, grabbed the pile of paperwork off my desk, and headed home.

❖

That night, after a dinner from one of the drive-thru burger barns, I dragged one of my dining room chairs into my bedroom closet and climbed up to survey the contents of the top shelf. The closet was an enormous walk-in with room to hang every garment I owned and enough floor space to host an elementary school slumber party. The top shelf held a stack of LPs, a pair of snow boots that were completely useless in West Grove, and a large cardboard shoebox.

I took the shoebox down and onto the floor. It was from a pair of size-eight Nikes I still owned. The original box had become so tattered through move after move that I'd replaced it a year ago. I took a moment to dust off the lid, then slowly spread the contents on the carpet in front of me.

Some things might have been worthy of a safe-deposit box. My grandfather was a collector, and the smattering of coins he'd sent me over the years had stayed in their respective cases under a few random birthday cards I kept just to cover them. Beneath those were the things that were really important to me: some photographs, a graduation card, a handful of letters, and a small stack of yellowed newspaper clippings.

I scanned everything, touching a photograph, a clipping, for seconds at a time, not reading any of the words. I rarely took anything out of the box, and when I did, it had nothing to do with nostalgia. After the weirdness in my classroom, I needed to feel safe. I needed to feel as completely invisible as I'd been for the first eighteen years of my life, before anyone knew my name, before anyone cared about where I'd been and what I believed.

I piled everything back into the box, careful not to tear the delicate newsprint or fold the corners on the photographs. I could have merely slid it back up on the shelf, but I took the time to get on the chair, to choose its exact position.

There was nothing worth pilfering in my classroom, nothing of value, nothing the slightest bit incriminating. Really, beyond half a shelf of novels that betrayed my sexual orientation and a well-stocked liquor shelf, there wasn't anything that anyone would consider worth finding in my apartment, either. The framed photos were of my family and my college friends. I was not a journal writer. Everything of real value, both the good and the bad, were tucked safely away inside my head where nobody would ever be able to come across them by accident. I knew that deep down and believed it completely, but for some reason, I still sensed that something was brewing.

❖

Thursday was burrito day. I meant to be early to lunch, but we packed up late and made it through the line behind Millie Johnson's kindergarten class. Jody's cafeteria duty shift was ending, so she got a tray along with Tina and me and started toward the door.

Oscar Muniz caught up with me first, wiggling a small blue slip of paper from the office. "Sign this, Ms. Smith? Ms. Ortiz won't let me go to recess until you sign it."

"Pardon me?"

He sighed and started again. "Would you please sign this, ma'am?"

"I would be happy to."

"I was at the dentist," he told me, smiling wide so I could see his teeth.

I balanced my tray in one hand, and Jody offered me a ballpoint pen from behind her ear. I told Oscar to turn and held the blue sheet against his back to scribble the general gist of my name on the proper line. "Happy recess."

"Thanks," he said, heading back in the direction of the office at a barely contained almost-run.

Tina held the door for us. "You spell your name with a Y?"

I nodded, sticking the pen back behind Jody's ear.

"A C and a Y?"

"Yes."

"That's different. Is it your real name?"

I felt my eyes go wide. "What?"

"I mean, is it short for something?"

"Oh," I said quickly. "No, just Cary. My father chose it."

"After Cary Grant," Jody inserted.

"Really?"

I shot Jody a look. "No. There's probably some story behind it, but my mom doesn't like to talk about him."

The staff lounge turned out to be like a seven-car pileup with multiple injuries and emergency vehicles. If I could've gotten away with it, I would have asked Tina and Jody back into the hall where we could sit on the nasty floor and eat our burritos in silence. Sally Schumacher's Jack Russell had given birth the night before, and she was busy sharing the story in blow-by-blow detail as everyone else attempted to eat without vomiting. I was almost done with my burrito anyway, trying to tune her out and feeling vaguely thankful that she hadn't gotten her film developed yet, when the door opened.

It was Mr. Dunlop, hand in his pocket, jingling change on his daily pilgrimage to the Coke machine. He scanned the table in a faraway manner as if we were his sheep, but he moved on quickly as soon as he caught wind of our topic.

"We're going to keep the two girls," Sally told us, finally beginning to gather her things.

Jody murmured an indistinct answer and nodded with big eyes.

"I was trying to think of good names, but I could only come up with Gertrude and Alice."

Daniel stared. "The only names you could think of were Gertrude and Alice?"

"Well, you know," she said, "for Gertrude Stein and Alice B. Toklas?"

Things became very quiet. A few shifty glances moved around the table, and Jody actually looked upward as if to determine whether Selena was listening. Mr. Dunlop stood silent, his eyes on the soda machine as if there were more than five flavors to choose from.

"Ms. Smith," Sally said in what seemed like an unnaturally loud voice, "who are some other famous woman couples?"

I felt the redness creeping up my neck fast. There had to be some way to divert attention from me, but I couldn't think of one. I couldn't even think of any other couples, not that naming puppy siblings after lesbians was something I would support in the first place.

Slowly, one at a time, Mr. Dunlop's coins slid into the soda machine. Daniel had covered his mouth with a napkin, although I couldn't tell if he was trying not to laugh or still visualizing dog placenta. I couldn't look at Jody or Tina. Both Sally and Bev were waiting patiently for my answer.

"You could call her Trudy," I finally suggested, more to my tray than to Sally. I heard a Coke can drop in the periphery.

Fortunately, Sally smiled. "Oh, I like that! Trudy's a great dog name. Maybe I will stick with that."

She and Bev left, still talking a mile a minute about dogs. While I was staring dumbly at the door, Dunlop moved through it. He didn't say anything but offered up a strange little smile.

The moment the door closed, Daniel dropped his jaw. "Please. How about Martina and Rita Mae? Ellen and Anne? Those Indigo Girls?"

"They're not together," Jody inserted delicately.

"What was that about, anyway?" he asked, leaning so low that his tie grazed his lunch tray. "Did you do something to piss her off, or is she just unbelievably stupid?"

"And in front of Dunlop," Jody whispered.

"Don't worry about it," I muttered, gathering my tray. "It's not like it would change his opinion of me."

"I'll love you forever if you return mine, too," Daniel offered.

I wanted to tell him to bite me, but I took his tray and didn't say anything.

Tina grabbed her tray and opened the door for me. "Come on."

I so wished that she hadn't witnessed that exchange. It wasn't that I didn't want her to know I was gay, I just hated that she'd seen me looking like such an idiot. I anticipated awkward silence all the way to the cafeteria, but I was wrong.

"You really think he doesn't like you?" she asked.

"He's wanted to see me fired since my very first day."

"Why?"

The question hung thickly in the air. There were so many answers, and at the same time, there were none. Our eyes met for a long time, even though Marvin the custodian was sweeping the floor barely twenty feet away.

"That's right," she finally said with what I could swear was a tiny wink. "You're a Yankee."

Chapter Five

My father, Lanny Smith, was indeed the one who'd insisted upon naming me Cary. Beyond that, I knew very little about him. According to two of the photographs from the shoebox in my closet, he was strikingly handsome, with dark eyes, an irreverent smile, and a strong, wiry build. He drove a battered red pickup, listened to The Grateful Dead, and painted houses for a living. He was also a high school dropout with a hot temper and a drinking problem.

He was five years my mother's senior. My grandparents did not approve of him and had been furious when my mother had gotten pregnant shortly before her high school graduation. My mother had married my father and started nursing school, trying her best to make things right, but by that February, just two months after I was born, he had moved out. They didn't officially divorce until three years later, but I did not remember my father, and only one picture of the three of us existed, a Polaroid taken in my grandmother's living room when I was five days old. It was the only photo of him that remained in any of my mother's albums.

My grandparents and my mother's three older siblings had been very good to her. They'd babysat and paid for my mother to finish school. They were understandably upset when she'd left Portland after the divorce, but their grudge was short-lived. They'd understood that she had to move on, to attempt to have the life she'd intended before getting mixed up with Lanny Smith.

Our first move was to Scranton, Pennsylvania, where my mother had taken a job at Mercy Hospital. I'd attended kindergarten there, but I remembered almost nothing aside from a small, dark, stale-smelling apartment and the entrance of my mother's second husband, Stanley the Rat. With his help, she'd managed to wash her hands of everything having to do with my father, save for half my genetics and my last name, which, curiously, she'd never sought to legally change.

What she'd chosen to do instead was call me by my middle name, Elizabeth. I didn't know if she'd resented that my father had chosen my first name or if she'd just preferred Elizabeth, but in any case, she'd introduced me to everyone in Scranton as such, and it had become the name to which I'd answered.

It wasn't easy. I was a shy kid, and it was awful to have to explain my name to my teachers every time we'd moved to a new school. I'd never considered that I could be anyone other than Liz, though, until my first college roommate had called to introduce herself the summer before our freshman year at the University of Illinois.

The moment she'd asked, "May I speak with Cary Smith?" it had struck me hard. I would be on my own. Nobody would be expecting my mother to come to conferences or sign permission slips. It was my opportunity to erase the confusion, the embarrassment, and the baggage. Liz Smith could drop off the face of the earth, and Cary Smith could appear out of nowhere three-hundred-and-fifty miles away. It was like something my mother would have done.

I'd always preferred my given name. Instead of correcting her, I'd simply agreed. "This is Cary."

Friday was a lovely day, sunny and hot for October, without a trace of the insistent wind that usually blew clouds of dust and tumbleweed down the street. We spent much of the afternoon outside on the back sidewalk, carefully potting bean seeds in Dixie cups in a variety of soils with and without fertilizer so we could study and graph our results as to which produced the tallest, strongest plants. It wasn't in the curriculum, but I didn't care.

At least we were doing work. I'd seen Chris's class out playing kickball on Friday afternoons more than once. After we finished with the plants, I let the kids lie on their stomachs in the scratchy brown grass beside the walk, journaling their predictions about the experiment's outcome. They were so happy to be out of the classroom that they mostly did what they were told, and I didn't care anyway if some of them were just sitting and talking.

Everything was fine, really. I'd spent thirty minutes on the phone with Amy the night before, planning our evening like a good sometime-girlfriend. We were going to make dinner together, something that would hopefully be busy and wholesome and more conducive to conversation than going out to a restaurant. I wanted to make up for being such a jerk over the past few weeks.

By the time we'd carefully grouped and situated our makeshift garden on the window ledge inside, put away journals, and washed up, it was ten of three. There was no point in hauling out math assignments at the eleventh hour. Everyone was tired and flushed from the sun. I was just as happy as the kids to wind down with a chapter of *Coral Sharkey*.

It was nearly dismissal time when the door clicked open. As everyone turned sleepily toward the noise, I lowered the book to my right side where I hoped it might disappear. It was a good call. Mr. Dunlop filled the doorway, and his eyes remained intent on me for what seemed like a very long time. He didn't say anything at all.

My finger slid out from between the pages. All eyes were on me, curious, anticipatory, yet not a single person gave me away. "Report cards signed and returned on Monday," I began as if he'd interrupted something important, "history museum permission slips if I don't already have them, and not one math book left in a desk tonight."

Dunlop cleared his throat loudly, and the smirk in his eyes told me I was absolutely pathetic. "I'll see you in my office," he said. "Fifteen minutes."

My heart was pounding as the door closed, and my cheeks felt hot. I picked up the book again and thumbed through quickly, trying to find where we'd left off, but I couldn't remember what I'd just read. I wanted to continue like everything was fine, but I just couldn't find the damned page. I wanted my class to think this meeting was about something else, something normal, something boring, or just be tactful enough to pretend it could be, but I knew that I wouldn't be so lucky.

"Why is he so mad?" Shannon asked, a beautiful note of defensiveness in her voice. "Because you're reading to us? Mr. Crenshaw used to read to us every afternoon."

I didn't look up from the book. "The problem probably isn't *that* we're reading."

There was a long silence. I could tell that my comment had gone right over several students' heads, but other reactions ranged from nervous shuffling to outrage. Nestor finally spoke up. "That's stupid. I know some people don't like those books. Like, my aunt won't let my cousins read them, but that's stupid. They're just books."

Someone asked why people didn't like them, and Chelsea glared indignantly back at the rest of the class. "Because of the vampires and witches and stuff. They think we're so impressionable that we're going to believe everything we read and start worshipping Satan."

I heard more than one gasp, so I leapt from my desk and grabbed a marker from the board before Selena, Dunlop, or God himself could strike us down. "Good word," I said, scribbling *impressionable* on the right corner. I thought about adding the word *censorship*, or maybe *Satan* but instead drew a box around the word and the homework assignment and added *do not erase*. My writing looked strange, and the box was crooked. I wanted to fix it, or maybe I just didn't want to face the kids again.

"We get to finish the book, though, right?" Brandi asked. The bell rang, but nobody moved.

"Right. Eddie, Cristal, David, permission slips on Monday."

Now, the room became a churning mass of chaos as if everyone wanted to be the first to escape. I watched them clear into the hallway, my crowd of *impressionable* babies, then swore and threw my red marker at the board. It hit the edge of the rail and fell to the floor, but I didn't move to pick it up. I had only thirteen minutes and thirty seconds to make it down to Mr. Dunlop's office, after all. When I turned to gather my things, I saw Christian standing at my desk.

He paused for a second, then bent to pick up the red pen. He set it in the rail gently and turned back to me. "Don't worry about it. It's not like after we read *Charlotte's Web*, everyone expected pigs to talk or something."

I tried to smile back at him. "Thank you. Have a good weekend."

I started down to the office early. I wanted to get it over with, and I knew that if I stayed in my room, I was just going to cry. I supposed there was a minuscule chance that this meeting really wasn't about what I thought it was, but that seemed unlikely. I wondered if Kathy would be pissed, too. I wondered if I'd shown enough good character to get assigned probation like Daniel.

When I reached the office, other teachers were signing out, laughing, and talking about their weekend plans. I flattened against the wall so they could walk past, trying to be invisible. As if she knew exactly what was going on, Selena's eyes narrowed as I passed her desk. I wondered if she'd been listening on the intercom.

"Coral Sharkey and the Bat, of all things? What were you *thinking?"* Dunlop paced behind his desk, his greasy hair flopping while I sat on my usual hard plastic chair front and center. I knew that if I just kept my wits about me, I could talk my way out of this or at least make him defer to Kathy. Still, my stomach hurt formidably. I felt like I was seven years old, caught in a lie or some other childish misdeed, waiting for my stepfather to smack me across the face and get it over with. "Where is the sense in that? This is trash, Miss Smith. *Trash*."

"That's not true."

He stopped pacing and stared straight at me. "I knew you were different, but I was under the impression that your brain still worked properly."

Humiliation and anger swirled through my body, but I forged on as if that comment had never left his mouth. "If we finish all our work early, we read a few pages and discuss the situations the book presents. It's about conflict resolution. We talk about making better decisions and problem-solving and—"

"It's about a *vampire*," he spat. "What am I supposed to say when parents call me complaining that their eleven-year-old is being taught about the occult? What am I supposed to say, Miss Smith?"

"Have you had any complaints?"

"It's only a matter of time. Our school library does not own that book. Our district does not in any way, shape, or form endorse that book. You are supposed to be a role model, Miss Smith. Parents entrust you with their children."

I'm not going to throw up. Really, I'm not. As the ringing in my ears grew, Mr. Dunlop's tirade became a dull, nonsensical drone. I could no longer hear the words, but his face grew redder and redder, and spit flew out of his mouth and lodged in his mustache. He leaned over his desk, barking at me, preaching a full gospel. *Thou shalt not, thou shalt not, thou shalt not.* I wanted to ask how he'd found out about the book, whether he'd seen it during his observation, if Selena had ratted me out, or if he'd let himself into my room the day before to dig through my things. I wanted to know if he'd actually read the book himself, but there was no way I could say a single word.

As suddenly as he'd started, there was silence. He stared at me, breathing heavily, very obviously waiting for an answer to a question I hadn't heard. The clock ticked. Kathy laughed about something outside the door. The clock ticked again and again.

"This could be worth a lawsuit, Miss Smith. Are you even listening?"

I hoped he wouldn't ask me to repeat what he'd said. "Yes," I agreed, then choked it out. "Yes, sir."

He let his breath out in a big sigh. Either I'd come up with the correct response for once, or he'd exhausted himself. "I'm going to speak to Ms. Sutton about this. Until then, I do not, under any circumstances, want to hear that this book is still on school grounds. Do you understand?"

"Yes, sir." As soon as he let me go, I scribbled the time in my out box and exited the office without so much as looking at Selena. She probably listened in to conversations in the principals' offices, too, not that anyone could have missed a word the way Dunlop was yelling.

It was darker and cooler in the main hall. I could feel my heart pounding, and my whole body was trembling. I was mad, really mad. I wasn't about to stop reading that damned book, at least not until Kathy told me I had to. I'd done far worse things in my lifetime.

"Hey, are you okay?" Tina Flores stopped a few paces away. She was wearing jeans, and they looked even better on her than the skirts, if that was possible.

I nodded. "I'm fine."

"Are you sure?"

"Yes. Dunlop just called me in again. It's nothing, really." All at once, I realized that I was about to succumb to the stupid, helpless, girly response of tears. "I should go."

Tina caught me by the arm. "What happened?"

"Nothing." I swallowed hard and blinked diligently at the far side of the wall. "I was reading the *Coral Sharkey* books aloud."

"So what?"

"He has a problem with—"

"He's an asshole, Cary. A pompous, pathetic asshole."

I wanted to tell her to move her hand before Dunlop found us and called her into his office, too, but her touch felt protective and warm and desperately necessary. "I know, but he's talking to Kathy and—"

"Kathy will take your side." She squeezed my arm tighter for a second, then let go. "Go home and try not to worry about it. It's going to be okay." She continued down the hall toward the office, and I spent one of my least-stellar moments staring after her, watching her ass in those tight jeans. I was in trouble anyway, so why the hell not?

Before she could disappear around the corner, though, the tears came, forcing me to duck back to my classroom, grab my backpack, and slip out the back door with my tail between my legs.

❖

"I had a really shitty day," I said, stroking Amy's shoulder distractedly.

"What happened?"

"Dunlop found out that I've been reading the *Coral Sharkey* books aloud. I've never seen him so mad."

Amy's brow furrowed. "Aren't those about witchcraft?"

"There are characters who are witches, but they're about so many more things. Loyalty, honesty, making the right choices. I mean, they're all about morality, if you ask me."

"But if there's witchcraft in them…"

I rolled over. "Just forget it, okay?"

"I'm not saying you're wrong. My niece and nephew love those books. Dunlop's probably just concerned about somebody taking offense."

"None of my kids are offended. They beg for another chapter every day. They've written these gorgeous essays. Like after reading a scene about bullying, I had them write about what they'd do if they were in that situation."

"If they're not offended, how did he find out?"

"What, you're saying that one of them ratted me out?"

Amy's hand moved gently across my forehead, smoothing my hair back. "No, but maybe one of them, who is okay with it," she added, "said something about it to someone in another class."

"I guess. He's been on my case, though. He observed my class for a full hour last week."

She frowned. "He can do that. I mean, you have tenure, he doesn't need to, but—"

"It just feels like he's waiting for me to screw up," I muttered. "It just feels like he's…"

Amy waited a long time for me to finish, but when I didn't, she nudged me. "It feels like he's what?"

"Somebody was in my classroom the other day."

"What?"

"I stepped out of my room for a while, and when I came back… God, this sounds really crazy."

She propped up on one elbow, her eyes narrowing. "Was there anything missing?"

"No, but I swear someone had been looking through my desk. I mean, I keep most of it locked, but the chair was pushed out of the way like someone had been there."

"And you think that has something to do with today?"

It sounded worse than stupid when I said it out loud. It didn't feel so stupid inside my head, but I still wished I hadn't mentioned it.

"You're so paranoid," she said, grinning. "Why are you always so paranoid?"

I didn't answer. For one, I was lying butt naked beside my female coworker. If Dunlop could come crashing into my classroom like he had today, what was stopping him from coming by Amy's house?

"Cary, the kids go through my stuff all the time. We've had custodians break into desks looking for money. You don't really think that Dunlop would dig through your classroom without permission?"

I continued to stare darkly at the ceiling. "No. I probably shouldn't even be saying any of this 'cause I don't know for sure."

"Why?" she asked, her voice quiet yet incisive. "Don't you trust me?"

I searched her soft face, her gentle blue eyes. Of course I trusted her. She was absolutely incapable of hurting me. I could hurt her over and over, and she would still never betray me, even if she could figure out some way to do it without betraying herself in the process. I couldn't answer.

"Look," she whispered, "I'm not asking if you love me."

"Amy…"

Her eyes met mine again. "I know you don't love me. I'm just asking if you trust me."

I nodded, feeling like complete shit. "Of course I do."

CHAPTER SIX

I decided when I was ten years old that I wasn't ever getting married. It had nothing to do with being gay and losing the big dream of the husband, the kids, and the huge church wedding. I knew by then that I was different from my friends, but I had no idea that had anything to do with who I would grow up to love. The reason was simple: my mother had a knack for choosing complete loser men who hurt her and hurt me and then left. We'd never stayed in one place long enough for me to really observe any good relationships or stable marriages, and I wasn't about to waste my life being miserable like her.

By the time I was thirteen, I knew that I was attracted to girls instead of boys, but that idea never seemed nearly as shameful as trying to build a life with a long line of jerks who didn't care. I learned to keep my distance, to never get too attached to friends, schools, or homes since we tended to uproot with little notice. I did crave emotional intimacy, but I feared it more intensely.

Truth be told, I was ridiculously lonely. The older I became, the fewer people I could find who wanted to share intelligent conversation and the entire night with no strings attached. I sometimes wondered how bad it would be to find that one person, the one I could spill all my guts to, the one I could wake up next to every morning for the rest of my life, but I'd never allowed myself to consider that option with someone I was actively seeing. It was much safer to date casually, never offer spare keys or an underwear drawer, lest I promise something to someone and break her heart a week later.

In that respect, West Grove was Mecca. West Grove was all about tiptoeing out of the closet for just long enough to enjoy some take-out sex, crumple up the wrappers, and throw them away in someone else's dumpster.

I still felt a bit bruised and swept aside over the weekend. I wasn't sure if it was Amy's reaction to what I'd said or just the fact that we didn't talk on Saturday or Sunday. Most days, I would have preferred the silence, but this time, I wished she would call me and tell me she understood or give me some ideas about how to deal with things. It didn't happen. When Amy finally snuck close enough on Tuesday afternoon, she just asked if I'd heard any more from Dunlop or Kathy, and it wasn't the right time to pick her brain or beg for reassurance.

I hadn't heard any more. Dunlop did gravitate around me whenever we were in the same part of the building, as if he was trying to get close enough to search my person for *Coral Sharkey*, but he had no further comment. What made me crazy, though, was that I didn't hear anything from Kathy, either.

By Wednesday, the silence was unbearable. When I went to check my mailbox before lunch, she was at the counter where Selena normally stood, paging through the absentee notebook. I gave her what felt like plenty of opportunity to begin, but she glanced up only long enough to see that it was me.

I started. "I assume you want to speak with me?"

Kathy looked up at the far wall with a slightly thoughtful look, like she wasn't sure what I was talking about. It threw me for a second, but I just knew that Dunlop had documented the incident in writing the moment I'd left his office Friday afternoon and copied her before leaving.

"Do you want to set up an appointment, or shall we talk now?"

"Now is good."

"All right, then."

Her office was larger than Dunlop's but far less cavernous. Sunshine spilled through a row of small, skinny windows at the top of one wall. Lamps in the corner and on the desk added a gentle, homey touch. While framed diplomas and awards hung on each of the walls between hulking gray filing cabinets, none of them were tacky or handmade. Bookshelves were packed with volumes on curriculum, leadership, and a variety of educational methods. Photos of Kathy's daughter and her dogs sat atop her desk, along with a coffee mug, three Diet Coke cans, and an impressive heap of paperwork. None of the chairs were cheap plastic.

She began before either of us had a chance to sit. "Frankly, Cary, I wasn't going to say anything, but you obviously need to get this out of your system."

"You weren't?"

She shook her head. "You'll do the right thing."

I stared at her, feeling a little light-headed. "I know what I think is right, but Mr. Dunlop—"

"His point is valid," she said, wiggling one of the soda cans as if to make sure it was current before taking a sip. "There's been a huge fuss over those books in some districts, and some of our students do come from fundamentalist households."

"But nobody's complained. They're great books. They're intelligent, they're entertaining, they're well-written. My kids can't wait to go to the library every week. Eric Sanchez came up to me the other day—mind you, this child has never in his life read anything outside of class—and asked me how he could find other books by the same author."

Kathy watched my discourse politely, then nodded when I was finished. "Well, it sounds like you've made your decision."

I could feel all of the smallness, anger, and stupidity Dunlop had forced upon me dissolving into a stew of nervous excitement. While I thought about it, a vague hint of the smile I'd thought I'd recognized in Kathy's eyes slid onto her lips. It made my nerves exponentially worse but not in a bad way. "That's it? You're okay with this? I mean, I'm not just reading to them. We've written essays and…"

"I think it wouldn't hurt to move on to another author," she said knowingly, "but just between you and me, I think your class would be pretty disappointed if you didn't finish the book."

I knew enough to steer clear of Dunlop in the interim. "Thank you," I whispered, getting up to let myself out.

I could have skipped down the hall. The way it was, I couldn't keep the smile off my face. I wanted to tell somebody, but the only person who knew details was Amy, and there was no point in tracking her down on the playground only to be shushed. I was on my way to see who was in the lounge when I bumped into Daniel.

He looked every bit as excited as I felt. "Oh my God, do I have news for you!"

"What?"

"Not here," he whispered, dragging me down the hall. "Have you eaten?"

I shook my head. "I just had this fantastic meeting with Kathy."

"So you're saying you need to go out back for a smoke? Seriously, grab your lunch and come with me."

Moments later, we were sitting in the cab of Daniel's big black truck, the windows rolled up all the way. The sweat stood out on both of our faces before I could even unwrap my sandwich.

"So," he said, pulling his knee onto the seat so he could face me. "What was your meeting with Kathy about?"

"She totally vetoed Dunlop on something. Made my day."

"Well, I'm about to make your week. Flores asked me which way you went."

"What?"

"You heard me."

"She did not!"

"She did." Daniel nodded, bouncing a little on his seat, his eyes wide and gleaming. "Bev and Sally took off before Jody joined us, and it was just the two of us for a moment."

"And she asked you which way I went?"

"She asked me if you were straight."

"Just out of the blue?"

He nodded. "I said, uh, no, and she said that she didn't think so after that whole excruciating lesbo dog scene last week, but she wanted to be sure."

My sandwich had made its way back into the plastic wrap. I was no longer hungry. "She wanted to be sure? Oh my God."

"Oh your God." He giggled. "What does that sound like to you?"

"She can't be, Daniel."

"She can't be gay? Or she can't be interested in you? Cary, come on. You're such a catch. Anyway, you're all sexy in your little thongs," he added, grabbing for my butt.

I inched out of his way. The way it was, I felt like this conversation belonged in seventh grade. We didn't need to be making underwear jokes, too. "Promise you're not lying?"

"I swear. Ask her out, Cary."

I stared out the side window, feeling the sweat running off my body and that dumb smile still on my face. "I don't know."

"Hey," he said, finally opening his door. The outside air flooded in, feeling cooler than midday Texas ever had before. "You know you'll be sorry if you don't at least try."

❖

By Friday afternoon, I hadn't found the guts. I tried to tell myself that it wasn't my fault. Tina and I were never alone, but even if we had been, I knew I wouldn't have dared. After she'd gone out of her way to question Daniel, I expected some secret looks, some extra vibes, maybe, but I wasn't getting anything. Maybe I was just nervous.

I had good reason to be. If I was bad at relationships, I was worse at trying to cheat on them. I ran into Amy in the restroom after dismissal and knew exactly what she really meant when she asked if I had big plans for the weekend. I made up something about having to clean my apartment that evening because a friend from college was stopping in on her way to El Paso. Amy's eyebrow did twitch when I called the friend a *her*, but she finished drying her hands, gave me a polite smile, and told me to have a good visit.

I did have big plans for the weekend, although they had nothing to do with anyone else. My class was about three-quarters of the way through *Coral Sharkey and the Bat*, and I needed a new author soon. I had a pile of tests to correct after school, but I planned to stop at the public library so I could spend the evening with a bottle of wine and a stack of candidates.

I had finished most of the papers when I heard a distant clicking down the hall. I didn't realize how late it'd gotten, but the clock read nearly five. I stretched my back and listened for a moment, trying to place the footsteps. Amy had left school directly after our meeting, and anyway, neither she nor Jody ever wore heels. Marisol and the fifth-grade teachers rarely stayed so late. I put my money on Kathy. As I checked answers on the next to last paper, the clicking got louder, then stopped.

The silence forced my attention away from my work. The window on my door was covered with construction paper, but I had the distinct feeling that someone was watching. I turned for a second to make sure nobody was looking in my windows from outside, but Tammy Wells's enormous SUV blocked my view of most of the parking lot. I glanced one more time at the door, then went back to my papers, even though my entire body prickled with a nervous energy.

I was working on the last test when I heard the clicking again, this time slower and louder, right outside my door. Surely, it was Kathy trying to determine whether my lights were on. I still didn't understand why she'd pause for so long without knocking, but I tried not to think about it as the noise grew fainter, back down the hall. I just finished the paper as quickly as possible and gathered up my things.

Kathy was indeed in the office when I signed out for the day. I bid her good night, then headed out of the building through D-hall. Tammy was gone by then, but a blue Chevy Blazer was parked two spots away from my car. Tina was slamming the tailgate.

"What're you doing here this late?" I asked.

She smiled. "Trying to get my act together. Daniel wasn't kidding when he said you're always here."

"Sometimes. I hate taking work home."

"So you stay here? There's a lot of homework in sixth grade."

"Yeah. I usually wind up taking some of it with me anyway."

I looked at her; she looked at me. Our conversation was inane, just silly small talk, but her eyes were right on me again, as if we were having some sort of intimate discussion. That was always the way she looked at me, like she was trying to eke a deeper meaning out of every word I said. It scared me a little bit, but I was starting to crave the danger.

"So anyway," I said, the words tumbling out of my mouth uncensored. "May I take you out to dinner?"

Now there was another silence, but it was very different. With that one stupid suggestion, we'd left the confines of flirtatious, electric, almost-about-to-say-everything and plunged headlong into an ugly, uncomfortable, one-of-us-should-probably-say-something. I couldn't believe I'd asked her out in exactly that many words, and, apparently, neither could Tina.

"Tonight? I can't tonight."

My grip tightened on my keys, and I tried hard to keep the wince off my face even as it traveled through the rest of my body. "Okay."

"I'm sorry. I have this stupid new teacher meeting in half an hour."

I'd sat through six during my first year, and not one had been on a Friday night. Friday nights were football nights. The district would never require anyone to attend anything opposite a football game. I nodded quickly. "I hated those. Once a month like clockwork."

"Tonight's about evaluations, I think. I probably shouldn't miss it."

"Of course not. That's a valid one."

For what must have been a solid minute, we both squinted down the street as if something traveling down South Fourth would somehow excuse us from the conversation. There were no ambulances, fire trucks, or aliens.

"Some other time, maybe?" she finally asked.

Now, I really couldn't look at her. "Oh. Yeah. Some other time. I should let you go."

"I'm really sorry."

"It's absolutely okay," I assured her in a classic super perky, definitely-not-embarrassed-off-my-ass voice. I opened the door to my car, threw my backpack inside, and told her to have a good weekend as I started the engine.

Stupid, stupid, stupid. I could not believe I'd been so stupid.

I realized exactly how thickly I was obsessing when I found myself heading west on South Fourth several blocks past my turn. The landscape became grimmer. People's mud driveways led to dilapidated, windowless skeletons of houses, half-dressed children, and the occasional chicken running from yard to yard.

The whole neighborhood seemed to be a study in tan, from the roads, to the yards, to the homes, to the children, to the clouds of dust and tumbleweed traveling down the street beside me. I thought about turning around, but there wasn't room in the street, and I didn't want to pull into someone's driveway. I probably should have been a bit nervous driving through the neighborhood with three hubcaps and a gas gauge registering one hair above empty, but it just made me feel angry and even worse. I hated that some of the kids in my classroom lived in that neighborhood without any of the creature comforts the rest of us took for granted. I hated that I was supposed to fear them because I was white and had a savings account. I hated that I was in this ridiculous city, in this ridiculous country, where there were such neighborhoods and attitudes.

I turned on Houston, which took me north along the western edge of town. I passed three pawn shops before the homes flanking the road began to sport glass windows, real doors, and a prickly pear cactus here and there in the name of landscaping. I didn't feel any better. There was an Albertsons on the corner of Houston and 29th, so I ran in to pick up a frozen pizza and a six-pack of Coke as if that would excuse the side trip. From 29th, I got back onto Grove, which turned into the highway, my usual drive home. It was past six, and I didn't feel like stopping at the library anymore.

One of the kids from two units down was busy dribbling his basketball through the labyrinth of cars at my apartment complex, nailing the side of a pickup, digging it out from under a sedan from time to time. It took more energy than I thought I had left to avoid him on my way to the mailbox, and by the time I'd forced my little key into its hole and jiggled it into the proper juxtaposition to spring the lock, I could fairly see the end of my rope dangling before me.

I extracted four bills and a *Newsweek*, wrestled the key back out, and climbed the stairs to my apartment. The basketball rolled out from between two cars, and its owner followed obediently, right into the path of a worn Chevy truck. There was a squeal of tires and a barrage of Spanish obscenities, then the *thump-thump-thump* of the basketball against the pavement once again. I didn't even bother looking back.

My neighbor, Lucy Hernandez, was busy draping her husband's work coveralls along our railing to dry. Their miniature Chihuahua skittered along, winding figure eights around her feet. It was a death trap if I'd ever seen one. "Hey, Cary. How're you doing?"

I forced a smile at her and managed to step over the dog without tripping. "Okay. How're you?"

"Oh, I'm good. I swear, that kid's going to get killed one of these days."

"Hope it's not on our watch. I'll see you later, okay?"

"All right. Bugsy, come!"

Halfway into my apartment, I looked down and saw two huge, bulbous black eyes gazing back at me, unblinking, tremoring in that nervous, micro-dog manner. I was sure Bugsy didn't know his own name, let alone a command as complex as *come*. "Go home, boy," I told him, egging him on as gently as I could with my foot.

"Come," Lucy tried again, then sighed, tossed a fourth coverall back into her laundry basket, and came to scoop up her dog. "Sorry," she told me, grinning sheepishly. "Are you sure you're okay? You look real tired."

I nodded. "Long week."

"Well, take care. Let me know if you need anything."

I need a drink. "Thanks."

I went about my business, putting the pizza in the oven, going through the mail, checking my answering machine. Nothing exciting, just a recording trying to sell me vinyl siding and two hang-ups. I tried to sit with my pizza and a Coke and read my *Newsweek*, but even bloody photos and stories of horrific car bombings in the Middle East couldn't stop me from feeling sorry for myself. A slice and a half into my cardboard pizza, I went into my office and consulted the calendar that hung above my computer. It was printed on salmon-colored paper and featured inspirational bible verses on each page, compliments of the West Grove Independent School District. Today's little box was blank, save for the location of the high school football games. The previous Monday read, *New Teacher Meeting – Administration Building.*

I returned to the kitchen, dumped what was left of my Coke into a glass, and filled the rest of it with rum. I tossed my magazine aside, sprawled lengthwise on my sofa, and stared blankly out my living room window, barely feeling the alcohol burn its way down my throat.

Lucy had gone back inside her apartment, but the dog was tethered to a pink cord and curled up in a minuscule heap next to her doormat. Through a gap in the stained gray coveralls, I had a straight shot through the parking lot toward the west side of the horizon. A teenage boy was working on a Camaro, Tejano cranked on the radio, looking sweaty and grimy and so damned proud of whatever he was doing. I wanted to be him, more concerned about my wheels than a date or even the football game. I just wanted to be anyone other than me.

I had been like that with my first car. I'd learned to change its oil and washed it every weekend. It was a primer-gray, fifteen-year-old Honda Civic that I'd loved desperately despite its rust patches, mismatched tires, and lack of functional air-conditioning. Mom had helped me pay for it as one of those sad, parental, don't-hate-me gestures when she was busy clearing up divorce number three and finishing our stint in Florida. I wondered if the kid outside was a high school sophomore like I had been, hormonal and angst-ridden and drunk with newfound freedom.

I had such history with that car. I'd had my first girl kiss in it, in the back parking lot of the Winn-Dixie where Mandy Freeman had worked. I'd done my first cross-country drive with it. I'd gotten my first two speeding tickets in it. It had its own history when I'd gotten it, too. Searching for an ice scraper on the first day we'd gotten frost in Memphis, I'd found a cast-iron crowbar tucked under the driver seat instead. I'd never had occasion to look there before, so I'd gotten on my knees on the driveway, dug farther, and had come up with a roll of gray duct tape, too.

Fascinated, I'd stuffed everything right back where I found it, used my jacket sleeve to clear the windshield, and spent my work shift at Blockbuster Video daydreaming about what mind-blowing adventures my car might have had. Maybe its previous owner was a cat burglar or maybe even a murderer. I had the real, honest-to-God getaway car.

So much had happened since then. Another car, three states, and five apartments later, the sky was beginning to turn pink-blue beyond the dead grass and dusty pavement. Thin, wispy gray clouds hung in the distance, and as I thought harder, remembered more, they began to blur into pink and brown. I didn't try to stop the tears this time, just took another sip of my drink and kept staring out the window.

Oh, I shouldn't have asked her out. I shouldn't have trusted Daniel. I should have taken more time, done more research. I was stupid to think she would be interested in me, stupid to think this was a good idea, stupid to even consider cheating on Amy. I didn't deserve an ounce of the polite hesitancy with which Tina had turned me down.

It was dark out, and I was quite drunk when I called Billy Jessen. We'd been best friends in college and roommates through grad school. He taught American history at a high school in Killeen, and we had spent countless hours on the phone commiserating. If there was a person in the world I could call up in tears, it was Billy. That didn't mean he would be nice to me, but I could do it, so I did.

"You are so lucky that the volleyball team's in Waco tonight," he told me right away. "Otherwise, you know what you'd get."

"Hey, this is Billy. Leave a message, and I might get back to you if I feel like it," I muttered. I could hear some ball game playing in the background. It wasn't like he was busy. "So what's up?"

"You called me," he reminded me. "And you don't sound so good."

"I did a dumbass thing today, and I don't really want to talk about it."

He sighed. I was ready for a lecture on wasting his precious time, but instead, I stopped hearing the TV. Knowing him, he'd hit the mute button but was still watching anyway. "So other than that dumbass thing, how's Cary?"

"Okay. Work's okay, I'm okay. You know."

"How's coach girl?"

"Okay."

"Well, that's not very interesting."

I closed my eyes and began to let myself settle back down. "What's going on with you? *Your* coach is in Waco tonight."

"Yes, and it sucks," he said. "We did dinner the other night, though. At her place."

"No shit."

"No shit. She wanted me to see the new digs. Isn't that cute?"

"Did she cook for you?"

"No." He laughed. "We had take-out Chinese. She says she's a pathetic cook."

"You should've cooked for her. She'd know you're a keeper."

"Aw. That's sweet of you. You must really be upset."

That made me smile. "So did you do her?"

"Cary!"

"Well."

There was an indignant silence, then laughter. "Okay, I would," he admitted, "but she's still all upset over the divorce, you know, so I was nice."

"What about a sympathy fuck? That wouldn't be nice?"

"Don't even start, Cary. Don't make my mind go there."

"The divorce is final, then?"

"I guess. She doesn't talk about it. I didn't even know she was married until this year. I never met the hubby."

"Is he still in Killeen?"

"Oh no, he took off right away. Moved back with Mommy or something. Nice, right?"

"Wait, I thought she came to that social studies people thing you had last year."

"My department party," he corrected. "Social studies people."

"And she didn't bring him?"

"No. That's why I didn't think she was married. She brought her best friend, and it was just weird. The friend was walking around like she actually knew me or something. And she sits all dainty on my sofa, turns to the picture of you and me from Marcus' party, you know that one?"

I had a copy of the same photo framed and sitting on the other side of the living room. "Yeah."

"Well, she says, 'is this your girlfriend?' and I'm like, 'uh, no, we're just friends.' That's the last thing I wanted Anita thinking—"

"Because you're scamming her?"

"Shut up. Well, yes. So anyway, this other chick totally wouldn't let it go. She kept asking where we'd met and if you were in Killeen, and I was finally like, 'okay, her name's Cary, she teaches in West Grove, and although I know we'd be cute together, we shared an apartment in Urbana for two years without consummating our relationship.'"

"You did not say that."

"Essentially. You're not crying anymore."

"You always make me feel better."

"I know it. Are you going to tell me about your dumbass thing already?"

I slid deeper into the sofa and stared at the ceiling, encouraging the sensation of intoxication to quash the feelings of idiocy. "I asked somebody out, and she totally dissed me."

"So? Like that's never happened to me."

"In the parking lot."

"At school?"

"Yes."

He clicked his tongue knowingly. "Was this another teacher person?"

"Yes."

"What variety?"

"New kindergarten teacher."

"What?"

"Don't think of your kindergarten teacher. She's really hot and really nice and…God, I fucked up."

"Oh no. Straight girl?"

"I didn't think so. I mean, I thought so, but then Daniel said—"

"Oh, Daniel. He's an idiot. So when you say she dissed you, are we talking loud, horrified rebukes for everyone to hear, or…"

"No, she was perfectly nice about it. I just feel like a moron."

"Look, everything's okay if she's still speaking to you Monday morning," he assured me.

"I guess."

"Now. You said things are good with coach girl, but you're seeing other people."

"Things are fine," I whispered. All at once, I was exhausted, and my tongue felt thick and uncooperative. "I shouldn't even be thinking about seeing someone else."

Billy sighed. He knew I was done talking about it. "Have one more, sweetie," he said gently, "then get some sleep, okay? It's going to hurt a lot less in the morning."

Chapter Seven

I slept most of the day Saturday. My head hurt, my stomach hurt, and I couldn't manage to drag myself out of bed for more than ten minutes at a time. I'd been hungover more times than I could count, but this felt different. There was an emotion gnawing at me, and the more I thought about it, the less it seemed to be the embarrassment or indignation that had flooded my veins the night before. This was definitely a sense of loss, although I wasn't sure what I could possibly be missing.

A lost opportunity, maybe, or a loss of ground as far as my ego was concerned. It didn't make sense, though, that one human being could appear from nowhere and cause such chaos in my psyche. It was as though I needed to get closer to Tina in an insistent sort of way so my story could continue on its prescribed course. Everything had been coming together so beautifully, so suddenly, in such a crazy rush. I should have known it was too good to be true.

On Sunday, I scraped my act back together. While the rest of West Grove was at church, I went to Walmart to pick up groceries. Since the public library wasn't open, I went home to scour my own shelves for books that seemed interesting but entirely noncontroversial. Nothing jumped out at me, but I pulled out some old standbys and began to peruse them.

I was up late reading. I just couldn't concentrate. Most of what I'd pulled didn't really interest me, and over and over, my eyes drifted to my bookshelf where eight more volumes of *Coral Sharkey* sat. At first, I was angry with Dunlop all over again, but then I began to dissect what Kathy had told me. She knew I would make the right decision, but it wouldn't hurt to move on to another author. I'd assumed that she felt the same way I did, but I wasn't even sure how that was anymore. If reading these books was the right thing to do, why did I feel guilty enough to back down? I'd felt all liberated and vindicated when I was merely allowed to finish the book I'd been reading, but there were seven books we hadn't touched.

People get fired over things like this. They refuse to submit to people's stupid intolerant fears, and they stand up for what they believe, even if it costs them their job. I thought about that for a long time. I was annoyed enough with Dunlop to consider taking a stand, that was for sure, but I wasn't so certain this was the issue with which I wanted to go down. There were plenty of other books out there. Still, I couldn't help but wonder what would happen if I shrugged at Kathy, stood my ground, and set the third *Coral Sharkey* book on the chalk rail to advertise what we'd be reading next. What if I'd begun the year with hobbits or talking animals instead? What if, what if, what if.

Stop it. I shut off the living room lights and went to check my shoebox on my way to bed. *Some things happen for no reason at all.*

The Commercial Appeal, Friday, May 31, 1991
"Memphis Man Found Slain in Drainage Ditch"

A woman walking her dog discovered the body of a 20-year-old Memphis man early Thursday morning in a drainage ditch near an East Memphis subdivision.

Jonathan McGrath was dead at the scene. As of late Thursday, a cause of death had not been determined, but police say the victim had been severely beaten.

McGrath was a 1989 graduate of Memphis University School and was attending Rhodes College.

No one was in custody Thursday. Anyone with information is asked to call Crime Stoppers.

❖

I was feeling better Monday morning. Sure, asking Tina out might have been a mistake, but life would go on. We really did seem to have a few things in common. If I could stop being weird around her, it would be nice to have another friend who lived for fifteen minutes outside the city limits.

I wasn't running particularly late, but I remembered being distracted Friday afternoon, and I wasn't sure I'd left everything the way I'd intended. I poured my coffee in a travel mug, grabbed a piece of toast, and ate on my way to work, going over the day's lesson plans in my head. I was pretty sure I had my act together, but the moment I pulled into the parking lot, that feeling disappeared.

There, in the spot closest to the door, was Mrs. Shore's eggplant Cadillac. Rusty chrome bumpers, flowered seat covers, and a sticker on the rear window inviting me to follow her to Grove Terrace Baptist Church. It was just the two of us there, Mrs. Shore and me, just like it had been every morning before Tina joined the faculty.

This is not what happens next. A sick feeling settled into my stomach as I dug my things out of my car. My fingers didn't want to work. I dropped my lunch, then my keys. I tried to assure myself that I couldn't have freaked Tina out badly enough to quit, for fuck's sake.

What if I had? What if that smile was just a polite cover-up, and sometime during whatever she was really doing Friday night, it had hit her that she didn't need to put up with getting hit on by an awkward, pathetic dyke? What if Dunlop was waiting in his office, hands folded on his desk, that huge, nasty smile spread across his face, just waiting for me to find the memo in my box informing me that I'd violated the morality clause?

I must've crashed through the door like an insane person because Mrs. Shore jumped when she heard me. She was most of the way down the hall by Marisol's room. *Leave, just get out of here. If you go, maybe she'll come back. I need one more chance.*

Completely oblivious, Mrs. Shore smiled warmly. "Why, good morning, Ms. Smith. Looks like it's just you and me again."

"Just like old times," I said, searching my pants pocket, then my purse for my keys. I thought for sure that I'd locked them in my car until I found them in the other hand.

"But we're neighbors this time."

Yes, she was standing there in the D-wing with Marisol's door wide open. A dizziness washed over me as her words began to make sense. *Everything is okay. It's all going to be okay.*

"Oh," I blundered. "Is Marisol out today?"

"The baby's sick. It's nothing serious, but her parents are out of town and can't stay with her. It's been a long time since I've had sixth grade," Mrs. Shore said, turning toward her room with a stoic look. "I should take a look at some of this stuff."

"You can do it in your sleep," I said, although she was inside Marisol's room by then, and I was halfway inside mine. I sat at my desk and looked around, stunned by the light, surprised at how badly I was shaking.

In just a few minutes, Tina's blue SUV entered the parking lot. The very sight of it gave me the oddest sense of comfort, as if my last contact with her hadn't left me in a huge funk. I didn't watch her climb out. Instead, I slid my attendance book front and center on my desk and turned the page to a new week.

❖

It was half an hour before the bell on Tuesday when Mr. Dunlop entered my classroom without knocking. His body language suggested that he was trying to be sneaky, but it didn't work.

David was absent that day, so I was sitting on his desk at the back of the classroom and Ashley was at the front, giving her report on the fur trade. She paused as he closed the door, walked all the way to the back wall opposite me, and sat on his usual shelf. I made a mental note to loosen the screws before he had a chance to come back.

"Go ahead," he encouraged. "Don't mind me."

Ashley stared at me as if I might let her finish at a later date. I wanted to kick Dunlop. "We're hearing presentations this afternoon," I said.

"Wonderful. Carry on."

Ashley looked like she'd rather step in front of a bus, but she found her place and began to discuss the Hudson Bay in a sleepy monotone. I clenched my grade book and turned my pen over and over in my other hand. I tried hard not to look toward Mr. Dunlop, but I couldn't help sneaking a glance now and again.

He didn't have his legal pad. That probably meant that I wasn't going to have to suffer through a meeting following this visit, but it made his intentions ridiculously obvious. I wasn't reading the damned book. It wasn't sitting on my desk, emitting tiny particles of immorality.

He continued to sit in the back of the classroom, listening with his head cocked to one side as Nestor, Morgan, and Eddie gave their reports. Chelsea and Shannon were passing notes. I silently walked up and confiscated a folded paper football that three of the boys were snapping back and forth. Eric had fallen asleep with his head on his desk.

I was about to call on Gina when Selena cut in with the afternoon's announcements. "A pleasure as usual, Miss Smith," Dunlop said, smiling his nasty little smile and winding his way back toward the front of the classroom. "We'll see you at the meeting."

"Yuck," Christian said the moment the door closed. "How come he's in here all the time lately?"

"Announcements," I reminded him.

"Blah blah blah, Nestor's parent pickup."

I laughed out loud. "Please. Quiet for one more minute."

They held off until the transportation list had been read, and Selena was busy rattling off the same messages about soccer and report cards that we'd heard the afternoon before. "Remember third grade?" Chelsea asked everyone. "He used to sit in on Mrs. Radcliff's class all the time."

"He's an asshole," Michael said flatly.

"Language," I started, but I was cut off.

"How come he calls you *Miss* Smith?" Cristal asked. "I thought it was *Ms.*"

The bell rang. "It is," I said. "Have a good afternoon."

I made sure *Coral Sharkey and the Bat* was buried deep in my backpack before I headed to the lounge for the staff meeting. We had one more chapter to go, and I was going to finish it tomorrow, assuming Dunlop didn't feel the need to share the end of the day with my class again.

I was about to round the corner toward the lounge when Amy caught my eye from her post by the cafeteria. Instead of looking away, she waggled one finger toward me, beckoning me closer.

I joined her against the wall, wondering what could be so important that she was willing to be seen within ten feet of me. Kids and parents were still moving past, but she began right away in an excited whisper.

"Daniel's having a Halloween party Thursday. I have to be at church to help with their party at seven, but we could go earlier."

"I have a meeting at the admin building that afternoon," I remembered.

Amy looked crushed. "On Halloween?"

"That is kind of irrational—"

Tina passed us on her way to the staff meeting. I'd avoided the lounge during lunch for the past two days, and we really hadn't had any contact since Friday. All at once, that made things even more awkward. She looked at me, I looked at her, my face went hot, and I assessed my proximity to Amy, hoping we weren't too close or too obvious. When I looked back, Tina threw me a tiny smile, rounded the corner, and was gone.

I turned my attention right back to Amy. "It can't last forever. I'll be there after it's over. If I'm invited, that is."

Amy grinned. "You're invited, silly."

When I hopped up on my usual perch, Daniel passed me a small slip of orange paper. The only other teachers who seemed to have them were Bev and Sally, so I took care to unfold it as inconspicuously as possible.

Inside was a crude drawing of a grotesque, toothy jack-o'-lantern:

Boo.
Wear a costume.
Thursday, October 31, 5:00 - ???
Daniel Crenshaw's house – 4912 Buena Vista

I was about to tell Daniel about my meeting, but a snippet of conversation from across the room caught my attention. Three of the first-grade teachers sat near the Coke machine along with Maggie McDaniel and Tina, listening to Jenny Welker rant in a high, riled tone. She taught second grade and was new to Bush that year. She was several years my senior, so I'd assumed she'd transferred from another school, but Jody had told me it was more likely that she had finally sent her youngest to kindergarten.

"I couldn't believe the nonsense," she was saying. "The presenter couldn't get in from Dallas, so they rescheduled the meeting for Friday night. Can you imagine?"

"Friday night," the crowd repeated obediently.

"They didn't let us know until last Monday," she went on. "I don't know about you," she said, looking at Tina, "but it's nearly impossible for me to drop everything and reschedule on that kind of notice."

Tina shrugged and murmured in agreement. It looked like it didn't make a hell of a lot of difference to her, but she wasn't about to challenge Jenny in all her indignant glory.

"They're mandatory, you know," she continued, "so I had to skip Cody's game. Wouldn't you know it, they played him for the first time all season, and I missed it."

As the crowd grumbled at the injustice, the meaning of their conversation hit me. Tina hadn't lied to me. The Monday meeting had been rescheduled, for real, for a Friday during football season, of all things. Granted, she hadn't offered up an alternative dinner date, but at least she hadn't lied to get rid of me.

She caught me staring. This time, she didn't smile immediately, so I turned to Daniel and wiggled the orange paper the slightest bit. "I have a curriculum meeting, but I'll come afterward."

"Good. I invited her, too."

"Who?"

"Who have you been gawking at for the past five minutes? You're not going to get a date eating lunch in your classroom, sweet pea."

Chapter Eight

Shortly before dismissal time Thursday, thick dark clouds moved in, completely obscuring the sun. By the time I was alone in my classroom, it was dark as night. What a wicked look for Halloween, I thought, assessing what I might need for my meeting and packing my bag.

Not that West Grove did Halloween. My first year, I'd made the mistake of asking who was going trick-or-treating, only to weather a horrific lecture from an eleven-year-old evangelist on how such things were the mark of the devil. Several of the churches held carnivals or "safe" parties, but hardly anyone in town went door-to-door. That made me sad. Regardless of where we lived, Halloween had been the best day of the year when I was a kid. We'd worn our costumes to school and had elaborate parties. I'd trick-or-treated wherever we lived, stocking up on months' worth of sugar and eating it in just days.

This year, I'd mentioned nothing about witches or pumpkins, but I tossed out miniature Hershey bars for correct answers during our math lesson. The foreboding sky was probably God's response, I decided, ducking into my car just as the rain started. By the time I reached the district administration building, it was coming down in fat heavy drops.

West Grove didn't do rain, either. The city's official position on the topic seemed to be that it never rained at all in West Grove, and therefore, there was no need for extravagant safety precautions like storm drains. The ground was baked to near impermeability, and there wasn't enough vegetation to consume any substantial amount of water, so each time the skies opened up, West Grove became the Venice of the great southwest.

Most of the water usually ended up at 29th and Alamo. I avoided that part of town at all costs, so I'd never seen it myself, but I'd heard stories of cars being completely submerged at the intersection. My route between Bush and the admin building didn't take me that far north, so I didn't run into significant trouble. Others were coming from the east side of town, though, and we got a late start waiting for them to splash in, muttering about how many blocks out of their way they'd had to go to avoid the flooding.

Once it began, the meeting wasn't bad. Since I was the only teacher from Bush, I got to sit next to Kathy Sutton, and it was fascinating watching her responses to presentations and comments. She took scrupulous notes on some things in her beautiful, loopy, almost illegible hand; eyed me sideways while someone from the district curriculum office spoke about potential evaluation processes; and actually wrote me a note when a teacher from Crockett Elementary asked a question that had already been covered: *He used to teach at Bush. First thing I did was fire him.*

It did drone on and on. I caught myself zoning out the bay windows at the storm more than once and noticed two of the other teachers checking their phones or watches from time to time. Since we'd started after four, I knew we wouldn't be done by five, but I didn't expect to go past six, either. I fidgeted for a while, trying to picture the fastest possible route to Daniel's, but by six fifteen, I knew there was no way I'd make it to the party before Amy had to leave for church.

We adjourned shortly thereafter. It was blustering so badly outside that my umbrella was useless, and my jacket was soaked through by the time I got the car door closed. The rain splattered angrily on the roof and flowed in sheets down the windshield. My car started, but there was tremendous resistance as I moved through the parking lot. I thought things would be better on the street, but Main was dark, and I could only guess where the curbs were based on the parking meters. I knew I had to find a better route when I came upon a stalled sedan abandoned in the middle of the street with its hazard lights blinking ominously through the current.

I found a dryer north-south street, but there were business lights casting an enormous glare off the water, and I'd moved from a two-lane road to a four-lane where none of the delineations were visible. The other poor travelers and I moved along at a crawl, skidding, sputtering, hoping to God the next traffic light would stay green. My knuckles were white, and my shoulders felt like cement.

I almost stalled at 35th. I'd been doing a decent job of gauging water depth by the cars in front of me, but a pickup moved in between me and the Chevy I'd been following, and all at once, I had no perspective. Halfway through the intersection, the water began to lap up over the sides of the hood, the engine chugged and coughed, and I felt the current begin to nudge me sideways. An ugly vision of being swept away, flailing helplessly past strip malls and car dealerships, flashed through my mind, then my tires caught ground again. The light was turning. I didn't know what to do other than to give it a little more gas.

This was ridiculous. The traffic signals were out at 42nd. Shopping carts were free-floating in the Albertsons parking lot. If I wasn't so close to Daniel's, I would have just gone home. I couldn't imagine that anyone else would have braved the weather, but when I finally reached his block, both sides of the street were lined with cars.

Daniel's house was a small, tidy, gray brick bungalow that usually sat behind a marginally green lawn and a row of six, small, equally spaced cacti set in a bed of crushed white stone. The landscaping was under several inches of standing water now, the top of each cactus looming like a prickly green iceberg. I had to take off my shoes and roll up my pants to navigate my way down the street and up his drive.

Things were hopping. Ella Fitzgerald was playing on the stereo, and several small groups of people congregated in various parts of the living and dining areas. Most of them were wearing costumes, aside from a guy named Pete, who taught science at one of the junior highs, and Daniel's drag queen friend, Lola. I was impressed to see several of his acquaintances from West Grove's gay bar, considering he'd also invited the likes of Bev and Sally.

Daniel himself was sitting on his sofa in one corner of the living room, dangling a beer bottle off the back and holding court with Jody, Tina, and two of his friends from elsewhere. One of them was a childhood buddy named Hector, the other was another teacher type whose name I didn't recall. Daniel was wearing skintight Wranglers, a plaid shirt, boots, and a black ten-gallon hat. "Well, look who's here."

"Hey, sweetie," Jody said, leaning backward to squeeze my elbow. "Where's your costume?"

Hers consisted of a pair of black plastic glasses attached to a bulbous nose and bushy mustache, so I didn't think she had much of a right to talk. Tina's costume was rather minimalist, too. She was wearing exactly what she had to work but had added a headband with floppy gray bunny ears that probably came from a stash in the kindergarten room. Hector was dressed as a pirate, though, complete with earring, eye patch, and a hook on his left hand, and the other guy was wearing a black cloak and had fake blood smeared all over his face.

Daniel answered before I had a chance. "She's wearing it. Bitchy dyke on the rag."

"Shut up, Rawhide," I told him, tipping the brim of his hat down over his face.

"Oh, excuse me. That's bitchy, not-getting-any dyke on the rag."

Jody began again as if Daniel hadn't said anything. "So where's your costume?"

"It went for the lifeboat around 35th, and I haven't seen it since."

Jody wrinkled her nose. "It's still raining?"

"Not much, but it's two feet deep out there. My curriculum meeting just finished. I didn't have a chance to get home."

"Well, you were supposed to bring a costume and change into it in the parking lot," Daniel decided.

"Sorry. I missed that memo."

"At least she's here," Tina said.

"Yeah, everybody's been asking about you," Daniel said. "Sally wanted to talk more about her lesbo dogs."

"I'm getting a beer," I muttered, heading toward the kitchen before Daniel could recount the whole story for the people who had missed the original scene.

To my surprise, Tina followed me. I half expected to see Jody trailing along, too, but it was just the two of us. I went to the fridge right away and browsed the selection.

"Want one?"

"Please."

I fished out a second bottle for Tina and opened it on the dishcloth hanging from the oven door. "Has it been excruciating?"

She grinned. "Not really. We all know more than we wanted to about what Daniel's into, but it hasn't been that bad."

"Who he's into?"

"Well, that, too. How was your meeting?"

"Oh, fine. Boring. Long," I said, grabbing a paper plate with a black and purple bat on it and choosing a few munchies. It was difficult to carry on a conversation without looking at Tina, but I was trying diligently. I had no idea where anything stood, and her bunny ears were painfully adorable.

"How'd you get stuck doing it?"

I grinned. "Kathy offered me up."

"Oh no."

"It's not so bad. She's on the committee, too."

"I really like her," Tina said warily. "She seems a bit more worldly than a lot of people here."

"I like her, too." I picked up my plate and my beer and was about to return to the living room when Tina stopped me.

"Cary…I want to apologize for last Friday."

"Why?"

For once, her eyes were anywhere but on me. "I didn't mean to come off like such a bitch. You kind of caught me off guard."

I nodded evenly, although my pulse was racing. "I'm sorry about that."

"Don't be. I just don't want things to be weird between us."

"They're not," I said quickly, absolutely refusing to step all over the conversation this time. "I didn't think your response was particularly bitchy."

"I'm glad. Three guesses as to what they're talking about now."

When Tina settled back where she'd been, Jody made room for me next to her on the love seat. We had a lovely conversation for a long time, just the three of us, while Daniel and Hector and the other guy talked about sex. It was long enough for me to finish my food and beer and to spend what felt like forever trying not to wish I was sitting next to Tina instead of Jody.

"Amy was here," Jody finally said. "She was really upset that she missed you."

"I know. I hate that she had to take off."

"Did she say she was going to church?" Tina asked.

Jody nodded. "They have one of the biggest parties in town, hundreds of kids each year."

"Is it one of those things people go to instead of trick-or-treating?"

"Yes. People don't trick-or-treat here," I said.

"Is it because they're too religious?"

"Some of them. The rest still think that someone out there has the free time to inject rat poison into a whole bag of peanut butter cups."

"That sucks."

"That's what I think," I said. "What's the fun in being a kid if you don't get to do things like that?"

"Yeah, everything's better in New York or wherever," Daniel interrupted.

"My church ran a carnival," Hector said. "It was better than nothing. Didn't yours?"

"My church? They ran one of those abortion fun houses."

Jody's head jerked toward Daniel, her eyes huge. "*What?*"

Daniel rolled his eyes and flailed his beer around as if searching for an explanation. "Not like, *whee, we're having abortions*, but like, you know, one of those haunted houses that's supposed to scare you into being pious? Fetuses floating in jars, guys dressed up as Satan running around with drugs and chicks and—"

"Beer and fags and sinners," Tina added evenly.

The only thing that shocked me more than the ease with which she said that was the giggle that came from Jody. Daniel nodded too, completely unfazed, spreading his arms as if to display his own personal abortion fun house. "Exactly. It obviously worked so well."

"See, if your parents had just let you dress up one day out of the year instead," I teased.

"My momma caught me in her heels more days than that, thank you very much." Daniel tipped the last drops out of his beer and sprawled back, taking up more than his share of the sofa. Hector didn't seem to care. "Ah, those were the days. Almost as perfect as when my dad found out that I'd auditioned for my first school musical."

Jody snapped her fingers. "Mark your calendars, guys. Auditions for *Peter Pan* are the second week in November."

"I'll help with props again, but you really don't want me hearing auditions," I told her.

"You were never in musical theater?"

I laughed. "No."

"I was," Daniel reminded us for the hundredth time. "Curly in *Oklahoma!* and Harold Hill in *Music Man*."

Hector nudged Daniel's arm. "Didn't you hook up with Donnie Jones during *Music Man*?"

"No, no, no. Football."

Hector murmured in agreement. The other teacher guy went out for a smoke.

"See," Jody said. "He doesn't want to hear it, either."

"What are you talking about?" Daniel asked. "Donnie Jones was my first time."

"Please. How many times do we have to hear this story?"

"Don't listen, then."

"I'm going to the restroom," Jody decided. "Anyone want another beer?"

"Yes, please," Hector said.

"Whatever," Daniel said, retaining his huffy act until she was out of earshot. Then, he leaned in toward the rest of us eagerly. His face was red, and his speech was profoundly slurred. "Tenth grade. I'm fifteen, and I can't take my eyes off this guy, right? Oh, he's beautiful. Big and sleek with a dimple right here and the most gorgeous blue eyes. He's a junior, the backup quarterback on varsity. Well, after practice one day, we—"

"Wait a minute," I said. "You were *on* the football team?"

"Of course. I had to be. My dad coached for thirty-two years, Cary."

"At Lee?"

"At West."

I had no idea he was from the less affluent side of town. Or for that matter, that his father had coached football. I'd known that his three older brothers had played, but I'd never dreamed that Daniel had. "Wow. I'm sorry."

"Me too, except for this incident," he assured me. "I sucked. Placekicker on JV for two years, then I broke my arm and got to quit."

"You broke your arm playing football?" Tina asked.

"No, roller-skating, but that's neither here nor there."

"Donnie Jones," Hector reminded him.

"The quarterbacks always held for extra points, so one day, my dad made Donnie and me stay after practice together. I kicked a few, he tried to help me out for a while, but that just meant that everyone else was gone by the time we hit the showers."

Tina caught my eye. "You're kidding. You did it in your high school locker room?"

Daniel smiled dreamily. "Not kidding."

"Told you that you didn't want to hear it," Jody said, handing Hector another beer and sitting back down.

"Mine was with Todd Hernandez at band camp," Hector offered.

"So, Ms. Flores," Daniel said. Though he was plainly speaking to Tina, his eyes were on me. "What was your first time?"

I wished he hadn't asked. It was too personal for someone who had known us all of a few weeks. We were just beginning to get comfortable around one another, and I didn't want her to hate my friends. I expected Jody to jump in, to tell her she didn't have to answer that, but even she looked interested.

Tina didn't flinch, but she did whack Daniel with her bunny ears. Instead of putting them back on, she fastened the headband to the arm of her chair. "I was a freshman in college. Just left home, first frat party. It's not even worth talking about."

"Frat party, huh," I said, trying hard to appear indifferent. Oh, I'd wanted her to be gay. "Tell me you remember his name."

"Justin. We dated for a couple months, then, well, sort of went in different directions."

I could feel her eyes on me, but that probably had everything to do with how desperately I was trying not to look at her. Daniel cleared his throat loudly, as if *different directions* could possibly mean the same thing coming out of Tina's mouth as it would coming out of mine. Sure, plenty of people played for both teams. I just knew that wasn't the case here. I wanted to drop it and move on.

Tina kicked my shoe gently. "What about you?"

"We were in Tampa that year. I was sixteen," I said, mostly addressing my beer bottle. "I ran track with Mandy Freeman. Used to drive her home after practice. We'd talk for hours. Shut up," I added since Daniel was giggling.

"Your very first time was with a girl?" Tina asked.

I nodded. "I dated a few guys when I was little, but I knew there wasn't any point."

"That is very cool."

"I think so," Jody agreed in a businesslike tone. "Do y'all suppose the water's gone down?"

Nobody mentioned that Jody was the only one in our group who hadn't shared. Daniel stumbled up and went to turn on some outdoor lights to see how bad his backyard looked, and Hector and Jody followed as if they cared enough to see it for themselves.

That left me alone with Tina. "It was pretty bad tonight," I began.

"Does it always flood like this?"

That wasn't what I was talking about, but I nodded. "Usually."

"It's absurd. I've been dreading trying to get home."

"Just avoid the middle of town, and you'll be okay."

"I live in the middle of town. My apartment's probably under three feet of water right now. Where do you live?"

"On the north side, off the highway. After you pass the golf course, there's an apartment complex on the right. I should get going."

She got up with me. We went to thank Daniel and said good night to Jody and Hector, then let ourselves onto the front porch. The water was still standing on people's lawns, but it had gone down enough to suggest that we might be able to get to our vehicles without removing clothing.

"If you have any trouble, call me," Tina said. "My car's higher than yours."

I waited in the street next to my Toyota as she scribbled a phone number on a scrap of paper from her purse. "Thank you," I told her, tucking it into my pocket. "Be careful."

"You too," she said. "Good night."

She waited to make sure my car started, which it did once again. I wondered where the gallantry ended, whether she was going to follow me part of the way home or what, but I turned west on 49th, and she turned east.

I got home at nine, far more exhausted than the time of evening warranted. I decided against bringing in the mail since there was a small lake surrounding the box and kicked off my wet shoes the second I had the door closed. I dumped my bag on the sofa and headed directly into my bedroom.

I wasn't at all surprised that the light on my answering machine was blinking. I'd been gone for fourteen hours straight. I pushed the button, and as it rewound, I dug Tina's cell number out of my pocket and set it on my dresser so I could pretend I might need it someday. The machine beeped to play back the first message, and I waited for someone to start talking, but it didn't happen. Nothing followed other than a moment of static, a click, then a dial tone. The second beep came, and the same thing happened. When the machine beeped a third time, and the silence began, I knew my machine had to be broken. I couldn't even remember how old it was.

I went to consult caller ID, certain that some important message had been eaten. No name registered on the most recent call, though, just *West Grove, TX, 230-9950*. When I began to click backward through the history, I found not just two, but three more calls from the same number between six and eight thirty that night.

That in itself wouldn't have bothered me much, but I knew I'd seen that number before. I remembered a hang-up call weeks earlier and began to filter through all the records from the box.

I was stunned. While I didn't remember getting hang-up calls on more than three or four days, that number appeared again and again. Evenings, weekends, times I surely had been home but ignoring the phone. The history was absolutely full of them.

Daniel and Jody both carried cell phones with 523 prefixes, same as mine. Amy's was district issue since she took the soccer, basketball, and baseball teams off campus, and its number began with 377. The number Tina had just given me had an East Texas area code. I flipped through my planner, then scoured the notes I'd made in the margin of my faculty directory from Bush, but nothing matched that number. I didn't have my student information at home, but surely, one of my kids couldn't be dumb enough to obsessively prank call me.

Without a second's hesitation, I picked up the phone and dialed 230-9950. It didn't occur to me to be nervous at first, but the moment the connection went through, and there was a click at the other end, I panicked. What could I say to this person? *Hey, it's Cary. I saw that you called me fifty-seven times?*

The voice on the other end was an automated one. I'd reached the mailbox of 230-9950, it said. The customer was not available.

I hung up before it gave me the opportunity to leave my own non-message. I was shaking. I needed to close my shades. I needed to make sure the door was locked. I'd just gotten up when the phone rang.

I leapt across the bed and grabbed the caller ID box before a number could even register. I stared at the screen, my pulse pounding in my ears, waiting what seemed like forever for that second ring. *Crenshaw, DJ,* it read.

God. I lay back on my bed and tried to catch my breath. I felt like I was beginning to lose my mind. I let it ring one more time, then answered.

"Hey, Cary," Daniel gushed, still sounding very drunk. "I just wanted to make sure you got home all right."

"I'm fine, thanks."

"So you and Tina left together."

I knew he wasn't really calling out of concern. Instead of locking the door, I spent the next ten minutes insisting for what seemed like the hundredth time that nothing was going on between Tina and me. I did not mention the slip of paper on my dresser.

CHAPTER NINE

The story about my first time had been a bold-faced lie. I never did have sex with Mandy Freeman. We'd just made out a few times. Given that information, one might think I was looking to appear wilder and more experienced than I really was, but the truth had a lot more to do with the fact that Mandy Freeman was a character I could discuss. We'd both been sixteen, giggly and terrified as we'd explored our ambivalent sexualities in my primer-gray Honda behind the Winn-Dixie where she worked. That story was sweet. The truth was, too, but I was afraid people wouldn't see it that way.

I was seventeen, not sixteen, in Memphis, not Tampa. We lived there barely long enough for me to complete my junior year of high school. Instead of losing my virginity to shy Mandy Freeman, I lost it to a nineteen-year-old college sophomore named Natalie in my own bedroom while my mother was pulling a twelve-hour shift at Methodist.

Natalie Broward and I had worked together at Blockbuster, renting videos on Saturday nights. I'd known that she was a biology major at the University of Memphis and that she liked old Hitchcock. I could see it in her eyes when she thought something was hilarious, even when her lips didn't betray it. Her eyes were green, a unique deep green with thick, dark lashes. Her smile was quick, almost boyish, and so intimidating that for several weeks, I didn't even have the guts to speak to her.

I got over my fear that March, when I was promoted from re-shelving movies to working next to her at the registers. We'd chatted a lot between customers, but it was mostly run-of-the-mill small talk until the day she'd looked over my shoulder at my homework assignment and asked what I was reading.

When I'd turned over my copy of *Heart of Darkness* so she could see the title, Natalie had given me a knowing grin. "For school, not pleasure, I assume. My sister's reading that."

"Who's your sister?"

"Chrissy Broward. She's a junior."

My breath had caught in my throat. "Chrissy Broward is your sister? She's in my math class."

"I don't think she knows I work with you."

"I don't think she knows my name."

Natalie had rolled her eyes. "What makes you think that?"

There was no point in explaining. My neck was still tingling with the shock. Now that I knew, I'd supposed Natalie looked a little like Chrissy, but their differences had far outweighed their similarities. Natalie had a comfortable jock build, wavy dark hair which she'd usually pulled back in a half-assed ponytail, and a casual, laid-back air. She'd initiated conversation easily and got along with everyone. Chrissy, on the other hand, was thin to the point of almost being skinny, with a thick, shaggy, shortish crop of bottle-blond hair that had offset her brown eyes in such a striking manner, I couldn't help but stare at her every day during math. She was ridiculously popular but sat silently in class, her eyes rarely straying from the top of her textbook. She was my usual kind of crush, someone who could sit right next to me all year and never so much as glance my way.

I was at once excited and horrified that Natalie even knew her, and everything that came into my mind had sounded stupid. "I don't know. Most people don't even know I'm here."

"Because you're new?"

I'd shrugged. "I'm always new."

Natalie had grabbed a handful of videos from the drop slot and continued in the same chatty tone. "Well, I don't see how anyone could help but notice you."

The next Saturday, she'd beckoned me into the alley behind the store during a smoke break and kissed me on the mouth. Two weeks later, we'd had sex. In the weeks that followed, we'd spent as many evenings as we'd dared in my bedroom but passed the bulk of our time together downtown on the cobblestones along the river, watching barges drift past, talking about absolutely everything.

We'd kept our relationship secret. I knew that my mother would hit the roof if she found out I was seeing a college sophomore. Since I was in school with Natalie's sister, we had to avoid her house and all of the usual hangouts for fear that someone would recognize me as being only seventeen. The biggest problem, though, was working around Natalie's boyfriend.

They'd been dating for three years, and Natalie had sworn that he'd been charming at the beginning. I'd seen nothing charming about the jealous, possessive person who'd belittled her in front of our coworkers and all too often left bruises on her body. Natalie had spent as little time with him as possible but stayed in the relationship because, as she'd explained, it was "the thing to do." His parents were influential in the community, and so long as she associated with such people, her parents had stayed out of her business and allowed her to come and go as she pleased.

I hadn't pretended that she would someday leave him for me. Even at the age of seventeen, I'd understood the futility in that. I had cherished every second we had together even more knowing that she was with me instead of him. One evening, during one of our talks on the riverfront, Natalie had explained in one sentence why she'd pursued me so: when she was with me, she could be herself. She might as well have told me that she'd loved me; nothing anyone had ever said to me had made me feel so beautiful and whole. I'd loved her for real, although I'd never managed to say it out loud.

That May, my mother had lost her job. Once again, we'd packed up everything we owned and moved on to another city, another job, another school. Just two and a half months after our first kiss behind the Blockbuster, I'd seen Natalie Broward for the last time. I would always lie; I would always rewrite the past because the truth was far too complicated.

❖

Friday was an ugly day. The rain had passed through West Grove, but it left winter in its wake. The temperature was a good thirty degrees cooler than it'd been two mornings before, and I had to switch my thermostat from air-conditioning to heat the moment I got out of bed.

We were not so fortunate at school. Marvin, the custodian, was tinkering in the boiler room when I arrived, but he didn't manage to get the heat working. We did an hour and a half of TAAS practice testing in the cold, during which I sat huddled at my desk and thought hard. Tina didn't want things to be weird between us, but she didn't say she wanted to date me, either. Amy deserved better than I was giving her. I knew that I needed to do the right thing.

I did eat lunch in the lounge but left a few minutes early, saying I needed to check something in my room. Instead of stopping there, I continued out the back door.

The wind hit me squarely in the face the second I stepped out onto the playground, and it somehow managed to travel through my sweater and jeans as if they weren't even there. Bev and Sally were lining their classes up, and as I eased past, their students vied for my attention. "Hey, Ms. Smith!"

"Ms. Smith! I like your hair that way!"

They managed to cause just enough commotion. By the time I rounded the edge of the building, I could feel Amy's eyes on me, and for just a moment, I felt really sexy. I ignored the fact that a jacket would have been nice and took my time crossing the field.

Amy extracted herself from a circle of kindergartners and moved just a few paces toward me. "Hey," she called, smiling nervously. "You're early."

I imagined the amount of distance we might have kept between us if we were straight and discussing the weather, then parked myself there and took a small step backward. It felt too close. "Just wanted to say hello."

I saw her jaw twitch. I hadn't just stopped by to say hello more than twice since we'd first seen one another outside school hours.

Her cheeks had been pink with the wind when I'd left the building, but they were rapidly turning scarlet. "You look really hot," she blurted, then glanced desperately around us.

"Thank you. The windblown look is good on you, too."

Her smile grew. She stared at the ground and went even redder, if that was possible. "Yeah, whatever."

We stood silently for a minute. She scanned the playground, checked her watch, blew the whistle on one of Daniel's boys. I hugged my arms to my chest and tried not to shiver.

"I'm really sorry about last night," I finally said. "I was stuck at admin forever, and with the rain—"

"It's okay. I was hoping to catch you, but I know how those meetings go."

"So are you busy this weekend?"

Her eyes lit up. "I need to be at my parents' house tonight, but tomorrow, I have the whole day."

"Can I take you to dinner? Maybe take the dogs out before that if it's warm enough?"

"Yes." She made an awkward jerky motion, like she wanted to touch me, then thought better of it. Before I could respond, her whistle was back in her mouth. "Crenshaw and Smith's classes, line up."

"I'll call you," I whispered, then took off for the D-wing door, arms clutched as tightly to my body as I could manage.

❖

Saturday was really, truly wonderful. I got to Amy's house around two, and we spent most of the afternoon at the dog park. It was really only an empty plot of land that was once slated to be an office complex, but the plans had fallen through, and the city didn't want it to become a dumping ground for dilapidated cars and trash. They had erected a fence around it, hooked up a few garden hoses to the water main, and let people set their dogs free where they were confined and protected from traffic. Rumor was there was a movement to turn it into a skate park instead, but I didn't see that happening. It was a lot less expensive to turn on the water and let people clean up their own dog crap.

I liked Amy's dogs a lot better than Bugsy the Chihuahua. Sylvia was some sort of brown and white bird dog mix; Chipper was a fat English bulldog she'd found huddled in a ditch outside her parents' house, one whole side of his body swollen and full of cactus needles; and Tank was a beautiful, three-legged rottweiler. We ran around and threw a tennis ball with Sylvia and Tank while Chipper spent most of his time rolling in the dirt. The dog park was a safe place where we could laugh and play together. If people struck up conversations, they were exclusively about dogs, and if we saw anyone we knew, we were involved in an indisputably wholesome activity.

We went to the Ranch Hand for dinner, sunburned and windburned and happy. Our table was surrounded by a large group of senior citizens who were talking boisterously amongst themselves, so our conversation was uncharacteristically easy. We enjoyed our steaks at a leisurely pace and shared dessert like normal human beings.

I didn't want to take anything for granted. Back at Amy's house, I hesitated on the front walk as she unlocked the door. I would have been satisfied to end the evening right then if she needed to return phone calls or take care of something, but she turned around quizzically. "Aren't you coming in?"

"Sure."

She scooped her cat out of the doorway and made room for me in the foyer. "Just sure? Brother." Amy locked the door behind us, barely glanced at her answering machine, and grinned at me. "You really don't have to."

"No, no, I want to."

"Really? 'Cause I could just go to bed." With that, she pulled her sweater over her head and left me there in the living room.

The sex that night was wonderful. We usually hurried through it once, then she'd throw me out of bed before I could catch my breath. This time, we snuggled, took our time, then watched TV curled up under her covers.

I remembered *Saturday Night Live* being on, but it wasn't anymore when Amy nudged me. "Hey. It's late."

I felt for my watch. It read a quarter past one. "Guess I fell asleep."

"Me too." Instead of being upset, she looked apologetic. "I have to be at the early service tomorrow."

I nodded, not even trying to suggest that I could let myself out in the morning. God knew her parents were probably coming at the crack of dawn to cook her breakfast or something. I found my jeans and started working my way back into them. "This was nice," I began hesitantly.

She gave me a shy smile in return. "It was. I've missed you."

I thought about that for a moment. It hadn't really been that long, but that summed things up nicely. "Me too," I told her. If we could be like this more often, enjoying our dinner, taking our time with everything afterward, not arguing, I'd want this every weekend or maybe even every day. "You want me to lock up?"

She shook her head and reached for her fuzzy blue robe. "I'll see you out."

Sylvia appeared to follow us to the door, and Tank sat up and gave a token *wuf*. Chipper, who was sprawled over two sofa cushions, opened one eye but didn't bother moving. Amy told them all to sit and stay while I pulled on my coat and found my keys. They were far better at their assignment than Bugsy the Chihuahua.

"Good night," Amy whispered, sneaking a kiss even though the door was open.

"Good night. See you Monday."

It was cold outside, ridiculously cold for the beginning of November. As I settled into my car, still in a sleepy daze, I toyed with wishing for snow, even though it'd be a waste on a weekend. The mere prediction of one inch would make the whole town come to a grinding halt, but the idea of curling up on the sofa with a puffy blanket and a cup of hot cocoa would be the perfect postscript for the evening.

God, I was tired. Once I got home, I took the stairs by twos and impatiently jiggled my key in the lock. I just wanted to be in bed again. I left my coat on the sofa, kicked off my shoes on my way to the bathroom, and did the world's quickest job of brushing my teeth and taking out my contacts. For only the third or fourth time in years, I skipped my route past my shoebox.

Bed felt wonderful. It was a rare thing that I snuggled deep into my comforter alone in my own bed, sober, and cherished it so much. It was warm and soft and late, and I felt absolutely wonderful. Without even the suggestion of ugly thoughts, my eyes closed.

What seemed like just minutes later, I was jolted out of a dead sleep. Heart pounding, eyes wide open to the darkness, I fumbled for the alarm, wondering why the fuck it was waking me at two thirty-seven in the morning. Then, the phone rang again.

I found the caller ID and held it close enough to read the digits. My first thought was that it was Amy, that something had happened after I'd gone. My second thought was that someone was dead. The caller ID told me nothing. It was someone's cell phone, a local number, no name. I didn't think it was the person who had been calling constantly, but my brain was so hazy, I couldn't be sure.

I picked up after the third ring. "Hello?"

There was a pause, then the most terrifying thing. "Cary, this is Kathy Sutton. I'm so sorry to call at this hour."

I groped desperately for my glasses, hoping that they might somehow help me make sense of what I was hearing. "What's wrong?"

"Oh Cary, I'm so sorry. I need you to come down here."

My glasses weren't helping. "To come down where?"

"There's been a break-in at Bush. I'm here with the police."

My breath caught in my throat. I knew the answer, but I had to ask anyway. "My classroom?"

"Yes. I'm so sorry, but we need you here right away."

"I'm on my way." I hung up without saying good-bye and started throwing on the first clothes I could find, mostly things I'd worn out with Amy.

It had never been so cold and dark in my apartment before. Surely, it was no different from when I'd arrived home, but I was wide-awake this time. *Thank God I didn't stay at Amy's. Thank God.*

I couldn't remember where I'd left my shoes, and every second felt like wasted time. I was swearing out loud by the time I found them, one underneath the kitchen table, the other on the opposite side of the sofa. I wondered for a sick moment whether Kathy would have known enough to try me at Amy's. I locked up and rushed back down the stairs, pulling my coat on as I reached the car.

By the time I turned onto Fourth, I was absolutely trembling with the cold. The heater refused to work, and I was wearing a T-shirt underneath a light jacket. My lips felt numb, my nose wanted to run, and my stomach was a raw, twisted knot. There was something about Kathy's tone that really worried me, something about the way she kept apologizing. There wasn't much worth stealing in my classroom. It had taken me all of two minutes to locate everything the other day.

What if it's because I'm gay? I chewed my lip and wiped my nose on the back of my hand. Jody and Daniel and Amy and Tina were the only ones who knew for sure. Bev and Sally assumed, but that didn't matter; this wouldn't have been a teacher. None of my students knew. None of them ever knew. I was so careful, always so damned careful that I barely felt like myself anymore.

I could see the blue flashing lights three blocks away. My stomach wrung tighter, but I pushed my glasses up on my nose, sat up straight, and tried to pull myself together. I conjured my best detached look and even checked it in the rearview mirror at the last stoplight. *Me? I've been in bed all night. Since nine. My bed. Not Amy Davis's bed. I wasn't having sex with her. I wasn't having sex with anyone. I haven't even* had *sex, 'cause I'm not married.*

The first thing I saw upon pulling into the main lot was Sally Schumacher's red Pontiac. It was parked haphazardly just beyond the police car, as if she'd come barreling in, squealing tires and all, and had skidded to a stop with a billow of smoke and dust. She was standing outside the D-wing door, arms firmly clutching a long coat over what looked like turquoise sweats, talking a mile a minute to Kathy and a young, good-looking cop. All the bullshit I'd conjured in my mind disappeared immediately. I wasn't the only one.

I left my car next to Sally's, only parked in a real space, and strode defiantly toward them, jaw still clenched but feeling immensely better. "Kathy, what happened?"

Nobody looked at me strangely for calling her by her first name. For a glorious moment, the principal's face softened into a luscious look of empathy, and she reached for my shoulder. "This is such a nightmare."

I nodded at Sally. "Is it just our classrooms?"

"That's what we think," Kathy said. "I haven't been past D-hall, but the officers cleared the building and didn't see anything else out of the ordinary."

Sally patted my shoulder, too. "Mine isn't too bad. The glass is broken out of the door, and my desk drawer was pried open, you know, like they were looking for cash? I don't keep anything important in there, though."

Yours isn't too bad? What about mine? The portions of my stomach which had previously relaxed seized up again. "May I go inside?"

The cop looked up from whatever he was writing. "You're D-6?"

I nodded.

He looked back at me for what seemed like a long time. "Please, ma'am. You'll need to let us know what's missing."

Kathy grabbed me by the arm. "Let me go with you."

Oh God. Oh God. Oh God. My feet felt like lead, but I followed Kathy across the lawn, through the D-wing door, and into the hall. Sally's classroom, the first on the left, was lit up, door wide open. I could see a bit of what looked like glass beneath my door, but it was closed, and everything else on the hall was dark as death.

Kathy stepped in front of me and grabbed the doorknob before I could. "Cary, I'm sure it means nothing."

Panic rose from my toes upward. The window had been knocked inward, the construction paper ripped out. "What means nothing?"

She didn't answer. "Watch the glass on the floor," she whispered, then opened the door and turned on the lights.

I couldn't breathe. I stood with Kathy in the doorway, broken glass all around us, unable to breathe, unable to move, unable to think. My desk drawers had been pried open and were hanging at awkward angles. The desks on the left side of the classroom were shoved out of the way, and the contents of my supply cabinet were scattered on the floor. None of that mattered, though. None of it mattered at all because there behind my desk on the whiteboard for God and Kathy to see were huge red letters that read, *I KNOW ABOUT YOU.*

Kathy stood somewhere in my periphery. I was fairly certain she was wearing a pained, almost frightened expression, but the panic had risen through my entire body, and I couldn't look away from the whiteboard. It felt like I was suffocating in my own silence.

"I'm sure it's the gangs. West Side Mafia tags the back of A-wing all the time."

"Yeah," I mumbled. "It's nothing. It's nothing."

"That's right. It's nothing," Kathy agreed firmly.

A huge wave of nausea engulfed my body, and my palms went wet. I knew I was going to be sick, and I knew it was going to happen right away. I think I asked Kathy to excuse me, but the next several minutes were hazy at best. I knew I wouldn't be able to find the bathroom in the darkness, so I ran for the back door and made it around the corner toward C-wing before vomiting.

I'd never felt so tiny and helpless and out of control in my whole life. I leaned against the building, gasping for breath, staring blankly up at the sky. Millions of stars were shining brightly, blurring together in streaks of light until I gathered myself enough to wipe my eyes on the bottom of my shirt. The brick felt cool and soothing against my back. I had never wanted something so badly in my life as to be back at home, sleeping safely in bed.

I was alone outside for a long time. I heard the crunch of boots around D-wing from time to time as the police officers went in and out, and I heard Sally calling to Kathy to say she was going home. She sounded far too chipper. I wanted to punch her. Shortly after that, though, I heard lighter footsteps coming toward me.

Kathy hesitated at the edge of the building. "Hey."

"Hey."

"Are you all right?"

"Yeah. I'm sorry I took off."

"It's okay. Take your time."

"No, I'm good."

We walked slowly back to my room together, not speaking but very close to one another. Kathy began sweeping the broken glass into a pile with her foot and allowed me to move through my room and take a mental inventory. My computer was still there, but my disc player was gone. The locks on my desk looked to have been pried off with a screwdriver or some other sort of rudimentary tool. There were gouges in the paint where it had slipped in the process. I used one of those drawers to store my purse during school hours, and it had been empty. The other was a catchall for things that would only appeal to eleven-year-olds: hall passes, extra pencils and paper clips, a few bags of cheap candy, a bottle of ibuprofen, and some loose change for the soda machine. While everything else seemed to be there, the coins were gone.

The two drawers that didn't lock had been searched as well, but I could account for everything inside. Apparently, my vandal wasn't looking for blank office referral forms or Tampax. By the time I went over to check my supply cabinet, Kathy had moved behind me and was trying to chip away at the words on my whiteboard. I deliberately did not look at her.

They had really riffled through the supply cabinet. Most things seemed to be there, but it was a crazy mess. I was scooping things off the floor and tossing them back into their approximate places to deal with another time when we were rejoined by the police.

It wasn't the same officer I'd met outside. This one was an African-American woman with short dark hair and striking gray eyes. I knew that Amy had once dated a cop, and I wondered if she was the one.

"Officer Williams," she said, holding out a hand.

"Cary Smith," I responded, my voice still coming out tiny and hoarse.

Her handshake was forceful and all business. "Do you have an idea of what's missing?"

"Not much," I said. "A disc player, maybe two dollars in coins, a package of markers, and half a dozen bottles of white-out."

The cop gave a contemptuous laugh as she wrote that down. "Kids," she said. "All this for a handful of change and a quick high."

Kathy wiped her hands on her jeans and picked her way around desks to join us. "What do you think about that, though?"

Officer Williams shrugged at the words, then turned a piercing gaze at me. "Do you have any idea?"

I finally forced myself to look at the whiteboard. Kathy had scraped away for ten, maybe fifteen minutes and had barely made a dent in the last U. At least ten possible meanings coursed through my head, but I couldn't say any of them out loud. "I don't know. It makes me…" I stopped, not sure how to finish that statement, either. Any expression of fear couldn't possibly cover it.

"It frankly scares the hell out of me," Kathy interrupted flatly. "I'm the last one in this building most days."

"Ma'am, I wouldn't worry so much," Officer Williams said. "Considering what was taken, I'd say it's definitely just kids trying to be intimidating. We think that was unlocked, right," she said, nodding back toward the entrance to D-Hall, "and these two classrooms are the closest to the door."

If the outside door was left unlocked, Marvin was going to be in a world of trouble. I assumed Kathy had already gotten in touch with him. I liked Officer Williams's theory, but I knew in my gut that it wasn't correct. "Why not write this in the interior classroom, then?"

Kathy's eyebrows jumped like that was a good question. "Almost nothing was taken from Sally's room."

"You can watch the road from here," Officer Williams said.

"I suppose," Kathy said, looking back one more time and shaking her head. "Marvin will come in tomorrow to take care of the desk and the board. It's some kind of paint, but surely, he can find a way to clean it. Do we need to replace the supply cabinet?"

I shook my head and closed the doors on the mess inside. "It's fine."

Officer Williams told Kathy that there wasn't any reason for me to stay. Kathy and I walked back to the parking lot together the same way we had earlier, not speaking but so close we bumped elbows.

"I'm so sorry, Cary," Kathy said once we reached my car, and for the first time ever, wrapped her arms around me. "I'm sorry I had to wake you, and I'm sorry you had to see this."

I held on tightly, too, but only for a moment. I didn't want to come off as some desperate little kid.

"Look," she said, letting go but keeping her face close to mine so I couldn't help but miss the gravity of her words. "I don't want you staying late, at least for a while, okay? They're probably right, this is probably nothing, but I don't want to take any chances."

"I understand."

"Are you all right to go home?"

I nodded mechanically, but inside, I knew I wasn't. I didn't know what she would do if I said no. Surely, she wouldn't take me home with her and let me sleep on her sofa with her terriers. I wondered if she'd tell me to stay with Daniel or Jody. I wondered if she'd tell me to go back to Amy's.

"Good. Try to get some sleep."

"You too."

It was after four thirty when I got home. I left the lights off in my apartment while I stopped in the bathroom to pee and brush my teeth, but my eyes were well adjusted to the dark, and it didn't help me feel any more restful. I checked the locks on my front door and windows three, four, five times and skimmed the top of the shoebox in my closet before and after stripping off my clothes. I got back into bed, but I knew it was futile. My thoughts were racing, and my eyes wouldn't stay closed no matter what direction I turned, even if I pulled the covers over my head. There was no way I could possibly sleep.

Chapter Ten

I KNOW ABOUT YOU.
    I spent the bulk of Sunday cleaning my apartment. I turned up the stereo and scrubbed everything from the shower to the blinds. I did not call Jody, Daniel, or Amy. I didn't want to talk about it.

I couldn't get the words out of my head. When I closed my eyes, I saw them, four or five inches tall, bright red against the white background. The writing itself was nondescript. I doubted that I could recognize anyone's hand from letters scrawled quickly with paint, but it didn't strike me as particularly similar to any of my students.

I KNOW ABOUT YOU.

Who knew what about whom? Sure, the cops thought it was random graffiti, but I had a nagging feeling that wasn't the case. I was positive that someone had been through my desk that other day, that I wasn't just imagining things.

You know I'm gay? You know about Amy and me? You know I'm finishing a book Mr. Dunlop forbade me to read? You know something else, something about where I've been, what I've done, who I've known? Who are you?

I arrived at school earlier than usual on Monday morning. I'd gotten about six hours of sleep over the past two nights, including what I'd had before Kathy's phone call, and my whole apartment was spotless. I still had plenty of things to clean up at school, though, that was for sure.

The glass was missing completely from my door, which meant I didn't need to use my keys. I expected to walk into the same trashed room I'd left the other night, but the student desks had been straightened, the shrapnel had been swept up, and all the contents of my desk were stacked neatly in the corner, a replacement desk sitting where the old one had been. It was by no means new. The top was worn, and the paint was scraped off the sides here and there, but there were two keys on a little ring inside the top drawer, and the locks worked.

The graffiti was no longer behind my desk. Nothing was behind my desk, actually, because the whiteboard was entirely gone. The wall was bare, save for an enormous swath of scarred, shredded drywall. Paint had come off in huge chunks, revealing the fuzzy cardboard-gray underneath, and there were residual swirls of crusty industrial glue here and there the color of snot. It looked as if Marvin had just taken a crowbar and pried the whole thing off the wall. While it was a big improvement over the last time I'd seen it, it still looked hideous. There was no way I could possibly pretend nothing had happened.

I spent a few minutes on my supply cabinet, then went down to the office. Dunlop's office door was closed, but Kathy was sorting through paperwork at her desk. Her tendency on normal days was to buzz in right before the bell, but it looked as if she hadn't gotten much sleep, either.

Instead of her usual generic greeting, she came out of her office and gave me a quick, one-armed hug. "Hey sweetie. How are you doing?"

"I'm fine. How are you?"

Kathy shrugged. "I've been better. I'm sorry about the wall in your room. Marvin said he tried everything he could think of to get rid of the paint, but the only thing that worked took off the surface itself. I did *not* say he could rip the whole thing down." She giggled as if the absurdity of the situation had just struck her funny, then cleared her throat hastily. "Sorry. That was inappropriate."

I shook my head, grinning back at her. "The whole situation's crazy. Sometimes, all you can do is laugh." *Or cry. Or drink.*

"Anyway," she continued, heading briskly back into her office, "I'll have him bring you a chalkboard until the new whiteboard comes in."

"Thank you."

I turned to leave and found Selena staring at me unabashedly. I couldn't read her look, but it seemed to be in the family of disgust. As head secretary, she surely knew what had happened, but I wondered if Kathy or Marvin had told her what the board had said. I was very sure Kathy had kept Sally out of my room the other night. Maybe Selena was mad because Kathy wouldn't tell her. Maybe she was mad because Kathy hugged me. Maybe she was just mad at me for the usual reasons, whatever those were.

I didn't need to prepare a current events' discussion. Instead of dropping off their jackets and backpacks in their lockers, every one of my students stopped short in the front of the room and gawked at the travesty behind me. I refused to answer questions until everyone had taken care of their belongings and settled into their desks for the morning. Not surprisingly, that happened a full five minutes earlier than usual.

"So what happened?" Nestor asked.

"Ashley, Eric and Adriana aren't here yet."

"That's what they get for being late," Christian said. "They can hear it later."

I still waited until the tardy bell rang. "Someone broke into the building over the weekend."

"And stole the whiteboard?" David asked.

I couldn't tell if he was serious or just being a jerk. "They stole a few little things and painted graffiti on the board."

"What kind of graffiti?" Cristal asked.

The PA system buzzed, and Selena began the morning routine. Unfortunately, the flag hung in the front right corner of the classroom, and I could no longer keep my back to the wall when we stood for the pledge. I knew that very few eyes were on the flag that morning, but I kept mine trained on it with a vengeance.

There were several more questions. Did I have to come in when it happened? Did they catch the people who did it? What did they steal? How did they get in the building? Not a single person asked if we were getting a new whiteboard. Honestly, that morning, I didn't care if we were or not. I didn't feel like teaching anything at all. It was a long time before someone asked about the graffiti again.

"Was it gang stuff?" Chelsea asked.

"That's what the police think."

"Bet it was a West Side Mafia tag," Zack said, his voice contemptuous. He turned to Fernando Aguilar directly to his right. "Your brother's Mafia, right?"

Fernando was a short, stocky boy whose hair was always painstakingly gelled so it stood up in the front with just the slightest hint of a wave. He never raised his hand, and aside from the times I'd called on him, I'd heard him talk about three times all year. He gave Zack a warning look. "Shut up."

"My cousins see him beside the skating rink all the time."

"Zack, enough," I said flatly.

Fernando responded in terse Spanish, too fast for me to try to translate. All I caught was *Ochos Loco*, the name of a rival gang. Whatever it was, it caused Zack to stand, lean over toward Fernando, and dare him to say it again.

I jumped off my desk, but Fernando was in the aisle so quickly, his chair fell to the floor. Before I could intervene, he'd grabbed Zack by the arm.

"Stop it now," I yelled, pushing between them and grabbing Fernando before he could take a swing. Zack had apparently been preparing a punch as well, because it landed squarely on my shoulder. I was immediately glad that Fernando was half a foot shorter than Zack. Otherwise it would've caught me in the face instead.

"You, by the windows," I told Zack. "You, against the wall." I let go of Fernando, hoping to God I hadn't made a mark. "Chelsea, get two referral sheets out of my bottom drawer."

I could hear both Zack and Fernando breathing hard at opposite sides of the classroom, but there was no movement anywhere else. It wasn't at all like Chelsea to ignore directions. Slowly, still trying to keep half an eye on the boys, I looked around the rest of the classroom.

Mouths were open. A few people were looking at Zack or Fernando, but most were staring straight at me, shock in their eyes. I felt awful for a second. It must have been the first time all year I'd yelled.

Before I could focus on Chelsea, she got up, sifted through my new desk, and handed me two pink sheets of paper and a ballpoint pen. "Ma'am."

I thanked her and stood dead center of the room for the next few minutes, filling out the paperwork. Nobody made a sound. "Christian, please take Zack down to the office."

"What? What about him?" Zack asked indignantly. "He said my cousin was a—"

"I'm not having the two of you in the hall at the same time," I snapped. "Nestor will bring him down in five minutes."

Christian came up to me and held out his hand. "Want me to bring both referrals?"

"Please. Tell Mrs. Ortiz that Fernando will be down in a few minutes."

"Yes, ma'am."

The uneasy silence continued throughout the morning. I spent my kids' computer lab time in the office, finishing paperwork and talking with Mr. Dunlop and Mrs. Aguilar. Fernando sat on the floor in one corner of Dunlop's office, head tucked into his knees. I'd never met Mrs. Aguilar before, but I could tell Fernando was going to be in big trouble when they got home. Nobody had been able to get in contact with Mrs. Carillo, so Zack sat on a chair outside Dunlop's office, flinching every time Selena's phone rang.

I had written them both up for disruptive behavior rather than actual fighting; this cost them a parent conference but no mandatory suspension. I could tell without looking that my shoulder was bruised where I'd gotten in the way of Zack's punch, but it felt wrong to mention it. The day had gotten off to such a messed-up start that I wished I could have gotten away with just telling them to sit down and shut up.

By lunchtime, my lack of sleep was catching up with me. I didn't really want to talk to anyone, but I knew I would never make it through the afternoon without caffeine. Unfortunately, I didn't have any change in my purse, and the stash in my desk was no more, so I headed to the staff lounge to make a fresh pot of coffee.

Daniel, Bev, Jody and Tina were huddled around Sally, and I knew they were talking about me because their conversation stopped the moment I arrived. I nodded hello, then felt five pairs of eyes watching me as I washed out the coffee pot, got it started, and searched through the cupboard for a mug that looked like it might not give me tuberculosis.

Daniel was the first one to find the balls to speak. "Hey," he said, his voice genuinely concerned. "Sally says your room got the brunt of it."

I nodded briskly. "It was pretty bad."

"What'd they take?"

"The disc player, my soda change, Sharpies, and white-out."

Tina squinted at me. "You're kidding. Someone broke in for that?"

"You have to want a high pretty bad to steal Sharpies," Jody muttered.

"Can you even get a high from a Sharpie?" Daniel asked.

"They just took change from my desk," Sally told everyone, trying to draw attention back to herself.

"I heard that Marvin left the D-wing door unlocked, and the alarm off," Bev whispered.

"The alarm had to be on," I said. "The police wouldn't have come if it wasn't."

"Two thirty in the morning," Sally said loudly. "Kathy called at two thirty in the morning. Bill and I had spent the day in Lubbock, and we were just exhausted after the drive."

"I'm so sorry," Tina said directly to me, completely ignoring Sally. "I'd be scared to death."

"Me too," Jody said. "Heck, it scares me, and it's not even my room."

"You know the worst part?" Sally asked, gathering her things from the table and starting to the door. "They painted something on her whiteboard."

Damn her. The coffee wasn't done, but I went back to the counter, deliberately turning my back to the conversation, and pulled the pot out from the machine to fill my cup. It kept dripping, and coffee sizzled angrily on the hot surface. I replaced the decanter more forcefully than necessary and watched what was left slosh inside it.

"What?" Jody asked, her voice so loud it made me jump. "What was it?"

"I don't know," Sally said sweetly. "Kathy wouldn't let me in there to see."

I turned to shoot Sally a look that said I wasn't going to tell her now, either, but apparently, she knew that. She and Bev were out the door.

"Cary," Jody said, "what was it?"

"Police thought it was just gang stuff," I said, sitting back down and taking a sip of coffee. It was scalding hot and burned my tongue.

"Gang stuff?" Daniel asked, screwing up his face in a you've-got-to-be-kidding-me look.

"Yes, and we just had a baby gang fight in my room. Mafia versus *Ochos*, right there in D-6."

"Holy shit, I thought I heard you yell!"

"Watch your mouth," Jody told Daniel, then turned to me, her eyes pained. "During class?"

"Yup. Fernando and Zack. It was awesome."

"Fernando's Mafia, right?"

"Daniel," Jody warned.

He shrugged. "Did anyone get hit?"

"Yeah, me."

"Where?" Tina asked. "This is insane."

I motioned to my shoulder, trying my coffee again. It was either a little cooler, or the first sip had destroyed my ability to sense pain.

"Here?" Jody asked, poking at my shoulder. I didn't see it coming and couldn't gather myself fast enough to keep from wincing.

She exchanged a look with Tina, and before I could say or do anything, Tina had slid the neckline of my blouse clear off my shoulder so they could look. I couldn't see the bruise, but I could see my bra strap. "Jesus, guys!"

"Wow," Tina said. "You need to ice that."

"It happened three hours ago. I'll be fine," I told her, struggling back into my shirt. My face felt like it was on fire.

"Yeah, that's gotta hurt," Daniel agreed.

"Do you think it was someone from one of your kids' families?" Jody asked.

"No," I said, flatly, straightening my shirt again and picking up my coffee. "Just one of those things, you know? I'll see you guys."

"Hey," Tina said, grabbing my other hand before I could leave. "One way or another, don't stay so late, okay?"

Her fingers were warm and soft. I'd been too stunned to think when she'd moved my shirt, but now a tingle of electricity ran all the way up my arm. Our eyes met just as directly, as if Jody and Daniel weren't sitting right there. I knew I should look away, but I couldn't. Even though I'd been doing a diligent job of trying to get over her, I realized that moment that I didn't want to.

"I know," I said, finally slipping my hand from her grasp. "Kathy told me the same thing."

❖

Tuesday morning, Marvin rolled a gigantic, antiquated chalkboard into my classroom during one of our TAAS practice tests. It squeaked when it moved, and it took five of us to navigate it around the other furniture and in front of the wall where the whiteboard had been.

It was apparently a good time for Marvin to install the new window, too. Even though I told him several times that my students needed quiet, he had his tools and the supplies with him, and that was when he was going to do the work, damn it. He had to remove some of the trim to replace the glass, so the pounding, ripping, and drilling noises were intense. I actually had the kids close their test books for twenty minutes until the worst of the noise was finished. When he was finally gone, I had them continue and went to work covering the new window with construction paper. I'd had enough of seeing straight into the hall.

I really thought the news had spread through the entire school on Monday, but I was wrong. When I dropped my class off for gym, Amy told them to run the perimeter of the field and shot me a piercing look. "Why didn't you call me?"

"Was I supposed to?"

"About Saturday," she said. "This morning, Bev brings her kids in, yapping at me about how they were finally getting around to replacing your window. I didn't know what she was talking about, Cary."

"I'm sorry. It's no big deal, really."

She threw me an exasperated look, then directed her attention back to my class. "Are you okay?"

"I'm fine."

"Was it because of..." She made an almost-invisible motion between the two of us.

I shook my head. "It was just a random thing."

"Why didn't you call me?"

"I didn't want to worry you."

She stared directly at me for what felt like an excruciatingly long time. "Are you seeing somebody else?"

I took a step back. It felt like she'd hit me. "What?"

"Nothing."

"Why would you think that?"

"No reason." She sighed and squinted back out at the field again. "I just sort of thought you'd tell me about something that big."

"I'm not seeing somebody else, okay?"

"Just forget it."

My kids were rounding the final corner, and I was sure my cheeks were flushed with guilt, even though I'd done nothing wrong. I nodded briskly and turned to go. "Okay. I will."

I wasn't sure whether to be hurt or mad. We'd had such a wonderful day on Saturday that I couldn't believe that thought could have crossed her mind. If I would have come running back to her at four in the morning, she would have freaked out. Since her cell phone was district issue, she didn't even bring it to church. Anyway, I hadn't actually told anyone at all. Everyone had either heard it from Sally or through the grapevine. I was mad, I decided, or at least frustrated.

I knew Amy would apologize. I just didn't know when. I half expected to catch her eye during the staff meeting that afternoon, but as soon as Kathy brought up the burglary, I focused on the floor. She informed us that until further notice, the school would be closing at five every evening, and we were all expected to be out by then. Nobody was in danger, she assured us, but she didn't want to take any chances and have someone in the building after dark. After that, Jody made a long, boisterous announcement about auditions for *Peter Pan*. Slowly but surely, the buzz began to quiet.

I arrived at school Wednesday morning to find a formal-looking white envelope in my mailbox. *Ms. Smith* was written on the front in black ballpoint, and the flap was sealed. I worried for a second that it was some kind of new, exclusive summons from Dunlop, but the writing was larger and sloppier than his. Ninety percent of the staff at Bush had unmistakable teacher writing, and I hadn't written myself a note. Amy had never done something so bold.

> *Cary-*
> *I'm sorry.*
> *Call me tonight?*

I tucked the note into my pocket and grabbed a slip of scrap paper from beside the sign-in sheet.

> *Amy-*
> *I will.*

Since I didn't have a fresh envelope at my disposal and reusing Amy's would blow her cover, I folded the paper in half and stuck it in her box.

I thought about the note most of the day and even made an extra trip to the office before lunch to make sure Amy had gotten it. Her box was empty, and Selena didn't give me any extra special nasty looks so I assumed Amy had just picked it up with a handful of other papers. I wanted her to believe me. I even toyed with the idea of calling her from school just to leave a message on her machine. I knew it was her church night, but I wondered if we could catch dinner beforehand or make plans for later in the week.

After school, Chris, Marisol, and I gathered in the staff room to go over lesson plans for the month. Although I usually did my own thing, we did bounce ideas off one another, and some months, when we were particularly short on time, we divvied up the subjects and shared plans. After an hour, Chris pointed out that it was past four thirty, and our curfew was looming.

"Want me to sign you guys out?"

"I certainly do," Marisol said, heading out. "Thank you."

Chris stood at the door, waiting for me. "Cary?"

I was still scribbling in my book. "I'll go down in a few minutes. Thanks, though."

He tapped on the door over and over again. I wasn't sure if he was just waiting on me or if he was trying to distract me into packing up. "You are going home, though, right?"

"In a few minutes. I still have to get my stuff together."

"I think you're nuts after last weekend. I'll see you tomorrow, assuming you're still alive."

"Thanks a lot," I muttered without looking up. "Have a lovely evening."

When I finished in another minute or two, the halls were deserted. I was sorry I hadn't left with Chris. The construction paper covering the brand-new glass on my door was dark, almost so dark I couldn't tell what color it was, dark enough to suggest another nasty storm. When I looked over to the door at the end of D-hall, though, I saw that the sun was only just starting to sink toward the horizon.

More confused than wary, I unlocked the door and nudged it open far enough to look around. There was no motion, nothing scurrying for cover. I flipped on the light, glanced one more time into the deserted hallway, and let the door close behind me.

My blinds were down. That was the problem. The entire bay of windows was covered, making it feel dark and stuffy in the classroom. During my tenure at Bush, I'd closed them only a handful of times, usually during winter break or particularly cold weekends to try to trap the heat. Now, every set was pulled down and turned closed.

I think you're nuts after last weekend.

A twinge of fear prickled through my body. I'd been uneasy around school since the beginning of the *Coral Sharkey* fiasco, but this was the first time I was flat-out scared. Someone was messing with me on purpose. I was obviously still in the building. My purse was in my desk…God, was it? I unlocked the drawer and checked carefully, actually opening each compartment to make sure nothing was missing. My grade book and a pile of papers were spread out on my desk along with half a Coke. I hadn't signed out. It was obvious I was coming back.

Marvin. It had to be him trying to be helpful after the weekend. He'd closed the blinds every night during my first month at Bush no matter how many notes I left him. I peeked into the trash can and found it empty, and the proper portions of my board had been erased.

One way or another, the claustrophobic feeling exacerbated my discomfort. I went to open them, beginning at the far end of the classroom. I was leaning over David's desk, trying to get to the cord without knocking over Dixie cups full of science experiments when I heard the door click behind me.

"Leave them down."

The cord slipped through my fingers and swung, back and forth, back and forth. I was afraid to stop it and even more afraid of moving my hand back to my side. The voice was female, but I couldn't place it. I wasn't crazy, I wasn't paranoid. I was trapped. The dirty metal blinds went in and out of focus. I was absolutely certain that there, in the corner of my classroom, I was about to die.

I heard nothing more behind me. I waited and waited, stock-still, ears ringing, until the silence became absurd. I was certain that if I turned, I'd find myself looking down the barrel of a gun, but I knew I had to do it. I'd been through too much to go down in a sixth-grade classroom in small-town Texas without a fight. Slowly, slowly, I turned my head, just a tiny bit, just to sneak a glance at what was about to become of me.

Tina Flores was standing there. I felt my jaw drop, and in my haste to turn completely, I knocked two Dixie cups to the floor. I scrambled to retrieve them, my eyes glued to Tina the entire time.

"I thought you promised me you'd leave at a reasonable hour."

"What?"

She raised one finger to her lips and as I stood there staring, moved back to the door and turned the dead bolt.

I had never locked the door from the inside before. "What are you doing?"

She didn't answer. While I remained frozen in the corner, clutching David's chair, she wound her way through the desks until she was right there with me.

"Please tell me," I begged, my voice barely more than a whisper.

"I think you know."

I didn't. Tina was just inches in front of me now, almost uncomfortably close. I could smell her perfume. I had absolutely no clue what she was talking about.

Her eyes dropped between us for a moment, and then she gazed back at me through her eyelashes, a tiny smile starting on the corner of her dark red lips. "You know."

David's chair gave way to my fingernails, and hard green plastic jammed up to the quick. I didn't move, didn't breathe. There was something desperately sexy about the way she was looking at me, but I couldn't begin to appreciate it. I'd never been so frightened in my life.

Her smile continued, and her eyes pried into me, through me, making me feel hot and cold all at the same time. I could not look away, could not blink until her visage blurred, and her lips met mine with an absolute defiance.

Panic began like swiftly rising waters, licking at my ears, my nose, threatening to swallow my body whole. *This should not be happening.* I tried to think, to reason, to act, but all I could do was stand there. *This cannot be happening.* Just as I was certain I was about to drown, I tasted her tongue and felt her hand against my breast. *Oh my God.* Kissing Amy felt nothing like this.

It took all the strength I had to pull away, and I made it only centimeters from her face. "We can't do this."

Her eyes flickered open for only a second. "Shut up," she told me, thickly. Her mouth returned to mine, and her right hand came under my sweater and moved upward.

"Ms. Smith?"

I lurched backward against the radiator with a deafening crash. Three seconds might have passed or perhaps ten minutes. One way or another, I was shocked to find that I was still in my classroom. The door remained closed, but the speaker hummed gently. My mouth opened, but no sound came out.

"Ms. Smith?" A second time, now. It was Kathy's voice.

Her face completely unemotional, Tina shrugged toward the speaker. I closed my eyes tightly and tried again, summoning the strongest voice I could. "Yes?"

"Just seeing if you're still here. I'm locking the front door."

I nodded at the speaker and clutched my arms tightly across my chest. "Thank you. I'm on my way out."

"Okay. Be careful."

I exchanged one direct look with Tina. She was most of the way back to the door, her expression still blank. *If we really were the only ones in the building, would this be so horrible?* I turned back to the speaker hastily, feeling sick to my stomach. "I will. Good night."

"Good night," Kathy returned, the buzz ending far sooner than it ever did when Selena was the one listening.

It was over. Whatever this was, it was over. Tina turned toward the door, and I took the opportunity to pull my sweater all the way back down. My face was on fire, my conscience aching.

"She's right," Tina said. "You should get out of here."

With that, she unlocked the door, stepped out into the hall, and disappeared toward the parking lot, all in a silence as disconcerting as that under which she'd appeared. She did not look back; she did not justify or apologize for what had just happened. She didn't even say good-bye.

I didn't raise my shades. I grabbed my purse, locked up, and stumbled to my car, but that was as far as I made it. Like a complete fucking idiot, I sat all alone in the parking lot at George Herbert Walker Bush Elementary School, in the bad part of town, as the clock passed five, then six, then later. Darkness fell completely, and I sat in my car trembling, tears drenching my cheeks at first, then, when I couldn't cry any more, enveloped in a cold numbness. I had no idea what had just happened. I hadn't felt so helpless and clueless and gutless since I was a child.

A distant crash registered somewhere in my periphery. Bottles breaking at the taqueria? *Damn.* I turned my key in the ignition and backed up without bothering to look first. *Could I possibly be any more irresponsible?*

A group of Latino men in their late teens and early twenties were loitering outside the taqueria, drinking and smoking. I rolled through the stop sign and made a right onto Fourth, not wanting to know if they'd been watching my car in the parking lot. The city's neon lights splashed across the hood of my car from cash advance and pawn shops and One Stop Western Gear, all bleeding together into an enormous collage of God-what-am-I-doing-here. I drove past them, up and down the streets, seeing nothing. I drove until my gas gauge registered empty, then filled the tank and drove some more. I didn't know where I was going, and I didn't know what I wanted. I just drove. It was ridiculously late when I finally found myself in front of my apartment.

My porch light was off. My intent had been to get home before dinnertime. Lucy Hernandez was kind enough to turn hers on when I came up the stairs, though, so in just another moment, I was locked inside my own apartment. I turned on the kitchen light, the hall light, the bedroom light, the bathroom light. I stripped out of the sweater and pants I'd been wearing and replaced them with a

T-shirt and sweats that hadn't been involved in the whole wretched scene. It felt like something had chewed a hole through my stomach, but I swallowed half a glass of vodka before acknowledging the answering machine.

The first two messages were hang-ups. The third call was Amy.

Oh, fuck. Amy. I set my glass down and lay back on my bed, hugging my pillow and bracing for the worst.

"Hey, it's me," her message began, agreeably enough. "Give me a call when you get in."

There was another hang-up, then a message from Jody. The machine beeped again, and Amy's voice played back a second time.

"Cary, it's me again. I'm leaving for bible study, but I should be home by eight. Leave me a message when you get in, okay?"

My machine then played back what seemed like enough static and silence to fill the rest of the tape. When I was certain no further messages could fit, it beeped one last time.

"Cary, it's Amy. I don't know where the hell you are, but it's eight forty-five, and I'm home, and I don't have a damned message from you. I don't know what's going on, if you're mad at me, if I did something—"

I slapped the delete button, and Amy went silent. I didn't want to hear it. I couldn't begin to deal with it. I reached over for the caller ID box and backed through the messages, seeing *West Grove, TX, 230-9950* over and over. Jody's number was in there, Amy's registered four times instead of three, and Daniel's cell number appeared early on as one of the hang-ups, but all in all, I'd received seven calls from 230-9950.

Why wouldn't this person leave me alone? Who the hell were they, and what did they want? Was this the person who had broken into my classroom, who *knew* about me, who had tipped Dunlop off about which books I was reading to my students? Was there someone out there who wanted to mess with my head even more intensely than Tina had that afternoon?

I didn't call Amy back. I should have, but I didn't. I should've had dinner, too, but I didn't. Instead, I curled up on the sofa with the vodka bottle and stared at the TV without noticing what I was watching.

The phone rang shortly after the end of the ten o'clock news. The TV was off by then, and I was getting ready for bed, making sure everything was locked and secure. *West Grove, TX,* it said. *230-9950.*

I was drunk and pretty much out of my head. With no deliberation whatsoever, I picked it up and pushed the on button. "Hello?"

Nothing. I repeated myself, waited, then repeated myself again. There was no response. The connection clicked, and in another moment, I was listening to a dial tone.

Please just leave me alone. I dropped the phone back onto the coffee table and checked again to make sure the door was locked. I peeked through the shades into the parking lot, but nobody was standing there watching me. I turned out the lights, moved into my closet, and reached for my shoebox. Even though everything else in my life was spinning out of control, it was exactly where it was supposed to be.

CHAPTER ELEVEN

The Commercial Appeal, Tuesday, June 4, 1991
"Memphis Woman Questioned in Beating Death"

Monday morning, Memphis police arrested the girlfriend of a slain Rhodes College student in connection with the crime.

The suspect had not been charged Monday evening.

Natalie Broward, 19, was detained by police for questioning in connection to the murder of Jonathan McGrath. He was found beaten to death May 31 in a viaduct near an east Memphis subdivision.

Broward, an honor student at the University of Memphis, has no prior arrest record. The victim's sister, Jessica McGrath, said that Broward had dated her brother for over three years but that they had been arguing recently.

"Jonathan was hoping to fix things with [Broward]," McGrath said. "They were going to dinner that night to talk."

Authorities found Jonathan McGrath's pickup in the parking lot of a restaurant half a mile away from where his body was discovered.

❖

I had really bad dreams again. I woke up shaking at five, and by the time I convinced my heartbeat to slow back down to normal, it was too close to six to bother trying to return to sleep. I squeezed my eyes closed, the previous evening drifting back to me as if it, too, had been a dream. A guilty shiver moved through me, like I was a slutty teenager again. I wondered what would have happened if Kathy hadn't buzzed my classroom. I couldn't believe another teacher had kissed me on school grounds after all the half-assed sneaking around I'd done with Amy. Amy, whose calls I hadn't returned.

Goddamn it. Amy was going to kill me. What was I even supposed to tell her when I didn't understand what had happened myself? I shut off the alarm and spent longer than usual in the shower, the water cranked so hot, it stung.

It wasn't as if I'd never cheated on Amy before. It'd only been once, when I'd gone to visit a friend from college over summer break, and we'd both been very drunk. My friend had hooked up with someone else right after I returned to Texas, so I hadn't felt the need to tell Amy about it. I didn't see why I didn't feel that way about what had happened with Tina. I hadn't even really done anything. Everything was pretty much done to me while I stood there paralyzed. I still felt like I'd committed a major violation.

My class had music instead of gym on Thursdays. If I was careful, I could make it through the entire day without running into Amy. I could write her a note or maybe leave her a message saying I was so incredibly sorry, that I'd gotten home late and felt sick, which was mostly true. Jody and Daniel would both vouch for me. They hadn't gotten ahold of me either. Honestly, I was certain that Daniel would vouch for me even if he knew I'd been making out with Tina in the middle of my classroom, but I absolutely did not want to get into it with him.

When I arrived that morning, my room looked like my room, only darker. I pulled the shades up hurriedly, then examined the corner by David's desk for signs of unrest. A few of the science projects looked a little worse for the wear, but nothing was dead, and they weren't the ones we'd treated with Miracle-Gro. Nobody expected much from them anyhow. David's desk and chair were intact, nearly in the same spot they'd sat the day before with David in them. Really, I assured myself, nobody would ever know what happened.

Current events, a spelling test, and a math lesson later, the clock moved to eleven fifty, lunchtime. I'd skipped breakfast that morning, and my stomach was growling. As I headed my kids toward the lunchroom, I was thinking exclusively about food and about avoiding Amy. The moment my kids were safely in the lunch line, though, I ran smack into Tina's class coming in the door. They had to be more than five minutes early. With all the worry about Amy, I hadn't even so much as considered what I would say to Tina.

She barely glanced at me, just a tiny, distracted gaze, as if she was merely tossing a token pleasantry to someone while focusing on her baby-duckling line of kindergartners. "Hey."

"Hey," I mumbled, squeezing out the door as quickly as I could. I knew she was wearing a blue blouse and a flowered skirt. I knew she looked beautiful as ever. That was all. That was plenty. I took off down the hall to my classroom where my lunch was waiting.

By the end of recess, I had scripted exactly what I was going to say to Amy, and I'd even practiced it a few times. I had no problem with lying. I just rarely felt so guilty, and Amy tended to be quite intuitive. Hoping for the best, I strode onto the field with enough time to talk but not enough time to get into details, squinting through the midday sun at the crowd of children, hoping I looked as irresistible as I had the other day.

As soon as I cleared the corner, my plan fell to pieces. Instead of hiding in the shelter in the center of the field like usual, Amy came straight for me. Her eyes were bloodshot enough to suggest that she'd spent a good portion of the night crying.

Oh, I was in big trouble. The gears in my brain ground, stuck, threatened to stop altogether. I couldn't even remember how my speech began. "Look, Amy—"

"Did you even get my messages last night?"

"I got them. I got home late and…"

"Shut up," she interjected darkly. "I don't want to hear it. I don't want to hear about how tired you were or how much work you had or whatever the hell it is this time. I'm sick to death of this being all about you."

I was the one to sneak a quick glance around us this time. "What are you talking about?"

"Oh, come on, Cary. I exist only when you want to get laid. Well, you know what? There's more to a relationship than that. I've got feelings. I'm sick to death of needing you because I know you only need me when you think you're going to get some."

"Amy," I whispered, "this isn't just about sex."

Her jaw tightened. "How stupid do you think I am? When was the last time we just hung out without ending up in bed? I need someone who can be there for me sometimes, you know? You're never there, Cary. I don't know where the hell you are. This emotionally unavailable thing got old a long time ago."

I stared at her, feeling stiff and cold and achy. Her stance was defensive but hurt, arms crossed tightly over her chest. I read several times about Jesus, over and over, on that lanyard. What *would* Jesus do, anyway? I licked my lips and started over. "Look, we need to talk. Let me pick you up after work, and we can get dinner and—"

She shook her head. "It's over. This is over. Do you understand?"

I understood. My throat went raw in that hyper-conditioned, junior high kind of way. I knew I should say something, but nothing came out.

Amy nodded decisively and turned on her toe. "Good," she said, as if I'd agreed. With that, she traveled a good twenty paces and blew her whistle. "Crenshaw and Smith, line up."

I tried not to think about Amy over the next hour, but it was difficult. Once I got the kids going on their seed graphs and charts, my only job was to travel lamely down the aisles, looking over shoulders, offering encouragement to some, reminding others they really did need to do actual work, all in a voice that didn't sound like my own. I couldn't argue with what she'd said about me being emotionally unavailable, but the part about wanting her exclusively for sex hurt. I'd never intended our relationship to be that way. I'd tried to talk to her about important things, and I'd really, truly listened to what she'd said. I was glad when the clock finally inched its way to music time.

Jody's door was open when we got there. She stood in the hall as my class filed in and raised her eyebrows pleasantly. "Did you talk to Coach D?"

I puzzled at her completely inappropriate demeanor. "Yes."

"Grab a book and take your space on the risers," she told my kids, then hung on the door for a moment, regarding me expectantly.

"What'd she tell you?" I asked.

Jody shrugged and watched the end of the hall as if something fascinating was happening there. "Oh, something about deep-sixing things."

"That about sums it up."

"You okay?"

"I will be."

"Hang in there," she said between her teeth, giving me a quick slap on the shoulder. "I'll take you for a drink later."

❖

I really didn't know what to do with myself that night. I had papers to correct, but I couldn't stand being at home, so I finally drove out to the city cinemaplex and paid seven dollars to see whatever was closest to starting. That turned out to be a perfectly disgusting mob picture. I sat in the back of the theater along with fifteen teenage boys, watching without emotion as bullets sprayed the screen over and over. For one hour and forty-seven minutes, I did not think about my life, with or without Amy Davis.

I should have just rented an armful of gory movies. I could have popped one after the other into my VCR until they numbed me to sleep there on the couch. The way it was, I tossed and turned and finally got up at two a.m. to work on the papers I'd neglected. That did put me to sleep. I awoke with a start at five of seven to realize that my alarm had already gone off.

I showered quickly and pulled on the first sweater and pair of jeans I found, thankful for the casual Friday policy. My hair still wet, I grabbed a Coke in lieu of breakfast, packed up the assignments I'd left scattered across the living room, and ran for my car. Even after rushing, it was still past eight by the time I signed in.

The rest of the day went just about as well. I stayed in my classroom for lunch, but Jody stopped in to tell me she hadn't forgotten about me. She really was going to take me out for a drink, but that night, she already had plans to take her parents to Lubbock for a concert at Tech. I assured her that was fine and told her to have a good time. Really, I didn't want to go out for sangrias with her and Daniel. I didn't want to talk about Amy, and I really didn't want to talk about who I should date next.

By dismissal time, I was exhausted. I wished that meant I could go home and flop on my bed and actually get some rest, but I knew that was unlikely, so I took my time packing up and putting things away. When I got to my car, Tina was loading something into the back of hers. I didn't speak, just went to toss my bag in the back seat.

"How're you doing?"

I wondered what she meant by that. The last time I'd really spoken to her, she was busy groping me. I could think of no appropriate response.

She shut her tailgate and moved around to the driver's side, closing some of the distance between us. "I overheard Coach Davis talking with Jody yesterday morning."

I closed my eyes. "Oh. That."

"I didn't know you and Amy were…" She glanced around us, then made a suggestive, half shrug gesture. "Together."

"It wasn't really like that," I said, watching Marisol as she left the building. "Look, we shouldn't—"

"Come to dinner with me."

I stumbled on that, shocked at how easily it had left her mouth. It was just as blunt as the other day when I'd asked her, but somehow, I managed to feel stupid on the receiving end this time.

"Do you have plans?"

"Well, no."

"Go home. Change. I'll pick you up." Tina glanced toward Marisol's truck, then threw me a sarcastic grin. "Don't worry. I promise it won't be anything like Wednesday."

There was no time to appreciate everything that statement acknowledged and implied. "I live really far north," I said.

"I know. You told me that the other night. What's the address?"

"2400 Parker. It's really out of your way."

"What apartment?"

"29 B."

"I'll see you at six."

The drive home wasn't long enough to clear my mind. Even a week earlier, I might have been excited, but after meeting Mr. Hyde the other evening, I wasn't so sure if going out with Tina was a good idea. Beyond that, I had no idea if this was supposed to be a date. Her mention of my breakup with Amy certainly smacked of moving in, but wasn't it a little weird to start dating *after* she'd jumped me?

She did tell me to change, which suggested we weren't going to a dive. I'd barely had time to get wet in the shower that morning, so I ran a bubble bath while I dug through my closet. An hour and a half later, I'd soaked, shaved, washed and dried my hair, and decided on a pair of black pants and a sweater that was fitted enough that I couldn't justify wearing it to school.

I told myself this wasn't in anticipation of anything, rather, if I took the time to look presentable, it might improve my attitude. That was probably bullshit, but I decided to ignore the times I'd arrived at Amy's house wearing my school clothes and three days' worth of stubble on my legs. She'd never know that I'd just spent more time preparing for dinner with Tina Flores than I'd spent getting ready for my senior prom.

Tina pulled into the parking lot right on time, as if she knew the neighborhood or had at least been circling the block. She told me I looked nice, which made me blush. Great way to start the evening.

"Thanks," I said dismissively. "You do, too."

She thanked me just as evenly, her face remaining the same color it'd been when I entered her car. She was wearing pants and a blouse underneath her coat, which surprised me after seeing so many short skirts at school.

"So where should we go? I've only been to drive-thrus and Denny's."

"Let's not go there," I suggested. "Steak or Mexican?"

"Either."

I pulled on my seat belt and weighed our options. "Head back into town. Everything's that way."

We were very quiet in the car, but that didn't bother me. I was busy scanning everything out of the corner of my eye, trying to get a better idea of who Tina really was. I hadn't pegged her as another neurotic neat freak, but her car was spotless and completely devoid of the stray papers and soda cans that littered the passenger seats and wheel wells of most of my other friends' cars. I wondered if she'd stopped to get it detailed on the way to my apartment. The radio was off, and I couldn't read the titles on the row of CDs tucked neatly into the console. A small black leather purse sat between us, and two keys on a UT chain hung from the ignition.

I chose Veracruz instead of the Ranch Hand. It wasn't quite as tacky and was farther east, which meant we were less likely to run into students. I expected it to be crowded at half-past six on a Friday night, but the Lee game was in town, so half the population was off tailgating or eating stadium food. We were seated in a quiet corner of the room.

I hesitated to peruse the beverage list. I was sure I remembered Tina with a beer at Daniel's Halloween party, but I didn't want to make things uncomfortable if I was wrong. Amy didn't drink and hated it when I did. When the server came, though, Tina ordered a margarita, so I followed suit. Neither of us were carded.

The silence as we looked over our menus started to make me nervous. I was afraid we wouldn't have anything to say once we ordered, and we'd spend the evening making stupid small talk, watching everyone else in the restaurant in the hope they'd do something interesting.

I longed to study Tina's face, but I didn't have the nerve. I watched her hands as I pretended to ponder what I wanted for dinner. They were small and delicate, less squarely built than mine. Her nails weren't particularly long but a dark shade of maroon and obviously professionally manicured. She wore a gold ring with a black stone on the ring finger of her right hand and a thin band with some sort of carved pattern on her left middle finger.

Before I could make out the detail, she closed her menu and looked directly at me. "I feel like I should clarify something."

"Oh?"

"About Wednesday."

I didn't know what to say. I certainly wanted her to clarify several things, but I hadn't expected it to happen right away. "Okay."

"I'm not that way. It was a really stupid thing to do after what happened to you this past weekend, and I'm sorry for it."

"Okay," I repeated vaguely, not entirely sure I wanted her apology.

"I'd been trying to get your attention. Not so subtly, I thought."

I shook my head. "What?"

"I gave you my phone number, Cary."

"I didn't think I was supposed to use it."

"Why else would I give it to you? Anyway, subtle obviously wasn't working."

"So you did that?"

This time, her self-conscious smile was accompanied by a gentle pink blush. It was absolutely lovely. "I said it was a stupid thing to do. I certainly wouldn't have done it if I'd known you were with Amy."

I didn't want to talk about Amy. "I wasn't really *with* her, per se. How did you get into my classroom?"

"Wednesday? The door was open."

"Not while I was in that meeting."

She sighed impatiently. "Okay, Marvin let me in. He had just emptied your garbage."

"He seriously just let you in?"

"After a few lies."

I returned to my margarita. "Okay."

"So you weren't with Amy?"

Damn it. "Well, we were sort of together, but not like…"

Tina's eyes narrowed, and an evil little smile crossed her lips. "Okay, I knew you guys were fucking, but I didn't know she was your girlfriend."

I closed my eyes tight, feeling my neck going hot again and willing it to stop before it became visible.

"Don't worry about it. I'm sure Jody and Daniel are the only ones who know."

"How did you know, then?"

"I pay a little more attention than most people seem to here."

Our food came. We went silent as our server transferred our dishes to the table and asked if she could get us anything else. We both assured her that we were fine. I waited until she was safely back across the dining room before continuing. "We were on and off for a couple years. It wasn't anything serious."

"She seemed to think so."

I couldn't help but think of how horrified Amy would be if she knew everything had been that obvious. "She's a good person. She deserved better."

"So why wasn't it something serious?"

"I don't know. Because I'm a jerk. I really don't know."

That made Tina smile. She watched me for what felt like a long time, especially while I was trying to negotiate my plate without dribbling ranchero sauce down my front. "I haven't heard anyone say that about you."

"What have you heard people say?"

"That you're passionate to a fault about work and bothersome-ly tightlipped about your personal life."

"Who did you hear that from?"

"Pretty much everyone. Jody also says that you're smart, kind, and a good friend, but I gathered that much on my own. Have you dated anyone else here?"

I shook my head. I wanted to change the subject so badly, I almost couldn't stand it.

"And you've been here two years?"

"This is my fourth."

"Really. You came here straight out of school?"

I'd never said that but supposed it wasn't a particularly strange assumption to make. I nodded, then tried to nudge the spotlight off myself. "You did your master's at UT?"

"Yes."

That made her three years younger than me, assuming she'd gone right to grad school after earning her bachelor's. I wanted to ask, but that seemed rude. She had a disarming sophistication, granted, but her looks agreed with twenty-four at most. "So did you grow up there?"

"In Austin? No. I certainly haven't moved around as much as you said you did, though. How often did you have to change schools?"

The ball was right back in my court, both impressive and annoying. I'd never met someone so disinterested in herself that she could play my game. "Every year or two. Different cities, different states."

"How come?"

"My mom. There was always some great new job somewhere else."

"Trying to climb the career ladder?"

"Sometimes, it was for promotions. She got laid off a couple times, and we just left some places."

"Did she ever move for your sake?"

Nobody had ever asked me that question, and I wasn't sure how to answer it. I stared at what was left of my enchiladas, hashing her words over in my head, trying to figure out what she could possibly be getting at. "Not really. Some of the schools weren't very good, but I never wanted to leave. I always wanted to stay just another year so I could have the same friends and the same bus route and the same syllabus."

"That must've been hard. Was it just the two of you?"

"Sometimes."

Silence. When I got brief and cryptic with my responses, most people stopped questioning, but Tina was not most people. She waited for me to elaborate, but when it didn't happen, she nudged harder. "Sometimes?"

"My mom was always in and out of relationships."

Tina frowned. "That's kind of a messed-up way to raise a kid."

I shrugged. "I guess. That's the way it was."

"Did she move to get away from them?"

"Well, we left Stanley the Rat in upstate New York and Michael the Lech in Milwaukee."

Tina's eyebrows jumped. She'd finally managed to get too much information. "I'm sorry."

"It's okay. Like I said, that's the way it was." I finished my margarita and missed it immediately, but Tina was still working on hers, so I didn't make a move to order another.

"Was living with your dad an option?"

"I never knew him." Tina's eyes grew again, and I couldn't help but smile. "You totally didn't mean to get into this."

She gave me an indignant look, although I sensed it wasn't real. "If I hadn't, I wouldn't have asked. Has your mother ever married?"

"Four times, counting my father."

"Holy shit."

I grinned. "She's been with the same guy for eight years now. Finally found a good one."

"None of the others were?"

"No."

There was another silence. We'd both finished our dinners, and there was really nothing to distract us from it. Tina finally laughed. "Well, comparatively, my childhood was entirely normal."

"Most people say that. Do you have brothers or sisters?"

Her gaze left mine and traveled across the restaurant as if searching for the server. "An older sister and a younger brother. He just enlisted in the Navy, can you believe it?"

"Now? He's going to wind up in Afghanistan or worse."

"I know. My dad was career military, and even he thinks it's crazy."

"Don't you worry about him?"

She shrugged. "I've always worried about him. He was kind of a messed-up kid. Had a hard time in school, always getting in trouble. Do you want another drink?"

I needed one, especially if we were going to continue talking like this, but I couldn't help but glance around again. "I shouldn't."

"Have another. You're not driving."

"I don't usually drink much in public."

"Why?"

"It's probably just morality clause paranoia, but this is a small town."

"So what exactly do they use this morality clause for? A *don't ask, don't tell* kind of thing, or what?"

I shook my head, leaning farther into the table and hoping she'd continue to keep her voice low. "It's totally open-ended. If someone sitting behind us hears us talking about anything, really, and deems that it's immoral, then turns out to be the great-uncle of one of the kids at school…"

"How likely is that?"

"Everyone in this town is related to everyone else somehow."

"But, like, anything? That's absurd. What if I started telling you about my boyfriend?"

I shot her a look. *If you tell me about your boyfriend, you have even more explaining to do about the other day.* "So long as you just talk about where you went to dinner and what church he goes to."

"You can't talk about sex?"

"Not out loud."

She grinned. "You are paranoid."

"We're supposed to be role models. Their kind of role models. If one of our kids sees us in the Walmart, we better be behaving like a teacher."

"Buying steak, Diet Coke, and a few bibles? Come on. They can't expect everyone to be an angel all the time."

"Well, that's at least what they want us to think it's about."

"It's really just carte blanche, then," Tina said. "If they want to fire someone, they can do it for no reason at all."

"Yes. Maybe I am paranoid, but I feel like people are looking over my shoulder all the time."

"Because you're…"

I nodded before she could say the word *gay*. "Dunlop has been itching to fire me since my first day."

"Do you really think he knows?"

"After what Sally said about her dogs? One way or another, it's obvious that he doesn't like me."

"You intimidate him."

"What?"

"You're competent, and you're beautiful. Of course you intimidate him."

I felt my cheeks growing red again. "We shouldn't be talking about this here."

"So let's go somewhere else."

Chapter Twelve

Outside, the wind had kicked up again. Crumpled paper and a few small stray tumbleweeds blustered through the parking lot in a low current of dust as we made our way back to Tina's car, and once we got in, she turned on the heat. "Do you want to get a movie or something?"

That meant we were going back to my place. I stressed about that for a while as we traveled down 49th toward the video store. Now I had to wonder where this was heading. Since my third or fourth date with Amy, I'd taken for granted that sex would be involved, but I had no idea what to expect in this case. *She began to undress me the other day.*

Tina found a spot directly outside the video store but didn't turn off the engine. After scoffing at the morality clause over dinner, she froze just as quickly as I did. The interior of the store was lit up as bright as day, and there, poring over the new releases, was Sally Schumacher. As both of us stared, two of her kids came running up from behind a display. The taller one was holding a video over his head, and the other looked to be screaming and punching at him. I wondered why they weren't at the football game.

"Do you want to leave?" Tina asked.

I shook my head. "You stay in the car. What do you want to see?"

She floundered for a moment, her eyes still on Sally. "Have you seen the new Jodie Foster movie?"

I prepared for a stealth maneuver through the store, but Sally's kids were making such a scene that she'd snatched up a movie and hurried through the checkout before I found what I was looking for.

Tina backed out of the lot immediately. "I hope her dogs are better behaved."

"They're incestuous lesbian Jack Russells," I said. "It's unlikely."

We drove up the highway in silence. Everything was awkward again. It was like we were okay until every time we were reminded that this might look like a date. Neither of us spoke until we were out of the car at my apartment. I led her up the stairs and onto the landing, hoping that Lucy Hernandez wouldn't pop out to say hello. I'd never pretended to be anything I wasn't around her, but I didn't quite know what to call Tina, and I was certain that when confronted, I'd stumble over it instead of just offering her name. Fortunately, Lucy's husband's truck was in the parking lot, and their TV was playing. Bugsy did yip frantically behind the door as he usually did when I came up the stairs, but nobody even peeked between the blinds to see what was happening.

I unlocked the door and was at once self-conscious about my mismatched furniture and packing crates. "Please excuse the Bohemian look."

Tina stepped past the two feet of foyer into my living room. "Don't apologize. It's comfortable."

The folding card table and the place where Billy's cat had started to shred the sofa seemed far more obvious than ever before. "A work in progress, I guess."

"No, it's lovely," she assured me. "May I use your bathroom?"

Once I'd sent her in the right direction and the door had clicked closed, I went into a mad scramble. I got rid of the movie I'd left in my machine, exchanged the overhead light for the lamp in the corner of the room, and went to inventory my cabinets and refrigerator. I had nothing worth nibbling on, but my beverage selection was okay. I also did a visual inspection of my bedroom to make sure I hadn't left any socks or underwear on the floor, then hurried back to a casual pose in the kitchen before Tina could return.

She took her time coming down the hall, examining everything on the way. "Have you lived here since you've been in West Grove?"

I nodded. "It's cheap, it's pretty quiet, and the neighbors on this side are nice."

"Mine's okay, but I pretty much grabbed the first place I could move into right away. You really don't mind the drive?"

I grinned. "No, okay? Can I get you something to drink?"

Tina joined me in the kitchen, and we discussed for a moment what might properly follow margaritas. I had Coronas cold, so we decided on beer, as frat party as that was. She finally moved to the living room with her bottle and examined the photos on my walls and end table. "Who's this?"

"My mom and her husband." I nudged the video in and curled up carefully on the far end of the sofa.

"Seriously? She doesn't look nearly old enough."

"She's forty-six."

She looked back from me to the photo. I assumed she was doing the math. "You must look like your father."

"I guess."

She tapped another photo, grinning back at me. "And who's this?" It was the one of Billy and me at someone's party, arms around one another, foreheads and noses scrunched together. Someone had once told us we had better engagement pictures than most married couples.

"Billy. He teaches American history in Killeen. We lived together in grad school."

"Your mom must've loved that," she teased, settling in at nearly the polar opposite end of the sofa.

"She knows better."

We were quiet and entirely respectful during the movie. I got up at one point to get myself a fresh beer, and we managed to end up a little closer together on the sofa, still far enough apart to keep from accidentally nudging hands or knees but close enough for me to spend the last thirty minutes of the movie thinking about it.

I'd been worse than freaked out the other night, but nothing she'd said or done since had suggested that was the real Tina. I was ready to write that off as a reserved person's crazy attempt at being forward or like she'd said, just a really stupid thing to do. I'd tried to squelch my crush on her since the day she'd turned down my dinner offer, but it was very much still there. She hadn't stopped being gorgeous, that was for sure. Maybe, just maybe, we could cuddle a little after the movie ended?

That idea didn't last long. The moment the credits started rolling, she got up to use the bathroom again, and I braced myself for what would certainly come next. She'd move directly to the foyer, grab her coat, thank me for the evening. If I was extra lucky, she might even offer to return the video. I tried not to be too disappointed, just gathered up the empty beer bottles and set them on the kitchen counter to go out the next morning.

Instead of heading for the door, Tina wound carefully around the packing crate coffee table and to my complete surprise, sat back down on the sofa. "So what'd you think?"

"I liked it a lot. What'd you think?"

"It was good. And anyway, I'll watch an hour and a half of Jodie Foster no matter what goes on in the movie."

I smiled at that but sat back down. "Well, she's an awesome actress."

"But just tell me you wouldn't be interested."

I stared at my hands and shrugged. "Well, of course."

"Cary, look at me." One of Tina's eyebrows had cocked, and she was wearing a darling smile. "You are so damned shy, it slays me."

I kissed her. I had the notion that despite her words, she'd been expecting me to do just that because she kissed back at once. Her lips were gentle, sweet, and sensual, so different from the demanding feeling I'd gotten the other day at school, and as we continued, kissing more and more deeply, our arms and bodies meshed graciously into one another. It was lovely.

We didn't stop. I felt a huge sense of immediacy, the warm, sexy kind that led somewhere, but just as I was becoming certain enough that half of it was coming from Tina, we parted just far enough to catch our breath and regroup.

My face felt hot and indulgent. "Do you want another drink or something?"

She shook her head and slid her lips slowly down my neck. "Want me to close the blinds?"

I shook my head and motioned in the direction of the bedroom. "Let's go in here."

❖

I woke up butt naked, daylight streaming in from behind the blinds. Tina was on the opposite side of the bed, buttoning her shirt.

"Hey, you." She paused long enough to sprawl back along the covers and kiss me quickly on the mouth. "Do you have to be anywhere today?"

I couldn't remember what today was. I tried to look at the clock, but I hadn't taken my contacts out the night before, and my eyes were raw and uncooperative. "I don't think so."

"Go back to sleep," she told me, stroking my cheek once and rolling back off her side of the bed. "I'll run and pick up doughnuts."

I tried to dislodge myself from the covers and force my brain to catch up with her. "Let me at least—"

She shook her head and smiled at me. "Don't get up. You look so perfect there."

A minute later, I heard Tina getting into her coat in the other room, the jingle of keys, then the sound of the front door closing. I lay back obediently, a residual warm, sexy haze from the night before covering me. It felt like I'd had more to drink than I really had. I didn't remember the last time I'd been dead to the world until nine.

Oh, last night had been amazing. I had forgotten how good sex could be. It wasn't that Amy was lousy in bed. I'd never faked with her; it was just entirely predictable, something comfortable rather than exciting. This had been fantastic sex, the kind of yelling, screaming, orgasm after orgasm sex that made me hesitant to ever face my neighbors again.

Although it'd taken up a fairly large portion of the night, we hadn't just fucked. We'd talked, we'd laughed, we'd cuddled together. I'd never been able to discuss work in quite the same way with anyone else. Jody and Daniel laughed about how ridiculous things were sometimes, but deep down, they were still so incredibly from West Grove that I had to watch my mouth.

Tina was not. When I'd told her about my first evaluation with Dunlop, her jaw had dropped, and she'd called him a misogynist pig. She'd reiterated what she'd said at the restaurant, that he was intimidated by me and had no idea how to handle himself in my presence. I'd asked why he didn't treat her the same way, and she'd laughed and told me that people like Dunlop didn't think she needed a brain to teach kindergarten.

The best part of the night had come at half-past two, when we'd both caught ourselves falling asleep as we lay under the covers, holding one another. Tina had craned her neck to see the clock and made a half-assed attempt to leave, but I'd caught her before she could get out of bed.

"It's so late. You can stay if you want."

The moment the words had left my mouth, absolute terror had washed over me. I couldn't remember the last time I'd spent the whole night sleeping next to someone other than Billy. I'd longed for it over and over again, but Amy's categorical refusal had stung so badly that I hadn't even suggested it in ages.

Tina had rolled over and stared at the ceiling for a long time. I could fairly see the wheels turning inside her head, but I had no idea what she was considering so seriously. I was about to clarify that I hadn't asked to marry her, but before I could, she'd tucked her arm back under her pillow, definitely not the act of someone wanting to leave. "Are you sure?"

I'd nodded. "Please stay."

She'd kissed me and cuddled up against me under the covers in the darkness. "Twist my arm."

It'd been beautiful waking up next to her, and it was beautiful now knowing she was coming back with breakfast. I couldn't stay in bed enjoying it for long, though; my eyes felt like fire, my mouth tasted fuzzy, and I needed to pee. After just a few more minutes of basking in Tina's scent on my pillow, I threw on a T-shirt and wandered out of my bedroom.

The shades were still open from the day before, and it was wickedly bright in the living room. The usual kid was out in the parking lot, dribbling his basketball between cars, so I tugged my shirt down as low as it would go and ducked quickly through my apartment before he could get a lesson in female anatomy. Once I was finished in the bathroom, I found a pair of boxer shorts, put on a pot of coffee, and lay on my sofa, feet up, watching traffic way up on the highway, daydreaming of what we could do with the rest of the day. I had no idea where Tina was going for doughnuts. There was a place on 83rd, but I guessed she probably didn't know about it. I knew it'd take her a while, but I didn't expect to be sipping my second cup of coffee by the time she returned.

"Hey," she said, shooting me a look and closing the door behind her. "I told you not to get up."

"Yeah, but I made coffee. Want some?"

She nodded and set down a box from Kenny's Donuts down on 49th. "You know how I was laughing at you yesterday for being paranoid when you said what a small town this is?"

I went into the kitchen to pour her a cup of coffee, delighting in hearing her keys jingling and her jacket coming down on the sofa again, the sounds of her staying. "Who'd you run into?"

"That David kid from your class and his father."

"It was truly providence that kept me from offering to join you."

"Exactly what I thought. Bad enough that I walk in there un-showered," she muttered, accepting her coffee and sitting across the card table from me. "So what do you want to do today?"

❖

Tina and I exchanged a promise Saturday afternoon that we would keep everything that had happened between us a secret. I didn't feel that either of us was the least bit ashamed, but we didn't want to chance that word might get back to the likes of Dunlop. Beyond that, I'd broken up with Amy all of two days prior, and I was fairly sure that Jody wouldn't look favorably upon that. I knew that Daniel would look very favorably upon it, but there was no way he would be able to keep from sharing with Jody.

I kept that promise all of twenty-four hours. When Billy called me Sunday after dinner and asked if things were better with Amy, I couldn't even pretend to be indignant about getting dumped. I gushed for nearly twenty minutes about the weekend, then listened distractedly for another twenty as he detailed several near encounters with Anita, the volleyball coach. At the end of the conversation, he told me that my woman had to be pretty wonderful because he hadn't heard me so happy in ages.

That summed everything up rather nicely. I awoke very early Monday after a wonderful night's sleep, made myself a pot of coffee, and sat outside on the landing in my pajamas, appreciating the nip of the wind against my cheeks, watching the world around me move from total darkness to the beginning of the gentle, dusky gray-pink of almost-winter morning.

When Bobby Hernandez left for work at six thirty, Bugsy the Chihuahua skittered out the door toward me, a crazed, determined look in his huge eyes. His toenails were orange that morning.

"Hey," I told him, offering him the back of my hand to snuffle. I didn't remember the last time I'd willingly communed with Bugsy, and that fact seemed to trouble his little dog mind at first. After a moment, he cocked his head to one side, goggled at me, and slurped his tongue against my hand.

I was scratching under his collar by the time Lucy made it onto the landing. I couldn't help but think that Bugsy would've found his way under a truck by then if I hadn't been out there, but I guessed if that were the case, Bobby might have taken a moment to stuff him back into their apartment. Anyway, he was so tiny, he would probably fall down the stairs and concuss himself before making it to the parking lot.

"Aw, Bugsy, leave her alone." Lucy sighed. "Come, Bugsy."

The dog didn't look at her. "He's fine," I assured her.

"Well, you've found yourself a friend, yes you have," Lucy cooed. "You little love slut, you."

I assumed she was talking to the dog. He still didn't pay any attention.

"I hope this is waking up early instead of staying up late," Lucy said, this time in a normal tone of voice. "Are you guys off today?"

I shook my head. "I should get in the shower, but it's nice out here."

"It's cold out here," Lucy corrected, rubbing her arms. She was wearing flannel pajama bottoms, but her top was sleeveless and skimpy, and her feet were bare. "Who's the girl with the blue truck?"

"She teaches at Bush."

"Does she have a name?"

"Tina."

"Bugsy, come," Lucy tried again. "She's cute," she added, grinning broadly.

I shrugged to myself and finished my coffee. Lucy's by-the-way-I-know-you're-queer-and-this'll-prove-how-tolerant-I-am banter trumped snide looks and prayer tracts stuck in my door frame any day. "Hey," I told the dog. "She's trying to get your attention."

"Come?" Lucy begged pathetically.

I got up off the ground and picked him up. He weighed less than my coffee cup. "Time to go home."

Bugsy gave me a look but made no other attempts to prevent me from returning him to Lucy. I thought about telling her that Bugsy might listen to her if she didn't emasculate him by painting his toenails, but I decided to let it go since she'd been really nice to me. Anyway, I needed to get in the shower in order to get to work at my usual time.

I must have ignored the pile of crap in my school mailbox Friday afternoon because I found it altogether too full for a Monday morning. A stack of information about the play from Jody. A reminder about yet another curriculum meeting later that week. A small pile of homework paperclipped together with a lavender-scented note explaining that Nestor was ill and wouldn't be in class. A third-of-a-page phone message slip.

I turned that over, hoping it wasn't some parent calling to complain. "Jeff Sanchez?" I asked aloud.

"From Zavala elementary," Kathy reminded me from her office. "He was at the meeting the other week."

If I'd realized she was in, I probably wouldn't have wondered aloud, but I did appreciate the reminder. I didn't think I'd spoken to him at all. "How did you remember that?"

"I took the message."

"Did he mention what he wants?"

Kathy set a paper down on Selena's desk, glanced toward the copy room as if checking on her whereabouts, and grinned knowingly. "He didn't say, but my guess would be a date."

I held her eye contact for as long as I could bear. "You're kidding," I finally muttered.

"Just a guess. Don't quote me on it."

I kept waiting for the wink-wink-nudge-nudge that Lucy had given me earlier, but it didn't happen. Granted, Kathy looked genuinely amused, but I wasn't sure what that meant. I turned hurriedly to leave.

"You know it's about the next meeting," I said. "I'll find out at lunch."

On my way back down the main hall, I ran into Tina. As teachers, parents, and students milled around us, a vision of her naked body flashed before my eyes.

Instead of ducking back down the hallway from whence she'd come, she gave me an altogether normal smile. "Ms. Smith."

I returned it in kind, barely nodding back at her. "Ms. Flores."

The absurdity of our exchange struck me funny, but I was glad I didn't laugh out loud. Three paces later, Amy snagged me from the cafeteria door.

"Hey," she called. "Give me a hand with this stuff?"

I followed her to a pile of equipment from the previous Friday's soccer game. Kids were eating breakfast at tables not far away, so I picked up a box without asking any questions.

Amy let me into one of the storage rooms near the kitchen, set her box on a shelf, and cleared room for mine. "Are you okay?"

I wanted to say I was wonderful but was afraid that would sound sarcastic. I just nodded. "Are you?"

She nodded, too. "I'm really sorry. I meant what I said, but I shouldn't have hit you with it in the middle of the day like that."

"It's okay. You deserve better, and I need to get my head together."

"It's not like that," Amy said, looking horrified.

I took advantage of the closed door and touched her on the arm for emphasis. "Really, it's okay."

She stared at me, her eyes wide and uncertain, like she couldn't believe I wasn't screaming at her. "I don't want things to be awkward between us."

Things were awkward while we were dating. "They're not."

"Really?"

I nodded. "I'm okay," I said for what felt like the thousandth time. "Do you need more help?"

She shook her head. "Thanks."

"You're very welcome," I told her, leaving the cafeteria without looking back.

I didn't understand why Amy wouldn't believe what I told her. Everyone else on the planet seemed to know I was in a great mood. Daniel slapped me on the back and told me I must've had a good restful weekend because I looked better. The moment we started current events in class, Gina announced that I must've had a date that weekend because I was all smiles. I didn't offer any information, but I didn't go out of my way to dissuade her, either, because frankly, that was the only current event in which I had any interest.

I'd barely settled in my semi-usual spot in the faculty lounge for lunch when Tina set down her tray. She said hello to Daniel, Bev, and Sally and barely nodded at me. She was good at this game. I chewed on my sandwich and uh-huhed at Bev and Sally as genuinely as I could.

They had left and Jody had joined us when the door opened. I expected Dunlop, but Kathy breezed through with change for the machine instead.

"So," she said to me, her voice all business. "Did you return that call?"

"I did," I said. "He wanted a copy of our current mission statement." He'd also asked me out, but I wasn't about to admit it.

Kathy threw me one tiny sideways smile on her way back out of the room. "He could've gotten that from me. He wants a date."

Daniel spit Diet Coke all over the table before the door closed. "What?"

"Yuck," Jody muttered, handing Daniel a napkin and glancing up at the speaker just once. "Who wants a date?"

"Some guy from the curriculum meeting. I nipped it in the bud," I assured everyone. Tina's foot slid against mine under the table.

Daniel was still stunned. "But she..." He turned to check the door, as if Kathy might still be standing there wearing the same look.

"She took the message. I don't know where Selena was."

"She's flirting with you," Daniel said eagerly. "Did you see that look?"

Tina's toe moved over mine and pressed gently. It sent a completely inappropriate feeling clear through my body. When I dared glance at her, her eyes told me she was trying her hardest not to laugh.

"She's teasing me," I muttered. "There is a difference."

Daniel sputtered and flailed for another second. Jody moved his soda out of the way. Before he could come up with another full sentence, Tina cut him off smartly. "Is she running Dunlop's route today or something?"

"She probably offered to get him a Coke just for the chance to needle you," Jody agreed.

"Oh my God, just imagine that coming from Dunlop." Daniel giggled. "He wants a date," he said, fixing his eyebrows into a glare and affecting a surprisingly realistic Dunlop-tone.

"Oh, it so wouldn't be like that," Jody said.

"Miss Smith," Daniel agreed, adding a stodgy walk to his imitation, "my office, right this minute."

"Come on," Tina told him. "Wouldn't he be thrilled? You two could get married and live right here, happily ever after."

Daniel flapped his hands excitedly. It looked as if he'd just eaten something hot. "And have babies! Lots and lots of babies! Cary and some random guy from the curriculum meeting, sittin' in a tree."

Tina grinned as though she was particularly proud of herself. For just a tiny second, her hand touched my thigh under the table and left a trail of fire in its wake.

Chapter Thirteen

I'd come out to my mother one month before I'd turned eighteen. It was the fall of my senior year of high school, and we were in Columbus then, just the two of us.

I hadn't meant to do it. I'd discovered the word that explained all of the jealous, possessive friendships and bizarre, out-of-place feelings I had around other girls, but I had no intention of explaining any of that to my mother until I was safely out of the house at college. She was fairly liberal as far as parents went, but I wasn't certain that she would be so okay with her only child being a lesbian.

My math teacher, Mrs. Wyse, was the catalyst. While I'd hated her bitterly at the time, I could probably thank her for the fact that I'd graduated that spring and gotten into college. Instead of allowing me to fail her class, she'd sent a note home at midterm time and followed up with a phone call to make sure that my mother had gotten it.

She hadn't. I'd signed her name to the note and turned it in, and wow, had that made my mom mad. What had made her madder yet was the grade itself. I'd generally done well in school, especially considering all the moving around we did, and she wasn't about to let me get away with an F.

For the first time in my life, we'd had one of those all-out screaming fights. She'd told me she hadn't worked so goddamn hard to see me fuck up my life like she had so many years before. I was so close. Couldn't I just do the right thing for a few more months and be done with it? I'd struck back, cursing her for my very existence, for being a shitty mother and moving us all over the country and ruining my life. I'd known that while she'd meant every word she'd said, I hadn't meant a single one. I'd felt horrible, but I wasn't about to back down. We'd yelled until I was sure we were both out of scathing words and profanities. We'd stared at one another for what seemed like forever, then she'd taken a very different tone, this one icy serious.

"I'm making you a gynecologist appointment."

"What? I'm not going."

"Oh, yes you are. You are not going to end up pregnant so long as you're under my roof."

I'd never been so angry and embarrassed. "I'm not going to get pregnant."

"Condoms don't always work."

"Mother," I'd interrupted, "I am not going to get pregnant. You have to listen to me. *I am not going to—*"

"I'm not stupid, Liz," she'd yelled back. "You're spending all your time with Dylan, and I know what that means."

"I'm not fucking Dylan, okay? We're just friends. I barely even see Dylan."

"What the hell are you talking about? You take off every night to go meet him."

I'd stopped short, breathing heavily. I'd made a big mistake.

Mom had looked at me through narrowed eyes. "Cary Elizabeth, where have you been going?"

"To Lauren's, okay?" I'd exploded, looking away. I was balancing on the very precipice of the big confession, and I hadn't wanted it to be this way. I hadn't wanted to come out to my mother screaming and cursing. I hadn't wanted to be the cartoon coyote, stranded in midair long enough to ponder his impending crash. "I've been going to Lauren's."

Mom hadn't caught the change in my demeanor. She'd thrown up her hands and kept right on yelling. "I'm supposed to believe that?" She'd shaken her head and interrupted herself with an exasperated sigh. "I give up, Liz. I have no goddamn idea what to do with you."

"Mom, I have been with Lauren," I'd whispered. "It's not Dylan I've been seeing, okay? It's Lauren." With that, I'd broken. Tears had come from nowhere, tears like I hadn't allowed her to see since I was a little kid. It had happened so quickly, there was no way for me to run.

There had been what seemed like an endless silence. I was sure she was going to curse me again, maybe even throw me out of the house. The silence had continued, though, to the point that I had begun to worry that she hadn't understood, and I'd have to spell it out for her. I was positive that I'd never be able to say the word *gay* out loud, and honestly, I was crying too hard by then to have spoken at all. When I'd dared to look up, I'd seen that her eyes were welling and spilling forth, too.

My mother had crossed the room, pulled me close, and told me she loved me more than anything else in the whole world. Neither of us could stop crying, and neither of us had let go.

Later, she'd told me that she was glad about it. She said she'd spent scores of nights lying awake, praying that I wouldn't become another statistic, following in her footsteps and getting knocked up before graduating high school. She had considered from time to time that I might be interested in girls, but whenever she'd come close to confronting me, I had gone off with a boy or made some comment that had stopped her in her tracks. She did ask if anything any of her old boyfriends had done to me could have affected my attitude toward men, but she'd listened patiently while I'd stammered that it had nothing to do with anything; I just liked girls instead of boys. There were no other awkward questions or disapproving statements. From that moment on, everything had been all right. We were back to being our formidable little team, stronger than ever before.

I knew enough to be thankful for Mom's response, but I didn't realize how lucky I was until I watched several of my college friends' Norman Rockwell families crumble to pieces under the weight of that same confession. I was thankful for it because from that point on, there had never been a need to hide who I was or who I loved from anyone. Until I moved to West Grove.

❖

The drama that was Tina and me continued through the week. We played off one another with straight faces, keeping everything that was going on between us under wraps like a subtle inside joke. If anyone guessed, they didn't say anything. She asked me to dinner Tuesday night, and we sat at the Ranch Hand discussing the merits of the bilingual program. I asked her to my place Wednesday evening, and we ordered pizza. Tina left at five thirty the next morning in order to get back home and make it to work looking presentable.

The whole thing was bizarrely whirlwind. What was even more unbelievable was how happy it made me. I caught myself daydreaming about Tina and went out of my way to bump into her in the halls just so we could exchange generic salutations. It had been a long time since I'd felt the manic energy of a brand-new relationship, and I had no idea that I could see so much of someone and still feel that it wasn't nearly enough.

I did feel bad that I hadn't seen my other friends. Daniel didn't seem to care, but Jody had started rehearsals for *Peter Pan* and was trying to design the Christmas program at the same time. She ran around looking flushed and haggard, and Kathy relaxed enough to give her permission to stay at school later than our 5:00 curfew. I offered to stay late for the rest of the week to help. I remained until five on Thursday helping block scenes, ran home long enough to grab dinner and change into more comfortable clothes, then returned to build props and paint scenery.

Friday morning, I arrived at school around my usual time, feeling particularly exhausted. I'd been up late correcting papers, and it didn't help that I'd gotten more exercise than sleep the night before that. The fluorescence of the office seemed even more obnoxious than usual, in part because Kathy's door was wide open, the overheads on. Something was not right.

Dunlop was sitting at her desk, talking on the phone very loudly in an extra important tone. I didn't know who on earth he could be talking to at that hour and imagined a dial tone on the other end. While I watched, he said something about a meeting and flipped obviously through Kathy's datebook.

Selena was in the copy room. It didn't look as if she was doing anything more complex than adding paper, so I poked my head in and spoke in a voice barely above a whisper. "What's going on?"

Selena looked up, saw it was me, and sighed deeply. "What?"

I'd obviously ruined her concentration, and it would be all my fault if she couldn't remember where things went. I didn't care. "Is Kathy out today?"

"She's in Dallas," Selena grumbled, her head back inside the copier. "Her father had a stroke."

"I'm sorry," I said, glancing back toward Dunlop. He usually usurped her office when she was gone, but it seemed ruder than usual today. "Was it a bad one this time?"

Selena pulled herself up on the paper drawer and spit her hair away from her face with an exasperated look. "I'm sorry," she said in a tone that disagreed with her words. "What do you need?"

"I just asked if he was okay," I said, trying to keep my voice civil. "Is she likely to be back?"

"Do you need to see her?"

"No, I was just hoping everything was all right."

"She plans to be back on Monday if he's stable," Selena finally answered. "If not, later next week."

I nodded, thanked Selena without adding any token obscenities, and left the office before Dunlop could finish his phone call, recognize my voice, and haul me in for some torturous lecture just because he could. I expected to see him in my classroom later that day.

He was everywhere, that was for sure. He was in the halls every time I passed from class to class, was monitoring the cafeteria when we went down for lunch, and he entered the staff lounge with his usual handful of change right as Jody was complaining that he'd spent the past thirty minutes in her back pocket.

It was a long afternoon. Our science lesson dragged, and everyone was restless and grumpy and wouldn't shut up. Once the bell rang, I was zipping up my backpack, grateful to finally be done, when I heard the door open behind me. The encounter with Tina popped into my head, and I whirled so fast that I stumbled into my desk and dropped my bag.

Mr. Dunlop stood in the doorway. "Miss Smith." His voice was completely even, as if he hadn't just scared the crap out of me. The small smile on his face betrayed that he'd enjoyed that fact more than a little.

"Mr. Dunlop."

"I found these in the office," he said, holding out something approximately the size of a small paperback. "I thought perhaps you might have misplaced them."

I might have been terrified that he'd found a problem in the book I was reading now, but his use of the plural confused me. He continued to stand in the doorway, so I had to do all the walking in order to even see what he was holding. As soon as I got close enough to see the box of Sharpies, an icy coolness moved from my outstretched hand into the pit of my stomach. "Where did you find them?"

"They were in the office," he repeated. "They are yours, right?"

The box read *Smith*, clear as day. I nodded and took them from him. "Yes, but…They were just sitting in there? Did someone turn them in or something?"

He looked at me blankly. "Where did you leave them?"

My fists clenched, and I heard the box crumpling. "They were taken from my supply closet during the burglary."

"Hmm," he said, like that was a little bit more interesting than the idea that I had irresponsibly dropped them somewhere, but not much. "Well, I don't know how they got there, but they were in the office. You know," he added, stopping at the door and checking his watch. "I was looking at the sign-out sheets. You might think about getting home before it gets too dark."

Is that a threat? That sounds like some kind of threat. My hands felt numb, especially where they clutched the box. "I've been helping Ms. Finnegan."

"I know," he said. "I just want y'all to stay safe."

"I understand." The moment he disappeared down the hall, I slumped in my desk chair and stared at the box of Sharpies. I took them out, one by one, turned them over in my fingers, examined them as completely as one can examine a permanent marker. They were all there. They all worked. They, or at least their box, had been touched by that person.

I KNOW ABOUT YOU.

Someone else was at the door, but at least this time, there was a tap-tap-tap on the frame. "Hey," Jody said.

"I'm sorry," I said. "I'm on my way, I just got stuck with a parent."

"Forget about it. Wendy's sick, Peter's gone to Lamesa for the West game, and Daniel only has half the Lost Boys to work with. I'm going to do a quick chorus rehearsal and call it a night."

"I can stay."

She shook her head. "We've got it covered." She looked back toward the hall for a second, then lowered her voice. "What'd Dunlop want? You look a mite distressed."

I nodded toward the Sharpies. "He gave me these."

Jody's eyebrows jumped. "Office supplies?"

"These are the ones that whoever broke into my room took."

"How can you tell?"

"My name's on the box. It's my writing."

"So they didn't take them?"

"No, Dunlop said he found them in the office."

Jody stared at my desk, her brow knit tightly. "I don't get it," she finally said.

"Yeah, me either."

"They probably dropped them in the field on their way out of here, and somebody found them and turned them in," Jody decided. "You should ask Coach D."

Both of us stared at one another.

"I mean, I could ask her," Jody stammered hastily, her cheeks going red. "I'm sorry."

"We're okay. I'll ask her," I assured Jody, although it wasn't going to happen.

I left Bush shortly thereafter. My intent was to go home and call Tina, but instead of turning off the highway onto Parker, I rolled down the driver's side window and kept going straight.

I KNOW ABOUT YOU.

After passing my apartment complex, fields of brown grass, packed dirt, and short, squat, skeletal bushes surrounded me. They continued as far as the eye could see, all the way to Lubbock, barely scored by the thin, ruler-straight double stripe of blacktop that was 669. The wind blew in, cold and thick with dust, forcing me to squint hard at the road ahead of me.

I had no idea where I was going. Nowhere, really, but my car was a crucible, a contained experiment, something simple for me to inventory, and I was undeniably the only person there. I passed a herd of muscle-bound brown cattle from time to time and watched them staring dolefully back at me through huge, damp, dark eyes, as if even they wondered what I was doing there. I had no answer, other than right then, tired and angry and frightened felt a lot less significant when the world around me was so enormous.

I drove half an hour or maybe forty-five minutes, until I was shivering with the cold, and the setting sun glared antagonistically to my left, spreading orange and yellow along the barren horizon for miles in each direction. The crossroads were few and far between, and each one would take me miles out of my way before offering a turnaround, so I finally pulled off the road in a gravel driveway. My tires sent forth a cloud of dust that obscured my vision completely as I settled to a stop. A placard in the middle of the sagging metal gate declared the drive the property of the oil company that owned the surrounding field. The gate was closed with one small padlock, but a huge amount of razor wire curled around the top of the fence, as if someone would be more likely to jump it than to snip the lock. I had no idea why anyone would want to go in there anyway.

I sat for a long time, watching the slow up-down, up-down of an oil derrick pumping about forty feet inside the fence. My life had been exactly that monotonous two months before. Monday, Tuesday, current events, fractions, TAAS prep. Up-down, up-down. *I KNOW ABOUT YOU.*

Far in the distance, there was a bark, then the eerie, plaintive howl of a coyote. I couldn't tell from which direction it came, but I thought about the cattle with their big sad eyes. I thought about the cattle and the endless fields and the immense expanse of nothing around them. They had nowhere to go, nowhere to hide. I had nowhere to go, nowhere to hide. There was no way I could run from something if I didn't know what it was or from where it was coming.

I could not change my identity or my history. I'd seen what I'd seen, learned what I'd learned, and done what I'd done. There was no rewriting any of that. All I could do was open a fresh volume and work my hardest toward being who I really meant to be.

I KNOW ABOUT YOU.

I was here, of all places, in the middle of such grandiose nothingness that I could lose myself if I wasn't careful. How could someone be here with me, someone hell-bent on punishing me for what I had never intended in the first place? It sounded crazy. It was undeniable that things were happening, weird things, frightening things, but could one person really be responsible for all of them?

I do not belong here. I do not belong here, but there is nowhere to go.

The coyote howled again, then was joined by another. I threw my car in reverse and turned to go home.

Chapter Fourteen

I was about ten minutes north of town when I fished my phone out of my backpack and called Tina.

She answered immediately. "Hey."

"Hey. What're you up to?"

"I'm at the gym, but I'm almost done."

"Have you had dinner?"

"Not yet. Do you want to come to my place? I don't have anything in the house, so we'd have to go out, but..."

"I could make you dinner," I offered.

"Are you serious?"

"Yeah. I'll pick up groceries. That'll give you time to finish up and get home."

"And shower," she reminded me. "How was play practice?"

"Okay. There wasn't much to do."

There was a silence. I wondered if she was trying to find a nice way of asking what the hell I'd been doing for the past hour and a half, then. "Cary, are you okay?"

"Yes. I'll let you finish. My phone's almost dead, and I don't have the charger with me."

She didn't ask where I was. That was fine with me. I didn't want to explain. I'd never been to her apartment, so she gave me directions. I stopped at Albertsons for groceries on the way. I hated being around people when I was upset, hated the vulnerable feeling of allowing others to peruse my emotions, but I was tired of being afraid and paranoid and crazy. If I could just have a normal evening with Tina, maybe all the other feelings would go away.

Tina's apartment complex was slightly older than mine but a bit classier. It, too, was a labyrinth of two-story buildings divided by crowded parking lots, but the staircases and landings were done in thick dark timbers, and the tiny islands of grass outside each unit were chemical-infused bright green instead of dead. Her apartment was on the second floor of the furthest building from the street with a shared landing like mine. Her neighbor had several wind chimes and a village of beautiful potted begonias and geraniums, but Tina's side of the porch was bare.

I pulled the groceries from the car, locked up, and climbed the staircase, all the while keeping my eyes on Tina's apartment for signs of motion. Her car was in the parking lot, but I didn't have a good idea of how long it would have taken her to finish at the gym, or for that matter, to which gym she belonged. Once upstairs, I threaded my way through the neighbor's planters, took one last second to gather myself, and knocked.

It took a moment for Tina to open the door, and she was still dressed in a tank top and shorts. "I'm really sorry. I just got home."

"It's okay," I assured her, nudging the door closed and instinctively sliding off my shoes. The carpet was white and devoid of the snags and stains mine had accumulated. "I guess it didn't take very long at the store."

Her eyes lingered on me. "You look tired. Are you sure you don't want to go out?"

I nodded. "I'll cook. It's fine."

"Really, are you all right?"

"Yeah. Just tired."

Her arms came around me, pulling me to her in a gentle, protective hug. Either by nature or thanks to the morality clause, my friends in West Grove were not physically affectionate, and I couldn't remember the last time I'd felt something so genuine and comfortable and beautiful.

"Sorry," she said somewhere past my shoulder. "I probably should have showered first."

Her shirt was still damp from the gym, but it made the moment feel more impulsive and authentic. "I don't care."

She laughed, then rubbed my back once and let go. "Pots and pans and utensils are in fairly normal places, I think."

I followed her, feeling numb and lonely. I missed her hug. "I'll find stuff. Take your time."

She kissed me quickly on the cheek, thanked me, and disappeared down the hall, leaving me alone in the middle of the living room. I meant to continue straight into the kitchen, but when I heard a door close, I stared unabashedly in every direction.

I wasn't sure what I'd expected. Something similar to what I'd had upon arriving in West Grove, maybe, a smattering of mismatched, exhausted-looking hand-me-down furniture, unpacked boxes, maybe even pilfered metal folding chairs and a mattress directly on the floor. I expected the home of someone straight out of school, still struggling to make ends meet, still trying to figure out how to run her own household.

It was sparse, granted, with no sign of the clutter that accumulated over time, but aside from that, it was perfectly lovely. Her sofa and love seat matched one another and were neither stained nor shredded. She had a real side table and coffee table. She had throw pillows, plants near the window, and an actual print hung on the wall. It was nice, really nice, in a very tasteful, established sort of way.

That wasn't the only thing that surprised me. It was lovely, but every inch was as impersonal as the interior of her car. I scanned the entire room for a framed photo or some small sentimental token, but there weren't even books to look through. Two magazines lay on the coffee table, and her purse sat on the arm of the sofa. It was almost like I was in a well-decorated Holiday Inn.

The kitchen was a little better. The day's mail was scattered on the counter, along with two rings of keys and Tina's gym card. Three photos hung on the refrigerator: two of them were pictures of the same two gorgeous little girls with huge brown eyes and bronze skin, the other a snapshot of a handsome young man in military fatigues. I assumed that one was her brother, although I didn't see much of a resemblance. His buzz cut was dark, and his eyes looked to be brown, but he was light-complected and squarely built. I squinted at the name on his uniform, but it wasn't clear enough to make out letters.

It wasn't as if I'd been digging through her drawers and medicine cabinet, but I felt guilty anyway. I began to prepare dinner quickly, hoping to be far enough along in the process for it to appear as if I hadn't been gawking. I felt a little better about myself seeing her kitchen setup. She had decent pots and pans and lovely knives but not many at all. Her wineglasses matched, but there were only two. It was enough for me to cook with, but I had to plan ahead as to what I was going to use when, and I had to keep washing my knife.

I did have a good start by the time Tina returned, this time wearing jeans and a gray T-shirt reading *Navy* in thick blue letters. Her hair was wet, and her feet were bare. She peeked into the oven, then wrapped her arms around my waist from behind and nuzzled into my neck and shoulder, kissing there very lightly.

"That smells wonderful," she said. "You can cook for real."

"I don't very often, but I can."

"Well, I can't, so it's a good thing you're doing it."

That explained things. She asked to help with something, and I had her make the salad and set the table. She had nice dishes and silverware, which made me feel stupid again. I was still eating off my mother's castoffs, and an embarrassing number of my utensils were official property of the University of Illinois dining services. "I can't believe it," I continued. "You've barely been here a month, and everything is so beautiful."

"You haven't seen the second bedroom," she assured me, grabbing glasses and pouring the wine. "I don't think I'm ever going to get through all the boxes in there."

"Well, what I can see looks great."

"Thank you," she told me evenly. "Are we ready?"

The chicken was done. Her table was small, barely large enough for us and the salad bowl, so we filled our plates and left the pans in the kitchen. I tried hard to focus on the food, but I was used to my cooking, and I couldn't help but gaze around the apartment, trying to memorize everything I saw.

"Cary, this is fantastic," Tina said. "Seriously, where did you learn to cook like this?"

"My mom and I cooked together when I was little. When she started working weird hours, I used to make dinner."

"My mother does not cook," Tina told me. "Throwing a roast in the oven was her idea of domesticity, and it happened once in a blue moon."

I knew Tina was waiting for me to elaborate on why I was out of sorts, but she had finished dinner entirely before she pointedly poured me another glass of wine. "Tell me about your day."

I shrugged. "It was okay."

"Oh?"

"Well, up until the end." My plan was to stop there, leave it at that, skirt every question, but something unprecedented happened instead. I came closer to spilling everything that was wearing on my mind than I'd ever come in my life. I started with Dunlop's impromptu observations the first week in October, then told her about the day my classroom had been upset and the whole *Coral Sharkey* issue. I gave a summarized version of the break-in without mention of what my whiteboard said, and by the time I explained that Dunlop had just returned my missing box of Sharpies, Tina was sitting back in her chair, nursing her second glass of wine, listening intently with a pained furrow in her forehead.

"So what do I do? Pull your shades and mess with your head. Awesome."

"It's okay," I muttered. "You understand now why I freaked out."

"Yeah. You, my dear, are having one shitty year."

I nodded lamely. "I just can't help but wonder if all this is connected or if I'm reading too much into it, you know?"

"Connected?" She considered that for a while, as if that idea surprised her. "Are there any parents who are pissed at you?"

"Not any more pissed than usual."

"What about Dunlop?"

"I could see him blowing the deal with the book out of proportion to get me fired, but I don't know if I can see him breaking into my room."

"He was totally out of control today with Kathy gone," Tina decided. "What did he teach before he went into admin?"

"Texas history, I think."

"Secondary, then. I assume he's playing assistant principal in primary school for the power trip?"

"Probably. He's such an idiot that I don't want to be afraid of him, but with all this happening, I don't know."

"There has to be some logical explanation. He's definitely the reoccurring character, but just handing back something he stole from your classroom? It would be so transparent."

"Jody suggested that they might have been dropped outside, and someone found them and turned them in, but it's been kind of a long time."

"Were they scattered around?"

"It didn't look like it. They were in the box when he gave them to me. Otherwise, he wouldn't have known they were mine."

"What if someone turned them in right away? The day after, say, and they've been sitting in the office since?"

"Just sitting there on the front desk?"

"Behind it or in Selena's stuff? Dunlop was snooping through everything today."

I felt some of the tension leave my shoulders. "That's the first idea that's made sense."

"I could be totally wrong," she said. "I mean, yes, I think he's trying to intimidate you, and I definitely wouldn't stay after hours at that building right now if I were you, but you know what Selena would do if some kid gave them to her. We all annoy the crap out of her, and getting up to put them in your box would waste a minute of her life."

I nodded. "That is so much better than thinking that the entire world is out to get me."

A smile twitched on Tina's lips. "There is medication for that."

"Yeah, I know," I muttered, getting up from the table. "My mom's tried to sell me on it for years."

She gathered our plates and followed me to the kitchen. "It's this place. You've been here too long."

"Forever," I muttered. "Might as well give in and call it home."

"Oh, come on. You were in Illinois for longer than you've been here."

Had I ever mentioned that I'd gone to college there? Maybe when we were talking about Billy? If it had come up in passing, nobody else would have remembered it. She had a remarkable knack for that, though, and it was beginning to make me nervous. "Yeah, six years, I guess," I said, trying to sound completely nonchalant.

Tina didn't buy it. She gave me a delicious, wide-eyed, teasing look and nudged me hard on the shoulder on her way to clear more dishes. "Don't freak on me, okay? You need to repaint the back of your folding chairs if you want to keep that one a secret. What is it, already?"

"What is what?"

"What is it that you're so afraid someone will figure out?"

It flashed in front of my eyes again, red letters on the whiteboard. *I KNOW ABOUT YOU.* Her words were teasing, but I didn't like the question one bit. I turned sharply to the sink and started rinsing dishes with a vengeance. "Nothing."

"Nothing? Come on." She wrapped her arms around my waist, sort of like she had before dinner. "Let's see. You're having a torrid affair with Daniel? Amy has your name tattooed across her boobs? You're an undercover agent with the CIA?"

Fortunately, her touch did a lot more for me this time than it had earlier. *Let it go. Just let it go.* "I could tell you, but then I'd have to…"

"You'd have to what?" She interrupted, kissing my neck.

"What do you want me to do?"

"Everything."

An hour later, I lay back on her sheets, staring at the intricacies of her ceiling fan. Her bedroom was nearly as hotel-impersonal as the rest of her house, but I hadn't noticed it for the first several minutes of our stay there. The furniture was large but weathered. A bookshelf was packed with novels, mostly quick reads. The walls were bare aside from an abstract print hanging on the near wall and a thin golden cross by the door. A pair of tennis shoes sat outside her closet, probably from the gym, and a towel hung on the back of the door. Beyond that, nothing was out of place other than the alarm clock and paperback we'd knocked off the bedside table at some point. I could learn nothing new about Tina other than she wasn't kidding when she said she was a neat freak.

That wasn't what alarmed me. I'd slept with several people I didn't know very well in college, and I'd gotten over the weird guilt about kissing Tina while I was still technically with Amy. The thing that baffled me was how comfortable this felt.

I lay there next to her, feeling her heartbeat, listening to her breathing as it began to steady. In so many ways, it seemed like I'd known her far longer than I had. We'd first gone out eight days ago, and I'd had no qualms about trusting her with everything that was going wrong in my life, just like that. We'd seen one another five times during the week. I loved that she listened to me, loved that she was impressed by my cooking, and loved that she felt so comfortable with me that she didn't need an invitation to come up and kiss my neck from behind. All at once, this little, tiny, brand-new relationship seemed very serious.

That scared the hell out of me. "May I ask you a question?"

She nodded.

"Where is this going?"

She barely glanced at me. "Where do you want it to be going?"

"I know what I want. I'm asking what you want."

A brief sardonic smile moved across her face. "I don't know. I enjoy your company, and I don't feel like a tremendous slut after spending the weekend in bed with you."

"But is this going to be okay a month from now?"

"Like, if nothing changes?"

I nodded.

"I'm not looking to move in with you, if that's what you want to know."

"Okay."

She stared at me until she was unable to contain laughter. "Cary Smith, I'm absolutely positive that you're relieved."

I rolled my eyes. "That's an exaggeration."

"No, you're definitely relieved," she said. "I'm not sure whether to be offended or what."

"I'm just happy with where we are now, okay?"

"Okay, okay, don't get pissed," she muttered, still smiling. "I just got out of a major relationship. The last thing I want is another commitment."

"Major like?"

"Six years."

"What? That's not dating, that's a freaking marriage."

She cocked her eyebrow at the ceiling. "Yeah, well, it was one of those things that shouldn't have happened in the first place."

But somehow continued for six years? I wanted to pry so badly, I couldn't stand it. "Is that why you came here?"

"I came here for the job."

"But it's why you left Austin?"

She shrugged. "One of the reasons. It was a perfectly awful relationship. It's not worth discussing."

As we lay there underneath the covers in her entirely impersonal bedroom, in her tidy, detached apartment, it struck me that there was a fine line between being mysterious and deliberately withholding facts. I told myself time and again that I wasn't lying to people if I simply left some things out, but it felt quite different to be on the other side of that theory. I wondered how Tina and I had managed to have so much sex while holding one another at arm's length.

"Really, you don't want to hear it," she assured me, snuggling into my shoulder. "Why haven't you found some nice girl to settle down with?"

"Commitment issues," I said vaguely. "I believe Amy called it emotional unavailability."

"That's pretty harsh and not entirely accurate, I think. You've dated a lot, though."

"Some."

"You started dating girls in high school. Don't even try to tell me that chick in Florida was the only one."

"She wasn't."

"So where do these commitment issues come from?"

I thought about reminding her that my mother was in her late thirties before she could settle down to a man, a job, and a home, but she surely remembered all of that like she did everything else I'd said. "I've had a few shitty experiences, too."

Tina propped up on her elbow then and studied my face for a long time. I mostly stared at the crown molding, but I could feel her eyes moving across me. When she finally spoke, her voice was quiet and gentle. "Have you ever been in love?"

Without looking back at her, I shook my head, as emotionally unavailable as ever. "No."

That was another bold-faced lie.

Chapter Fifteen

The Commercial Appeal, Sunday, June 23, 1991
"Murder Suspect Found Dead"

A Memphis woman was found shot to death in the 5900 block of Great Woods Drive late Saturday evening, according to the Memphis Police Department.

Natalie Broward, 19, had been shot once at close range. She was pronounced dead at the scene. The death was ruled a suicide.

Broward was detained and questioned earlier this month regarding the death of her boyfriend, Jonathan McGrath. McGrath's body was found May 31 in a viaduct less than one mile away from Broward's East Memphis home. He had been beaten to death. While no formal charges were filed against Broward, she remained the only suspect in the case.

Absolutely nothing out of the ordinary happened that week. Dunlop was still reigning supreme, but he did not appear out of nowhere in my classroom. Nothing went missing, and nobody returned any more of my stolen property to the office. Kathy was back on Wednesday. Play practice went into full swing. I had a few more phone calls from the same old number, but they didn't bother me nearly as much as usual. Tina and I went out together on Monday and Wednesday nights. Slowly, finally, I began to settle back into a lovely complacency.

Friday was Jody's first big scenery cram session. I, along with several other teachers, brought old clothes to change into directly after school, and others ran home for a few minutes and returned wearing grubby jeans and sweatshirts. Chris brought his two teenagers, two of the second-grade teachers brought their husbands, and one of the first-grade teachers brought a gigantic hairy dog that lay in a heap near the office and looked irritated when people came anywhere near him.

Jody and Daniel ran student rehearsals in the cafeteria for an hour after school let out, then Jody joined the rest of us. She said that Daniel had to be at his parents' house for dinner, but all of us decided that he just didn't want to get dirty. Tina had a get-together with the kindergarten teachers and Mrs. Shore again, but she told me to call her when I was leaving and come over.

I was covered in sawdust in no time. Javier Sotelo and I spent the first couple hours in the storage area behind the gym where tools were set up, creating the facade of a pirate ship. I'd just started to help Bev with painting when Domino's pulled up with a huge stack of pizzas and cans of soda.

Everyone sat on the sidewalk to eat, just feet away from the dripping pirate ship, shoveling in pizza like we were kids. I was rooting for a nice conversation about football or TV shows, but nobody could go five minutes without talking about work.

"I heard that Mr. Dunlop wants to move Mr. Crenshaw down to third grade again," Bev said.

I really couldn't see Daniel with eight-year-olds. "How come?"

"It's the first year for TAAS," Javier said. "His kids score well, so every few years, they pull him back to third grade to start off a new crop."

"Does it work?" I asked.

Marisol shrugged. "It's stupid because they don't keep him there. They wind up having to shuffle the GT kids around so they don't get him twice."

"The gifted and talented kids don't all need to be in the same class anyway," Bev said defensively. "I thought you were on Atkins."

Marisol glared between Bev and her third crust. "I was for a while."

Javier nodded solemnly at me. "If your scores stay where they are, Dunlop's going to give you fourth grade."

Jody waggled her finger at me. "That's very true. Bet that's why he's in your classroom all the time this year."

Kids any younger than my sixth graders made me nervous. Anyway, fourth grade was TAAS hell year. They took a writing test in addition to the reading and mathematics that the third, fifth, and sixth grades had. "I doubt it," I said. "Anyway, that's just Dunlop, right? Doesn't Kathy have more say over that stuff?"

"Ms. Sutton has the final say over that stuff," Bev said. "And if people are working well where they are, she doesn't like to mess with it. Anyway, the new test is going to be bad for fourth *and* fifth grade."

For the rest of the meal, the conversation deteriorated to a discussion of passing and proficiency, raw scores, and the Learning Index. I bowed out graciously, the same way I did every time TAAS came up in conversation, just murmured along with the others while my mind wandered. I thought about what Javier had said but came to the same conclusion each time. Dunlop would never expect me to raise scores in fourth grade or any grade because I was, as he said, different.

I was there until eight o'clock. I thought about calling Tina from the car, but I had paint on my shirt and jeans and wanted a shower before seeing her. I'd had a terrible time keeping her off my mind during the last hour or so. The moment my brain went complacent, I felt her arms around me and her lips against mine. It really wasn't late for a Friday, I assured myself. In another hour, those things could be happening for real.

I saw the flashing blue lights the moment I turned onto Parker. They played off the windows of the complex and everyone's cars like a disco ball. It was a bit disconcerting, maybe, but nothing worth interrupting my fantasies until I saw that the police car was parked very close to my apartment. I wondered if someone had finally run over that kid with the basketball. Maybe Mrs. Delgado in the next unit had found the guts to call the cops on her husband.

By the time I pulled into a spot between a junker Chevy and Bobby Hernandez' truck, though, all my previous thoughts had melted into an ugly, nauseating numbness. The commotion wasn't in the parking lot, nor was it front of the Delgado's door.

CHAPTER SIXTEEN

L ucy came flying down the stairs far too quickly to be
wearing flip-flops and clutching her dog to her chest. I
watched Bugsy's little head bounce, up and down, side to side, and
wondered how much brain damage was occurring. I wondered if it
would even be apparent in a Chihuahua.

"Oh God, Cary, I couldn't remember your cell number." She
gasped for breath. "We tried you at work, we tried you at Jody
Finnegan's, but nobody answered."

I moved slowly out of my car, staring lamely at where the
window to my second bedroom, the one I used as an office, used to
be. The screen was cut, and there was a gaping hole in the bottom
pane. It had been raised to allow access to the apartment, scattering
glass shards along the sill and onto the landing. The door, too, was
wide open, and I could see a police officer moving around inside.
Bobby Hernandez stood just outside in a wifebeater and a pair of
Levi's, poking his head in hesitantly. The scene from three weeks
ago came flooding back to me, the phone call from Kathy, the feeling
of complete violation as I stood in my classroom door staring in
disbelief at the whiteboard. *Three goddamn weeks ago.* I wanted to
close my car door again, drive right back out onto the highway, and
hand this mess off to someone else.

I KNOW ABOUT YOU.

"We heard it, you know, this big crash, and we would've called
the cops sooner, but we figured it's the neighbors fighting again or
something. Bobby finally went to see."

"It's not your fault," I told Lucy. My legs didn't want to work, but I forced myself to climb the stairs. I didn't want to look, didn't want to see what had happened this time, didn't want to find another fucking message painted on my living room wall.

The cop met me in the foyer. He was a short, chubby, white boy with rosy cheeks and a blond buzz cut. He looked as if he was about twelve. "Officer Hays, ma'am. Do you live here?"

I nodded and tried to move past him, but he smiled and offered me his hand as if this was a cocktail party instead of a crime scene. "Cary Smith," I said, shaking it mechanically. It was large and sweaty, and his grip was painfully firm.

After the niceties, he stepped out of my way and followed me through the apartment at a respectful distance, holding a pad and pen at the ready in case I had anything to say. I didn't. Absolutely nothing came to my mind except how very strange it was. Everything seemed to be where it was supposed to be, in the same state I'd left it that morning.

Every door in the apartment stood open, though, and I could tell that the entire place had been painstakingly cleared. I had no trouble picturing Officer Hays peeking around each corner, gun drawn, sweating bullets, not so sure that he really wanted a Wild West shoot-out.

As I moved from room to room, closing doors, opening cabinets and drawers to check the contents, I began to realize that the scene was even stranger than it had originally seemed. Though nothing was obviously out of place, everything had been very carefully perused. Items in drawers had been shuffled, things I'd recently used mixed up with things that were normally pushed to the back. The towels in my linen closet were moved from the left side toward the middle. While the drawers on my filing cabinet were closed, a few papers inside were askew, and my computer mouse had been moved from the edge of my desk where I'd set it to make space for paperwork to a position much closer to the screen. Nothing was missing, but someone had searched everything and made an epic effort to put it back exactly as they'd found it.

Terror flowed urgently through my body as I moved into the bedroom. I didn't care if this person had gone through my silverware drawer or touched all my underwear, but I desperately needed to make sure everything in my closet was still there. I snapped on the light and moved back to see the top shelf as best I could, wishing Officer Hays would back up and leave me alone. I slid the shoebox down and paged through it briefly, accounting for all the newspaper clippings and photos.

"Coin collection," Officer Hays murmured somewhere behind me. "Good thing they didn't find that. Easy to pawn."

Thank you, Columbo. I'd appreciate it if you'd remove yourself from my anus now. I realized that was the only thing I'd really sorted through, so I pretended to shuffle through my shoes and look behind the hangers, then led Officer Hays back into the living room.

"Nothing stands out to me," he said helpfully. "Did you notice anything missing?"

My entire sense of security. I felt nauseated all at once and headed back outside quickly. "Excuse me," I told him. "I need to make a phone call."

Lucy was waiting out there, still bouncing Bugsy. "You can come into our apartment, baby. Bobby can get you a drink, you know."

"Thanks," I told her, walking past their door and to the stairs, away from the crowd and the broken glass and the chaos. I sat on the top step and called Tina.

"Hey! Are you done?"

The moment I heard her voice, tears came into my eyes, and my mouth went dry. I didn't know what to say. "I need you to come here."

There was a confused pause, and her voice was very different when she started again. "To school? Cary, what's wrong?"

"I'm at home," I said. "Somebody broke in. I just need you." I'd never said those words in my life, and as soon as they were out of my mouth, I wanted to take them back. It was true, though. I needed her desperately. I just wished I'd had the presence of mind to keep from admitting it.

If she understood the significance of that statement, her voice didn't betray it. "I'm on my way."

Neither of us said good-bye. I listened to the click and the dial tone for a long time before folding up my phone and resigning to more conversation with Officer Hays. At some point during our journey through the apartment, a second cop had appeared, this one tall and Latino with huge biceps, sexy dark eyes, and a pair of sunglasses inexplicably propped on top of his head even though the sun had gone down. Lucy had joined her husband and was speaking with the new officer, bouncing up and down like she was cold. I imagined that she was since she was wearing a skinny tank top and obnoxiously short shorts. Bugsy jiggled tremulously, his bulbous eyes fixed intently on the officer, his pink toenails standing out boldly against Lucy's shirt.

Bobby nodded toward the window, his arms crossed protectively over his massive chest. "Ten after eight. I seen the clock."

New Cop scribbled at his report. His name tag read *Ayala*. I wondered if he was related to Marisol's husband. "You heard it?"

"We hear a noise, yeah, and the dog goes crazy."

"Did you call emergency then? Go out to see what was wrong?"

"Well, not right away. The dog goes crazy over anything," Bobby admitted, his eyes lighting apologetically on me. "It sounded like something big, though, so in a minute, I got my gun and went to see what happened."

"It was enough of a noise for you to get your gun."

Bobby nodded. "It was a real big crash. I run back and tell Lucy to call 9-1-1 right away."

"And the call came in at…" Officer Ayala checked something on his report and muttered to himself.

"We called at eight fifteen maybe," Lucy said. "I was so scared you were still home until I saw your car was gone."

I nodded distractedly, then her words played back in my head. "What do you mean? I haven't been home since this morning."

Officer Ayala looked up at me, his pen hovering above the paper.

Lucy's brow furrowed, and she squeezed the dog tighter against her chest. He made a tiny, involuntary squeak. "I heard you come in this evening. I was sitting right there watching *Seinfeld*. Heard you come up the stairs, heard your keys in the lock."

My phone slid out of my hand and landed with a crash on the cement of the landing. I didn't move aside from touching my fingers together where it had been. "I've been at Bush since seven thirty this morning," I said. "We were working on props for Jody's play. I haven't been home."

Officer Hays bent to retrieve my phone, and I stuffed it back in my pocket this time. There was silence while he straightened, and for a moment, we all stared at one another.

Bobby and Lucy both started in hurriedly. "Now, I know I heard people going up and down those steps this evening."

"I swear to God, Cary, I heard someone go in. I was right about to go over and say hi when my friend Elle got here."

Officer Ayala went back to his notepad. "Do you know what time that was?"

"I sure do. It was six. She was supposed to have already picked me up for Jazzercise, but she was running late."

"And you left then?"

"Yeah, we were totally late. You know," she said, turning back to me, "I didn't see your car when we left."

"Did you notice any other cars?"

Lucy frowned at the officers. "I don't know. Maybe some others on the far side of the lot, but I don't really remember."

"Do you go to Jazzercise on a regular basis?"

Lucy looked offended, as if the cop was questioning the state of her abs. "Every Wednesday and Friday."

Officer Ayala turned to me. "You're usually home by that time?"

I shrugged, my brain completely fuzzing over. "Usually, but not always."

"You're not normally this late, though."

I shook my head. "I go out some evenings, but I almost always stop in first."

I knew where we were headed, but the cop's words still bothered me. "Who knew you were working late?"

"Not that many people. The teachers who were there and maybe some of the students who were practicing."

"Where do you work?"

"Bush Elementary."

"Park your car in plain view?"

I nodded.

"People know it's yours?"

"Probably."

"People know where you live?"

I was tired of that ambiguous *people*. "Not many."

That was when Tina's blue Blazer nosed through the parking lot. I'd never felt so thankful to see someone in my life. As the cops continued to question Bobby and Lucy, I pressed along the railing back toward the staircase.

"Jesus, Cary," Tina said, pulling me to her right away. "Are you okay?"

Her hair was still wet from showering after the gym, and she smelled warm and clean. I buried my face in her shoulder as deeply as I could and did not care who was watching. "I wasn't here. I just got home."

"But are you okay?"

I nodded. I knew that had to be the answer, at least until the police left, and I could get out of there for the night.

"You just came home?"

"The cops were already here."

"We called them," Lucy said, offering Tina a hand over her dog. "Lucy Hernandez, my husband, Bobby, and this is Bugsy. We live next door."

"Tina Flores. I work with Cary." She shook their hands distractedly, then turned right back to me. "Did they take anything?"

"Nothing," I muttered. "They went through everything, but they didn't take anything."

Both officers frowned. "No cash?" Officer Ayala asked. "No jewelry?"

"Nothing, but I swear to you they looked through everything. Closets. Drawers. Everything."

"Damn," Tina said, peering into the door hesitantly, as if she really didn't want to go in there. "It isn't anything like what happened to your classroom, though, is it?"

I closed my eyes. I really hadn't wanted to bring that up. "No."

Officer Ayala heard. I could fairly see his ears prick up. "Your classroom?"

"My classroom at school was broken into the other week. They think that was gang related, though."

"How long ago? Did they take keys or any personal information?"

"Three weeks ago," I said, avoiding the officer's eyes. "They didn't take anything personal. Stuff to pawn and get a quick high." There was no way I was going to mention the whiteboard.

"Bush Elementary? Way across town," Officer Ayala said, adding that information to his report. His handwriting was nearly illegible. "A lot of gang activity in that area, too. It's probably not related, but I'll check it out. Three weeks is mighty close."

No shit. Mighty close indeed.

"This doesn't make sense," Officer Ayala finally muttered, exchanging a glance with Officer Hays. "Mr. Hernandez, you say the window was broken at ten after eight, and you called it in around eight fifteen. That doesn't leave but five minutes for all this to happen."

I rubbed my head wearily, begging it to stop hurting. "I don't understand."

"I've seen guys in and out of places in less than that for drugs or money, but if they went through everything like Ms. Smith says, there's no way it happened that fast. Now, Mrs. Hernandez here says she heard someone getting in around six. I'm thinking that this had to have happened earlier."

Bobby shook his head. "I'm telling you, I come home from work at six thirty, and I know this window wasn't all busted in then."

Tina spoke up delicately from beside me. "So if someone was in here earlier, but the window was broken at eight…"

"They broke the window on their way out," I muttered.

"If someone had keys to your apartment," Bobby said excitedly, "but didn't want it to look like they had keys."

"Does anyone else have keys to your apartment? A roommate? A boyfriend?"

I'd never even had a duplicate made in case of an emergency. "Nobody."

"Are you sure?"

"Yes, I'm sure," I snapped. I felt Tina's hand against mine, maybe reassuring me, maybe telling me to cool it. I let our fingers intertwine and held on tight.

Officer Ayala went on quickly. "Do they change the locks between tenants?"

"They're supposed to," Bobby said.

"Had any work done lately?"

"Not that I know of."

"We got sprayed for bugs today," Lucy remembered. "Drunken asshole probably left the place wide open for someone to bust in."

I winced a little at Lucy's words, and I noticed Tina frown, too. The police officers didn't react. "I'm going to try to get in touch with the maintenance man and the landlord," Officer Ayala said. "Are you staying here tonight?"

I gave him Tina's information while Lucy went to get the landlord's pager number. After that, Officer Ayala turned to go.

Bobby threw his hands up in the air. "That's it? Aren't you going to dust for prints or something?"

Officer Ayala smiled wryly, as if Bobby was a silly little boy who had watched too much *CSI*. "There's a ton of traffic in a place like this. You, your friends, your boyfriends, your landlord, your maintenance workers, the tenant before you, their friends, the tenant before that."

Yeah, we get the picture, lazy ass. Nobody mentioned that we could rule out any boyfriends, even though Tina was still holding my hand. I wasn't about to let go. I'd chewed my lip raw, and my throat hurt badly.

"I'm going to go try this number," he said, taking the information from Lucy. "If you notice anything missing or have any other problems, give us a call, all right?" Before anyone could tell him whether it really was all right, Officer Ayala was down the stairs and talking on his radio.

Officer Hays looked a bit more sympathetic. "Two things this could be. Either an addict looking for quick money or someone trying to get your account numbers."

Tina turned to me. "Is any of that stuff missing?"

I shook my head. "They went through it, though."

"You need to call your bank and credit cards right away and cancel your accounts," Officer Hays said. "Most of them won't hold you responsible for any charges you didn't make. One way or another, I don't think you're in any danger here, but you probably want to stay somewhere else until you get that window fixed and the locks changed."

"Yeah," I said sullenly. "Thanks."

"You're welcome," Officer Hays said brightly, shaking my hand again, sealing the business deal. "I'm sorry about all this. Let us know if you have any more trouble, okay?"

I didn't watch Officer Hays leave. My fucking police report was a nicety, a mere going through the motions to document that they'd answered the emergency call. It was just like at Bush; they didn't really care who had done this. They didn't care how far this person had gotten inside my head. What could possibly come next? Was I going to slide into my car next week to find someone in my back seat? Would everything start to make sense, or would I wind up dead in some alley before anyone would care enough to ask why?

Thankful that the interrogation was over, I kicked some of the glass out of the way and headed inside.

"I'm so sorry about all this," Lucy said from the landing. "Me and Bugsy should probably—"

"Of course. Thanks for everything," I told her.

"Listen, I'm going to go make sure the landlord knows they need to fix that window," Bobby said. "I'll come by tomorrow and put in another dead bolt for you."

"That'd be great. I'll pick one up."

I did like Bobby and Lucy, and they were just about the best neighbors in the world right then, but I was really relieved to see them go. I wished I could leave, too, but I steeled myself and went into my office. The bulk of the broken glass had landed inside and was spread all over the carpet. I looked at it only long enough to keep from stepping on it. While I worked my way through my filing cabinet, pulling credit card information and phone numbers, Tina carefully picked up some of the larger shards.

"You seriously think they went through all this?"

"Positive."

"Start calling."

I was about to pick up the phone when a horrible ruckus started on the pavement below. Both Tina and I jumped, then peeked hesitantly through what was left of the window.

A huge piece of plywood was bobbing up the stairs, *thunking* on the railing with every step. In another moment, Quentin, the maintenance man, set it down with a clatter on the landing. "Ma'am? I'm fixing your window."

I felt stupid talking through the hole. "I'll let you in."

Shortly, Quentin dragged his tools and a flashlight up next to the plywood. He was a small, scruffy, middle-aged black man with a wandering eye and a speech impediment. While none of my repair requests had been taken care of particularly promptly, he usually did adequate work, and the few times I'd been around while he tinkered with an appliance or mowed the lawn, he'd been entirely pleasant. I thought Lucy's characterization was harsh, but I did feel a little uneasy knowing that he'd let the exterminator into the apartment that day.

He went to work, humming to himself, seemingly unaware that Tina and I were both pretending not to watch him. After he'd done quite a bit of drilling and pounding, I went to check it out from the landing. The outside of my apartment looked like an abandoned crack house.

I began in as nonjudgmental a tone as I could conjure. "Did you spray for bugs today?"

He paused in what he was doing and consulted the sky. "I let the guy in at nine thirty, maybe ten o'clock. Didn't look like this, though. That policeman asked me if I locked the door. Well, nobody would've needed to do this if I done left the door open, you know?"

I nodded.

"This a mess," he said, shaking his head at me. "I told him if I see anybody around here, I'll take care of them for you."

I tried to smile. "Are you going to change the lock?"

He nodded and stood back to survey his work. "When it's light. Glass company ain't coming till tomorrow anyway."

I thanked him, he gathered his things, and Tina and I were alone again, closed back in the apartment that was no longer my safe haven. I brought all the paperwork into my bedroom and sat on the bed, feeling beaten. Tina sat next to me and without saying a word, pulled her arms around me. It made the tears come back into my eyes, but I didn't let them fall. I had just started to pull myself together again when I felt her body tense.

"What's that?"

I let go and looked up from my Mastercard statement. "What's what?"

"That."

I followed Tina's gaze to my dresser where I'd left several sweaters after doing the laundry. I'd folded them neatly just the night before and placed them in a single pile, ready to go on their shelf in the closet. Now, something was sitting on the pile, something dark that looked like metal. Before I could even think let alone move to stop her, Tina got up, crossed the room and reached for it.

When she turned back toward me, she was holding a large rusty crowbar.

CHAPTER SEVENTEEN

All I could do was stare. There were no words; there were no actions. All I could do was stare at that old rusty crowbar, wonder why, and feel the dread seeping into my bones.

Tina finally broke the silence, her voice hoarse. "Do you want me to see if the cops are still there?"

I shook my head. "I just want to get out of here."

She didn't argue. She set the crowbar back down like it was on fire, then fumbled for a moment, realizing she'd put it in front of the sweaters instead of where it'd come from. She finally placed it gently on top of them as if tucking the evidence in like a small child at bedtime would turn it into something pleasant, or at least something benign. She helped me gather my things off the bed and followed me as I threw a change of clothes, my toothbrush, and my glasses and contact lens case into a plastic grocery bag.

"Do you think that's what they used to break the window?"

"I don't want to think about it."

We didn't exchange any more words as we locked up and climbed downstairs and into Tina's car. She turned on the heat, but it didn't make me stop shaking. I stared out the window at the lights and the houses and the cars and the broken white lines between lanes. The silence continued until we had nearly reached the center of town.

"You're very quiet," Tina said hesitantly.

"I feel like I'm going to throw up."

She nodded. "We're almost there."

At her apartment, I locked myself in the bathroom for what must have been twenty minutes. I didn't throw up, but I did cry, with the faucet running and my face buried in a thick green bath towel, until I felt worse than sick to my stomach. I still couldn't stop shaking no matter how hard I tried. I finally took out my contacts and splashed my face a few times, but it didn't help. I wished I could just stay in there all night, but I was painfully conscious of how long it'd already been.

When I finally returned to the living room, Tina was sitting on the sofa, flipping channels on the TV, but she turned it off when I sat. She barely glanced up, just scooted her phone across the coffee table toward me.

"Are you okay?"

I nodded and concentrated on sifting through my account information. I knew it had to be obnoxiously obvious that I'd been crying, and the last thing I wanted to do was start in again in front of her.

"Can I get you a drink?"

"Yes, please."

"Beer? Tequila?"

"Whatever."

She returned from the kitchen while I was explaining my situation to Pat from my Mastercard company, carrying a Guinness, a bottle of Jose Cuervo, and a shot glass. I considered the beer but poured myself a shot of tequila while uh-huhing in all the right places.

Tina watched, grimacing, as I finished it in one swallow. "You want a chaser or something?"

I shook my head, listened to Pat typing away at his computer, and poured a second shot. I downed that one, too, and kept going, working my way through my purse and my paperwork, throat burning, my mouth coated with the taste of alcohol.

Tina removed the cap from the Guinness and sipped at it delicately, watching me all the while. "You're going to be sick if you don't slow down."

"No, I won't," I assured her, although I'd lost count by then. In another half hour, I finally set the phone down and pushed it across the coffee table. "I have to go to the bank tomorrow morning."

She ignored that. "You drink a lot, don't you."

"Sometimes."

"How come?"

This was not the time for a flippant answer, but I knew that if I started to say anything honest, I was drunk enough to share far more than I should. I kept my mouth shut.

Fortunately, Tina looked away after a moment, smiling gently. "I'm sorry. I didn't mean to sound like your shrink. I'm just gone after one glass of wine. I'm a cheap date, you know?"

That didn't quite explain the question, but it excused it somewhat. I let a half-smile come onto my lips for the first time all night. "I know."

"I tried to drink in college," she said, "but after a few beers, I'd always wake up puking on the floor of some frat house, not quite sure where I was or who I'd slept with."

"You never drink enough to forget where you are."

"Well, nobody told me the rules."

I grinned sardonically at her and filled the shot glass one more time.

As if reading my mind, she nodded at the bottle. "How many has it been?"

I had no idea. "I know where I am, and I'm not going to yack on your floor." I finally leaned back against the couch. "Is this it? I can't believe I shouldn't call anyone else."

"I don't know how there could be anything else. You're remarkably organized."

"Or something."

"Are you sure you're okay?"

"Yeah, I'm good." The alcohol was finally coursing through my entire body, and for a moment, I really did feel good. I closed my eyes, and all the ugliness disappeared. All the fear went away. I felt warm and cozy and very interested in falling into bed with Tina. I knew that wasn't going to solve anything, and that very soon, I'd be too drunk to move. I kept my eyes closed in the hope of savoring that sensation as long as possible.

"If you say so," she said, touching me gently on the knee and getting up. I heard her in the kitchen rinsing her beer bottle, getting something from one of the cupboards, opening the refrigerator. When she returned, she set a large plastic tumbler of water in front of me.

The happy feeling started to dissipate. I was still uncomfortably warm, but everything else just melted into heavy, fuzzy, intoxication. "Have you ever just wished you could be somebody else, just for a few hours?" I asked. "Anybody else. Driving some big-ass rig through Tulsa. Delivering pizzas in Tucson. Ignoring your butt-ugly dog while somebody breaks into your neighbor's house."

She grinned indulgently. "That really is an ugly dog."

"I just want it to be three o'clock again. Finish school, tell Jody I can't stay after all. Go home and it wouldn't turn out this way."

"Don't. You wouldn't want to be in the middle of that."

"It wouldn't have happened if I was home."

"You don't know that. Jesus, Cary, the last thing you need is to walk in on some fuckup going through your apartment. Suppose he had a gun?"

Of course he had a gun. This is Texas. I'm the only person in this entire state who doesn't have a gun. Amy had a gun, although the very idea terrified her, and I'd heard that Jody was a disturbingly sure shot. Even Daniel had one, although he kept it more to accessorize than to defend himself. I knew it didn't matter. I had no idea who was terrorizing me, but I did know beyond the shadow of a doubt that this person was not about breaking into my house in my presence. "It's not like that."

"What do you mean?"

"I can't explain it. I just know."

"I'm still not following you. Are you saying this isn't a random thing?"

"They were looking for something in particular. I'm positive they were."

"What?"

I didn't want to think about that. Had they found it? If so, who the hell were they, and how had they found me in West Grove, of all places? "I don't know."

"And the one at school?"

"Do you know what they wrote on my whiteboard?"

I saw her jaw twitch. She shook her head.

My tongue felt thick, and though I could barely hear them beyond the ringing in my ears, I knew my words were slurring. "I know about you."

"What?"

"That's what it said."

Silence. The warm, cozy feeling had returned, but this time, it didn't extend below my shoulders. *That's what it said. I KNOW ABOUT YOU.*

"About you being gay?"

"That's probably what Kathy thinks," I said. "But God, look on my bookshelves. Ask my friends. Call my mom, you know? There's really no need to dig through my underwear drawer."

Tina smiled, but I couldn't tell if it was about what I'd said, or because sober people thought sloppy drunk people were funny. "I guess."

"I suppose if someone wanted me fired," I mumbled, but my train of thought was gone before I could finish.

"Someone's messing with you."

Her statement echoed in my head over and over. *Someone's messing with you. I know about you. Messing with you. Fucking with your head. I know about you.* Before I could stop them, words tumbled out of my mouth. "I'm really scared." With even less warning, I felt tears on my cheeks.

"Oh honey," Tina whispered, hurrying next to me on the sofa, wrapping her arms around me, tucking my head against her shoulder. "I know it, sweetheart. I know."

❖

When I awoke, it was very dark. It took me a long time to realize that I was lying on Tina's sofa, but as soon as I had that down, everything else came rushing back to me in a huge, sickening wave.

I hadn't been drunk enough to black out in years, but I assumed that was what had happened since I didn't remember many details after finishing the phone calls. I was pretty sure that we'd had a conversation, during which I'd said things I shouldn't have. I hoped I hadn't thrown up.

I couldn't remember where I'd left my glasses, either. I felt around the side table, then the coffee table, to no avail. I could barely see without them, but I needed to pee far too badly to continue the search, so I abandoned it and set my sights on finding the floor instead. I was still spinning drunk. My head swam when I got up, and I had to steady myself on the sofa, then, two woozy steps later, the armchair. I knew there was a wall that ran the entire distance from the kitchen to the bathroom, so if I could just find that, I would be home free.

Knees still shaking, I moved very slowly, feeling in front of me every centimeter of the way and inexplicably slammed my toe into something solid. I didn't trip, which told me it was probably the cabinet under the kitchen counter. It smarted like crazy, but I managed to refrain from cussing and caught myself on the countertop that led me to the wall, and that supported me for the duration of what felt like the longest journey in the history of the world.

I was pretty sure I hadn't thrown up. My mouth felt fuzzy but in a rather generic sort of way. After using the bathroom, I brushed my teeth and spent a moment feeling thankful that I'd remembered to take out my contacts. I had to lean close to the mirror to get the full effect, but my eyes were formidably bloodshot and stung insistently in the light. I remembered well why it had been a long time since I'd gotten that drunk.

The return trip went faster. The darkness felt much better than the light had, and though everything was blurry without my glasses, enough moonlight was spilling in through the blinds for me to find the sofa. I was about to crash right back where I'd been when I heard Tina's voice from the bedroom.

"Cary? Come to bed."

I looked longingly at the sofa. My knees wanted to give, and I knew I'd have been out again upon landing. The bedroom seemed forever away. For just a moment, I considered pretending I hadn't heard but knew that would make me feel rotten in the morning. I felt my way to the edge of the sofa, to the wall, then found the door.

The next several minutes might have been sensual if I wasn't completely incapacitated. My approach to the bed was less than graceful, so with the patience of a saint, Tina helped slide my clothing off and pulled me close under the covers, her arm resting gently around my waist. Somewhere in my haze, I sensed her lips on my shoulder, just once, and heard soft words before I passed out again: "I'm so sorry."

Falling asleep the night before really had been too fortunate. I was wide-awake at four in the morning with a massive headache, my eyes still feeling angry red, but I got up only long enough to find a bottle of ibuprofen in the medicine cabinet and swallow six pills. The shades blocked out far more light from the street and the parking lot than mine did, so I closed my eyes again, hoping the darkness would coax me back to sleep.

It didn't. The cocktail of pounding and pondering in my head was far too strong. I was thankful to have Tina next to me. Hearing her steady breathing and feeling her arm next to mine calmed me immensely.

I had plenty to think about. When I'd first gazed through the broken window and noticed the subtle disarray in my apartment, I'd imagined someone smashing the glass, raising the window to climb inside, and rifling as quickly as possible through my things. After the police had pointed out that the timetable didn't make sense, though, the entire picture had changed. Now, I imagined someone calmly walking in and taking plenty of time to sift through every possible place I might have hidden something. I imagined someone wearing street clothes, completely unconcerned that the blinds were up, and people were milling around the complex. Paging through my books, my kitchen cabinets, reaching into the back of my T-shirt drawer. I imagined someone sitting at my computer desk with a latte, calmly paging through my files and reading my email. The person did not have a face or even a gender.

How could anyone have possibly let him or herself into my apartment? The management had handed me one key to the door and one key to the mailbox when I'd signed my lease, and since there was only one of me, I'd never bothered to duplicate either one. I kept them on a ring with my car key and my work keys, and they were always with me, either in my pocket or hanging on their hook next to the door. I didn't have pets to care for when I left town, so I'd never had a reason to lend them to anyone, not even my closest friends. There had to be another way. Quentin had to have left the door unlocked, but how would this person have known unless they were sitting in the parking lot all day, every day, just waiting for an opportunity?

No, they had to have keys. Quentin was having the locks changed, but if they got a copy once, why should I think for a moment that they couldn't get one again? What was stopping them from showing up when I was home? From standing over my bed until their stare awakened me? Had they found what they wanted, satisfied their curiosity, come to their own conclusions, or was this going to continue until they had details?

Finally, there was the crowbar. How could someone who was so careful to return all my things to the correct places forget something like that? If they had keys, why would they need that in the first place? If leaving it was intentional, this person knew something for real, something I'd spent ten years trying to erase. They knew it'd jog my memory and drive me crazy with worry. Even though it'd never been on purpose, I'd really thought I'd done a diligent job of covering my tracks, and that memory existed in my head alone.

Tina and I didn't exchange many words that morning. I could tell that she knew I felt like crap, and she treated me very gently until I'd tried to apologize one too many times for getting drunk, crying all over her, and blacking out. Then, she looked at me tiredly and told me to knock it off. That felt much better than being handled with kid gloves. We picked up breakfast sandwiches from a drive-thru, then spent nearly an hour at my bank trying to explain my situation. Everything seemed to make far more sense to my credit card companies, or maybe I was just testier now that I was hungover instead of actively drinking.

By the time all that was through, most of the morning was gone. I felt horrible for dragging Tina through this bullshit. Brand-new relationships like ours were supposed to be about fucking all weekend, not picking up broken glass and working through my issues. "Look," I told her as she pulled into a parking space in front of my unit. "You don't have to waste your time with this. You've already done so much—"

"It's not a waste of time. Anyway, I'm not leaving you alone in there if they haven't changed the locks."

"I'll be fine," I promised. "Lucy and Bobby are right next door."

She stared at me for a minute. "Do you want me to leave?"

Honestly, I did, just for a little while, so I could be alone with my thoughts and my subtly trashed apartment, but the last thing I wanted was to upset her. "No. That totally came out wrong. This is just a really lousy way to spend your weekend."

"For you, too."

The window was still covered with plywood, but Bobby met me on the landing with a new key. He told us that he'd be home most of the day and would be happy to install the dead bolt I hadn't remembered to buy. I thanked him again and told him I'd let him know when he could come over to take care of it.

Everything looked far less frightening in the daylight without the strobe of blue lights playing off every angle of every room. It did seem more depressing, though, that was for sure. I spent the first few minutes walking through all the rooms again. Nothing was so disheveled that I couldn't have just picked up where I'd left off Friday morning, but I felt like I needed to go through everything myself, especially the top shelf of my closet. Tina followed on my heels, though, and I couldn't spend more than a token moment anywhere.

"Are you sure you don't want me to call the police back?"

"What for? Nothing's gone."

She nodded toward the bedroom. "The pry bar."

I shook my head, trying to keep my countenance grim. "I was thinking about that this morning. If they didn't give a shit about getting prints off the window, they're not going to give a shit about that."

"I was thinking about it, too," she said timidly. "They couldn't have used that to break the window unless that was how they got in. If they used it on the way out, it wouldn't be in here."

I sighed, feeling defeated. "You're right."

"So either they really did climb in the window, or at least intended to use it, but found the door open?"

"This is making my brain hurt," I said. "Could you kick in a window like that without cutting yourself?"

"Maybe. It's at the right height. I'd look for DNA evidence just in case, but the West Grove boys in blue aren't into that kind of stuff."

"DNA evidence," I muttered. "You watch too much TV."

"What are you going to do with it?"

"The crowbar? I don't know. Get it out of here."

Tina shrugged like that was as reasonable as anything else. "Look, I know your head hurts, and I'm driving you crazy," she finally said. "Do you seriously need a few minutes alone?"

Yes. I looked around the apartment again, pretending to consider her words. "Maybe. I just need to wrap my head around this and figure out what to do next."

"I will run to Walmart and pick up a dead bolt and grab some lunch. Sound good?"

I nodded. "Is Bobby still here? The black pickup is his."

"Yes. Do you want me to take the crowbar?"

I shook my head as gently as I could. "Let me think about it a little more, but I'll probably just put it out in the trash."

I brought a roll of paper towels and my vacuum cleaner into the office and legitimately spent the next several minutes cleaning glass shards out of my carpet while Tina got back into her coat. I dumped the larger pieces in the trash can, picking them up with the paper towel until I became brazen and impatient enough to forego the protection. Of course, I sliced an inch-long gash in my finger and had to run to the bathroom for a bandage.

It was one of those clean, razor-blade cuts that bled a lot. I probably should have spent a while with a washcloth pressed against it, but I didn't dare take too long. I wound the largest Band-Aid I could find around it tightly, hoping that would stop the blood, and started in with the paper towel again until I'd picked up enough large pieces to warrant running the vacuum over the rest. I was sure I'd still slice the hell out of my feet anyway the first time I went barefoot in there. I set the trash can in the hallway, double-checked that Tina's car was gone from the parking lot, and went into the bedroom.

It was still there, of course, right where Tina had left it. I set my sweaters aside, moved the crowbar onto my bed, and examined it carefully. This couldn't be the one. There was no reason for someone to have kept it for ten years. This had to be something random that was left behind by accident. It had to be.

The thing was, I couldn't be positive, and if I couldn't be positive, I couldn't call the cops and turn it over. With my luck, the illustrious West Grove police department would find age-old prints on there or something, even though they weren't interested in looking for them in my apartment. What even happened when you turned over evidence from a *different* crime?

My mind spun, my cut finger throbbed. Second-guessing myself over and over, I brought it into the living room, set it gently in the bottom of my trash can full of glass, and headed out onto the landing. I locked the door and spent a long time scanning the parking lot, the apartments across the way, the drive all the way up to the highway. Nobody. It was chilly and overcast, an uncommonly yucky day in West Grove.

I didn't go to the dumpster closest to my unit. I cut behind into the back side of the complex and walked the fence to the opposite end where a second one sat. I considered throwing it as far as I could over the fence to rust anonymously in the field on the other side. I considered jumping in the car and driving a few miles up the road and throwing it in a different field. Finally, I convinced myself that if people could discard dead bodies in the trash and get away with it, I could get rid of a crowbar in a dumpster without getting caught. Before I could talk myself out of it, I slid the side door open and emptied the contents of the trash can amongst plastic garbage bags, crumpled fast-food wrappers, and broken, discarded household items. Some of the glass pierced one of the bags, but the crowbar fell out of sight.

Back in my apartment, I pulled down the shoebox and went through it far more thoroughly than I had the night before with the cop standing right beside me. If this person had perused it, they'd taken even greater care to put everything back as they'd found it than they had in the rest of the apartment. Everything was in order: the coins, the photos, the clippings, the card, none of them crumpled or dog-eared or sitting at a bizarre angle.

I'd just put the box back on the shelf and dragged the chair back into the dining area when the phone rang. I hoped it was Tina and felt better because I did. I found the phone and was ready to flop down on the sofa and apologize for being a jerk when I saw the readout. *West Grove, TX, 230-9950.*

Goddamn it. I threw the phone, dreading the sound of the answering machine, dreading the anticipatory silence that would follow. It hit the wall and left a big dent. *Are you watching me right now? Do you know that I'm alone for the first time since I came home to find this? Did you watch me clean up the glass, throw out the crowbar, and put a hole in my fucking wall?* I stared wildly out the window into the parking lot, searching every car, every landing for a sign of motion. Something caught my eye, but it was just the neighbor kid and his basketball, weaving blindly along the blacktop. As I watched, his ball hit a maroon lowrider squarely on the door and set off its alarm. The kid took off in the other direction, but after several cycles of whooping and honking, the alarm stopped without anyone so much as looking outside to see that everything was all right.

I didn't understand the object of this game. What was the use in wearing me down, of causing me to break if I had no idea to whom I was supposed to confess? *If you want me out of here, you're close to getting your wish. If you want something else from me, I'm afraid that you'll have to spell it out a little more clearly.*

I got up and very deliberately replaced the phone in its charger, then played back the predictable non-message. I hadn't heard from that number in a while, I realized. *Missed me, huh?* I turned my back on the end of the static and returned to the living room.

Chapter Eighteen

I spent the next two nights at Tina's. I felt safer there, although it turned Monday morning into a logistical nightmare. She dropped me off with just enough time to shower, throw on clothes, and jump into my own car to leave for school. I hadn't so much as touched my paperwork or lesson plans since I'd left school Friday.

I closed myself in my classroom, fished last year's binder of lesson plans out of my filing cabinet, and copied verbatim what I'd done during the correlating week onto this week's blanks. It was a short week due to Thanksgiving, but I still felt guilty. I reasoned that was better than taking the plans straight from the textbook like some of my colleagues did every week.

Jody stopped me on my way back from the office. "Hey. Are you okay?"

I looked around, not sure how to answer that question. I found it odd that Tina would mention something to Jody before I could, and I was sure that nobody else knew what had happened. "Um, I guess."

"Good," she replied briskly. "I was a little worried. It's not like you to forget."

I was about to ask what the hell she was talking about when it hit me. "Oh my God, I'm sorry. I said I'd come back Saturday to put on another coat of paint."

She grinned a little and waved her hand as if absolving me of my sins. "Don't worry about it."

"No, I feel terrible." It wasn't the time or the place to explain what had gone on that weekend, but I didn't want her to think I'd blown her off. "I got broken into on Friday, and I kind of lost the rest of the weekend."

She grabbed me and pulled me down the hall and into her classroom. "What?"

"When I got home Friday, the cops were already there."

"Oh my Gosh, Cary. Are you okay? Did they take anything?"

I gave her an abridged version of the story with the promise of more details later, but Jody's brow still furrowed hard, and she wouldn't let go of my arm.

"Does Kathy know about this? It could have something to do with the burglary here. You must be a mess, baby. Why didn't you call me? It makes me sick to think about you there all alone."

I chewed my lip for a second and glanced at the speaker on the ceiling. "Tina came over and helped out. You were busy with the play, and I didn't want to saddle you with one more thing, you know?"

My attempt to bury that half confession didn't work. She watched me for a second, the furrow gone from her brow, her lips wanting to twitch into a smile. "That's a good thing," she finally said, squeezing my arm, then letting go. "Let me know if I can do anything for you."

I didn't bother to worry about whether she was going to tell Daniel. If she did, so what? I couldn't imagine Tina being mad. She knew they knew about Amy and me, and they hadn't gone running to the superintendent.

Honestly, I didn't worry about much that morning. I faked my way through current events, a writing assignment, and math, then led the class down to the computer lab. After getting things started, I let the aide take over and sat in the back correcting papers.

Twenty minutes into the period, Dunlop entered the room. He wandered through the aisles for a minute, looking over students' shoulders, then pulled out a chair next to me. "Miss Smith."

"Mr. Dunlop."

"Do you have some lesson plans for me?"

"I do." Barely looking up from my papers, I fished out my notebook, turned to the proper page, and handed it to him.

I watched as he read through the week, but if he thought my plans seemed contrived, he didn't react at all. He pulled out a pen, signed his initials in the corner of the page, then made a note in his own book. "All right, then," he said, getting up and pushing in his chair. "Do you have a language arts lesson coming up? I'd like to sit in and listen."

It just doesn't stop. I was about to be really mad, but right then, I happened to catch sight of the small black cell phone attached to his belt. I wondered what the number was. "We already did language arts this morning," I told him, looking up quickly lest he think I was checking out his package. "Nine o'clock tomorrow morning."

"Thank you," he said, nodding at me. "I look forward to it."

❖

Tina followed me home that afternoon. It was partially to make sure everything was okay, but mostly so we could catch dinner together.

Lucy was busy hanging Bobby's coveralls on the railing again. Bugsy stood on the landing at her feet, stuffed into a wooly, cable-knit, blue sweater. I didn't think it was cold enough to worry about him freezing, and apparently, he felt the same way. As Tina and I inched past him, he sat, cocked one leg up, began to scratch at it, and promptly got a toenail caught in the stitching.

"Hey, y'all," Lucy called, smiling broadly at Tina and giving me a sneaky, knowing look. "Bet you're psyched about the holidays."

"Short week," I agreed, looking from Lucy to Bugsy, who had nearly tipped over trying to free his foot. I thought about saying something, but it was easier to kneel and remove his claw from the sweater myself.

Lucy didn't notice. "Well, everything looks good on this front," she said, nodding toward my brand-new window. "We'll keep an eye on things while you're gone."

"Thanks," I told her, righting Bugsy and patting him on the back. He gave me a pleading look, as if I might take the stupid sweater off him. I gave him a sympathetic look and closed Tina and myself in my apartment.

She nudged me right away. "I totally thought you were going to lose a limb."

"He's harmless. That sweater," I muttered, rolling my eyes. "She just needs to get knocked up. Once she has a baby to dress, she'll leave the dog alone."

"So where are you going?"

"For Thanksgiving? Ithaca."

"To see your mom?"

I nodded. "You're not staying in town, are you?"

She shook her head. "My brother's shipping out to Kuwait in two weeks."

"God, I'm sorry."

She tossed her purse down and raised her hands. "I don't want to talk about it. He got himself into this mess."

That seemed sort of harsh, but I could tell she was serious when she said she didn't want to talk about it. I wanted to hold her, to tell her I could only imagine how worried she must be, but I couldn't force myself to ignore her request. "Let me check my messages," I said, changing the subject as abruptly as I could. "Then we can get going."

She followed me into my bedroom while I monkeyed with the answering machine. The first message was from Daniel saying that I just had to call him back to hear what Bev had said in the hallway after dismissal. The second was a hang-up.

"You may as well return that call," she offered. "It's really early for dinner."

While Daniel giggled about Bev cluelessly referring to school as "my good old Bush," Tina lay next to me on my bed, stroking my hand absently. I was fairly sure where she hoped that would lead, but once I was through on the phone, I sat back up and moved to the dresser.

West Grove, TX, the caller ID read. *230-9950.* The call had come in just five minutes before we'd arrived. I tipped the box so that Tina could see. "Do you recognize that number?"

"It's not Daniel?"

I shook my head. "There was a hang-up afterward. The same number's been calling me incessantly."

She sat up and took a better look at the number. "Since Friday night?"

I shook my head. "Only twice recently, but for a few weeks, it was like four, five times a day sometimes."

"Do they always just hang up?"

I nodded. "I picked up once, and they didn't say anything."

"You should've mentioned *that* to the cops," she muttered. "Have you called the number back?"

"Yes, but it always goes straight to voice mail."

"Nice. You should try at like two in the morning, when they're not expecting it. God, Cary," she said, pulling her arms around me from behind. "You don't need to think about this shit right now."

That was nice. I felt her hand moving under my sweater and her lips against my neck, returning to where we were when I got off the phone with Daniel. When I went to set the phone back on my dresser, I caught sight of us together in the mirror, and my whole body went numb. I knew my mind was just playing tricks on me, but it was so real, so bizarrely real that it took every ounce of energy I had to return to the moment at hand.

For just a second, the face I saw beside mine was not Tina's.

CHAPTER NINETEEN

My last flight left Dallas-Fort Worth at three o'clock Sunday afternoon. The Midland Airport, where my car sat waiting, was barely four gates, and it only accommodated a few large jets each day. My plane was a prop of the noisy, rickety ilk that could conjure airsickness in even the most seasoned of travelers.

I hated flying under the best circumstances, and I'd been terribly ill upon arriving in Dallas after my prop flight out of town. I was thankful to see that this flight was full. When they weren't, the flight attendants sometimes had to ask people to move to the rear seats so the nose of the plane could get off the ground. I didn't feel particularly safe in a contraption so easily manipulated by its contents, so after clenching the armrests until my knuckles were white as the plane wobbled into the sky, I closed my eyes, tried to stay as still as possible, and hoped that sleep would distract me from the unending turbulence at such a low cruising altitude.

This was the first Thanksgiving I'd been away from West Grove. I usually cooked a turkey and spent part of the day with Jody and Daniel and Amy, working around their families' celebrations. This year, getting out of town had been a welcome diversion. My mom and Dave, her husband, had invited me to Ithaca since they were planning a cruise over winter break to celebrate his fiftieth birthday. We had a nice, laid-back weekend with plenty of food and an early Christmas celebration. I did worry from time to time that my apartment was sitting empty, but I wasn't concerned enough to call Lucy and Bobby about it. It was the first time in two months that my blood pressure remained stable when I heard the phone ring.

I liked Dave. He was nothing like the other men my mom had married. He was a shy, tubby high school principal with thinning salt-and-pepper hair and a conscience. We'd spent several hours watching football together and several more talking shop. I hadn't shared that I was under Dunlop's constant supervision that year, but I had mentioned that I'd gotten in trouble for reading *Coral Sharkey* out loud in class.

"That's the problem with you liberals," he'd teased. "Encouraging those kids to read. Next thing you know, they'll be studying and wanting to go to college."

My mother and I had also spent plenty of time sitting together on the porch, bundled up against the cold, holding mugs of hot tea. We'd watched it snow and talked like we always had, more like friends than mother and daughter. She'd asked if I was still seeing Amy, and I told her that we'd split up.

"You dated for a long time," Mom had observed.

"It ran its course."

"Are you seeing someone else?"

"Sort of. Kindergarten teacher."

"Does she teach at Bush?"

"Yes. She's new this year."

"Where's she from?"

I'd realized that I'd never gotten a solid answer. "She was in Austin for a few years, but her parents are in Arkansas somewhere, I think."

"Not from West Grove, in any case."

"That's all that really matters."

"Is there potential?"

I'd thrown her a look. "Don't you think it's a bad idea to enter every relationship assuming it has potential?"

Mom had shrugged, smiling slightly. "If it doesn't, what's the use?"

"Okay, every relationship has some sort of potential, but I'm not really in a place where I can be concerned about the long-term."

"You might in a few years."

"Mom," I'd said, looking straight at her and allowing one eyebrow to cock, "when you were my age, you had a ten-year-old and two failed marriages."

Her smile had broadened considerably. "I taught you so well."

"You taught me not to define myself by my relationships."

"Maybe in a roundabout way." She'd nudged my knee. "Does she make you happy?"

I'd nodded.

"That's all that really matters."

I had missed Tina with a vengeance, no matter how quiet and comfortable the weekend was. I'd finally broken down and called her during my layover. She was on the road, just east of Abilene, and barring any unforeseen troubles, she was likely to beat me back into town. I'd asked if I could see her when I got in, and she'd told me that she'd like nothing more.

As I watched the terrain glide past, the dread of what I was returning to began to seep in through the cracks. The month between Thanksgiving and Christmas was traditionally a mess thanks to wired children, holiday programs, and preparations for the school play. Add to that Dunlop's watchful eye, the insistent anonymous phone calls, and the consuming threat that someone—who seemed to have or want too much information—could burst in on another facet of my life at any moment, and I had an ulcer waiting to happen.

Maybe something would fall off the plane, and we'd have to turn around and return to Dallas. Maybe I could be stuck there for just a few more days, just long enough to take the edge off returning to real life.

Okay, something better not fall off the plane. As we closed in on the familiar landscape of dry, prickly brown, I could feel the wind gusting and tossing the plane violently side to side. I glanced out the window just long enough to see the matchbox buildings and cars begin to increase in size, then closed my eyes tightly again.

We were surely inches away from the runway when the plane shuddered, teetered, and nosed upward again. The captain came over the loudspeaker to explain that the wind was bad, and we'd have to make another pass at landing.

A nervous titter moved through the plane. Even the big, broad, oil company executive-type across the aisle was sweating through his shirt. There was the unmistakable sound of someone vomiting several rows ahead. This time, I concentrated hard on the view out the window, as if the bobbling scenery didn't scare the hell out of me. We did manage a landing this time, and I had almost stopped shaking by the time we taxied to a stop at the terminal.

The drive from Midland wasn't nearly long enough to settle my stomach. I called Tina from the road and barely had time to drag my suitcase into my bedroom before she arrived at my apartment. "God, I missed you," I said, falling into her arms right away.

"I missed you, too. Have a good Thanksgiving?"

"Yeah. Did you?"

She shrugged. "I'm glad to be back. How was your flight?"

"Wretched. I've never felt so sick in my life."

"I guess dinner's out, then."

"Not necessarily, just not in the next few minutes."

"Why don't you get in the shower? I could stand to crash for a while myself."

"Tell me you didn't drive all the way from Hot Springs today."

She shook her head. "I stayed near Austin last night."

"That's not really on the way."

"No, but I can only spend so much time with my parents."

Tina curled up on my bed while I got in the shower. She was right. I did begin to feel better almost immediately. I took my time, assuring myself that Tina wouldn't mind another few minutes of rest. I expected to find her asleep when I returned, but instead, she propped up on one elbow when I entered the room.

"Your mom called," she said. "She wants to know that you got in all right."

"I'm sorry. Did the phone wake you?"

She shook her head. "You should call her back."

I felt marginally guilty returning the call, but Tina dropped my towel and began to rub my back. "I'm home, flight was fine, thanks for the nice time," I told my mother. "Gotta run."

We did end up going to dinner, just an hour and a half later. I hoped that this was a sign of things to come. I'd never intended to lean so heavily on Tina or to allow her to see me at my worst. I wanted to jump back into the fun and spontaneity.

Of course, the point of no return was often a lot closer than expected. Tina and I sat through much of our meal at Kang's China House in near silence. I couldn't help but think about what she'd said earlier, that she was glad to be back. I wanted to believe that just meant she'd missed me, but her mood was more brooding than all that.

"Not a good visit?" I finally asked.

"It was tense."

"Because of your brother leaving for Kuwait?"

She nodded. "My mother kept randomly bursting into tears, saying she couldn't bear to lose him, too. He kept saying he'd be fine, but it was not pleasant. I took off on Friday night."

I wasn't sure who else her mother had lost. Tina hadn't mentioned a grandparent dying recently or anything. I hesitated to ask for fear of dredging up something even more uncomfortable. "So it was you and your parents and your brother. Was your sister there?"

"No."

I'd somehow managed to do just what I'd hoped to avoid. There was absolutely no emotion on Tina's face, but the bluntness of her answer resonated between us, letting me know exactly how stupid a question that had been. I hadn't heard much if anything about her sister. I'd assumed that she was married with kids, probably the two in the pictures on Tina's refrigerator, and that she was the one Tina spent so much time visiting in East Texas. Now, I wondered if any of that was true or if I'd just made it all up inside my head. The silence was absolutely deafening.

"I'm sorry," I finally said. "That you had a lousy time and that I brought it up."

She shook her head. "It's okay. Yours was better, I assume."

"It was nice," I agreed, almost feeling guilty. "Quiet."

"Did you have snow up there?"

I nodded. "It was gorgeous."

"I'm jealous," she said, touching my hand quickly as if to apologize. "Just you and your mom?"

"And her husband."

"You don't call him your stepfather?"

"I was out of the house before they met. I just call him Dave."

Tina nodded. "Say, along those lines, how come your mother calls you Liz?"

I didn't see that coming at all. Time stopped, and all motion was suspended around me. The bustle of staff, the din of patrons, the hokey, pseudo-Asian background music all disappeared into a thick void, spawning a tense grand pause into which I knew I was supposed to come crashing. I asked her to repeat herself.

She didn't. "When she called, I thought it was a wrong number at first."

Mom had called. Right. Tina was in my bedroom when she'd called and heard her message. It wasn't like the whole Liz business was a huge secret. Daniel had come across my high school yearbooks while I was busy cooking him dinner once and had decided to call me Liz just to piss me off. I countered by calling him Danny, and it'd never happened again. "My middle name's Elizabeth," I said briskly. "It's what she's always called me."

"Okay," Tina said, squinting as if she was trying to wrap her brain around that. "Your mother calls you by your middle name, but everyone else uses your first name?"

"Everyone called me Liz when I was little."

"Why don't you go by Liz now?"

"I prefer Cary."

"How did you…" She paused, searching for a word. "Switch?"

"I started going by Cary in college," I said, setting down my chopsticks. I was no longer hungry. "I wasn't living at home anymore, so it wasn't that confusing."

"Do your friends from high school still call you Liz?"

"I'm not in touch with any of them."

"None of them?"

That shouldn't have been so strange. I'd been out of high school for nearly ten years, and West Grove was nowhere near any of the places I'd lived. Even Billy, who had spent the first eighteen years of his life in the same house, was still in touch with only two of his high school buddies. I shook my head, feeling defensive. "We moved so often, I never got very close to anyone."

"Never?"

"Not really."

"Does your mother know you go by Cary now?"

"Yes, but she still calls me Liz. Is this really so weird?"

"Kind of," Tina said, her tone implying it was far weirder than that. "So you finished high school and just..." She threw her hands in the air lightly, as if cleverly evaporating something. "Disappeared."

"I never disappeared from anywhere."

Our eye contact continued in the most formidable of standoffs. I had not meant to be short with her, and I wasn't certain that she had intended to imply anything leading, but in case she had, I remained ready, hands clenched under the table, heart pounding.

She shrugged dismissively but continued to stare me down. "I guess I just meant that if Susie who ate lunch with you in third grade decided she wanted to look you up, it wouldn't be easy."

Well, apparently it wasn't that hard. As soon as I heard the words inside my head, I felt my cheeks burning, and every ounce of the sick feeling from earlier that day returned to my stomach. "I'm in touch with some people from college," I said softly, "and I can't imagine anyone prior to that caring."

"You never know," she said, her voice sounding at once less interrogative and more earnest, her smile sweet. "You tend to sell yourself a bit short sometimes."

Tina dropped me back at home shortly thereafter. It didn't seem to bother her, but our conversation left me shaken. There was so much I didn't know about her and too many things I'd admitted about myself. I lay on my sofa for a long time, watching the darkness out the window, my mind working overtime.

It was past midnight when the knock came at my door. "Liz?"
I'd heard Mom rattling around in the apartment for twenty minutes by then. She'd been late in getting home, and since she hadn't burst into my room right away, I'd sort of thought there wouldn't be any confrontation. Now, panic slid through my body. Her tone wasn't quite in the neighborhood of *what-the-hell-have-you-done*, but it was serious. I continued to lie there on my bed, staring at the ceiling, heart pounding, hoping she'd think I was asleep, hoping she'd just go away.

She knocked again, louder this time. "Liz? I need to talk to you."

Oh God. I inched my way out of bed, scanning my room for telltale signs of what had happened earlier that evening. My car keys were on my dresser; my closet door was closed. In the laundry room, the dryer was still running. "Be there in a minute," I called, my voice sounding surprisingly normal. I pulled on a T-shirt and a pair of sweats, stared at my reflection, ran my hands through my hair. It'd been wet when I finally lay down, and it was kind of messed-up now.

Go, she'd said.
I remembered almost nothing between slamming my car door on the street near the viaduct and opening it again in the carport outside my mother's house. I didn't remember whether I'd taken Poplar or Park, if any of the lights had been red, or how fast I'd gone. All I could see was the blood, and it was all I could think about. It had been everywhere. On my hands, on the steering wheel, on my clothes, probably on the outside of the damned car door. I'd had no idea how I was going to clean all of it up before Mom got home.

Go. I'll take care of everything.
I'd tried to scrub the bloodstains out of my clothes, but there were still telltale spots on both my T-shirt and shorts. I'd gone over my car with spray cleaner and paper towels until the only remaining

patch was an ambiguous dark stain about the size of a nickel on the carpet under the brake pedal. I'd backed it up onto the drive again to where I usually parked and half-assed washed it with the garden hose since the driver side door looked a lot cleaner than the rest of it.

I'd retraced my steps, front door to bedroom, bedroom to bathroom, more times than I could count, scrubbing anything I might have touched or that looked suspect. I'd flipped between the network affiliates during the ten o'clock hour, but none of the news anchors had mentioned anything about Jonathan McGrath or about that particular street. Nothing at all. I'd showered a third time before lying to stare at the ceiling and listen to my pulse.

I didn't understand how my mother could know something that the news didn't, but I supposed it was possible. At this point, anything was possible. With no idea of what I could say to explain, I opened the door to my room and headed lamely out into the kitchen. I found Mom sitting at the table, still wearing her scrubs. One hand rubbed her temple, the other nursed a drink.

"Mom?"

She didn't look at me. "Liz." She shook her head and paused as if auditioning words for the remainder of that sentence.

Her hesitancy made my skin crawl. My eyes traveled toward the front door. Had I missed a spot? Had the neighbors told her I was out washing the car at nine p.m.?

"I lost my job today."

Blood rushed to my head so quickly, I felt like I might pass out. "What?"

"Budget cuts," she said, her voice nearly a whisper. "They're closing the unit at the end of the summer. I did see it coming. I've got my resume out again, but…" She shook her head. "I'm so sorry, honey."

Her tears surprised me. She'd both quit jobs and been laid off before, but this was the first time she'd shown such emotion. I slid into the chair beside her and touched her hand shyly. "Mom, it's okay. You've applied at Baptist?"

"Yes, but it's more likely that we'll have to move again."

The dizzy feeling returned. "So we move again. We'll be okay."

She sighed deeply and looked directly at me for the first time. Her eyes were badly bloodshot. This wasn't the first time she'd been crying. "Things are different here. You have such good friends. I really hoped you could finish school here."

I had, too, until six hours prior. I hadn't considered what it'd be like working next to Natalie for the rest of the summer or how I'd feel upon going back to school in the fall. I hadn't even started to think through what would happen if the truth came out, and I wouldn't be *going* back to work or school. Now, Mom's words came as a huge comfort, as exactly the solution I needed.

"It'll be okay, Mom," I whispered, hugging her tightly. "Look where you need to. Don't worry about me."

Chapter Twenty

I wanted CliffsNotes or maybe something like the Shakespeare editions with translations to modern English for each page. I always did well in literature courses, but I was clueless as to what was happening in my life. I turned each plot twist around in my head to no avail. I flipped backward through the annals of my memory, searching for the bit player whose name I'd forgotten, the one who would make a sinister reappearance in what I prayed wouldn't be the final chapter.

I could not help but acknowledge that the craziness had started very close to the time that Tina had arrived in town. I went through my lesson plans, recalling which days Dunlop had observed me, which days my classroom had been violated. I reviewed my caller ID, noting that my first calls from 230-9950 had occurred shortly after Tina's appearance. They'd made a frightening crescendo around the time she'd coerced Marvin into unlocking my classroom, and there had been fewer since we'd been dating. I couldn't remember if I'd gotten any calls from that number when I was physically in the same place as Tina, but I didn't think so.

It was absurd to picture her breaking and entering, but the longer I thought about it, the more I realized I did not know. Tina was worse than evasive about where she'd come from, what she'd done, and who she'd known prior to her arrival in West Grove. I couldn't imagine that she had half as much to sweep under the rug as I did, but the graceful, polished way she'd sidestepped so many questions made me extremely leery. I knew that if I could just be certain that the Tina Flores I'd fallen so hard for was the real deal, I could come up with a way to exonerate her.

Really, there was no way that someone who was such a mystery to me could know too much. There was no reason why someone I'd never met before would just show up one day to riffle through my life and cause such unrest. I racked my brain for our common denominator, the circumstance under which we might have previously met, the acquaintance we might share, or how I might have somehow wronged her. I came up with nothing.

I curled up on my bed for a long time Sunday night with my junior yearbook, the one from Memphis. I searched for the name Flores in my class, then the other three, but I found no one who matched Tina's description. There were a couple Floreses, a boy a year my senior and a girl two years my junior, but neither looked enough like Tina to be related. I even went through each page, examining face after face.

This all made me feel certifiable, especially because I wanted so badly for my own suspicions to be wrong. I wanted to believe that Tina was face value, interested in me for the company, the conversation, or even just the sex. I wanted to believe it, but no matter how I turned things around in my head, I came to the same conclusion. There was no way everything could be coincidental. She had to have something to do with it.

I did not know the real reason the tides had turned, whether Tina had legitimately meant the words that had frightened me or if I was merely psyching myself out, creating a reason to run from yet another person whom I'd allowed too close to my heart. Whatever it was, I knew that until one of us broke down and told the truth, we would continue this face-off, this slow, deliberate dance, each of us prying without using nouns, each of us taking another step back and to the side until we became a nonsensical blur, nothing more than two agitated, exhausted animals chasing our own tails.

❖

On Monday morning, I found a note from Kathy in my box requesting to see me during my prep hour at one thirty. It was a very official-looking memo, small and yellow, with the district insignia header, similar to those she sent after required observations. Since she hadn't observed me, and my brain was floundering in all kinds of ugly directions anyway, I could think of no reason she might send an official summons other than that she'd discovered my relationship with Tina.

From that moment on, I was an attention-deficit poster child. The note was on my mind, then Afghanistan, then Tina, then the vision of seeing that crowbar sitting on my dresser. Eddie's leg jiggled furiously as he worked on his writing assignment, wearing on my nerves until they were stretched taut. I was thinking about Tina again when the computer aide buzzed me to say that the lab was down. Another forty-five minutes to fill with the nothingness in my head.

I paced the room maniacally as we neared midmorning, reviewing the concept of barter economics. I realized I'd forgotten my lunch but remembered a valid tidbit that would have been useful two hours earlier during current events. I couldn't remember what we actually had discussed and wondered if I'd remembered to say the Pledge of Allegiance. I'd heard that people had gotten fired for forgetting it. I decided that Nestor certainly would have reminded me. As I assigned the class pages to read from their social studies book, I noticed motion in the parking lot.

Tina walked purposefully to her car, hair flowing behind her, eyes squinting into the sun. As if I hadn't spent the entire previous evening exploring her role in my personal nightmare, I wondered where she was going and longed to have a prep hour so I could go with her. *She cannot have anything to do with it. She just walked into my life at the wrong time and started asking completely reasonable questions, the exact kind I avoided when they came from Amy.*

Instead of getting into her car, Tina opened the tailgate and started rummaging around. The wind licked gently at the hem of her skirt, lifting it barely a notch, just a little tease. I turned back to my class, back to economics, back to work. I picked up the chalk and began to write down terms to discuss after reading. When I glanced out again, she was carrying a large box and two plastic grocery bags.

"Nestor, Dana," I said, "please go to the D-wing door and help Ms. Flores with her packages."

"Ms. Smith?" Gina's hand was high in the air.

"Gina?"

She brought her arm back down onto her desk very primly and leaned forward. "Who do you think is the prettiest teacher in the school?"

"I've never thought about it. What does this have to do with barter systems? Are you going to trade three goats and a llama for Ms. Spardo?"

Someone made a gagging noise, and Christian started to laugh uncontrollably. When Gina gave him a dirty look, he pulled the back of his shirt up over himself, ducked downward, and smacked his forehead on his desk, hard.

"We could take a poll and graph the results," Chelsea suggested without missing a beat. "I think it's Ms. Flores."

Dana had left the door open. Tina passed by then, my students carrying every bit of her load. She threw me one tiny, lovely grin but continued down the hall without hesitating. I did not register my vote.

"While that would make an interesting graph," I said, "we wouldn't want to hurt anyone's feelings. Suppose nobody voted for me? How would I feel?"

Several girls laughed self-consciously, as if I'd tapped right into their own insecurities. Eric turned bright red and bent studiously over his textbook.

Her smile was so genuine, I thought, staring through the open door, wishing I could have one more glimpse of her. The notion of doubting her sincerity for even a second stuck hard in my throat, and I wondered why everything had seemed so different the night before.

I stopped next to Christian's desk and patted him on the shoulder. "Are you okay there, bud?"

"Yeah," he muttered, wiping his eyes on his shirtsleeve. "I'm good." There was a thick red mark on his forehead, but he was still giggling intermittently, so I could tell the tears were about Bev's dowry. I was glad he'd missed the looks Tina had given me.

My head was still spinning by one thirty. I'd considered going out to lunch with Marisol and Chris but opted instead to chew on a school corn dog in the staff lounge with Tina. She laughed at me and touched my wrist for emphasis, telling me that my kids were so sweet. I told her they were probably just excited to get out of class and did not mention Gina's proposed poll. Daniel watched Tina's fingers close on my arm with a carnivorous look of anticipation, but he did not ask any questions, and I did not offer any answers.

By the time I dropped my class off at art and reached the office, my palms were wet, and the corn dog was sitting heavily in my stomach. Selena looked up from the phone when I entered, scowling in a way that let me know just how completely I'd interrupted her conversation.

Kathy's door was open. She was bent over some sort of paperwork when I entered, but she looked up right away and squinted at the clock as if wondering if it could possibly be one thirty already. A small smile spread across her lips, and she reached to remove her reading glasses. "Good afternoon."

I felt Selena's eyes on my back, so I closed the door. I knew that committed me to whatever was going to happen, but I couldn't bear the thought of Selena listening to an accusation or reprimand.

Oddly enough, Kathy's smile did not suggest this was going to be a serious conversation. It was entirely too pleasant, and she just kept watching me and using it. To make matters worse, her blouse was unbuttoned two, possibly three digits, and my eyes desperately wanted to sneak toward her cleavage. It was all I could do to continue eye contact as I sat across the desk from her.

She finally tossed her glasses down on her desk. "I've summoned you here to ask what I'm sure is going to be a stupid question."

I shifted nervously on my chair. "Okay."

"Are you happy with your current assignment?"

I stared at her blankly. The entire contents of my chest clenched, as if a disembodied hand had snatched everything it could reach and was planning on rending its catch from my body. *My assignment in this building? My assignment in this district?* "I'm sorry," I stammered. "I'm not sure what you mean."

"With sixth grade."

I nodded warily. "Yes. Of course."

Kathy nodded. "That's what I knew you'd say. Most people would rather chew off a limb than face a classroom of twelve-year-olds, but you're fantastic with that age."

"Why do you ask?"

"Mr. Dunlop would like me to consider moving you to fourth grade."

The constricted mass of my insides wrung mercilessly. I could barely breathe. "What?"

Kathy held up her hand. "It won't happen if you're not comfortable with it."

"But what have I done? I mean, if he thinks I shouldn't be teaching this level—"

"Oh, it's not that there's a problem. Quite the opposite, actually. We're all concerned about the new testing regimen, and fourth grade is the big year. His idea is to place the strongest teachers at the most crucial levels, and in his opinion, that means you."

"*What?*"

Kathy laughed. It wasn't much more than a tiny snicker, and she almost managed to cover it but not quite. She raised her hands as if to tell me she couldn't believe it either. "He's been in your classroom several times this fall, hasn't he?"

"He's been on my case all fall," I corrected, then wished I hadn't been so blunt. It was out there, though, so I dropped my glance and muttered the rest. "He hates me."

"He doesn't hate you," she said, then snuck a glance in the direction of Mr. Dunlop's office as if he might be listening with a glass pressed against the wall. "Between you and me, he has some major issues where independent women are concerned, but he thinks you're doing a great job."

So he wants to pull me from my grade? It seemed like backward logic to me, but it was exactly what Javier had said. I nodded awkwardly, feeling a blush working its way up my neck and onto my face. I wanted to thank Kathy for the compliments, but since they were technically from Dunlop, I wasn't sure if that was the right thing to do.

"I gather I should tell him you're staying put?"

"I'll go wherever you think I should go," I said, trying to keep the hesitancy out of my voice. Sixth graders were hormonal and catty, sure, but fourth graders were little and squirrely.

"I think you should stay where you're comfortable," Kathy told me knowingly. "It's not as if sixth grade isn't crucial as well. Preparing them for junior high is a big deal."

I was about to thank her this time, both for refusing to move me and for acknowledging things I took so seriously. Before I could find the words, though, the door opened without so much as a warning knock.

"Dr. Levin is on line one," Selena announced like I wasn't sitting right there.

A look of distaste crossed Kathy's face. "Do you have another minute?" she asked me, confirming that I had not disappeared. "I really should take this call."

The blouse was unbuttoned three digits. I caught a glimpse of a lacy, dark-colored bra as Kathy made her way out of the office. I glanced backward at her, long enough to see her pick up the phone on Selena's desk, but Selena shot me a defensive glare, as if to warn me about narcing on her eye candy. I turned to the back of Kathy's office at once, cheeks still burning, thoughts spinning out of control.

Dunlop thought I was a good teacher? The notion was insane after all the nasty critiques he'd given me. I'd really thought that he was moments away from firing me. He thought I was a good teacher. Kathy said so. All at once, I had no idea what to think.

Kathy was back in the room before I managed to recover from the shock. I didn't know what more there was to say on the subject, but she closed the door and pulled her chair just a little closer to her desk. It made the neckline of her blouse gape farther. "There's something else I want to talk about."

I nodded and hoped she hadn't noticed my stare. Her smile was gone, and her tone was far more serious than it had been. I wondered if she'd had a bad conversation with Dr. Levin.

"I overheard something the other day. Mind you, I don't usually pay much attention to lunchroom gossip, but it concerned me. Is it true that someone broke into your apartment?"

I let out my breath. Of all the things she could have overheard, this was sadly the least complicated. "Yes. The weekend before Thanksgiving."

"I'm so sorry," she said. "Is everything all right? Are you able to stay there?"

I nodded. "There wasn't much to take care of. Financial stuff, mostly."

"Do the police think this has anything to do with what happened here?"

"They're checking into it. I didn't lose any keys from my classroom or anything. Do they still think this was gang related?"

She nodded. "Someone from the neighborhood, most likely. What still bothers me, though…"

I closed my eyes and my mood absolutely crashed. *I KNOW ABOUT YOU.* "What they wrote."

"I can't get it out of my mind."

"Me either."

"Cary." Kathy paused for a second as if she wasn't sure how to phrase what was on her mind. Her jaw was tight, and her eyes were very serious. She always knew just what to say and exactly how to say it.

"Yes?"

"I don't know if you remember this, but when you were hired, you were asked to sign a statement, an ugly statement about living a morally sound lifestyle."

Oh God. Oh God. Here it comes. I never expected it to come from Kathy. I'd always pictured being in Dunlop's office in the hard plastic chair, staring at his stupid plaques. I tried to calm myself, to keep from feeling betrayed, but I could barely force the words out of my mouth. "Yes, ma'am. I remember."

"Cary, I trust your judgment completely, and in turn, I will not judge you, but I must ask you something."

I swallowed carefully, looking straight back at Kathy Sutton. I sat stock-still and waited for it. *Are you a homosexual?*

"Has anything happened outside school that might cause you to be in trouble?" She stopped as if to clear her head, to try again. "I don't want to know details, Cary. I just want to know that you're not in any kind of danger."

Holy crap. My principal didn't want to know if I was gay but wanted to know if I'd picked up a hitchhiker or made a bad drug deal or chatted up the wrong guy at the laundromat? *What the hell?* The trouble was, I did feel like I was in danger. I didn't know how to answer that question honestly. "I don't think so."

"Are you safe?"

I wanted to say yes. It was the only reasonable answer, really, but I couldn't say it, and once I'd hesitated, I knew Kathy wouldn't accept a lie. "I don't know."

"Is there anything I can do?"

I shook my head. "My prep is almost over," I whispered.

"Do you need somewhere to stay?"

"No. Really, I'll be fine."

Without a moment's hesitation, she tore a page off her notepad and scribbled a phone number on it. Her contact information was not published, even in the faculty directory. "Please use it if you need my help."

"Thank you," I mumbled, holding the paper intact on my lap. It felt sacred somehow, like I really shouldn't fold it or stick it in my pocket.

"I need to know what's going on," she said. "Both for the children's sake and for yours."

I nodded. I had nearly forgotten the bewildered, relieved feeling I'd had when she'd left to take Dr. Levin's phone call, and I couldn't look anywhere near the buttons on her blouse. "Thank you," I repeated and let myself out of her office.

The principal didn't care whether I was gay, and Dunlop's scrutiny had been a grooming project rather than potential grounds for dismissal. I'd finally dared to add the digits and accept the sum, but now it was clear as day that I did not even understand the problem.

Chapter Twenty-one

Tuesday was my birthday. In many places I'd lived, I could count on a lovely dusting of snow or at least pleasantly nippy winter weather on December third, but West Grove was overcast and stagnant, the usual compromise when anywhere else in the country would get rain.

I didn't expect any sort of festivities, and I hadn't been approached with any plans. I assumed that meant Jody and Daniel would remember later in the week and take me out for sangria on Friday as if that was the plan.

The moment I sat on my desk to discuss current events, Nestor's hand shot into the air. When I called on him, he gave a huge smile. "Mr. Crenshaw said it's your birthday."

"And so it is," I said.

After a brief cacophony of birthday greetings, snippets of singing, and other random comments, the inevitable question came from Christian. "How old are you?"

"Never ask a lady her age," Shannon told him.

"Oh, come on," Chelsea said. "We'll guess anyway."

I shrugged. "Maybe. Did anyone watch the news last night?"

"Enron blah blah blah," Christian said. "You are…twenty-five."

"Nope."

"Forty-five?" David asked. I gave him a dark look. He giggled.

"Thirty?" Cristal asked.

"Nope." I gave up on current events and tapped that morning's writing prompt. The chalkboard squeaked and threatened to swivel. *What I really want for my birthday is a new damned whiteboard.* "Open your notebooks and get going."

"Are you old enough to be our mom?"

Since my back was turned, I wasn't sure who had asked that one. I would have credited it to David, but the voice was female. I did not answer.

"Did you go to graduate school?" Nestor asked.

I sighed, but at least it was a better question. "Yes, I did."

"And you've been here since we were in third grade. You're at least twenty-seven, then."

I loved Nestor. I didn't answer him, either. "That is the end of our guessing game. Notebooks open, pencils moving."

"I wish you would have told us yesterday," Nestor said, digging out his notebook and pencil. "My mom could have made a cake."

I was still feeling warm and fuzzy after school. After a brief staff meeting, I stayed an extra half hour working with Eddie and Samantha on reading comprehension, then gathered my things and went to the office to sign out. On my way back, I ran into Jody, who was juggling a huge box of rhythm sticks and sleigh bells as she pushed a coatrack full of costumes down the hall. Before I could offer some help, she let go of the box to flag me down. It clattered to the floor, and a deafening *splat-jingle* echoed down the hall.

"Ow," she muttered. "What're you doing here?"

"The teacher thing," I said, taking hold of the coatrack. "Where does this go?"

"My classroom, in front of the big closet," she said, handing me an enormous glut of keys with one digit sticking out like a thumb. "You're supposed to be home now, getting my message."

"And what would that message say?"

"That Tina's picking you up in less than an hour so you can meet all of us at the Ranch Hand for your birthday."

I threw a look behind us to see that the halls were empty. "I might as well just meet you guys there. It's on my way home."

Jody sighed loudly. "If you drive," she said through her teeth, "you can't get piss drunk. Tina will pick you up in under an hour to help facilitate said intoxication."

I didn't get a chance to argue. Just moments after I let myself into the music room, I heard a muffled, electronic rendition of the "William Tell Overture." After some shuffling, I found the source tucked under the front flap of Jody's bag. "Finnegan," I called down the hall, "you're ringing."

There was a *crunch-jingle-jingle* just outside the door. "See who it is."

I dug her phone out and checked the tiny screen, then nearly dropped it onto the floor. *West Grove, TX*, it read. *230-9950.*

Rossini had played thrice by the time Jody burst through the doorway and dropped the box onto her risers. "Well?"

"Do you know who this is?" I asked, stumbling over to her.

Jody barely glanced at it. "It's Amy," she said, taking it from me. "Hey. What's up?"

I remained in the middle of the classroom through the entire conversation, arms dangling limply at my sides, head swimming. I really couldn't believe what I'd heard, but Jody was indeed discussing the hours she'd need the gymnasium. I wanted to tug on her sleeve and beg her to stop, to tell her that this couldn't really be Amy, to tell her that she was stuck in the middle of this now, too.

"Hey," Jody said to me finally, holding the phone away from her ear. "It's okay if she comes, right?"

I couldn't make words come out of my mouth. It wasn't that I didn't want to hang out with Amy. I knew it would be awkward with both her and Tina there, but that wasn't it, either. I finally shrugged because I had to give some sort of answer.

Jody rolled her eyes. "Of course it's okay. See you at five thirty." As soon as she hung up, she turned on me. "Hon, you guys really need to get over this and learn to be cordial."

"It's not that. I just…that's Amy's number?"

"Yeah. I thought for sure she got it before you guys—" She stopped abruptly. A strange look crossed her face, and she looked toward the ceiling. I hadn't heard her name, but the speaker above our heads was humming busily. "Pardon?" Jody choked.

"Ms. Finnegan? I'm locking the office." It was Kathy.

"Yes, ma'am," Jody agreed, her voice all business. "I'm on my way out."

"Okay. Good night."

Jody winced as the buzzing stopped. "Shit."

"She didn't hear anything," I said. "Even if she did, you didn't say anything obvious."

"Right," Jody agreed lamely, turning to sort her instruments into boxes inside one of her cabinets. "I guess."

"You didn't," I assured her. "Look, I didn't mean to be a jerk. Everything is fine between us."

"Really?"

I nodded. "Does she know Tina's coming?"

"Yes."

"Does she know about…"

Now, Jody glanced sideways and cut me off. "No. I haven't told Daniel, either."

"Thank you."

"You're welcome. Now go home so she can pick you up already."

I had just enough time to get home, change into jeans, and check my answering machine before Tina's arrival time. Jody's message was the only one. Nothing at all from 230-9950.

I locked up when I saw Tina's car turning in and met her in the parking lot. Since Jody was so agitated that I'd thrown off her plans, my intent was to hurry things along, but the moment I closed the door and settled in, Tina slid an arm around my shoulder and kissed me with a surprising intensity. My initial reaction was one of embarrassment since absolutely anyone could have been watching, but when nobody knocked on the car window wielding a shotgun, I relaxed enough to enjoy it.

"God," I muttered once she let go. "I haven't done that since I was in high school."

Tina smiled to herself and threw the car in reverse. "You didn't tell me it was your birthday."

"Another one of those things that I assume won't interest anyone."

"So how old are you?"

"Twenty-eight."

"Old," she agreed, glancing sideways at me with a teasing grin.

"Shut up."

"Well, older than me, anyhow."

Her age was yet another thing I'd merely assumed. I wanted to ask, but she tossed me another delicious mocking smile, turned up the radio, and the opportunity was gone.

"Jody knows about us, right?"

"I never said it, but she figured it out after the stuff with my apartment," I said. "I'm sorry."

"If she's cool about it, I don't care."

"She is. She hasn't said anything to Daniel or Amy."

Tina's eyebrows jumped. "Is Amy coming?"

"Yes. I know it's weird."

"Not necessarily. I just haven't spoken to her except in passing."

"She's really very nice."

Now, Tina nudged me hard. "So I hear."

The parking lot at the Ranch Hand was full, considering it was a Tuesday and early for dinner. When we entered the restaurant, we found Amy and Jody waiting in the foyer. "There's some awards banquet taking up half the tables, and Daniel's late as usual," Jody said. "My name's on the list."

Tina nodded. "Good enough. What do you want from the bar?"

"I'll go with you," Jody said. "Sangria? A beer?"

"Gin and tonic," I replied, reaching for my purse.

"Don't you dare," Tina said. "You shouldn't have even brought that. Amy? Can I get you anything?"

"No, thanks."

"I'll get you a Coke," Jody decided, heading toward the other side of the restaurant with Tina.

Amy and I sat together on a lumpy cushion covered in blue vinyl to wait for our table and our drinks. "So I understand you have a designated driver," she began brightly.

"Not really. I mean, Jody dreamt up all of this. I don't mean to make you uncomfortable."

"Don't worry about it. It's your birthday. Anyway, I'm trying to loosen up a bit in my old age."

"Yeah?"

She grinned back. "Yeah. How're you doing?"

"Okay. You?"

She nodded. "Have a good Thanksgiving?"

"Definitely. I went up to Ithaca to see my mom and Dave. Did you cook?"

"No. We went to my sister's in San Angelo."

We were quiet, then. A couple entered the restaurant, inquired about the wait, and left without placing their name on the list. Amy watched the entire exchange like it was very interesting, elbows on her thighs, folding and unfolding her fingers distractedly. I finally couldn't stand it anymore. "Get a new cell phone?"

"What? Oh, yeah," she said, pulling it off her belt. She wore it in the same place Dunlop kept his, but I hadn't seen it during school hours. "I felt weird using the district phone for personal stuff, so I finally broke down and did it."

"I didn't mean to be weird when you called Jody earlier, I just didn't realize that was your number."

Amy turned away, elbows still on her knees. I could tell she was considering my words carefully, and I knew the exact moment when their meaning hit her. Her jaw went tight, she glanced around us, and she slowly folded her phone up and hitched it back onto her belt. I didn't think she was going to say anything, but in another moment, she dared to glance back at me, just for a second.

"You recognized it," she said quietly.

It was a statement, not a question, but I nodded anyway.

"I'm so sorry," she whispered. "I kind of lost my head for a while, and I didn't want you to think I was stalking you."

But you kind of were. "It's okay."

"There were some days that I just needed to hear your voice. I know that makes me sound really crazy, but—"

"Hey," I said, nudging her knee with mine. "Stop. It's okay."

"Really?"

"Really."

I was not hungry. I sat back from the table during the bulk of dinner, allowing the conversation to happen around me, making sure to insert a comment here and there so as to appear interested. I mushed my steak around on my plate, chewing a piece or two from time to time, washing each bite down liberally with gin and tonic. I started to get a little bit buzzed, but I couldn't worry about it for once since it forced the thoughts in my head to bounce around a little more slowly.

I was not getting fired, Dunlop was not on my case, and my phone stalker was no more than poor Amy, checking my whereabouts all those times I'd broken my promises about calling her. What did that leave me with? Two separate burglaries three weeks apart and a disgustingly thick paranoid streak.

Jody told story after story about the mishaps during her play rehearsals, and Daniel finished a fourth beer, laughing boisterously. Amy listened politely to Jody, concentrated on her meal, and looked quite uncomfortable. Tina poked me and gave me a pointed look as if to ask if I was okay.

I nodded, but that wasn't the case. I was scared, maybe even more scared than I'd been before my conclusion began to unravel, and the last thing I wanted was to alert my other friends to my funk. Jody would surely just refer me to her shrink, and while I sometimes thought that might not be a bad idea, I couldn't imagine sharing a therapist with my coworkers. Daniel would tell me to have another drink. Amy would shrivel up with guilt, worrying that her phone calls had sent me over the edge. Tina squeezed my hand under the table once, then let go.

Jody dragged me back into the conversation to see what yesterday's meeting with Kathy was about, and I explained briefly that Mr. Dunlop wanted to switch me to fourth grade.

Daniel groaned. "I hate that man. Every single time I get settled, he pulls that shit with me. I had third grade once before, and so help me God, if he ever does it to me again…"

Tina grinned. "I cannot picture you with third grade."

"It's really quite funny," Amy assured us.

"It's pathetic is what it is," Daniel said. "I hate teaching phonics, I go around with a bad attitude for the entire year, and nobody's test scores come out any better in the long run."

Jody glanced at Tina knowingly and cocked an eyebrow at Daniel. "You should try kindergarten. That'd be hilarious."

"Oh no, I shouldn't."

"Don't you need a separate certification?" Amy asked.

Tina said something in return, but I didn't hear it because Daniel was busy bitching and flailing. "Can you even imagine that? No, ma'am. I like my students potty-trained, thank you."

"The kindergartners are potty-trained," Amy muttered, then exchanged a look with Jody and Tina. "Well, most days."

"You'd be the hilarious one with the babies," Daniel told me. "Or, that is, you *will* be hilarious next year."

"Kathy isn't going to move me."

"What? Like you have any say in the matter."

"She said she wouldn't."

"Apparently, Kathy likes Cary better than she likes you," Jody told Daniel sweetly.

"Ha. Bet she knows your secret."

All eyes moved from Daniel to me in a very unnerving sort of way. "And what would that be?" I asked.

"Whatcha wearing under those Levi's? Do you know," he asked, leaning over the table toward Tina, "that my girl here wears a thong? We've had this conversation before," he said to Jody, then waved dismissively at Amy. "And we all know you know."

Oh, I felt bad. Amy did not say anything, but her face turned absolutely purple, and I could tell that she wanted to kill Daniel. She avoided my eyes, but I did catch her glancing at Tina shyly, as if begging her to be stupid enough to misunderstand.

Tina didn't look at me, either. Instead, she smiled at Daniel. "Is that so?"

"I know," he agreed emphatically, as if Tina had expressed any degree of surprise. "You'd never expect that from her. You'd think she's a little conservative if you didn't know how she votes."

I took a large swallow of my drink. "How do you know how I vote?"

Jody blinked at me. "Have you ever listened to anything that comes out of your own mouth?"

"Anyway, it's not conservative in a political sort of way," Daniel blathered, "more in a social way."

"You're saying I'm uptight," I clarified.

Daniel nodded. "A little bit," he said, holding up his thumb and forefinger to demonstrate.

Now, Tina shot me a luscious little grin. "You know, I wouldn't call Cary particularly uptight."

I kicked her under the table. It just made her giggle. Amy glanced at me apologetically, just for a second, as if it could be her fault entirely that she could make an educated guess as to what kind of undergarments I might be wearing.

Jody's voice dropped several notches. "She's not uptight, Daniel. She's just not as sloppy drunk as you are."

"It's your birthday." Daniel said, appealing to me with his palms in the air. "Have another. Now you," he said, pointing to Tina, "you are not uptight. Twenty bucks says you're not wearing any panties at all."

Amy's eyes went wide. Jody's nose flared, and she snuck look after look at the table next to us. My whole face burned, and when Tina's only response was to give a tiny, noncommittal shrug and nudge my leg with hers, the sensation slid rapidly through the rest of my body. Jody just would not stop worrying about that table.

I turned just a tiny bit to look back, and my eyes locked with those of a woman somewhere in her fifties with a formidable hairdo sponsored by Aqua Net and severely penciled-in eyebrows. She did not look pleased. Before I could look away, her companion, a gentleman with a graying comb-over, meaty jowls, and tiny dark eyes, turned to stare at us, too. He looked enough like Dunlop to make my breath catch in my chest.

I couldn't hear many words, but the couple did do us the favor of emphasizing the important ones. I caught *embarrassing*, *ridiculous*, and *disgusting*. It wasn't as difficult as it could have been since all conversation had stopped abruptly at our table.

Amy buried her face in her hands. "Brilliant. Just brilliant."

"Shut up," Daniel told her. "You could've warned me."

"Here's your warning," Jody said. "Every last time you get drunk in public, you make an ass of yourself. Good enough?"

"I think maybe we should go," Tina said lightly, reaching for her purse.

Amy, Jody, and Daniel stopped bickering for about five seconds, long enough to get the bill from Tina, then started in again about who owed what. It was an excruciating several minutes before Jody told Tina and me that we were set and that we could go on home.

Tina and I couldn't get to the car fast enough. She turned up the heat, and I stared out the side window, hoping to God we'd be gone before the others left the restaurant.

"Hey," she said, touching my elbow. "Are you okay?"

"I'm sorry my friends are such assholes."

She took my hand and squeezed gently. "They're my friends, too."

She didn't let go. We were quiet on the drive back to my place, but her thumb stroked absently, melting some of the tension. I still couldn't believe how ridiculously uncomfortable the evening had been, but the longer she held me, the less it mattered. When we reached my apartment, I asked her in, hoping for a few minutes of cuddling and reassurance that maybe, just maybe, she and I were okay.

I was still pressing the door closed behind us when Tina brushed my hair out of the way and kissed my neck slowly and deliberately. I felt her hand moving around my body to the front of my jeans, working the button, sliding the zipper down. I caught it there and held it fast but only long enough to engage the dead bolt and shut off the lights. Then, I turned, kissed her on the mouth, and led her hand back on course.

Sex had not been my intention, but I was a bit drunk and entirely willing. Instead of ending up in the bedroom, we only made it as far as the sofa, clothes strewn haphazardly around the room, blinds open. I didn't notice if Tina was wearing underwear or not. We lay together for a long time afterward, our limbs tangled around one another, Tina's head on my shoulder. It was lovely, and I was about to suggest we move into the bedroom when Tina kissed me on the cheek and began to free herself from our pile.

On her way to the bathroom, she gathered what clothing she'd shed. "I'll be right back."

Headlights had splashed across the room one too many times while we were on the sofa. As soon as I heard the door latch, I pulled my shirt closed and worked my way to the window to shut the blinds. That made it way too dark, so I fumbled with the lamp on the end table and knocked something onto the floor before managing to turn it on.

It was Tina's purse, a small, tasteful thing made of soft black leather, barely large enough to hold car keys and a pocketbook. Our conversation on the way to dinner played through my mind, and before I even considered what I was doing, the purse was in my lap, unzipped, and I was paging through a handful of credit cards for Tina's driver's license.

It was a new one, listing her address on Redbud in West Grove. *Christina Lee Flores*, it read. Her birthdate was May sixth, nineteen seventy-four, barely five months after mine.

While I was puzzling over that, I noticed that a small white slip of paper had fallen from the purse. I picked it up quickly and went to stash it back inside, but in doing so, the print caught my eye. It was a receipt dated the Saturday before from a restaurant in Killeen, Texas.

I knew I'd stared too long. I thought I heard the water running, and heart pounding, I slid everything back inside the purse and fumbled to zip it again just as the bathroom door clicked open.

Tina crossed the living room, a questioning look on her face. It could have just been that I was on the love seat instead of the sofa, but she looked at me, over at her purse, then back at me again. I had no idea how she could have known where she'd left it in our haste, but I began talking quickly, trying to divert her attention.

"I had to shut the blinds. I can turn this back off if you'd like."

She shook her head. "It's okay. I should go." Her glance dropped to the end table again, and this time, she picked up her purse.

I watched in horror as she slid the zipper open, waiting for her to notice that her credit cards were in the wrong order or that I'd accidentally crumpled that receipt upon stuffing it back in, but she found her keys, zipped it up again, and reached for her jacket.

"Sleep well, sweetheart." She bent to give me one last kiss, used the side of one finger to stroke my chest where my shirt had come open again, then turned the new dead bolt Bobby had installed and opened the door.

❖

So she's twenty-seven. She never said anything to lead me to believe otherwise, except that she'd just finished her master's degree. Plenty of people went back to school, I reminded myself, or just took a long time to finish. Daniel was the one who'd assumed she was fresh out of her undergrad. She didn't particularly look twenty-seven, but people said I didn't look my age, either.

It was fine that she was older than I'd thought. If anything, I was used to dating older women. I'd taken care to let Tina lead in every encounter we'd had so as not to drag her unwillingly into a situation that was over her head. *Really, this is a good thing.*

My nerves were too jangled to sleep. Billy had called while we were out to dinner, but it was after ten at that point, and I knew his school started at some ungodly hour in the morning. I finally decided that he was likely to just ignore the phone if he was asleep already and dialed his number.

He picked up after two rings. "Happy happy birthday, baby! Where were you?"

"Out."

"With?"

"Jody and Daniel and Tina and Amy."

"Wait a minute. Amy's the coach, right?"

"And Tina's the kindergarten teacher."

His voice went conspiratorial. "Do they know about one another? Ooh, Cary, a ménage à trois would make a really nice birthday present."

The thought interested me momentarily, but it was so inane, it made me laugh. "Amy and I broke up," I reminded him. "And no, she doesn't know about Tina."

"Awkward," he said, still sounding fascinated but less so than when he'd mentioned the threesome. "So you're saying you didn't get any?"

"I didn't say that."

"It was a good birthday."

I laughed. "It was okay. How're you?"

There was a silence. "Nah. Let's talk about you."

"Oh no. What's wrong?"

"No, really, it's your birthday."

"Billy."

"How was your Thanksgiving?"

"You're incorrigible. It was great. I was in Ithaca with my mom and Dave. What is going on?"

"Nothing. Have I reminded you lately that Killeen is so not Illinois?"

"At least you're somewhere near a real city."

"What, Waco?"

"I was talking about Austin," I said. "How far is it, anyway?"

"About an hour. Why?"

"Are you on the way from Austin to West Grove?"

"I guess, sort of. How come?"

"No big deal. Someone I work with drives to Austin sometimes."

"And you're thinking of tagging along to see me?" He sounded hopeful.

I felt a little guilty. "Not in the near future. I do want to meet Anita, though. Did you two have a nice Thanksgiving?"

There was another silence, this one long enough to make me wonder if we'd gotten disconnected.

"Billy?"

"It sucked, okay?" he finally muttered. "I invited her and Mike Thomas and his wife and kids over and cooked a fucking turkey."

"Um, that sounds nice. What went wrong?"

"Mike's family finally left, and it was just us, and we kept drinking, and then she started talking."

"Oh no."

"Oh yes. Cary. God, you're going to laugh at me."

"I won't. I promise, I won't."

Another silence. "She's gay, Cary. I feel so stupid. Like, hello, after living with you forever, some of the gaydar should've rubbed off or something."

"I don't think it works that way," I said delicately. "I'm sorry, Billy."

"Yeah, me too," he said tersely.

"Wait. Hold on. I thought you said she was married. She lied to you, too?"

"Oh no, she was married, just to a woman."

"How?"

"Some churches will marry gay couples. They apparently had a huge wedding, this big storybook thing, and her wife legally changed her last name to Anita's."

"Wow. That's…wow."

"They got together during their undergrad, Cary. They were together forever. That chick she was with at my party?"

"The wife."

"Right. I feel so, so stupid."

"At least you didn't try to kiss her or something."

"Yeah," he said, softly. "Yeah, that would've been bad. Anyway, to make things even more festive, the ex was back in town, and they had to hash over more crap. Just divvy up your shit and be done with it, you know?"

"I'm so sorry."

"Yep," he said, abruptly, like the case was closed. "I probably have to find a way to stay friends since we work together, but that is the end of any relationship with Coach Flores."

I nearly dropped the phone. Ears ringing, I sat up straight, staring into the darkness of my bedroom. *There must be fifty Floreses in the West Grove phone book alone.* Still, an ugly churning had begun in the pit of my stomach. "Wait, that's her name?"

"Anita Flores. Yeah."

"What's her ex's name?"

"I don't know. She said it once, but she just calls her the bitch from hell. Some girly name. Candy or Bonnie or something. I don't know. Why?"

I stared at the ceiling for a long time, and Billy waited on the other side of the line with tremendous patience, especially considering he'd been close to tears a minute before. "No reason," I said softly. "Forget I asked."

CHAPTER TWENTY-TWO

The standoff was coming. I didn't know how or where or which one of us was going to force it, but it had to happen. I needed some definitive answers about where Tina had been for the past several years and with whom she'd had her huge relationship. I needed to know if she'd really grown up in Arkansas or East Texas or somewhere else, who her friends were, and if there was any chance she might have come in contact with Liz Smith somewhere along the line. I needed to dissolve the character I'd fleshed out and accept every detail of the real Tina so I could stop making up crazy shit inside my head.

I spent the entire night tossing and turning, rolling over to stare at the clock every twenty minutes. Logically, I understood that there was nothing I could do about the matter at one, two, or three in the morning, but my head pounded with the edgy, desperate feeling that even as I lay there, time was running out. I needed to get Tina to talk. Alcohol was always a good facilitator, since it didn't take much with her. After little more than a glass of wine, her voice started to slur in a lovely sort of way, and it was usually a matter of minutes before we fell into bed together. Even if she was a cheap date, though, I was a master of avoidance. I had no idea how to remain strong enough to ask blunt questions and expect complete answers. I wished there was an easy way out, but no matter how long I thought about it, I came up with nothing.

Of course, the second the bell rang to begin class, my eyes wanted to close. Nine people didn't turn in all their homework, and half the class wouldn't freaking stay seated, let alone do their writing assignment. During math, I managed to botch a word problem. When I got notice that the computer lab was still down, I knew it was time for desperate measures. I sent Eric to knock on the staff lounge door to see if someone would pour me a cup of coffee.

That just meant that by the time we put away our math books, I had to pee so badly, I thought I'd surely die before the end of the morning. I'd planned for a science quiz, but the last thing I wanted to do was read questions about the water cycle. I tabled that in favor of working on spelling, but that wasn't much better. I still spent the last twenty minutes of the morning staring down the clock. When Daniel's kids burst out of their classroom on their way to lunch, I had everyone pack up, and we beat Bev's and Sally's classes to the cafeteria. I didn't wait to see if Jody noticed that we had entered the line completely out of order, just herded them in and left for the restroom.

Just as I approached the ladies' room door, it opened fast, straight into me. It hit my shoe instead of my face, but my assailant didn't stop to make sure. Selena stalked out, barely muttered, "Excuse me," and continued briskly down the hall without looking to see who she'd smacked.

She'd forgotten her purse. It was sitting on the little ledge above the sinks, right next to the extra paper towels, obvious as ever. I knew it was Selena's since it spent most of the day sitting in plain view on her desk like a prissy shih tzu. On any other occasion, I would have called down the hall to return it, even if she had crashed into me with no remorse, but I had to pee, right then, no negotiation. I left the purse where it was, set my lunch on the ledge next to it, and locked myself in the back stall.

It was then that the thought came to me. I did an admirable job of trying to talk myself out of it, but by the time I finished and returned to the sinks to wash up, I couldn't get it out of my head. It was my plan, the easy out for which I'd lain awake searching, the one thing that could save me from a confrontation. After drying my hands, I pulled down a second paper towel, grabbed the purse with it, and shook it gently. I heard keys. *She's an idiot for leaving it.* Without a second thought, I opened my lunch cooler. It was substantially bigger than my lunch that day, and Selena's purse fit handily.

I knew it would only make Tina suspicious about the night before if I didn't eat in the teacher's lounge. Moving quickly, I let myself back into my classroom and turned my back to the windows. I slid my shirtsleeve down over my hand, removed Selena's purse from my lunch, and tucked it into the very bottom of my backpack. Once that was locked in my drawer along with my own purse, I made sure that my shirt was hanging straight again and went to the lounge.

I still beat Jody, but Daniel and Tina were halfway through their meals. To my relief, Tina gave me a completely normal smile, and Daniel kicked a chair out from the table toward me, same as always. "I figured you were being a snob again."

"Not today."

"Well, you're late."

"The computer lab was down again."

Daniel laughed. "Another marathon morning without any port-a-potties along the way."

Tina squinted at him. "What?"

I tried not to look at her. She was wearing a clingy top, and it was chilly enough in there to see nipples. Honestly, I didn't want to think about Tina at all, but I knew I had to appear to be just as full of cloaked desire as usual. I took one fleeting glance directly at her chest, then shrugged and took a bite of my sandwich.

"All morning, no time to pee," Daniel said smugly. "From time to time, she's actually stupid enough to add a Coke to the equation."

"Coffee this morning. I couldn't stay awake."

Tina gave me a tiny grin. "Up too late last night, or were you just all worn out?"

I kicked her under the table, but Jody entered and set her tray down with a clatter at the same time. Daniel didn't seem to notice. "Have you guys heard?"

Daniel, Tina and I exchanged a look. I did not like how hushed and serious Jody's voice was.

"Kathy's father died."

The lounge became very still, and nobody knew where to look or what to say. The copier hummed industriously, and the Coke machine cycled. "That's awful," I finally said. "When did it happen?"

"Early this morning. She's taking off for Dallas after school."

Tina frowned. "She's still here?"

Jody nodded. "She's not sure how long she'll be gone, and she wanted to tie up as many loose ends as she can first."

"That's crazy," I said. "She needs to be with her mother."

"They knew it was coming," Jody reminded me. "Honestly, I think it was a relief."

We all pondered that for quite a while, chewing on sandwiches, keeping a reverent silence. It was finally Daniel, as usual, who annihilated the moment. "So when does the 'Lop assume power?"

Jody's nose wrinkled. "Can't you smell it already?"

It was a quiet afternoon for once. I didn't think the kids had heard, but everyone was strangely subdued anyway. By dismissal time, I had a headache and was exhausted. I'd intended to stick around to do some extra work, but I knew it was useless. Twenty minutes after the bell, I went to the office to sign out.

I was immediately sorry. Kathy was leaning on the counter looking absolutely wiped out, her hair mussed, her arms crossed, and Selena was crumpled in a heap at her desk, crying. I felt a nasty twinge of remorse and considered turning right back around, but it was too late. Both of them had seen me.

"I'm so sorry about your father," I said.

Kathy smiled tiredly. "Thanks. We knew it was coming. It was just a question of when."

"Is there anything I can do?"

She shook her head, but I felt her eyes lingering on me as I signed out and pulled a memo out of my box. "Thank you, though."

I nodded and stood there awkwardly. I couldn't just ignore Selena, but I wasn't sure what to say to someone who hated the very sight of me when she was busy bawling her eyes out in public in front of someone whose father had just passed away. Finally, I nodded toward her. "What's wrong?"

Kathy shook her head. "Her purse was stolen."

I let my jaw drop just a little and turned my focus back to Selena. "From here?"

Selena threw her hands in the air. "I don't know what happened. I had it before lunch, then this afternoon, it was just gone."

"Did you leave it here during lunch?"

Kathy nodded. "We think so. Anyone could have walked in off the street."

"All your credit cards?"

Selena's eyes went wide, eyeliner smeared two inches down her face. "All my credit cards, my driver's license, and my checkbook."

"Oh, man," I whispered. "Make sure you call them right away."

"I did." She sniffled. "The credit card companies and the bank and the police. That's what I've been doing all afternoon."

Instead of filing your nails. "I'm sorry."

"Keys, too," Kathy murmured in a voice that reminded me of our talk just days before.

"Keys to the building?"

"The building, the office, everything else," Kathy agreed.

"Can maintenance do anything about that?"

She sighed. "Eventually, we need to have the whole building rekeyed, but I don't see that happening until the summer. Physical plant can't even change the office locks until next week."

"Wow," I said, then turned to Selena one more time. "You're sure it's gone? You couldn't have just left it in the staff room or something?"

Selena sobbed. "We've checked everywhere. I know I didn't take it anywhere with me today."

Okay, just trying to help. I nodded gently, maintaining eye contact for just one more moment. "Can I do anything? Do you need a ride home?"

Selena stared at me, her face contorted into an expression of complete shock. I wouldn't even call her *ma'am,* and here I was offering to take her home? "My husband's coming with spare keys to the truck," she told me. "Thank you, though."

I nodded, finally turning to go. "Get some rest. Both of you."

That tiny twinge of guilt plagued me during the ride home, but by the time I'd arrived at my apartment, it was mostly gone. Selena was a pretty big idiot for leaving her purse out on the ledge in the first place, let alone for forgetting it there. Mine never left my locked bottom drawer during the day. Obviously, anything could happen in a place like Bush.

I didn't go through the purse until after dinner. With the TV playing and the shades pulled, I emptied its contents onto my packing crate coffee table and perused them with a dull interest.

The keys were all I cared about. Only the secretaries, principals, and two of the custodians had keys to the office, and those were what I needed. I did tuck Selena's driver's license away for future use. The picture was one of those really bad ones that could be mistaken for anyone at all. After that, I sat with my scissors, cutting Selena's checkbook and credit cards into little pieces. When they were sufficiently unrecognizable, I fed them into my kitchen garbage along with a smattering of coffee grounds, orange peels, and leftovers past their prime and brought the whole works to the trash. After a few minutes of correcting homework, I went to bed earlier than usual.

❖

I did sleep that night, which probably said something rotten about my character. I was out of bed by five thirty, and I showered and ironed my clothes as calmly as if it was any other day of the week. It was barely six by the time I grabbed a piece of toast for breakfast and got on the road.

The highway was dark and still save for an occasional eighteen-wheeler. The heater in my car refused to cooperate, and I was shivering by the time I began to pass under streetlights and the lonely neon of the heart of town. I did not feel afraid, though, just cold. I took a roundabout route, driving past liquor stores, pawn shops, and abandoned homes in the neighborhood surrounding Bush until I found a tiny Mexican grocery two blocks east of the school. The drive was dirt and gravel, and one of the windows was broken and patched with a haphazard combination of plywood and duct tape. It was just what I was looking for, something completely unremarkable from the street with a large dumpster out back. I pulled in as far as I could and left the car running while I opened the top and tossed in Selena's purse, empty of everything but the pocketbook itself. My heart began to pound only as I backed out onto the street through a cloud of my own dust and watched the grocery loom still and silent in my rearview mirror.

I circled the block before pulling onto the grounds at Bush. Both parking lots were empty, but I spotted Marvin's truck on the street near one of the back doors. Luck still on my side, I left my car across the parking lot from my usual spot, where it wasn't so easy to see from Fourth, and unlocked the D-wing door.

It was easy enough to set up my desk and lock away my purse without turning on the lights in my classroom, but the main hall was much darker, and I could only hope that nothing was in my way. Morning was just a suggestion outside, and the hints of ambivalent gray peeking through the windows at the end of each wing were too dim to be of any help. The section of South Fourth visible through the large bay of glass doors in the front foyer was absolutely still. I didn't like not knowing Marvin's whereabouts, but I didn't have time to go searching classrooms and the boiler room for him. My minutes were numbered.

The third key I tried opened the office door. It was pitch-black in there, even darker than the hall. I made sure the door locked again behind me, then felt for the counter to get my bearings. Several faint mechanical humming sounds came from the copy room to my right, and the clock atop the intercom system ticked loudly. I slid Selena's key ring back into my left pocket and took one last look behind me to make sure the foyer was still empty.

I had a little flashlight on my key chain, a freebie from one of the textbook publishers. It had come in handy on the nights Amy had kicked me out of bed at one in the morning, and I'd forgotten to leave the outside light on at my apartment. That morning, I'd taken it off the ring so I wouldn't have all my keys jingling as I went about my business. Its tiny beam didn't do much in the way of lighting my path, but it was at least enough to confirm that I really was alone.

Student files were in cabinets behind Selena's desk, but I was certain the staff files were housed elsewhere. Dunlop's door was closed, and I couldn't picture where he might keep something like that, so I decided to start with Kathy's office. Using the flashlight sporadically, I moved across the room, past Selena's desk, past the mailboxes, and nudged Kathy's door with my elbow. It swung with a tiny sweeping sound, metal against carpet. Once inside, I returned it to its almost-closed state and shined the flashlight across the room with far less caution. Against the wall to my left were three tall gray cabinets with a glass bowl of candy and several framed photos of Kathy's dogs on top. The second drawer of the third one read *Active, A-M.*

I did not anticipate that the drawer would be standing open, but I really had no idea if any of the small keys on Selena's ring would work. *Don't make me pick the lock. I'm in way too deep to leave without getting what I want.* I swallowed hard and pushed that thought out of my head as one of the small keys fit, and the lock turned.

I'd been careful not to touch the cabinet itself, but once I was inside, I pushed my sleeves out of the way and leafed through with my bare hands, feeling hot and cold and sweaty and slightly nauseated all at the same time. It was difficult to read anything in the dull beam from my flashlight, and I considered turning on the desk lamp if not the overhead light, but it was twenty of seven, and I was cutting it dangerously close. If someone was looking over my shoulder wherever I went, I knew it was naive of me to think they'd stop for a few minutes now to give me the upper hand.

Jody had been there forever; the file marked *Finnegan* seemed to go on for miles. By the time I passed it, my hands were trembling, and I had a wicked paper cut down the side of one finger. *Flores,* the next one read. I pulled the drawer open all the way and slid out the whole file.

It wasn't thick at all, maybe ten pages. Tina hadn't reached an evaluation period yet, and all the paperwork in there looked to be copies of transcripts, recommendations, and the forms she'd filled out upon being hired.

I turned to one of those pages and scanned it carefully, sucking on my finger before it could bleed. *Flores*, it read, *Christina "Tina" L.* I pondered for a moment that she'd gone to the trouble of specifying what people should call her. No maiden name was listed. The date of birth was the same one I'd seen on her driver's license. She had, in fact, completed her master's degree at University of Texas, Austin, in May of 2001, but her bachelor's was from Vanderbilt and dated May of 1996. I flipped back to look for her resume, wondering what she'd done and where she'd been in the interim, but on the way, I came across an address in Austin. I grabbed a sheet from Kathy's notepad, scribbled it down hastily, and stuffed it in my pocket along with Selena's keys. There was an evaluation from outside of Nashville and a few references, all referring to Christina Flores. Somehow, I knew I really didn't want to see any more, but I turned the last page and found a small stub of paper with emergency contact information. I completely expected to see Anita Flores' name on it, but that was not the case. *Carl and Peggy Broward, Memphis, Tennessee*, it read, clear as day. *Parents*.

Chapter Twenty-three

I KNOW ABOUT YOU. The words rang shrilly in my head. I stuffed the file back into the drawer, not stopping to look up or even breathe until everything was back exactly where it belonged. I slid the drawer in and felt it click. As I stood there, reeling from what I'd just seen, that click echoed somewhere outside Kathy's office. The screaming inside my head stopped abruptly.

Before I could make a move, the main office door squeaked open, and the lights flickered on. Adrenaline shot through my body. I searched the room desperately but found no way out and no good excuse for my presence. For lack of any solution whatsoever, I snuck behind another filing cabinet, hoping whoever it was would just go away. Then the thought hit me: *Selena doesn't have keys.*

I stood there in the corner, light-headed and sick to my stomach. I was terrified to breathe in case it might be audible. A chair scraped outside in the office, a few desk drawers opened, then closed. Papers shuffled. I touched the file cabinet next to me, steadied myself, and forced a breath. It felt shaky, rattly, and made me feel even more like I was going to pass out. Listening intently, I forced it out again, way out, to ensure the next breath would be deep enough to keep me upright.

If it wasn't Selena, it had to be Dunlop. If it was Dunlop, I was screwed. I hadn't seen him in Kathy's office the afternoon before, which gave him even more reason to come in early and piss on the territory. I knew I had about thirty seconds before he'd waltz in, flip on the lights, and catch me there.

I scanned the room with a new fervor. There was a strip of windows near the top of one wall, but they were only about a foot tall. If I could even figure out how to get up there and open one, it was unlikely that I'd be able to scramble through. I considered hiding under the desk but feared Dunlop would sit and park his crotch in front of my face, and I'd be stuck all morning. There was a small closet on the other side of the room, its sliding door standing partially open. It didn't look roomy, but I thought it might be my best bet.

There was more shuffling of papers outside Kathy's door, then the sound of someone flipping switches on the PA system directly on the other side of the wall. As the unit began to hum gently, I heard a distinct clicking sound against the plastic control panel. It sounded like fingernails.

Oh thank God. When I heard the footsteps retreat, I peeked just a tiny bit around the edge of the door and saw Selena messing with the absentee notebook on the counter. I leaned back against the wall feeling relieved. At least it wasn't Dunlop.

The seconds were ticking, though. Sweat began to run down my back, and it took all the self-control I had to keep from staring out the gap between the door and the frame. I heard Selena sharpen a pencil, open and close a desk drawer, and shuffle more papers. Then, to my absolute horror, her footsteps came directly toward Kathy's office.

I ducked back behind the file cabinet, my stomach lurching. I tasted my breakfast and swallowed hard, willing it to stay put. The lights snapped on, and the door swung open. I hugged the side of the file cabinet as hard as I could, praying for just one tiny moment of invisibility. Selena breezed in, set the papers on Kathy's desk and just as quickly breezed right back out without even looking in my direction.

When I dared to let out my breath this time, the edges of my vision began to go red. I thought I heard another door open, then a click, a whirr, and an even thicker humming sound. When I finally dared to peer back out the door, Selena was in the copy room, monkeying with one of the Xerox machines. Her back was turned to me.

I had to do it. Knees shaking worse than they did after my meetings with Dunlop, I made a break for it. I left Kathy's office and rounded the corner by Selena's desk in three steps.

She turned. "Oh, Miss Smith," she said, clutching her chest and almost smiling. "You scared me! I didn't even hear you come in."

I snatched the pen from the sign-in sheet so quickly, my hand got tangled in its chain. I had to look at the clock three times before I could process what it said. "Oh, I'm sorry," I mumbled, trying to smile back. "Did you ever find your purse?"

She sighed. "No, Marvin let me in this morning. The police think it was just one of those things, you know? I'm locking it up from now on."

I nodded briskly and started for the door. "That's a good idea."

"Miss Smith?"

I stopped short. "Yes, ma'am?"

If she noticed it was the first time I'd called her *ma'am*, Selena didn't show it. "Are you feeling all right? You look a little pale."

I swallowed again, shrugging innocently. My chest and throat had begun to tighten, and I could feel my lower lip wanting to tremble. "Didn't get much sleep last night, I guess."

"Well, have a good day."

"Thanks. You too."

The moment I stepped into the foyer, I sucked in the cool, dark air desperately. My eyes stung and threatened to spill over. It was still very early, but I set off for my room at once, begging the tears to wait until I was behind closed doors.

I might have made it, but not ten paces later, I ran smack into Amy. I had no idea what she was doing there at that hour, but she was carrying a huge hoe with a splintery wooden handle and seemed to be on her way to B-hall. Fortunately, she was paying attention to where she was going, so we didn't physically collide.

"Hey," she said. "What're you up to so early?"

"I had some stuff to take care of," I said, my voice very small and strained. I barely had the words out before the tears started.

"Honey, what's wrong?" For the first time in our acquaintance, Amy Davis did not scan the building for potential onlookers before acting. In a beautiful, fluid motion, she leaned the hoe against the wall and pulled me close, wrapping her arms around my body in such a selfless, protective manner that it only served to make me cry harder.

We remained that way for a long time. I couldn't stop crying, my stomach ached mercilessly, and I was terrified of what would happen if someone like Dunlop came by because I knew I was going to have a hard enough time explaining my meltdown to Amy. All I could do was hang on, and Amy didn't make a move to let go until I had to straighten to catch my breath.

"Walk with me," she said, picking up the hoe again and leading me down B-hall. "It'll help to get some air."

We moved slowly down the hall, past the second and third-grade classrooms, all the way to the very end, where Amy let us outside onto the back lawn. The horizon was barely turning pink and yellow, and someone's rooster was crowing in the distance.

"I'm sorry," I whispered. "I don't know what's wrong with me."

"You're kind of warm," Amy said. "You're probably coming down with something."

I shook my head. "Everything is just really fucked-up all of a sudden."

Amy watched me for a moment as if expecting me to elaborate on that. When I didn't, she shrugged and squinted toward the back fence. "I still think you're coming down with something."

"What're you doing here so early?"

"Jody has her stuff all over the gym for the next few weeks, so we're outside again." She slapped the handle of the hoe against her empty palm once and nodded toward the lawn. "I'm back on rattlesnake duty."

That was a repulsive thought. I was glad that Amy was keeping the blade a good distance away from me. "Nice."

She grinned for just a second at my disgust, then checked her wristwatch and reached for her phone. "Look, it's still really early.

I don't know what's going on, but you don't need to be here, Cary. Just call in and go home."

I stared at her cell phone, the very one she'd used to unwittingly torment me so. I'd called for a sub only once in three and a half years. "I don't even know the number."

She dialed and handed me the phone; I had no choice. I did appreciate it when the woman on the other end said she'd try Mrs. Shore, but I still felt like a gigantic fraud as I hung up and handed the phone back.

"There. That wasn't so hard, was it? Get out of here. I'll tell Selena you're gone."

"I already saw Selena."

"Looking like this? I'll tell her you're gone."

"Thank you," I told her, hugging her tightly again despite the hoe.

"You're welcome." I knew the look in her eyes. I'd seen it many times before. She wanted so badly to know what was going through my mind that she could hardly stand it, but as always, she did not ask. She merely squeezed my shoulder and turned me in the direction of the parking lot. "Now go home."

❖

I didn't want to know. I didn't want to know, but it was out there now. The mantra was back, the one from my whiteboard, blending in with the engine sounds and the traffic, creating new variations, each at least as hollow as the original. I tried turning up the radio until it was so loud, my car shuddered with the bass, but even that could not drown out the words. It made my head hurt worse, so I turned it off again and let the mantra flow freely until I could see and taste it.

I waited patiently for the shiny red lowrider ahead of me to creep over the railroad crossing near 21st, watching its too-small tires disappear entirely beneath the undercarriage of the car, listening for the scrape of the tailpipe against the pavement. I heard the strains of Tejano even though both of us had our windows rolled up, and I wondered if this guy was trying to get rid of an earworm, too.

I stopped at the traffic light at Grove, stuck behind another car so I couldn't make a right. My turn signal pulsed rhythmically, creating an accompaniment to the words. A woman was walking an obese, hairy spaniel down the sidewalk next to me, her hair teased into a perfect duplication of every seventh-grade cheerleader in my Central Illinois junior high school, circa nineteen eighty-six. She was wearing a T-shirt covered with a sequined American flag, probably a home job courtesy of the Bedazzler, and blue jeans hiked up so tightly into her crotch that it hurt to look at them. For the first time ever, I did not wonder what was wrong with this person. I didn't so much as roll my eyes. I looked at her furry dog, thought nothing new, and waited for my light to change. It was barely seven thirty in the morning, and it felt like I'd been awake for a week.

Amy had been right in forcing me to go home. After a drive home full of emptiness, I spent an hour tucked into a little ball on the bathroom floor, willing my stomach to settle and my tears to stop. I hoped dimly that they'd gotten Mrs. Shore to cover my class after all.

Once I dared to leave the safety of the chilly tile floor, I abandoned my school clothes in a damp, wrinkled heap and changed into sweats and a T-shirt. I lay in bed, pulled the covers all the way over my head, and tried to sleep, but it didn't happen. The words pulsed through my body like blood or oxygen, like something essential, and visions of the past two months played back in my mind without invitation. Our first date at the Mexican restaurant. The way she'd looked at me, held me, touched my body. I felt betrayed and so incredibly, incredibly stupid. She'd surely been playing me from the very beginning.

It was much later that I crept back out from under my covers and to the front of a bookshelf that housed a King James Bible, Tolkien, and Ayn Rand, half a dozen old photo albums, and all of my childhood yearbooks. I settled there on the floor and slid my junior year annual off the shelf as I had just days before. Its textured green and white cover was far less worn than those from most other years. Up until the previous weekend, there had been nothing inside it that I'd wanted to see. I perused the black-and-white photos of Memphis, of the school itself, of homecoming, and glossed over the few signatures I'd collected. Most of them were versions of the same thing written in different hands with different ballpoint pens: *I don't know you very well, but it was good having you in class. Have a great summer.*

I moved past the candids and the group shots and turned to the junior class. She was at the top of the second page, third from the left. The small dark font in the margin read *Chrissy Broward*. It was a fair picture, but according to my dim, piecemeal memories, it did not do her justice. Her hair was short, strategically messy in that perfect, popular-girl sort of way, and very blond. Her smile was lovely but subdued under a generous amount of visible teenage angst. I would have been certain there was some mistake, that this could not possibly be the same person if it wasn't for the eyes. They were huge and dark, imploring in such an insistent, personal way that staring into them on an eleven-year-old black-and-white photograph gave me the same chills I'd felt when Tina held my eye contact that first day in the staff lounge.

My real interactions with Chrissy had been minimal. I'd spent more time watching her than the chalkboard in math class, but she'd sat ahead of me and two rows over, so I was far more familiar with her silhouette, the back of her shoulders, and the detached, almost surly way she'd regarded the top of her desk throughout every class. She'd never raised her hand but always knew the answer when the teacher called on her. I'd seen a very different side of her in the cafeteria with her friends, giggling amid their requisite cans of diet soda and minimalist lunches, flirting with the cutest boys. We'd spoken literally six words to one another, once upon entering our math classroom, the other time the only day Natalie had ever brought me inside the Broward home. Frankly, I could not believe she had recognized me.

My photo was several pages later. According to it, Liz Smith was small, with mousy, shoulder-length hair, shy dark eyes, and nondescript, girl-jock clothing. I still wasn't used to having the braces off my teeth, and I'd just barely exited that awful phase where my face was a constant mess, and my breasts felt awkward. I'd run cross-country that fall, so I did have a few friends, but they were nowhere near the social status of Chrissy Broward.

I wondered how on earth she'd found me. Billy had once mentioned that Anita's friend-turned-wife, the one with some completely unremarkable girly name, seemed to have an odd fascination with the picture of us from grad school, but the notion that somebody I knew for just a few critical moments could have married someone that my college roommate fell in love with ten years and several hundred miles later seemed completely absurd. It was the stuff of fairy tales, an impossible story based entirely upon far too many coincidences. Maybe other people's lives were like that but not mine.

I slid the yearbook back into its place on the shelf, an entire year of other people's stories documented concisely and tucked between Tampa and Columbus. Somewhere, Tina had the same green and white book, identical to mine, aside from having twenty times the signatures. I wondered if it was hidden somewhere out of view in her apartment or if it sat in a dusty box in the attic of her parents' house. I wondered if she'd pored over my picture, marveling over how much or how little I'd changed. I wondered if she'd pored over that picture, hating my guts.

I was still in the same spot, knees pulled to my chest, staring at the colorful row of annuals without seeing them when I heard a knock on my door. I was not in the mood to see anyone, and I almost ignored it, but I decided it would be just like Dunlop to leave school on his lunch hour to make sure I was, indeed, sick in bed. I dragged myself up and through the living room, both of my legs thanking me for reinstating their blood flow with pins and needles.

Lucy from next door stood on the landing wearing tight, faded jeans and a soft-looking leather jacket. Bugsy was, as always, under one arm. "Hey, girl. Are you okay? We just got back from the vet, and I saw your car in the lot."

"I stayed home sick."

"Are you contagious?"

If you're worried, just turn around and go home. "I doubt it."

"Let me run home and make you some soup, then. You've been having such a rough time, and me and Bobby keep saying we should do something, you know, have you over for dinner or something."

Though my stomach still felt angry, lunch sounded good. I considered the offer but shrugged shyly. "Really, you don't have to do that."

"No, let me," she insisted. "I'll be right back."

I wasn't sure what to expect, but twenty minutes later, Lucy and I were sitting on my sofa eating Campbell's chicken noodle out of tan pottery mugs and watching the travesty that was midday television. At first, Bugsy whined and jiggled so intensely, I was afraid he was having a seizure, but Lucy sighed and told him to quit begging. Once he accepted the idea that neither one of us was going to share with him, he curled up between our feet on the carpet and let those enormous eyes close. I was jealous.

"So what's wrong, girl?" Lucy finally asked. "Your mind's been on something for a long time."

I stared dully at a commercial promising to consolidate my debt into one easy monthly payment. "You know when you're totally convinced you want to know the truth about something, then you're sorry when you learn it?"

"What kind of thing?"

"Something about someone."

Lucy considered that for a while. "I always thought Bobby's aunt Maria really liked me, but I made some joke once when we were with his mom, you know, something about what those guys really think of me. So she out and told me that Maria thought I was stupid and dressed like a whore."

While it wasn't quite what I was getting at, I did feel Lucy's pain. "I'm sorry."

"Yeah, we don't get along so well anymore. To think we've been married for four years now, and she's been putting on the nicey-nice face all this time. The second you learn what somebody thinks or what they're really like? It changes everything."

I nodded, turning back to the television. "It does."

"Is this about the chick with the blue truck?"

I nodded again.

"Did you guys break up?"

"Not yet."

"Was it something you did or something she did?"

"Both."

"Maybe you guys can just forgive one another and make up."

That was entirely logical, but I knew I didn't deserve forgiveness, and I wasn't so sure I could forgive her. Instead of trying to explain, I sort of nodded as if to imply that would be nice.

"You're a good person, Cary," Lucy told me. "It's going to work out with someone."

❖

Amy called at five. I'd just let the machine take a call from Tina, and I felt a little guilty about answering one and not the other, but I didn't know what to say to Tina yet, and I felt like I owed Amy one. She asked me how I was doing, and when I told her I'd probably be back at school the next day, she laughed.

"I wouldn't bother if I were you. The 'Lop called a staff meeting after school."

"On a Friday? What for?"

"'Cause if Kathy's back on Tuesday, he won't get a chance to run one."

"That's ridiculous."

"I know it. Look, I don't want to keep you, but I just wanted to know that you were feeling better."

"I am," I told her. "Thank you so much for this morning."

"You're welcome," she said softly. After a moment of silence, she added, "Take care of yourself, okay?"

I wasn't stupid. I could tell by the tone of her voice that she wasn't anywhere close to over me, and for once, I found immense solace in it.

It was the Thursday after school got out for summer, a beautiful, sunny day, warm, without a hint of the oppressive heat to come.

Neither Natalie or I was scheduled to work that day, and the very air smelled like freedom. My mother didn't leave until three, so we went to Natalie's house for the first time ever.

It was a large, brick two-story with a porch swing and intricate shutters flanking each window, the epitome of southern decor. I was a bit nervous about being there, so I left my car a good distance down the block. Natalie's room was on the second floor, so it was unlikely that I would be able to pitch out a window and pull off a clean escape if her parents arrived home, but the idea did make me smile.

Natalie's parents did not come home, and we were together through the afternoon. Her sister did come home, but by the time we heard her downstairs, we were clothed and on our way back out.

We met on the staircase. It was a long one with dark, shiny wooden banisters. I hugged the wall a little tighter as Chrissy passed, although there was plenty of room for both of us. I could tell that she'd just finished her lifeguard shift somewhere. She was carrying a towel and a backpack, and her skin was very tan.

She looked straight at me for a second, just long enough for a tiny flicker of almost-recognition to register in her eyes. "Hi," she said, her indifferent tone suggesting that even if she did place my face, she didn't actually know my name.

"Hi," I whispered back, wishing I could disappear into the wallpaper pattern.

Our exchange was over just like that. Chrissy turned directly to her sister and continued in a very different tone. "Jonathan just pulled in, and he looks pissed."

"Whatever. I don't have anything to say to him."

"Well, I'm not getting rid of him," Chrissy warned.

"I didn't ask you to," Natalie returned lightly.

I intended to get out of the way, to let Natalie and Jonathan hash out whatever was the problem this time, but I didn't get a chance.

The bell did not ring, there was no knock, no asking. The front door flew open so hard and fast, it smacked against the wall, and Jonathan McGrath was in the foyer, his face red with anger. "Where the hell have you been?"

Natalie stepped deliberately between Jonathan and me and folded her arms over her chest. "I'm fine, thanks. Of course you can come in."

I heard the floorboards squeak somewhere above us. When I looked back, I caught a glimpse of Chrissy retreating to her room.

"Shut up with the cute shit. Where have you been?"

"That's none of your business."

"None of my business?" he continued in a loud, mocking rant. "It's Thursday? Todd's band is playing at the HiTone tonight, and you said you'd be there for the sound check?"

"I told you a week ago that I'd think about going," Natalie said, her voice going so low, it made Jonathan's yelling sound even more out of control. "The last time I heard from you was Monday, and we were fighting about something—"

"And you said you'd go."

"I did not say that."

He flung his baseball cap at the wall and threw his hands in the air. "What the fuck is wrong with you?"

"Just stop it, okay?"

The room fell frighteningly silent, and Jonathan bent to pick up his hat. On his way up, his eyes landed on me for the first time. "Who the hell are you?"

I had no answer. Emily Dickinson popped into my head, but Jonathan struck me as the type who wouldn't appreciate my waxing poetic. I could smell alcohol on his breath, and his pupils were huge.

Natalie glanced at me, her face absolutely without emotion. "That's Liz. I work with her."

Jonathan threw me an impatient look, as if he didn't remember me existing at Blockbuster, and I wouldn't matter even if he did. "You weren't working today."

Natalie's eyes narrowed. "You went looking for me?"

"What am I supposed to do when you don't show up?"

"Look, if all you're going to do is yell at me, you can leave. You're making an ass of yourself."

He stared at her, an ugly look of disbelief on his face. "Like your sister's paying attention."

Wow, I really am invisible. A voice came from upstairs: "Get out of the house, Jonathan."

"Look," Natalie said, holding the screen door open for him. "You don't need to know where I am twenty-four hours a day."

"So you can go whoring around with other guys?"

"*Fuck you.*" Natalie turned to me, her jaw clenched tightly. "You better go."

I looked between them, wanting to help, but I was scared and uncomfortable, so I jumped at the opportunity. "I'll see you."

"Yeah, run on home," Jonathan muttered to me.

His condescending tone made me seethe, but what I saw out of the corner of my eye made even madder. Natalie followed me out, and as she passed Jonathan, he grabbed her by the wrist. When she wrenched her hand away, he shoved her on the shoulder, hard enough that she hit the door frame.

I stopped on the stairs, but Natalie looked at me with empty, disengaged eyes and nodded for me to go. I turned and left, wanting to run the distance between the front step and my car. Down the block, I could still hear them arguing, although I could no longer hear words.

Run on home. *Goddamn it.* I'd just turned my keys in the ignition when Jonathan's pickup roared past. I expected him to be alone, especially since he was still in such a huff, but Natalie was sitting in the passenger seat. Where the hell was she going with him? The sound check? His house? Some other place where he'd get drunker and higher and beat her up? Without considering what I was doing, I pulled out after them.

I stayed a good distance behind but kept Jonathan's truck in my sights. He turned onto one of the main streets for a few blocks, then, to my dismay, made a right onto another residential street, forcing me to hang back even farther. Now, I really wondered where they were going. I didn't know where Jonathan lived, but I had in my head that it was a wealthier neighborhood. Even so far back, I could tell they were still fighting.

I was nearly two full blocks behind, hoping Jonathan wouldn't turn and disappear from my radar, when he stopped so suddenly, the brakes squealed. The door swung open, and Natalie began to climb out. Had she seen me? Did she know I was following them and could take her home again?

Before I could panic or even pull to the side of the road, Jonathan gave her a push, forceful enough to send her sprawling on the pavement, and stepped on the gas again. He began to take off, the passenger side door hanging open, but halfway down the block, I saw brake lights again. For a sickening moment, I thought he was going to back over her, but he pulled to the curb, got out of his pickup, slammed the passenger side door, and stalked back toward where he'd left Natalie.

I nosed quickly toward the side of the road and ducked behind a parked white sedan. It blocked my car from view, but it also prevented me from getting a good look at what was going on. I saw Jonathan yank Natalie off the ground and heard yelling, but I couldn't make out words.

I unbuckled my seat belt and strained to get a better view until I was kneeling with my head pressed against the roof of the car. They'd stopped between houses where a cement drainage ditch cut under the street. At the edge of the pavement was a guardrail, tall enough to keep cars on the road but short enough to easily facilitate a nasty fall. Jonathan had backed Natalie up against the railing and hit her across the face.

I couldn't stand it any longer. I climbed back into the driver's seat and considered pulling up next to them and trying to get Natalie into my car, but I felt very cold and tingly, and instead of putting the car in gear, I took the keys out of the ignition. My left hand drifted between the seat and the door frame, touched metal, and curled around what it found.

Slowly, silently, I slid out of the car and pressed my weight against the door to close it without slamming. I walked past the white sedan, the crowbar in my hand, past three houses, across a street, past five more. Now, I could hear words.

"Who're you fucking?" The neckline of Jonathan's shirt was wet with sweat, and both his hands were tight on her shoulders.

Natalie sniffled and gasped for breath, but it was impossible for her to struggle too hard and keep at least one hand on the railing behind her. "Let go of me, you asshole," she said. *"Let go."*

His voice rose. "Who are you fucking?"

"I'm not fucking anybody."

"Don't lie to me, you goddamn bitch." His voice was like ice, and as he said the words, he let go with his right hand and slapped her hard across the face. She was already bleeding.

I was standing just down the street, maybe one house down. The adrenaline rose higher and higher, past my chest, past my throat, until I was dizzy with it. I couldn't feel my legs or arms, but oh, I could feel the adrenaline. "Let go of her."

Both of them jumped. Natalie's eyes focused on me for just a second, and in the midst of such a horrible look of surrender was one tiny ounce of pleading. I could not tell if she was asking for help or merely begging me not to watch.

Jonathan, on the other hand, turned slowly, very obviously intending to hide his surprise. His words were mocking. "You're going to make me?"

I didn't answer. I took several steps forward, the crowbar still at my side. "Let go of her right now."

I could see the exact moment when he realized what I had in my hand. I didn't expect a reaction, perhaps just more derision. Something made him back up, though. Maybe there was a look in my eyes, maybe it was the way I was advancing on him. One way or another, he backed up, tripped over the curb, yanking Natalie with him as he steadied himself.

"I said, right now."

He stumbled down the embankment into the drainage ditch. I followed along, my legs working on their own. Natalie was somewhere behind me. I couldn't remember when he'd let her go. The ditch was dry except for a trickle of muddy water in the very middle. It was dark where it tunneled under the street, but we weren't in there. We were in the waning sunlight, our shadows long against the concrete walls.

I'd never hit something so hard in my life.

The impact made Jonathan crumple to the ground and nearly knocked the crowbar out of my hands. I looked up, expecting to see horror in Natalie's eyes, but they were empty, cold, somehow agreeable. The side of her face was dark red where he'd hit her.

She looked at me.

I looked at her.

In a stilted, staggering motion somewhere down between us, Jonathan's hand moved to his head. There was blood. He didn't look up, but his words were anguished. "What the hell?"

I raised the crowbar and hit him again, again, again, until he did not move anymore.

CHAPTER TWENTY-FOUR

At seven thirty in the morning, I pulled into my usual parking spot in the back lot at George Herbert Walker Bush elementary school. I struggled with the D-wing door, let myself into my classroom, and continued down the hall to sign in. I paged through the notes Mrs. Shore had left from the previous day, checked my lesson plans, and went to monitor the hall as children started filing in from outside.

It was just another day.

I took attendance, collected homework, led the Pledge of Allegiance, and sat quietly while Selena read the morning announcements. I was about to ask about what had gone on in the world over the past two days when Eddie's hand shot into the air.

"Where were you yesterday? Were you sick?"

"Indeed. I assume you didn't give Mrs. Shore a hard time?"

"My mom had her for third grade," Morgan said wondrously.

"You really were sick?" Nestor asked. "When my brother had you, he said you were never gone, not even one day."

Christian made a zombie face and pawed at Nestor with his hands spread like claws. "They say she's not real."

"Oh, I'm real," I muttered, strolling down the aisle until I reached his desk. I stood there, arms folded, keeping one eye on him. "What did I miss?"

"Twelve sheets of practice TAAS," Christian said. "Don't get me wrong, we don't want you to leave ever again."

I didn't mention that they would've gotten those pages one way or another. "What else?"

"Colton Terry's brother choked on a sour ball at lunch," David announced. "Ms. Finnegan had to do CPR."

"She had to do the Heimlich maneuver," Chelsea corrected in a *duh* tone, as if that completely negated the validity of his statement.

"Well, if it hadn't worked, she would've had to do CPR," David insisted. "His face totally turned purple, and everyone thought he was kidding at first."

Shannon raised her hand. "What happens when you're not married, and you get sick? Did your mom come over?"

"Nope. It's very quiet," I told her. "I got a lot of sleep. My neighbor did bring me soup yesterday," I added, lest they think I was some freakish hermit.

Gina exchanged a sly look with the other girls. "Is he cute?"

"She's married," I said, "but her husband's pretty good-looking."

We made our way through language arts, math, and library time, then worked quietly on group assignments until lunchtime. That was the moment I'd been dreading. I could pretend this really was just another day until I had to sit six inches from Chrissy Broward's side and act like I had half an idea of what to say. I considered returning to my classroom like I had so many days before that October, to duck the whole issue and eat lunch alone.

When we reached the cafeteria, Jody waved from the middle of the room and gave me an anticipatory look, asking wordlessly if I was all better. I gave her a thumbs-up, then made a Heimliching motion back at her. Her eyes went wide, and she waved her hands excitedly, telling me she'd share the details later. I turned to go, but that extra ten second delay brought me to the door at exactly the moment the bilingual kindergarten was joining the lunch line.

My stomach clenched the moment I saw Tina. I looked straight at her as she bent low to speak with a little girl dressed in striped purple pants, but I did not see the long brown hair, the dark makeup, the Friday jeans and almost-conservative blouse. I saw that yearbook photo, the short blond locks, the ripped denim, the angry, heartbroken teenager who had been left behind. I blinked hard, willing that vision to go away. It would not.

"Hey," she said, cutting her class loose and returning to the hall with me, thankfully oblivious to the drama playing out inside my head. "How're you doing?"

"Okay," I said, although I knew there was no way that would seem authentic when I couldn't even look at her. "Much better."

"Good. I got worried when I didn't hear back from you."

"I'm sorry. I was trying to get some sleep, so I turned the ringer off. By the time I saw that I had messages, it was really late."

"Well, I missed you. What're you up to tonight?"

I nodded distractedly at two of the fourth-grade teachers as they passed close enough to hear our conversation. "We have a staff meeting, don't we?"

One of Tina's eyebrows jumped. "At three fifteen. How long do you expect it to last?"

I tried to laugh. "Well, knowing Dunlop, we could be here all night."

"You want to catch dinner?"

I didn't. The only thing I wanted to do less than go out to dinner with her was have sex with her. I had no excuses, though, so I shrugged. "Okay."

She paused for a second before the staff lounge door. "Don't sound so excited," she muttered, then nudged my arm, *just kidding.* "I'll pick you up at six."

The afternoon was not fantastic. Marisol and I had to diffuse an argument between two groups of students in the hallway directly after school, and we were late to the staff meeting. Dunlop chastised us for that, then barked at Jody, Daniel, and me to get off the cabinets. By the time he'd discussed two issues Kathy had already covered and read through a revised schedule for the week before Christmas break, my feet hurt, and I just wanted to go home. Dunlop ended the meeting by asking us to be more vigilant about locking up our valuables and monitoring the hallways. In the past week alone, a parent volunteer's phone had gone missing, and Selena's purse had been stolen.

It would have been nice if I could have avoided Selena entirely, but she was taking up a collection to pay for flowers and a donation in Kathy's father's name. There were several people crowding around when I slipped her a check, but she still caught my eye.

"Glad to see you back, Miss Smith."

"Thanks," I told her, sneaking away as quickly as possible. Her words sounded genuine enough, but Dunlop was close by, and I didn't want to take any chances that she'd mention how strange it was that I'd been in the building before calling in sick the previous morning.

I'd just tossed my bag into the back seat of my car when Amy caught up with me. Her car was across the lot, but she made her way between mine and Jody's. Doors were slamming, and engines were starting all around us. "Hey," she said, publicly placing her hand on my shoulder for the second time ever. "How're you doing?"

"Better."

"I'm glad. You sound a lot better than you did last night."

I heard a jingle of keys and turned to see Tina passing behind us.

It wasn't Amy's fault, but I still could have kicked her. "Thanks," I said quickly, giving her hand an apologetic squeeze to signal that our conversation was over. "Have a good weekend."

❖

Damn it all. After the trouble I'd taken to get ahead of the game, all it took was one poorly timed comment, and I was back to playing defense.

I honestly didn't know if Tina would even show up at six. I was ready to the point of pacing, but I wouldn't have blamed her for blowing me off entirely. I considered, as I trod from the living room to the kitchen, from the kitchen to the bedroom, from the bedroom back to the living room, what might happen if she suspected I was gravitating back to Amy. If we broke up, could we continue to work together knowing what we knew? As impossible as that sounded, it certainly seemed more reasonable than attempting to continue our relationship. I was running the route from the bedroom to the living room when Tina's SUV entered the parking lot.

She gave me a quick dry kiss when I climbed into her car. "Ranch Hand?"

"Sure. It's sangria night."

Tina turned left out of the parking lot, and I watched the needle on the speedometer as it climbed gradually and finally settled somewhere around seventy-five. I watched the dry brown landscape pass, glanced inside a late model Chevy as we dodged it to the left. I wondered if there was any chance that she hadn't heard what Amy had said in the parking lot. The actual physical contact was bad enough.

"You were right about this afternoon," she finally said. "I do believe Dunlop called that meeting just so he could be in charge of one."

"He gets really irritated about the way Kathy runs things," I said. "He's been dying to kick us off that counter for years now."

"That was absurd. I can't believe he yelled at you guys for being late, either. Does he expect us to rush in there at the bell and leave everyone unsupervised?"

Our conversation went on hold as we crossed the parking lot and got a table. The Ranch Hand was fairly busy, and I noticed one of the third-grade teachers sitting near the kitchen with her husband and children. For the first time, I didn't care. She was facing the other direction anyway, and the hostess seated us at the opposite side of the restaurant. As we settled into our booth, she asked if she could start us off with something from the bar.

"Sangria?" Tina asked me.

"I shouldn't."

She rolled her eyes. "Please. It's Friday. You need to relax."

"Two?" The hostess asked.

"Two," Tina confirmed.

I glared at the hostess as she left our table. That made Tina laugh.

"What's wrong? I've never known you to turn down a drink."

I stared at my menu as if there might be something tasty and exciting that I'd missed all these years. "That in itself is a reason."

"So what, you're randomly on the wagon now? Did you find Jesus yesterday or something?"

"Forget it. My stomach's still not quite right, that's all."

"You'll be fine," she assured me. "And if you're not, you can blame it on me later."

"I'll remember that."

"Okay," she said, folding her menu and giving me her undivided attention. "How come you're pissed?"

"I'm not pissed. I thought you were pissed."

"Why would I be pissed?"

"I don't know. Last night…This afternoon…"

"Oh, that."

The woman who had seated us returned with our drinks, removed a notepad from her pocket, and looked at us expectantly. I ordered the same thing I always ordered and once the server left, tried to explain: "Amy called after I turned my phone back on and…"

"Don't."

I stared at Tina. Her expression was completely blank. "I'm sorry."

"Look, I don't care who called who. I don't own you, and I'm not threatened by her in the first place, even though she is still in love with you."

"She is not."

"Look up from the floor the next time she talks to you. Are you still in love with her?"

"I was never in love with her."

"Hence the breakup." She nodded. "That's right."

"So this afternoon, Marisol and I had to separate a bunch of the boys," I said, deliberately changing the subject. "That's why we were late to the meeting."

"Were they fighting?"

"They were close. Two big groups of them. It was kind of scary."

"Gang stuff? Were those two kids from your class in the mix?"

"Somewhere in there. I'm just glad I didn't have to break up anything physical. Both Jody and Amy have gotten hit trying to pull kids apart."

"You did the other week," she reminded me. "Some of the boys are big enough to flatten Amy."

"I know. I can't imagine high school."

Tina said nothing about her ex-wife the volleyball coach. "This is one of the reasons I teach kindergarten. At that age, they're still portable."

I smiled. "True. I've heard some awful stories from my friend Billy. You know, the one in Killeen? He teaches tenth grade."

"I bet."

"He'd been there less than two months when he got in the middle of a fight and got decked. Seventeen stitches in the face, and he had to go back to school with a shiner."

"That just sucks."

"Yeah, he's a little bit particular about his face."

"Gay man?"

"Nope, just a pretty boy."

"Does he have a wife?"

No, but he was trying to do yours. I shook my head and calmly cleared a place for my steak as the server returned. There was no response from Tina, but it wasn't my goal to take her down all at once.

The server picked up Tina's empty glass and assessed mine. "Would you like another?"

Tina agreed. I requested more water, and for the time it took the server to return, we ate in silence. I wondered if Tina knew how inseparable Billy and Anita had become. If she did, I wondered if she was sleeping with me just to get back at Anita.

"You're quiet this evening," I finally said.

I expected her to blow that off or deny it, but she nodded. "I know. I'm sorry. I've been kind of off all week."

"How come?"

"I should be home this weekend."

A twinge of awkward guilt slid through my stomach. "Your brother ships out when?"

"Monday."

"How come you're not home?"

"Thanksgiving was bad enough. My mother's sure to spend the whole weekend wailing about how he's going to get himself blown up, and I just can't think about it, you know? He's just a baby."

"How old is he?"

"Twenty-one, but he's still twelve in my head. Of course, he acts like he's twelve most of the time, so that doesn't really help."

"What does your father think of all this?"

"He's worried, but he doesn't put up with my mother's melodrama anymore. He just goes off to watch TV and leaves my brother and me to deal with it. She constantly anticipates the worst. It's like she isn't comfortable until she's miserable."

"I think that's diagnosable."

Tina nodded. "I can't stand being around her, but that just makes me feel guilty." She took a long drink and stared broodingly out across the restaurant at nothing at all.

"Does anyone get along with her?"

"My sister was the only one who really did, but then my sister got along with everybody. She was a pleaser."

I nodded patiently, trying to encourage her confessional. She'd never before mentioned her sister in the past tense.

She shook her head, though, her eyes still very far away. "I should shut up. You don't need to hear this shit."

"It's okay," I said quickly. "Everybody has a totally dysfunctional relationship with their mother on some level. Jody still has Sunday dinner with her parents every week, and she has stories you wouldn't believe."

Tina finally grinned again. "Is that the reason for the asexuality?"

"Pick a reason. Her parents, her church, the deplorable lack of decent people to date."

"She has to be queer. If she's straight, her parents and her church wouldn't be an issue."

"There's still the deplorable lack of decent people to date."

"I think she's a bit sweet on you."

I felt the control slip from my fingers once again. "No, she's not," I muttered.

"She's very protective of you."

"She's protective of all her friends."

"True, but I still think she has a crush. I don't know that she knows it, and it certainly isn't as out-of-control obvious as Amy's."

"Stop it, already."

"What *would* Jesus do?"

"Shut up." I caught myself feeling thankful for the return of Tina's smile, even if it was catty, then was mad that I'd fallen for it again. *There will be time later.* She was most of the way through her second drink, and the tipsier she got, the more confidence I had.

By the time I finished my sangria, Tina was on her third. Most of my steak was gone, and my water glass had been refilled three times. I had to get up to use the restroom before dinner was over, but my head was remarkably clear. Our conversation was light from then on, with no more mention of her sister, Killeen, or Billy. So far, so good.

I was torn as to what to do when we took care of the check. I didn't want to call attention to the fact that I was far more sober than Tina, but I also wasn't crazy about the idea of letting her drive. Memories of ugly battles with Daniel almost swayed me toward the reckless, but as we crossed the parking lot, I finally asked for the keys.

Tina handed them over with no argument whatsoever. "Thanks," she said, settling into the passenger seat. "You know I'm a cheap date."

She sat quietly during the ride, watching the lights, holding my right hand over the console. I hadn't driven something so large in years. Once the newness wore off, the powerful feeling of being high up and in control seeped into me as if the upholstery was soaked in testosterone. I told Tina I loved how it drove, and she returned something in a distracted, sleepy voice about it getting shitty gas mileage.

When we reached my apartment, she asked to use the bathroom, and I asked if I could get her a drink. I had water, I told her, Coke, and the usual array of wine, beer, and liquor.

"I'm drunk anyway. Red if you have it."

I took my time in the kitchen, selecting a nice bottle of merlot. I poured a generous serving and was working the cork back in when Tina joined me again. She reached into the cabinet for another glass.

I shook my head. "I don't need any more tonight."

"Just a little," she encouraged. "So I'm not drinking alone."

Before I could complain a second time, she stroked my cheek gently and kissed me on the mouth. *Damn it, she is not going to derail me anymore tonight.* I couldn't think of a good excuse to push away from her until her hand slid up my shirt.

Rude as it felt, I stepped away gently, trying to smile. "Go ahead and sit down. I'll take care of this."

When I returned to the living room with her ample glass and my conservative one, she was sitting at the far end of the sofa, her head back against the wall, eyes closed. When I set her drink down, she thanked me and sat up long enough to take a deep sip. Apparently, she was an even cheaper date than I'd thought. In no time at all, she'd swung back to brooding.

"Would it help to call your brother?"

She shook her head. "He's probably not even home."

"If you want to talk, I'll listen."

Her eyes locked with mine. The alcohol had taken the edge off their intensity, but her gaze was formidable nonetheless. "About what?"

I shrugged. "Him, your mom. Whatever's got you down."

"There's really nothing to say."

"You were talking before."

She looked away. "You get along with your mother."

"Usually."

"Do you actually talk to her about your life?"

"Sometimes. She wants me to find some nice girl and settle down."

"Have you always been able to talk to her?"

"I didn't much when I was a kid. She worked weird hours, and I kind of did my own thing. We had to get along, though. It was just us."

"I guess."

"I can see how things would be different if I had a brother or sister," I said. "You said your sister got along with your mom."

Tina took another drink, then examined her glass carefully. "Things were different then."

I allowed the silence to fester for a moment. My heart was pounding. "Different how?"

"My sister is dead," she said, her voice very precise, her eyes still on her wineglass. "But I think you know that."

I nodded hesitantly. She'd alluded to it, after all. It did throw me that she'd jumped right to the point and said it so bluntly, but I hoped that made me appear surprised and concerned.

"Ten and a half years ago," she continued, taking another sip. When she lowered her glass, her eyes finally rested on me. "You know that, too."

My mouth went dry. I refused to look away, but I did not answer this time. *Now what?* I'd been so busy hatching my scheme, working subtle prompts into our conversation, that I hadn't even considered what I was going to do once I had her confession.

My falter was apparently just as grandiose as I'd imagined. Tina gave a short, derisive laugh. "I've told you my story. Now, I want to hear about Cary or Liz or whoever the hell you are tonight."

Instead of returning the serve evenly, I flailed and smacked wildly. "You haven't mentioned Anita."

"She's a lying, cheating bitch, but your pal Billy will discover that for himself soon enough."

"You were married to her."

Now, she looked right back at me. "There are a few things you've swept under the rug as well."

I couldn't stand it any longer. "Why are you here?"

"Oh, darling, there you go, discounting your own charisma again." She grinned slightly in a way that made my stomach clench. "Why do you think I'm here? Surely, you have some idea."

I hated that we were at my apartment. I hated that this was happening in my space so I couldn't leave. I sat without answering, feeling small and frustrated and frightened.

The smile disappeared as quickly as it'd come. "My sister is dead," she continued softly, "because they would not leave her alone. They had no proof that she did it, no proof she was even there. They just had no other suspects, so they kept at her. She couldn't eat, she couldn't sleep, she couldn't think. They kept at her, pushing and pushing and hoping she'd break. Well, she did."

"I'm sorry," I whispered. "I can't imagine how that must—"

"No, you can't because you conveniently disappeared into thin air."

"I have never intentionally disappeared from anywhere."

"You can say that over and over again," she said, setting her empty glass on the table, "but that won't make it any truer. You're the only one who could have made a difference, and you took off."

"I didn't just—"

"Stop lying," she muttered. "I know you were fucking her."

I stared back. I had never felt so disgustingly selfish.

"The night it happened, she gave me her diary, his car keys, a bag full of bloody clothes, and the crowbar. Told me to get rid of them and say I'd never been home. I got rid of the clothes," she continued tersely. "She liked you a lot. She wasn't in love with you, but she did like you a lot. Enough to cover your ass, anyway."

Tears sprang to my eyes, but I was sure as hell not going to let them fall. I wanted to scream at her, to run to my closet and thrust my shoebox into her hands. For ten years, that night had haunted my waking hours and my dreams. I'd wondered every single day if things would have been different if Mom and I hadn't left town, if I could have been there for Natalie, or even if she hadn't been so good to me. I didn't run for the closet, though. I got up, grabbed our glasses, and brought them to the kitchen as calmly as I possibly could.

"Yes, he hit her, and yes, he would've killed her if he knew about you two. What I need to know," she said, "is what really happened that night."

I turned to find her right behind me, blocking my way out of the kitchen. It scared the hell out of me.

"Did he find out?" she asked, her voice growing tighter. "My guess is that he found out, and she killed him trying to defend herself. Either that, or you killed him so you guys could be together."

I could lie. It would be so easy. "It wasn't like that," I whispered before I could stop myself.

"Then what was it like?"

There was no answer to that question. Anything I said was going to be wrong, even the truth.

"What was it like, goddamn it?"

Her palm connected with my face, hard. I'd been looking elsewhere and hadn't even seen it coming, and the impact knocked me off-balance. I was unable to think, to speak, to catch my breath.

She pulled away as if wanting to take it back. "Fuck it, Cary," she said, tears starting down her cheeks. "I came here because I needed to know, and I screwed up bad, okay? I didn't mean to get close to you. I didn't mean to fall for you. I didn't mean any of that, but it happened. If I could take it back, I would."

Her words made no sense to me, but they somehow made me feel even worse. When I touched the side of my mouth, my fingers came off wet with blood.

"You have to say something," she pleaded. "You were there, weren't you?"

"Yes."

"Tell me what happened."

I just couldn't think. For ten years, it had sometimes felt like I could think of nothing else, but now that I had my audience, my moment on the stand, there was nothing there. I was still stunned, and my cheek stung mercilessly. "I don't know what to—"

Tina looked me in the eye for a moment, letting my sentence drift into nowhere. "We were good, Cary, you and I," she said. "I don't want to have to do this." With that, she reached next to the sink and selected one of the good knives from my block. She examined it, turned it over with shaking hands, assessed her choice. It might have taken three seconds, but it seemed like forever. "Let's start here," she said, taking a deep breath. "Did she do it, or did you?"

I watched the knife until it disappeared under my chin. "Please," I begged. "Please stop."

"Did you kill him?"

I grabbed her hand with my left and tried to push her away with my right, but my terror was nothing compared to her desperation. She caught me by the shoulder, and the blade of the knife pressed hard against my neck.

"Did you?"

"Yes," I whispered. My skin was taut against the blade, and when I swallowed, I felt it give just a tiny bit. "I didn't mean to."

"Goddamn bitch," she said, something very different igniting in her eyes. All at once, they were sharp, angry, crazy, and they looked straight into mine as her fingers dug deeper into my shoulder, and the knife slid the tiniest bit. "You let her take the blame."

I don't want to die this way. Please, God, don't let me die this way. "I didn't mean to. She told me to go."

"I don't goddamn care what she told you," Tina yelled. As she lost control of her words, her right hand moved, forcing the blade into my skin. "She covered your goddamn ass. She died for you, and you're here, going on like nothing ever happened. She fucking *died* for you."

I didn't feel pain, but my pulse was pounding in my neck. I reached desperately behind me with my left hand, searching for something, anything at all. I felt the cabinets, the counter, and then something cool and round. The angle was awkward, but I wrapped my fingers around it best I could and swung the wine bottle wildly.

Tina barely had time to duck. Her head jerked back into the wall, stunning her for just long enough for me to break free from her grasp. I had no idea what to do with the bottle, but it separated the two of us nicely and gave me the space and time to be sure my legs would carry me. Without another second of hesitation, I flung it at her, snatched my purse and keys, and bolted out the door.

Chapter Twenty-five

I stumbled down the stairs, opened the car door, and crammed the key into the ignition. For once, luck was on my side. I'd parked in the middle of the lot that afternoon, in a spot where I could pull all the way through. I yanked the car into gear and stepped on the gas.

My tires squealed as I turned onto Parker and again as I started north on the highway. I grabbed for my seat belt, struggling with it as I floored the accelerator. Fifty, sixty, seventy. If Tina had seen which direction I'd gone, I had only seconds. Her car's engine was bigger than mine, and she drove way too fast under normal circumstances.

I tried to focus on the road ahead, but my eyes kept flickering to the rearview mirror. I was such an idiot for heading north. If I'd just turned south, there were so many places to go. Jody's. Daniel's. Even Amy's. Any one of them would bolt the doors and call the cops.

What could I even tell the cops, though? She was trying to kill me? She'd been stalking me for months because I'd killed her sister's boyfriend and caused her sister's death? What could I even say? I continued north, eyes on the mirror, the needle on my speedometer threatening to bury.

The road darkened quickly, and minutes passed. My mind began to clear somewhat, and my pulse stopped pounding so violently in my neck. I wanted to look at it or at least to touch it, but I was driving so fast, my poor little car was shuddering, and I didn't dare take either hand off the steering wheel. I passed a pickup, then an El

Camino with New Mexico plates. That one had only one headlight, which comforted me greatly. I could finally look back and be certain the car behind me was not Tina.

I still didn't trust that she wouldn't catch up to me. I saw the sign for a crossroad coming up, and slowed to turn without signaling. The road was barely wide enough for two cars to pass and had no lines painted down the middle or along the edges. Fortunately, it, like every other road in the area, seemed to be entirely straight, so I made it back to eighty regardless of how insistently my car shook.

I followed that road for ten, maybe twenty minutes until I found another crossroad. I turned north on 1205, then east when I saw another sign, then what I thought was north again, this time on an unmarked road. There were no headlights behind me now, no taillights in front of me, no lights anywhere within view. There was nothing there at all, actually, other than barren fields full of scrub, cattle, and a few lonely oil derricks. Finally able to breathe, I slowed to sixty, forty, twenty.

On either side of the road, two lengths of barbed wire stretched between rudimentary wooden posts. I rolled slowly alongside them until I saw a gap on the right where the fence ended just enough to fit a truck through. Four metal poles were set lengthwise across a shallow ravine in the middle of the dirt drive to keep the cattle from leaving the property. Though I probably could have just stopped in the middle of the road, I pulled into the dusty little drive and turned off the engine and the lights.

Crickets were chirping adamantly, but it sounded like complete silence now that my car had stopped shuddering, and the panic was no longer screaming in my ears. I flipped the dome light switch to off and threw open the car door, feeling the chilly air against my face, smelling dust and manure and my engine, which was smoking a little. My legs were stiff and shaky, like I'd been driving for hours, but I forced them to take me up onto the pavement. The terrain was flat as a pancake, and I knew I'd be able to both see and hear a vehicle a mile away. The sky was so full of stars that it looked gray.

I sat on the edge of the road, elbows on my knees, head in my hands, for a very long time. I could tell I'd been crying at some point because my lip still stung with the saltiness. My eyes had adjusted thanks to the clear sky, and I could see blood on my shirt and jeans. There was quite a lot on my left hand, too, and the more I thought about it, the more it stung. I didn't remember the blade of the knife on anything other than my neck, but I supposed I might have gotten cut in the struggle.

It struck me then that I'd never felt so depressingly, debilitatingly alone in my life. I had no idea where I was, no idea how long or how far I'd driven in any direction. I was barely familiar with the largest roads, and I had no map. I had a quarter tank of gas, and my engine still smelled hot. I had no idea if I had my phone or any cash with me. I needed to make it to a town, to a gas station, to somewhere I could spend the night. I really wanted to go home, but I knew I couldn't on the off chance Tina was waiting for me to return.

I knew I was a mess, sure, but when I finally returned to the car, turned on the overhead light, and flipped the visor down to look in the mirror, the sight made me gag. My lip was split and purple where Tina had hit me, and I still couldn't tell where all the blood on my hand had come from. My neck, though, was really what shocked me. As far as I could tell, the cut ran from a few inches below my right ear to close to the middle of my neck. Blood had run, smeared, and dried, and the entire area was so swollen, it was impossible to see how deep it was. I was upright, though, upright and breathing, so I tried to convince myself it really wasn't that bad. *She could have killed me if she'd really wanted to. She could have cut so much deeper.*

Before getting back on the road, I took a screwdriver out of the tool kit in my trunk and removed the license plates from both the back and front of my car. I placed the back one on the ledge between the back seat and the rear window and the front one on the right side of the dash where they were not readily visible in traffic but could possibly be excused if I got pulled over. It might have been a ridiculous precaution, but there were plenty of late model Toyotas out there either the same shade of blue or a similar dark color. Now, my hands were grimy as well as bloody.

I continued along the direction I'd been going, hoping to see any sort of road sign. It took a long time, but my headlights finally hit on something in the distance. I'd never felt so relieved as when I turned northbound on Highway 84. I didn't know where it would take me, but it was a divided highway, and that suggested it would eventually end up somewhere other than someone's barn.

I'd been on it no more than ten minutes when I arrived in the town of Post, population 3,708. It was a quaint little place with a small, historic downtown strip, long closed for the evening. Everyone who lived there was surely tucked happily in bed without gaping gashes across their throats and crazy girlfriends after them. It did have a nice obvious gas station, though, so I filled my tank quickly and got back on the road. I would have loved to stop in the restroom to wash the blood and grime off my hands and clean up my neck and face, but the convenience store was lit up brightly, and the attendant was sitting behind her counter right next to the door.

Soon. Everything will be okay.

I wasn't sure where to go next. Farther north? Farther east? Lubbock was somewhere to the north, and Tina could be there looking for me. Perhaps north wasn't such a good idea.

This whole fucking thing wasn't such a good idea. I felt angry tears sliding down my cheeks again and wiped at them with the back of my right hand. I continued west, everything stinging.

Half an hour later, I reached Brownfield. While it was not exactly hopping at that hour, it had what I needed. I circled three fast-food restaurants before I found one that was both open and had a separate entrance near the restrooms. I found a nice, poorly lit parking space and took a moment to assess the situation. Back in Post, I'd found forty-seven dollars cash in my purse; that would have to cover a motel. Now, I just needed to find a way to make myself presentable enough to check into one without being shipped off to the emergency room by some well-meaning desk clerk.

I got out of the car, popped the trunk latch, and started to search.

The tool kit, minus the screwdriver still sitting on the front passenger seat. An umbrella. A full quart container of oil and two empties. A duffel bag I'd forgotten about on the night of the apartment break-in. That was the day I'd changed into jeans and a T-shirt directly after school to paint props and scenery. I had clothes.

A scarf or a huge turtleneck would have been better, but at least I had clothes that weren't covered in blood. I grabbed the duffel, slipped inside the restaurant, and went directly to the bathroom.

It was small and cramped and smelled like piss, and the fluorescent lighting made me look hideous. I'd been covered in as much blood once before, but at least that time, it hadn't been mine. I rolled up my sleeves hurriedly and started scrubbing at my hands, but no matter how much it hurt, my conscience ached more. I was seventeen again, watching what seemed to be an endless stream of red wash down the drain. I didn't understand how I could be here again, ten years later, scrubbing away like some community theater Lady Macbeth.

Three of the fingers on my left hand were cut where I must have grabbed the blade of the knife, and there were two good-sized nicks on the side and top of my hand. My lip was split near the left corner of my mouth, and my cheek was bruising. The gash on my neck looked far better now that it was no longer caked in blood, but was still ugly and just itching to leave an obnoxious scar. My back felt tender where Tina had pushed me into the counter, but I couldn't get to an angle where I could see anything, and I didn't want to spend too much time standing topless in a nasty burger joint restroom anyway. My jeans and sweater were some of my favorites, but I stuffed them in the trash can. Experience told me that some bloodstains never came out, no matter what.

I stood before the smeary mirror, staring at the thing that looked back at me. My clothes were wrinkled yet presentable, and if I hunched, the collar of my shirt mostly covered the cut on my neck. There wasn't much I could do about anything else, but the dark circles under my bloodshot eyes did suggest that I'd been involved in a garden variety domestic dispute rather than some wild battle for revenge.

I returned to the car, threw the duffel into the back seat, and went in search of somewhere to sleep.

I longed to stop at one of the large, sparkling chain hotels, but I didn't want to use my credit card in the same town in which I was staying in case Tina had called the cops. A tired-looking

Mom-and-Pop establishment advertised free long-distance calls and color TV for just twenty-nine dollars a night, and that was where I stopped.

Before I left the car, I removed forty dollars and Selena's driver's license from my purse, so I wouldn't be juggling inside. I ducked as deeply as I could into my shirt, which made sense since the night had become cold and windy. With one last deep breath, I let myself into the office, an immaculately scrubbed, starkly decorated place with faux-wood paneling and a deer head mounted on the wall.

It took a moment, but a skinny, elderly gentleman wearing a plaid shirt and suspenders answered to the bell hanging on the door. "Ma'am?"

"Yes, I'd like…" I had to clear my throat and start again. I hadn't spoken since leaving my apartment, and I felt my lip split again with the motion. "I'd like a room, please."

I wished the man was a little more subtle. His brow furrowed, and his eyes squinched a little as he looked me up and down. "Single or double?"

"Single," I said, working on the registration sheet he placed in front of me. My fingers were shaking, and the pen was on a little chain that only made things more impossible. Without missing a beat, I registered under Selena's name and used the address I'd memorized from her license. When I slid my cash across the desk along with her ID, the man took my application wordlessly, barely glanced at the card which declared my name to be Selena del Arroyo Ortiz and my age to be thirty-seven, and went to get a key.

Headlights splashed against the front window, and I turned wildly, my heart stopping short. It was an SUV, but I couldn't tell the make. The driver's side door opened, and I caught just a glimpse of red paint in the residual glow from the office. A man let himself into one of the close rooms without so much as glancing our way.

"Ma'am?" the innkeeper asked hesitantly. "Are you all right?"

I tried to let out my breath slowly and evenly before turning back to him. I nodded and conjured a Daniel-thick twang fast. "If I might could get a room facing the back. Me and my boyfriend got to arguing."

The old man nodded sadly at me. "You got marks on your face. You done called the police on him?"

I shook my head. "I just need to be away from him right now."

The man's lips went tight, but he nodded. "Back of the building, right next to the office. You can pull your car back there."

"Thank you, sir." I clutched the key and turned to leave.

"You need anything, you holler. Otherwise, I ain't never seen you."

I tried a smile, but I tasted blood from my lip again. "Thank you."

I pulled my car behind the building but left it at the opposite end of the complex from room 16. It felt strange to let myself into a hotel room with no luggage, as though my only reason for being there was some illicit, hour-long tryst. I wished that was my plan, quick sex, maybe even with someone whose name I'd never know. Honestly, I just wished I *had* a plan. I locked both dead bolts, slid the chain, tugged the curtains until they covered the window completely, and turned to face my hideaway.

My room was small but warm and clean. An ancient heater hummed underneath the windowsill. The bedspread, carpet, and wall art were throwbacks to the seventies and the much-touted color TV was a monstrosity bolted to the top of the dresser. The toilet wore a sash informing me that it had been sanitized for my protection. Everything smelled heavily of cigarette smoke and room deodorizer, but I didn't care. For the first time in hours, I felt safe.

I sat on the bed with my cell phone and ran through the numbers I had programmed. I couldn't call Jody; she'd know too much. I couldn't call Daniel, either; he wouldn't keep his mouth shut. I couldn't possibly bring Amy into this mess. I finally found the Hernandezes number, hit dial, and huddled on the edge of the bed, counting rings until there was a click on the other end.

"Lucy, it's Cary," I said, trying to keep my voice steady. "I'm so sorry if I woke you."

"You didn't, but how come you didn't just come over?"

"I'm in Brownfield or Brownville or somewhere," I said. "I need you to do a…"

Lucy cut me off hard. "Wait, you're where?"

I closed my eyes. "I don't even know. I need you to do me a favor."

"What do you need?"

"I need you to go over to my apartment and see if there's anybody there."

"Like, who anybody?"

Oh, come on. "Tina, okay? We got in a fight."

"And you think she's still there? Is she, like, dangerous or something?"

"I don't know."

Silence, then Lucy answered hesitantly. "Cary, Bobby's at the plant. I'm here all alone."

"I'll stay on the phone with you."

"Well, at least let me get his gun."

I listened patiently as she moved through her apartment, opened a drawer, slid something out, and moved back toward wherever the television was playing. "Got it?"

"Yeah."

I heard Lucy unlock her door, then a long silence. I imagined her creeping around the corner, gun first, like one of Charlie's Angels. In another moment, she let out her breath.

"Your door's locked, Cary, and the blue truck isn't here."

I could feel my heartbeat slowing. "Is it the dead bolt or the knob?"

"The knob doesn't move, like when you turn the lock from the inside."

"Perfect. Thank you. That's all I need."

I heard a door slam again. Lucy was breathing very hard. "Cary, are you okay?"

"I'm fine."

"Are you sure? You sound really weird."

"I'm sure."

"When are you coming home?"

"I don't know," I whispered. "Look, I have to go."

"What do you mean, you don't know? You can't just take off and—"

"I'm running out of charge," I said. "I'll call you when I know more."

"Cary—"

"Thanks for everything. Get some sleep, okay?"

I hung up and tossed my phone onto the dresser, surely to Lucy's utter consternation. It wasn't nearly as close to dead as I'd told her, but I didn't have the charger with me. No charger, no toothbrush, and eighteen dollars left in my purse. What a brilliant fugitive I was.

I tried to sleep that night, but I failed miserably. No matter how exhausted I was, I couldn't settle down. Instead, I spent the night shivering, my neck throbbing, jumping at the smallest noises outside. For the millionth time in my life, I wanted to go home, but I had no idea where that was.

❖

I snuck out long enough the next day to withdraw one hundred dollars from an ATM and pick up a few essentials from Walmart. I half expected a drove of undercover cops to descend upon me, but nothing happened. Nobody stopped me, and I saw no familiar faces. Upon returning to my motel, I paid cash for another night and locked myself back into my room. With the curtains pulled, I could barely tell day from night, which was good because the sleep I hadn't gotten the night before caught up with me fast.

When I was awake again, I lay on the hard, lopsided bed, staring at the ceiling, listening to traffic noises, the plumbing, and the drone of the cartoon channel next door. I knew I had to return to West Grove at some point. All my things were there. I was expected at work on Monday morning. I just had no idea how I could do it without getting myself killed or arrested.

I really could call the police. My face and neck were obvious evidence that Tina was dangerous, and in a place like West Grove, surely someone could place us together at the Ranch Hand. I had no idea how I could file a report without incriminating myself, though. Explaining to a redneck cop in a small town that I had a relationship with another woman would surely destroy my reputation and end my career, but that wasn't what concerned me. There was no way that, upon interrogation, Tina would refrain from mentioning my confession. To my knowledge, the Memphis police had closed the McGrath case when Natalie died, assuming that she was the assailant rather than an eyewitness, but if Tina really did have Natalie's journal, choice details about our relationship could surely constitute a lead worthy of reopening it.

I thought about calling Billy or my mother for advice, but I couldn't think of a way to do that without telling the whole story from the beginning. There really was no other solution than to go home and face Tina and the cops and everything I'd done. Instead of spending another night in Brown-whatever, I screwed my license plates back where they belonged for everyone to see and bought a road map to find the most direct route.

An hour later, I pulled into the parking lot at my apartment complex. There were three cars in my end, none of them a blue SUV. I took the stairs slowly, feeling ashamed and not at all looking forward to the scene I'd find inside.

Lucy was right. The knob had been locked from the inside, then pulled closed. I let myself in, set my purse down gently on my packing crate, and moved through my apartment in a thick silence. I expected to see a disaster in the kitchen, merlot splashed everywhere, the knife tossed haphazardly on the floor, but it was spotless. All the knives were back in the block, and my wineglasses had been washed and were sitting on the shelf where they belonged. The bottle was gone, and the trash emptied. It was as if the evening before hadn't ever happened, aside from one thing. A single key lay on the counter. I knew without comparing it to mine that it would match.

Insanity. This was insanity. I sat on my bed, considering calling Lucy to tell her I was home and to thank her again, but the message light on my answering machine was blinking. It made me feel guilty for some reason, the way I had after avoiding Amy's calls.

Slowly, warily, I tipped the caller ID and scanned the readout. Only one number registered: Tina's.

I sat silently, not moving, staring at the answering machine for a very long time. I wasn't sure I wanted to hear the message at all. What was there to say after slitting someone's throat?

I sat there and stared. My palms were wet, but I didn't feel fear or worry or panic. The inanest thoughts crossed my mind. I thought about going to see a movie. I thought about going to pick up dinner. I thought about throwing the machine away without listening to the message. I knew I had to do it, though. I couldn't not do it. Without further hesitation, I steeled myself, and pressed the button.

"Cary," Tina's voice said, "I just needed to know."

❖

Nobody showed up to teach the bilingual kindergarten class that Monday morning. They had Amy cover while Kathy tried to get in touch with Tina, but Mrs. Shore had taken over by lunchtime. When Kathy went to check Tina's apartment two days later, she found it empty, with no forwarding address. People asked me if I knew where Tina was or why she'd left, and I shook my head and looked properly bewildered because I was. The cops did not show up at my doorstep. It was like she'd never been there, like the past several weeks hadn't even existed, like my secret was still intact. This whirlwind relationship had disappeared into thin air just like the rest of my history.

Five and a half months later, I graduated my sixth graders in the usual ceremony in the gym, complete with crepe paper and Jody pounding away on the upright piano. Three days later, I tucked my letter of resignation under Kathy Sutton's blotter and put an identical one in the mail addressed to the administration building.

Too much had happened. My car was packed, and although I was unsure as to where I would spend the next school year, I knew it couldn't be in West Grove.

About the Author

Erin Kaste was born and raised in Minneapolis, Minnesota, where she got in trouble at school for writing instead of doing the rest of her work. She began violin lessons at the age of four, went on to earn a degree in violin performance from the Eastman School of Music, and became a professional musician. After a brief public school teaching stint, she settled in Memphis, Tennessee, where she is currently a member of the Memphis Symphony Orchestra as well as their personnel manager.

Away from writing and music, she loves running, hiking in the mountains, road trips, and channeling her grandmother as she raises African violets and Christmas cacti. She shares a home with her wife, their two teenagers, two dogs, and two cats.

Books Available from Bold Strokes Books

Hands of the Morri by Heather K O'Malley. Discovering she is a Lost Sister and growing acquainted with her new body, Asche learns how to be a warrior and commune with the Goddess the Hands serve, the Morri. (978-1-63679-465-5)

I Know About You by Erin Kaste. With her stalker inching closer to the truth, Cary Smith is forced to face the past she's tried desperately to forget. (978-1-63679-513-3)

Mate of Her Own by Elena Abbott. When Heather McKenna finally confronts the family who cursed her, her werewolf is shocked to discover her one true mate, and that's only the beginning. (978-1-63679-481-5)

Pumpkin Spice by Tagan Shepard. For Nicki, new love is making this pumpkin spice season sweeter than expected. (978-1-63679-388-7)

Rivals for Love by Ali Vali. Brooks Boseman's brother Curtis is getting married, and Brooks needs to be at the engagement party. Only she can't possibly go, not with Curtis set to marry the secret love of her youth, Fallon Goodwin. (978-1-63679-384-9)

Sweat Equity by Aurora Rey. When cheesemaker Sy Travino takes a job in rural Vermont and hires contractor Maddie Barrow to rehab a house she buys sight unseen, they both wind up with a lot more than they bargained for. (978-1-63679-487-7)

Taking the Plunge by Amanda Radley. When Regina Avery meets model Grace Holland—the most beautiful woman she's ever seen—she doesn't have a clue how to flirt, date, or hold on to a relationship. But Regina must take the plunge with Grace and hope she manages to swim. (978-1-63679-400-6)

We Met in a Bar by Claire Forsythe. Wealthy nightclub owner Erica turns undercover bartender on a mission to catch a thief where she meets no-strings, no-commitments Charlie, who couldn't be further from Erica's type. Right? (978-1-63679-521-8)

Western Blue by Suzie Clarke. Step back in time to this historic western filled with heroism, loyalty, friendship, and love. The odds are against this unlikely group—but never underestimate women who have nothing to lose. (978-1-63679-095-4)

Windswept by Patricia Evans. The windswept shores of the Scottish Highlands weave magic for two people convinced they'd never fall in love again. (978-1-63679-382-5)

An Independent Woman by Kit Meredith. Alex and Rebecca's attraction won't stop smoldering, despite their reluctance to act on it and incompatible poly relationship styles. (978-1-63679-553-9)

Cherish by Kris Bryant. Josie and Olivia cherish the time spent together, but when the summer ends and their temporary romance melts into the real deal, reality gets complicated. (978-1-63679-567-6)

Cold Case Heat by Mary P. Burns. Sydney Hansen receives a threat in a very cold murder case that sends her to the police for help where she finds more than justice with Detective Gale Sterling. (978-1-63679-374-0)

Proximity by Jordan Meadows. Joan really likes Ellie, but being alone with her could turn deadly unless she can keep her dangerous powers under control. (978-1-63679-476-1)

Sweet Spot by Kimberly Cooper Griffin. Pro surfer Shia Turning will have to take a chance if she wants to find the sweet spot. (978-1-63679-418-1)

The Haunting of Oak Springs by Crin Claxton. Ghosts and the past haunt the supernatural detective in a race to save the lesbians of Oak Springs farm. (978-1-63679-432-7)

Transitory by J.M. Redmann. The cops blow it off as a customer surprised by what was under the dress, but PI Micky Knight knows they're wrong—she either makes it her case or lets a murderer go free to kill again. (978-1-63679-251-4)

Unexpectedly Yours by Toni Logan. A private resort on a tropical island, a feisty old chief, and a kleptomaniac pet pig bring Suzanne and Allie together for unexpected love. (978-1-63679-160-9)

Bones of Boothbay Harbor by Michelle Larkin. Small-town police chief Frankie Stone and FBI Special Agent Eve Huxley must set aside their differences and combine their skills to find a killer after a burial site is discovered in Boothbay Harbor, Maine. (978-1-63679-267-5)

Crush by Ana Hartnett Reichardt. Josie Sanchez worked for years for the opportunity to create her own wine label, and nothing will stand in her way. Not even Mac, the owner's annoyingly beautiful niece Josie's forced to hire as her harvest intern. (978-1-63679-330-6)

Decadence by Ronica Black, Renee Roman, and Piper Jordan. You are cordially invited to Decadence, Las Vegas's most talked about invitation-only Masquerade Ball. Come for the entertainment and stay for the erotic indulgence. We guarantee it'll be a party that lives up to its name. (978-1-63679-361-0)

Gimmicks and Glamour by Lauren Melissa Ellzey. Ashly has learned to hide her Sight, but as she speeds toward high school graduation she must protect the classmates she claims to hate from an evil that no one else sees. (978-1-63679-401-3)

Heart of Stone by Sam Ledel. Princess Keeva Glantor meets Maeve, a gorgon forced to live alone thanks to a decades-old lie, and together the two women battle forces they formerly thought to be good in the hopes of leading lives they can finally call their own. (978-1-63679-407-5)

Murder at the Oasis by David S. Pederson. Palm trees, sunshine, and murder await Mason Adler and his friend Walter as they travel from Phoenix to Palm Springs for what was supposed to be a relaxing vacation but ends up being a trip of mystery and intrigue. (978-1-63679-416-7)

Peaches and Cream by Georgia Beers. Adley Purcell is living her dreams owning Get the Scoop ice cream shop until national dessert chain Sweet Heaven opens less than two blocks away and Adley has to compete with the far too heavenly Sabrina James. (978-1-63679-412-9)

The Only Fish in the Sea by Angie Williams. Will love overcome years of bitter rivalry for the daughters of two crab fishing families in this queer modern-day spin on Romeo and Juliet? (978-1-63679-444-0)

Wildflower by Cathleen Collins. When a plane crash leaves eleven-year-old Lily Andrews stranded in the vast wilderness of Arkansas, will she be able to overcome the odds and make it back to civilization and the one person who holds the key to her future? (978-1-63679-621-5)

Witch Finder by Sheri Lewis Wohl. Tamsin, the Keeper of the Book of Darkness, is in terrible danger, and as a Witch Finder, Morrigan must protect her and the secrets she guards even if it costs Morrigan her life. (978-1-63679-335-1)

A Second Chance at Life by Genevieve McCluer. Vampires Dinah and Rachel reconnect, but a string of vampire killings begin and evidence seems to be pointing at Dinah. They must prove her innocence while finding out if the two of them are still compatible after all these years. (978-1-63679-459-4)

Digging for Heaven by Jenna Jarvis. Litz lives for dragons. Kella lives to kill them. The last thing they expect is to find each other attractive. (978-1-63679-453-2)

Forever's Promise by Missouri Vaun. Wesley Holden migrated west disguised as a man for the hope of a better life and with no designs to take a wife, but Charlotte Rose has other ideas. (978-1-63679-221-7)

Here For You by D. Jackson Leigh. A horse trainer must make a difficult business decision that could save her father's ranch from foreclosure but destroy her chance to win the heart of a feisty barrel racer vying for a spot in the National Rodeo Finals. (978-1-63679-299-6)

I Do, I Don't by Joy Argento. Creator of the romance algorithm, Nicole Hart doesn't expect to be starring in her own reality TV dating show, and falling for the show's executive producer Annie Jackson could ruin everything. (978-1-63679-420-4)

It's All in the Details by Dena Blake. Makeup artist Lane Donnelly and wedding planner Helen Trent can't stand each other, but they must set aside their differences to ensure Darcy gets the wedding of her dreams, and make a few of their own dreams come true. (978-1-63679-430-3)

Marigold by Melissa Brayden. Marigold Lavender vows to take down Alexis Wakefield, the harsh food critic who blasts her younger sister's restaurant. If only she wasn't as sexy as she is mean. (978-1-63679-436-5)

The Town that Built Us by Jesse J. Thoma. When her father dies, Grace Cook returns to her hometown and tries to avoid Bonnie Whitlock, the woman who pulverized her heart, only to discover her father's estate has been left to them jointly. (978-1-63679-439-6)